A
LOG CABIN
Christmas
COLLECTION

9 Historical Romances during
American Pioneer Christmases

A

LOG CABIN

Christmas

COLLECTION

Wanda E. Brunstetter
Margaret Brownley, Kelly Eileen Hake, Jane Kirkpatrick,
Liz Johnson, Liz Tolsma, Michelle Ule, Debra Ullrick, Erica Vetsch

BARBOUR
PUBLISHING

All scripture quotations are taken from the King James Version of the Bible.

This book is a work of fiction. Names, characters, places, and incidents are either products of the author's imagination or used fictitiously. Any similarity to actual people, organizations, and/or events is purely coincidental.

Cover photograph: Klammet & Aberl/Taxi/Getty

Published by Barbour Publishing, Inc., P.O. Box 719, Uhrichsville, Ohio 44683, www.barbourbooks.com

Our mission is to publish and distribute inspirational products offering exceptional value and biblical encouragement to the masses.

 Member of the
Evangelical Christian
Publishers Association

Printed in Canada.

Contents

Snow Angel

by Margaret Brownley

Dedication

To Courtney Rose. Angels come in all guises,
but none are sweeter, more talented, or delightful than you.

In the shadow of thy wings will I make my refuge,
until these calamities be overpast.

PSALM 57:1

Chapter 1

Miss Parker's Class of 1885

*When Jesus was born, Mary wrapped him in
swatting clothes because of all the flies in the stable.
Priscilla, age 8*

Maverick, Texas

Sheriff Brad Donovan knew trouble was brewing the moment the three-member school board stomped into his office. Whatever was on their minds had to be pretty serious to bring them out in this wintry storm. All three men wore heavy coats covered in snow, their noses and ears red from the cold.

Head of the school board Tim Griffin battled to close the door against the blustery wind. Swinging his bulky body around, he pulled the woolen scarf away from his neck.

Elbows on his desk, Sheriff Donovan greeted him with a wary nod. "What has she done this time?"

It wasn't just a wild guess. The new teacher from Boston had been nothing but trouble since the board had hired her two months earlier. Lately, he'd spent more time handling complaints about the schoolmarm than chasing outlaws.

Griffin practically sputtered. "Miss Parker kept my daughter after school." He wore lumberman's pants and calf-high caulked boots. Hands in tight fists, he added, "In this weather!"

Donovan pinched his brow in an effort to chase away a fast-developing headache. It was the end of the day, and he was tired. The unprecedented storm had created one problem after another. All he wanted was to go home to the boardinghouse and sink his teeth into Mrs. Langley's venison stew. But judging from the men's solemn demeanors, he'd be lucky if he arrived home in time for tomorrow morning's flapjacks.

Chuck Walters made a snorting sound. A blue knit cap covered his bald head to his eyebrows, his red beard almost white with snow. "That woman ain't got the sense God gave a woodpecker. Anyone who would steal pews from the

Lord's house ain't to be trusted."

Donovan blew out his breath. "She *borrowed* the pews." Far be it from him to defend the woman, but in all honesty, it was their fault for failing to order desks. "Miss Parker moved the pews to the schoolhouse so her pupils would have something to write on." She'd paid the preacher's son to move them for her, which didn't sit right with church elders. That had caused Donovan more trouble.

Chuck scoffed. "Borrow, steal, whatever. She still ain't got no right doin' what she did. I had to stand for two solid hours on Sunday morn to hear the preacher tell us we ain't nothin' but sinners. That's hard enough to take sittin' down, let alone standin'."

"That's nothing," Jake Penman added. A short man with a round face and an even rounder pouch, Penman was a shoemaker and barber. He liked to say he took care of a man from the top of his head to the tip of his toes. "That mural her class painted should be outlawed."

Donovan blew out a stream of air. Not the mural again.

"You're just peeved 'cuz Judas looks just like you," Chuck said.

"It's not just the mural," Penman argued. "Miss Parker don't know beans about discipline. She lets the Madison boy run wild. As for the mural—"

"I don't care about no mural," Griffin roared. "I want to know what the sheriff is gonna do about my daughter."

Donovan folded his hands on his desk. "The last I heard, keeping pupils after school is not a crime."

"Maybe not," Griffin huffed. "Miss Parker sent a note home yesterday saying she wanted to keep a couple of pupils including my daughter after school for rehearsals. Now they're snowed in, and no one can get to them!"

Donovan grimaced. No wonder the board was all up in arms. The original schoolhouse, along with pretty much the whole town, had burned down in the August fire. While the new school was under construction, classes were being held in an old miner's cabin, away from the hammering and sawing that would interfere with learning. It was a drafty, isolated place that should have been condemned long ago.

"Who else is out there?"

"Jimmy Madison and the little Jones kid," Griffin said. "Mrs. Jones is frantic with worry."

Donovan could understand why. Five-year-old Brandon was the only family Mrs. Jones had left since she was widowed by the recent fire.

Chuck Walters chimed in, "The road is completely blocked, and not even a mule can get through." Walter's droopy mustache twitched. "This sure is unusual weather. I ain't seen nothing like this since leaving Minnesota."

Unusual didn't begin to describe the recent snowstorms. The Piney Woods area was known for its humid summers and mild winters. The most snow they'd ever had in the past was perhaps a few inches—nothing like they'd had so far this last month.

"You have to do something, Sheriff," Griffin said. "I'll not have my daughter spend a night at the schoolhouse with that. . .that woman!"

"All right, I'll see what I can do." He stood, his six-foot-two form towering over all three men by at least four inches. Eager to get started before the last bit of daylight was gone, he plucked his Stetson off a hook and set it square on his head. He then shrugged his massive shoulders into his long duster.

"Good luck," Walters said.

Donovan responded with a nod. He opened the door to a blast of wind, snow, and icy-cold air. Something told him he would need all the luck he could get.

※

Drat! Where were they?

Maddie Parker tried not to let her anxiety show, but the wind lashing against the outside of the schoolhouse was hard to ignore. What began as a few snow flurries had now turned into a full-fledged blizzard.

The rehearsal for the Christmas play had ended more than two hours ago. Her other pupils had their parts memorized, but "Mary" and "Joseph" still needed work. Little Brandon was one of the angels. He needed no more practice, but he took his role seriously and chose to stay on his own accord, and Maddie didn't have the heart to dissuade him.

In her note home to parents, she had clearly specified when rehearsal would end, and still no one had come to pick up the pupils kept after school. Surely they didn't expect the children to walk home in this weather. If it weren't snowing so hard, she would attempt to walk the children home herself, even though Jimmy Madison lived a good five miles away.

Her patience at its limit, she sprinted forward to confiscate Jimmy's script. Folded in dart-like fashion, the script was aimed directly at Sophie Griffin's back. His endless capacity for making Sophie scream never failed to amaze her.

Eleven-year-old Jimmy was her oldest and most challenging pupil. Tall for his age, he was always in motion. During the rare occasions his hands and feet were still, his gaze darted back and forth as if looking for a place to light. He could wield a rifle, throw a knife, and shoot a slingshot with chilling accuracy, but something as simple as holding a pencil or adding two numbers together mystified him.

Giving Jimmy the part of Joseph had been a mistake. Worse, it had failed to produce the change in attitude Maddie had hoped for.

Sophie stuck her tongue out at Jimmy. A pretty child with long blond hair, delicate features, and expressive blue eyes, Sophie's constant complaints were every bit as tiresome as Jimmy's restless nature.

Catching Sophie's attention, Maddie shook her head in disapproval.

Sophie plopped herself on the floor and folded her arms across her chest. Her tongue vanished but was immediately replaced by a pouty bottom lip. A year younger than Jimmy, she played Mary, but she and Jimmy couldn't look at each other without fighting. Not only did the two of them refuse to stand next to each other, but they also resorted to name calling. The manger scene was a disaster. Peace on earth? Hardly. It was more like the Battle of Gettysburg.

"He won't leave me alone," Sophie complained. Blue eyes flashing, she tossed a blond braid over her shoulder. As difficult as Jimmy was, Sophie was Maddie's most worrisome pupil. Her father was head of the school board, and Sophie took great pleasure in reporting her teacher's every misstep to him: real, imagined, or otherwise.

"You started it," Jimmy said.

"Did not."

"Did, too."

"Quiet, both of you!" Maddie groaned. She dreaded to think of the awful tales Sophie would carry home at the end of *this* day.

Maddie sucked in her breath and fought for control. It wasn't like her to lose her temper. Smoothing down her skirt, she straightened her shirtwaist and pushed hair that had escaped her bun behind her ears.

Taking the teaching job following that terrible fire had been a mistake. At age twenty-six, she was an experienced teacher, but teaching in Boston with its well-maintained and well-equipped schools was a whole lot easier than teaching here in the wilderness. Had she not borrowed church pews and scrounged around for pillows, the children would still be sitting on the rough wood floor with slates on their laps.

If the lack of books and supplies wasn't bad enough, most of her pupils were still traumatized by the fire. Some even suffered from nightmares. At times it seemed that she spent more time calming their fears than teaching the three Rs.

The problems she tried to escape when leaving Boston were nothing compared to the difficulties she now encountered. Never could she imagine a more inhospitable classroom or more trying circumstances.

Five-year-old Brandon Jones stood shivering, his lips slightly blue. Small for his age, he had reddish-brown hair, hazel eyes, and a freckled nose. He still wore the angel wings Maddie had fashioned out of wire and muslin. He'd insisted on wearing them nonstop during the past week. Hopelessly bent out of shape, the wings no longer bore any resemblance to their original form.

It *was* cold, but thinking they would be home by this time, she'd hesitated to add more fuel to the fire. The school board was adamant about her following their endless rules, which included dousing any flames before leaving the building.

Now, she lifted the last log out of the bin and tossed it into the stone fireplace.

"You can't leave a fire burning overnight," Sophie said in her singsong voice.

"I'm quite aware of that, Sophie," Maddie replied. They didn't even have enough firewood to burn an hour, let alone overnight.

Despite her best efforts to plug the holes with fabric scraps, the wind rattled the ill-fitting door and whistled through every joint and gap in the place.

She poked at the log until flames climbed up the stone chimney. She turned just in time to see Jimmy knock over the Christmas tree. Diving forward, she managed to grab it before it fell into the fire. Fortunately, it was a small tree, cut from the piney woods surrounding the school.

Silently counting to ten, Maddie clapped her hands. "The last one in their seat is a big purple frog!"

Sophie and Jimmy scrambled to their makeshift desks ahead of Brandon, who started to cry, huge tears rolling down his cheeks. A knowing look spread across Sophie's face.

"You're an angel, so you can't be a frog," Maddie said, ruffling the boy's hair.

"He's a snow angel," Sophie said.

"Why a snow angel?" Maddie asked.

Sophie rolled her eyes as if the answer were obvious. "Because snow angels can't talk."

"Brandon can talk," Maddie said. He just didn't want to. According to his mother Brandon hadn't said a word since his father died in the August fire. She took his hand and led him to his seat. Tears continued to roll down his cheeks, his silent sobs vibrating the wires at his back.

Maddie felt a tug in her heart.

"Your mama will be here soon," she said. *God, please let it be so.* After Brandon stopped crying, she cracked open the cabin's only door. The wind swooshed in with a roar, splattering her with snow and ripping essays and drawings from the wall.

It took all her strength to close the door again. It was pitch black outside, and she doubted that anyone could find the windowless schoolhouse even if they tried. Panic began to rise but was quickly forgotten in the din of the clanging school bell.

Jimmy had lifted the brass bell off her desk by its wooden handle and now ran around the room ringing it. The clamor was far too loud for the small confines of the cabin, and Maddie covered her ears.

"Jimmy, please put that down!" No sooner were the words out of her mouth when she changed her mind. "On second thought, do ring the bell," she said. "Ring it as loud as you please."

Constantly criticized by his father and others, Jimmy seemed confused by Maddie's approval. Sophie gleefully pointed to the list of school rules posted on the wall.

"The school board says we're not to make any unnecessary noise," she said in her high-pitched voice, referring to rule number eleven.

"A very good rule indeed," Maddie replied. "But you see, this *is* quite necessary. Come along, Jimmy. Ring, ring, ring."

She grabbed the lantern and opened the door just wide enough to extend her arm outside and swing the lantern back and forth. The roof overhang kept the door somewhat protected, but even so, the porch was covered in snow. Like it or not, she would have to do some shoveling. She held her face away from the wind, but there was no escaping the blast of cold air that assaulted her.

She encouraged the children to make as much noise as possible. The chances of anyone hearing them seemed remote, but it was worth a try. The wind howled, but the school bell was louder. "That's it. Good boy. Keep ringing. Come on everyone, clap."

Sophie shouted, little Brandon stomped his feet, and Jimmy kept ringing the bell.

Maddie thought she saw something move on the outer edges of the lantern light. "Shh!" She signaled for quiet. "Hello, is anyone there?" she shouted. The wind snatched her voice away, so she called again, this time louder.

A dark shadow hovered just outside the circle of light. Maddie squinted her eyes. "Helloooo." All at once a black bear loomed up in front of her, teeth bared, its loud roar turning her blood cold.

Maddie gasped and dropped the lantern. Pulling Brandon away from the door, she slammed it shut and fumbled to slide the bolt in place with trembling hands. Only after the door was securely locked—or as secure as the rickety door allowed—did she dare breathe.

Now that she'd dropped the lantern outside, the fire provided the only light. The classroom was cast in flickering shadows that added to the gloom.

All three children stared at her with rounded eyes. Jimmy had dropped the bell, and it rolled slowly into a corner.

Mouth dry, Maddie swallowed hard. It wouldn't do to panic or let her pupils know how much the bear had scared her. Hands tight at her sides, she said a silent prayer. *Please God, send help, quick!*

She managed a smile. "That was interesting, wasn't it?" Her voice unnaturally high, she continued, "Can anyone tell me what kind of bear that was?"

Jimmy wrinkled his nose as if the question was beneath him. A skeptical look crossed Sophie's face. Apparently the child wasn't fooled by Maddie's cheerful facade.

"It was an American black bear," Jimmy muttered.

Sophie's gaze wandered over to the rules on the wall. Her mouth turned down in disappointment, probably because no rules existed regarding bears. Apparently, the stuffy, all-knowing school board couldn't think of everything.

Chapter 2

Miss Parker's Class

God told us to pass our trash as we would have others pass their trash to us.
That was before they invented wastebaskets.
Elizabeth, age 7

Sheriff Donovan was fit to be tied. Plodding through the woods on his horse during the storm of the century was the last thing he wanted to do. If the labored breathing was any indication, his horse, Morgan, wasn't too keen on it either.

If he was lucky enough to reach the schoolhouse without freezing to death, Donovan prayed he had the presence of mind to keep from wringing the schoolteacher's pretty neck. He blew out his breath. Pretty? Now where had that come from?

Drat! The cold had already affected his brain.

Anyone foolish enough to get herself stranded in a snowstorm with a bunch of children can't be all that bright. He knew hiring a woman from Boston would be a mistake. What did a big-city woman like her know about teaching children in a small Texas town? His had been one of the few dissenting voices, but the school board hired her anyway, though he suspected it was her pretty face more than her academic ability that swayed them. There it was again, the word *pretty*.

He pulled the collar of his duster another notch higher and gritted his teeth. All because of the fool schoolmarm, he was forced to fight fierce winds and knee-deep snow on a rescue mission.

Worse, it was now completely dark. If his lantern went out, he'd be in a heap of trouble.

Wind howling, Donovan urged his horse onward through the wet and sticky snow. He'd never seen anything like it. Droughts, tornadoes, fire, thunderstorms, and humidity were the norm for Maverick. Snow like this was a different ball of wax.

Tall pines swung back and forth, sweeping the sky and slapping boughs against tree trunks. Every so often a branch snapped off, missing him by inches.

16

In the darkness his lantern barely penetrated the thick whirling flakes. He was cold and wet and hungry and tired. It seemed like he'd been riding through the woods for hours. He thought he'd followed the road, but now he wasn't so sure. Was he going in circles? Hopelessly lost? What?

This latest storm had already dumped another couple of feet of fresh snow on top of what was left over from last week's storm.

His horse faltered. "Whoa, boy." He lifted his lantern high. The snow had given way to reveal a deep gulch. Thank God his horse had found his footing in time.

It was no use. It was too dangerous to go on. Searching probably wouldn't do much good anyway. He had no idea where the log cabin school was. For all he knew, it could be miles in the other direction.

He hated to give up, but what purpose would it serve if he got lost? Or if his horse was injured? As long as the schoolmarm and her pupils stayed inside, they should be all right. He'd come back for them first thing in the morning.

No sooner had he started back than he heard something—or thought he did. He reined in his horse and strained his ears against the howling wind.

Was that a school bell?

❄

A gust of wind whipped across the roof, but Maddie kept reading, holding the McGuffey book to the light of the fire.

"I Pity Them" was a good Samaritan story about an emigrant family traveling west and meeting tragedy. It was her pupils' favorite story and especially comforting on a night like this, when they needed rescuing themselves.

"You see, God sent help to the emigrants, and He'll send help to us," she said. *Just let it be soon, God; just let it be soon.* She sat in front of the fireplace with all three children huddled next to her trying to stay warm. The fire was almost out, and she could barely see to read. What if they were forced to spend the night at the cabin with no light or fire? Maybe she should try to retrieve the lantern dropped outside. The thought sent a shiver up her spine.

Brandon clutched her arm, fingers digging into her flesh. Eyes wide, he watched the dying cinders as if expecting the flames to jump out at him.

Making Brandon sit by the fire was almost as difficult as persuading Jimmy to give up the school bell. He'd insisted upon ringing it to scare off the bear, and her head still throbbed from the noise. At least she'd talked him out of going outside with his slingshot to confront the animal.

A thump came from outside the cabin, and all four jumped.

"What's that?" Sophie gasped. In her panic she inadvertently grabbed Jimmy's arm. Oddly enough, he didn't seem to notice.

"The bear's coming to get us," Jimmy said, his voice low. He flung out his hands, pushing Sophie back. "I told you I should have chased him off with my slingshot. Boo!"

Sophie screamed, the color draining from her face. Brandon buried his head in Maddie's skirt.

Maddie was just about at her limit. "Jimmy Madison, if you don't behave yourself I'll—"

Another bang was followed by a man's voice. "Open up. It's Sheriff Donovan."

Hand on her chest, Maddie gasped in relief. "Thank goodness. Come on, children. It's all right." She lifted Brandon's head and gave his nose a gentle tap. "See, everything's fine. We can go home now."

She jumped to her feet and hurried to unbolt the door. "Am I ever glad to see you!"

She never thought to say such a thing. Bad blood existed between her and the sheriff ever since he'd stood in front of the school board and objected to the town hiring a "greenhorn from Boston." Since then, she'd simply ignored him except for when he tracked her down to deliver the latest complaint lodged against her. Ignoring him was no longer an option. Not only did his presence seem to absorb the air in the room, but she was now completely dependent on him.

He slammed the door shut and glared at her, his lantern providing welcome light even as it revealed his displeasure. She was ready to bury her grievances, but his brusque manner told her he was not. Never mind. He didn't have to like or even approve of her. He just had to take them all home.

"You must be frozen," she said. "Come over by the fire." Not that the dying flames offered much warmth, but it was something.

He was dressed in a long black duster and a wide-brimmed hat that made his tall form appear much more impressive. A woolen scarf covered his mouth.

He yanked the scarf off his face, but his eyelashes and eyebrows were white with snow. He set his lantern down on the ironing board she used as a desk and pulled off his gloves. He then ambled toward the fireplace, pushing church pews out of the way to clear a path. The cabin was only ten by fifteen feet wide, but now it felt even more cramped.

He rubbed his hands together and blew on them.

"Did you see the bear?" Sophie asked.

The sheriff stared down at her. "Bear?" His breath came out in a white plume.

"A ferocious one," Jimmy said, holding up his hands claw-like to demonstrate.

18

"And he charged after us," Sophie said in an indignant voice.

"No one told me there were bears here," Maddie added. Or that a Texas winter could be so brutal.

The sheriff shrugged. "We're in the woods. That's where bears live." He met her gaze, his eyes challenging her. His rugged square face was anchored by an intriguing cleft chin. Unlike most men in town, he was clean shaven, with just a hint of a shadow at his jaw.

"Don't you have bears in Massachusetts?"

"Yes, but they have the good sense to hibernate in the winter," she replied, retaining her cool composure.

"Probably woke from all the racket you made. Bears don't like to be disturbed."

Sophie brightened. "I told you we shouldn't have made so much noise."

Maddie patted her head. "Yes, but then Sheriff Donovan wouldn't have found us." She clapped her hands. "Gather up your things, everyone. We're going home."

Sheriff Donovan turned away from the fireplace, hands at his waist, feet apart, an incredulous look on his face. "Ma'am, I hate to break it to you, but we're not goin' anywhere. Not tonight, at least. It's wicked out there. The road is blocked. We'll see how it looks in the morning."

She gaped at him. "You mean we have to stay here?" She glanced around the cold and drafty cabin. Despite her best decorating efforts, it still looked more like a dungeon than a classroom. She swallowed hard. "All night?"

He shrugged his massive shoulders. "Unless you have a better idea."

"We can't stay here," Sophie said. "A teacher cannot spend the night with a man that's not her brother or father. Pa will be furious."

Maddie folded her arms across her chest. Sophie knew the rules not only for pupils but teachers, too. "What do you have to say about that, Sheriff?"

He glanced at the three children before settling his gaze on Sophie. "Would your pa like it any better if we were all eaten by a bear?"

Brandon shuddered and clutched at Maddie's skirt.

"It's not necessary to scare the children," she scolded in a voice usually saved for her most unruly pupils.

He lifted his gaze to her without apology. "Do you have any more firewood?"

"Out back, but I doubt you'll be able to reach it for all the snow." Every morning before class began, she carried in wood from the woodpile. "I didn't expect to spend the night."

"That makes two of us," he muttered. He looked around. "This cabin has as many holes as a sieve. Do you have modeling clay or school paste?"

"In the cabinet," she said. Cabinet was a fancy name for the wooden crate housing what pitiful few school supplies she'd managed to collect.

He pointed at Jimmy. "How are you at plugging holes?"

Jimmy's face brightened. "I once plugged up the town water pump so no one could get water."

"So you're the culprit, are you? Sounds like you're the right man for the job." Donovan pointed to Sophie. "We need something to mix clay in." He laid a hand on Brandon's shoulder. "You're the chief stirrer."

Brandon stared at him on the verge of tears, and Maddie tucked the boy's hand in hers.

"Brandon will make a perfect stirrer," she said.

Minutes after arriving, Donovan managed to put all three children to work. "While you're getting things ready, I'll see to my horse and look for the woodpile."

"There's a lean-to in back. You'll find hay there," Maddie said.

Donovan gave a curt nod and left, taking the lantern with him.

By the time he returned a short time later, Maddie had managed to melt just enough snow to add to the clay. Donovan pulled off his duster, hanging it on a nail. He was dressed in dark pants and blue shirt, a silver star pinned to his leather vest. A gun holster looped with cartridges sagged from the weight of his double-action revolver.

"The lantern outside is broken, and I can't find the woodpile," he announced.

Heart sinking, Maddie washed the clay off her hands in a basin of water. "The last log is about to burn out." In his absence, she'd thrown a couple of wooden rulers into the fire to keep it ablaze.

Donovan grabbed the Christmas tree and tossed it into the smoldering cinders, paper ornaments and all. Crackling flames leaped up to engulf the tree, and the room grew bright.

She glared at him. "The children made those ornaments."

"I guess they'll just have to make more." He quickly moved the pews away from the walls and into the center of the room. After the clay was adequately softened, he gathered them around to explain what to do.

"It's called chinking. You take a handful of clay and push it between the logs." He demonstrated, and the children quickly caught on. They filled some but by no means all of the lower gaps. The holes up high were left for the sheriff to fill.

"I'm hungry," Jimmy said.

Donovan glanced at Maddie. "Do you have anything to eat?"

"Just some crackers and beef jerky," she replied.

20

She pulled out her supply of food from a box she kept beneath the ironing-board desk. She broke the dry meat into bite-sized pieces and set out the crackers. It wasn't much, but it was all she had.

"Rule number seven says we're not to eat in the classroom," Sophie said.

"I dare you to go outside," Jimmy said, playing with a loose floorboard next to the ironing-board desk.

Sophie made a face at him and plopped down cross-legged in front of the fire to daintily eat a cracker.

Shivering, Maddie ran her hands up and down her arms. "We're going to have to figure out a way to keep the fire going. Otherwise, we'll freeze to death." The Christmas tree created a bright blaze and filled the cabin with a pleasant pine smell, but it would soon burn out.

Donovan glanced around, his gaze settling finally on one of the church pews. "We have all the wood we need."

Maddie raised an eyebrow but made no comment. Let *him* handle the church elders when they found out their precious pews had been used as firewood.

Brandon tugged at Maddie's skirt. "It's all right," she said, wrapping her arms around the boy's trembling body, crushing his wings even more.

"It's warmer over here," Donovan said. "I won't bite."

"The fire makes him anxious." Maddie knelt down to look Brandon square in the face. "You don't have to be afraid. The sheriff will protect us." Her eyes locked with Donovan's. "Isn't that right?"

Donovan nodded for Brandon's sake, though in reality it seemed like a lie. Some protector. He hadn't been able to save his family three years earlier in December from the scourges of smallpox, and he certainly had no control over the weather. Worse, now he had to spend the night at the schoolhouse that was decorated from the floor to the rafters for Christmas—a holiday he'd sooner forget.

At least he didn't have to look at the Christmas tree anymore. That was a relief. All it did was remind him of his loss. The last happy memory of his family was decorating a tree with strings of popcorn and cranberries and little paper angels cut from packages of Arbuckles' coffee. Days later his wife, son, and unborn child were dead. Still, had he stopped to consider that the pupils made the ornaments, he would have been slower to toss it.

The children did a decent job of chinking the cracks between the lower logs. But they couldn't reach the high logs, and he didn't want anyone falling and getting hurt. That was all he needed.

He dragged a pew to one side of the cabin and stood on it, ducking his head beneath a string of red-and-green paper chains. The cabin was booby-trapped. Practically every wall was covered with pictures torn out of magazines or pupil essays written on brown paper or pieces of flour sack. He had to give the schoolmarm credit. She'd done wonders with what little she had to work with.

He slapped a handful of wet clay against a corner crack. The place should have been condemned long ago. The fire that had destroyed most of the town and part of the woods had failed to reach this cabin and others like it. What a pity. And whatever happened to the old miner who once lived here? One day the man just up and disappeared.

Saying the cabin was poorly built was a mite too generous. The logs were round and bark covered, and not one wall intersected at a right angle. At least the miner hadn't skimped on the stone foundation. The foundations of most log cabins in the area measured eighteen inches from the ground. That was higher than any termite could climb, or so the locals believed. This one was twice the norm. How strange that the miner would overbuild the foundation and skimp on the rest. Either he overestimated termites or got carried away.

While Donovan worked, Miss Parker gathered the children around her to sing carols. Just what he needed. Another reminder of Christmas.

Jimmy tried to outsing Sophie, but that little Brandon fellow didn't open his mouth. The boy was about the age that his son, Jeffrey, would have been had he lived.

Donovan slapped his hand hard against the wet clay. The clay stopped the unwelcome cold air from blowing inside, but not the memories. Nothing could stop those.

" *'Let heaven and nature sing. . . .'*"

He tried to ignore the singing, but he couldn't help but notice that Miss Parker had a nice voice. It was soft and clear and reminded him of spring. He shook the thought away. The cold had definitely affected his thinking.

He didn't realize he was staring until her gaze locked with his. The flickering light of the fire turned her blond hair into liquid gold. She wore it in a tight bun, but enough wisps escaped to hint that perhaps she wasn't quite as stiff and unbending as she seemed. He could almost envision her hair tumbling down her back. Would her hair feel as silky as it looked? As soft?

Shaken by the thought, he quickly refocused on the crack between the logs, and that's where his attention would have remained had Miss Parker not lifted her skirt to step over a pew, revealing a slender ankle below a lace-trimmed petticoat.

He quickly averted his gaze. Annoying woman. It wasn't bad enough that she had caused him so much trouble. Now she was making him think things he didn't want to think. Maybe even feel things he didn't want to feel.

First thing in the morning, he would escort the pupils and Miss Parker home, and he'd avoid all the cheerfulness of Christmas just as he has done every year since his family's death.

After that, he would have as little to do with Miss Parker as possible.

Chapter 3

Miss Parker's Class

The three wise men brought Jesus francis and mirth for his birthday,
but he really wanted tin soldiers.
Robert, age 9

Maddie couldn't sleep. The floor was hard, and the howling of the wind sounded louder without the children's chatter to drown it out. Sheriff Donovan kept the fire ablaze, but she was still cold. Though she'd covered herself with her cloak, the floor felt like a layer of ice.

Brandon was curled up next to her, his breathing soft. Sophie slept on the other side of Brandon. She muttered in her sleep much as she complained during the day. No doubt somebody had broken a rule in her dreams.

It had been a fight getting the children to bed down, mainly because Sophie insisted Brandon sleep on the "boys' side" with Jimmy and the sheriff. Brandon was adamant about sleeping next to Maddie. Sophie finally relented but not without threatening to report Brandon to her father.

Maddie yawned. Just about to fall asleep again, a thud at the front door made her jump. Sitting up carefully so as not to disturb Brandon, she called to the sheriff in a soft voice.

"Sheriff, I heard something."

Donovan groaned and rolled over. "What?"

"I don't know what. Something. Maybe the bear is back."

He reached for his pocket watch, holding it up so he could read it in the light of the fire.

"It's 2:00 a.m.," he said as if the time were relevant in some way.

"I don't think bears can tell time," she said. She whispered so as not to wake the children, and he whispered back.

"Only in grisly situations."

His unexpected pun made her smile. The grim-faced sheriff had a sense of humor, after all. Or did he?

"I can't bear the thought," she said, unable to resist.

24

"And I can't bear to be awakened in the middle of the night. Turn over, and go to sleep."

The last was delivered in his usual brusque manner. Sighing, Maddie turned over.

❄

She was on the way home for Christmas, the carriage swaying back and forth. She could almost smell the roast beef and gravy. The carriage suddenly hit a bumpy road, and it was all she could do to hold on.

Maddie opened her eyes and was disappointed to find that she wasn't in a carriage on the way home for the holidays. Instead, she lay on the floor of a drafty old log cabin. Brandon leaned over and shook her.

"I have to go."

She groaned. The sheriff had rigged a private place in a corner by leaning two pews against the wall, but it required walking near the fireplace, which Brandon refused to do unaided. He initially refused to use the tin bucket altogether, but need eventually overcame reluctance.

Hand on her sore back, she stood, her legs stiff. She felt like she'd been battered by a bull.

Predictably, Jimmy was a restless sleeper. Sometime during the night he'd managed to travel the length of the cabin and now slept on the "girls' side."

While Brandon took care of his business, she tossed a piece of oak into the fire. She hated burning up a perfectly good pew, but it was better than freezing to death. Let the sheriff handle the church elders.

She yawned and stretched her back. She had no idea what time it was. What she wouldn't give to be in her own bed. She reached for a second length of wood.

An ear-piercing scream sent the tiny schoolhouse into a panic. Maddie spun around, wielding the plank like a weapon. Sheriff Donovan jumped up, gun in hand. Brandon shot out from behind the pews, and Jimmy sat up, rubbing his eyes.

The scream had come from Sophie, who stood pointing at Jimmy. "You're on the girls' side," she shrieked. She then glared at her teacher. "And you're on the boys' side."

Donovan slid his gun back into its holster. "Some people just don't know their places," he said, sounding surprisingly pleasant given the early morning hour.

Maddie dropped the wood. "And I suppose you do." She pointed to his hat, which was clearly on the wrong side of the yarn barrier Sophie had stretched down the middle of the cabin to divide the girls from the boys.

"Hats have free rein." He settled back on the floor as if he had every intention of getting more shut-eye.

Hands at her waist, Maddie stared at him in disbelief. Obviously the sheriff had little experience with children. Already Jimmy was jumping from pew to pew, slingshot in hand. Sophie checked the school rules posted on the wall, and Brandon tossed a rubber ball up and down. Sleep was out of the question—even for the sheriff.

❄

The moment daylight broke, Donovan went outside to assess the weather. He returned moments later looking grim. "The drifts are at least ten feet high, and it's still snowing. It looks like we're stuck here for at least another day."

Maddie's heart sank. "We're almost out of food."

He tossed a nod toward the young ones. "Give it to them. I'm going to see if I can dig through the woodpile."

After he left, Maddie broke half the jerky into small pieces. She made the children wash their hands and faces in melted snow heated by the fire before divvying up the portions.

"Is that it?" Sophie complained. "We'll starve to death."

"I'm sure that we'll be rescued before that happens," Maddie said. "Eat slowly and—"

The food disappeared before she completed her sentence, and an argument broke out between Jimmy and Sophie as to who got more.

"Your piece of jerky was bigger," Sophie insisted. "And that's not fair."

Nerves on end, Maddie reached for her Bible. She started each school day with a Bible lesson and prayer. This wasn't a normal day, but she decided to keep the same routine.

"Let's pray," she said loud enough to gain everyone's attention. She waited for the three children to join her and bow their heads. "Dear heavenly Father, please protect us as we wait for rescue. Guide us in deed and thoughts, and keep us all safe."

"And send food," Jimmy added.

"And send food," Maddie repeated. "Amen."

Sophie pointed her finger at Brandon. "He didn't close his eyes. You have to close your eyes when you pray. That's the rule. Even if you're mad at God."

Brandon never bowed his head or closed his eyes during morning prayer, but Maddie hadn't made an issue of it. "Why do you think Brandon's mad at God?"

"Because God took his pa away," Sophie said in a matter-of-fact voice.

"God didn't take his pa away. The fire did that." Maddie took Brandon's cold hands in hers, rubbing them until they were warm.

"God would never take away people we care about because He loves us." She tried to think how to explain it in terms Brandon could understand. "It's like when you fall and hurt yourself and run to your mother. What does she do?"

"She takes care of you," Sophie replied.

"Yes, that's right," Maddie said. "God greeted your pa with open arms and is taking good care of him. Like He takes care of all His hurting people." She squeezed Brandon's hands. "Do you understand what I'm saying?"

Brandon stared at her but said nothing. She was suddenly aware of a terrible blast of cold air. Donovan had returned and stood by the door watching them, his arms empty. Apparently, he still hadn't found the woodpile. He studied her for a moment before slamming the door shut and shaking snow off his duster and hat.

"Is your horse all right?" she asked.

He nodded. "The chimney keeps the lean-to fairly warm."

"That's good," she said.

For the rest of the morning the blizzard raged outside, and tempers flared inside. The sheriff didn't help matters. He was distant and barely spoke except when absolutely necessary. At times she caught him watching her, but his thoughts remained hidden behind the gloomy mask of his face. No doubt he blamed her for the situation. As if she were responsible for the weather or remoteness of the cabin.

Now he knelt by the fireplace, breaking up the last of a church pew with blows of a well-aimed ax.

Sophie punched Jimmy in the arm. "He won't leave me alone," she whined for perhaps the hundredth time.

"Come along, children," Maddie said, feigning a cheerfulness she didn't feel. "Tomorrow will be Christmas Eve, and something magical always happens then."

At least it always did in Boston. The day before Christmas was when friends and relatives arrived bearing presents and food to share. There was always plenty of roast beef, potatoes, and fruitcake to go around—and what would Christmas be without oysters? Sighing, she pushed such thoughts away. She was homesick enough without making herself more miserable. If only the wind would stop.

"What about the Christmas program?" Sophie asked. "What if no one can come to see it?"

"We'll just have to wait for another day," Maddie said. "Perhaps after Christmas."

"We should do it at the Fourth of July picnic," Jimmy said, crawling beneath a pew to retrieve chips of wood. "We'll have Christmas in July."

"That's not funny," Sophie stormed. "Christmas plays should be at Christmastime. That's the rule."

"I tell you what," Maddie said. "Let's play charades." Whenever she'd suggested playing the game in the past, her pupils had responded with raised hands and loud shouts of "Me first." Today her suggestion was met with stony-faced indifference.

"I'm hungry," Sophie complained.

"Me, too," Jimmy said.

"It's nice to hear that you two agree on something. See? Already we have a Christmas miracle." She reached into her supply box for the last of the beef jerky and broke it into three small pieces.

While handing a piece to Brandon, she inadvertently knocked against Donovan's arm. The cabin was small, and the ironing-board desk and the remainder of the long, narrow pews took up most of the space, leaving little room for its occupants. It seemed like she could hardly move without bumping into the sheriff, rubbing against his arm, brushing him with the flared hem of her skirt. Earlier they even reached for the poker at the same moment, her hand meeting his on the brass handle.

Now she quickly pulled away and tried to pretend that nothing had happened. She glanced at him to see if he'd noticed but was unable to tell by his expression. He simply donned his duster and walked outside, presumably to check his horse or the weather. Again.

Maddie didn't need to go outside to know that the storm hadn't let up. Not even Jimmy and Sophie's shouting match could mute the wind that threatened at times to carry away the roof if not the whole cabin.

She reached into her supply box, where she kept her special stationery. She used it for progress reports home to parents. It was expensive paper, but desperate times called for desperate measures.

"I want you to draw a special picture for Christmas," she said, passing a sheet of foolscap paper to each child, along with a well-sharpened graphite lead pencil. Even Jimmy brightened at the prospect of drawing on real paper rather than on odd pieces of feed sack or whatever cardboard she could find.

While the three of them drew, she knelt by the fire, enjoying the relative quiet that had descended inside the cabin. Donovan returned and dumped an armload of chopped wood on the hearth and pulled off his duster and hat.

"You found the woodpile," she exclaimed.

He gave a curt nod. The silver star on his leather vest looked bright and cheery in the light of the fire, an odd contrast to his serious demeanor.

"You could try to be a little more pleasant for the children's sake," she said, keeping her voice low.

He met her gaze. "I don't like Christmas."

"That's a surprise. I thought it was me you didn't like." When he failed to comment, she ventured to ask, "Why don't you like Christmas?" Christmas was her favorite holiday—or it had been before coming to Texas.

He took so long to answer she had almost given up hope that he would. "My wife and son died on Christmas Day three years ago," he said at last.

She sat back on her heels. "I–I'm so sorry. I had no idea."

She'd lived in Maverick for only two months and didn't have much time to socialize. As a result she knew very little about its citizens. Widow Hancock had been kind enough to let her board in her home. The woman couldn't hear worth a bat's wing, so chitchatting was out of the question. Due to the number of complaints about her lenient teaching methods, she stayed away from the townsfolk as much as possible, except to go to church. Even then, she felt like an outsider and left the moment the service was over, not socializing like the rest of the congregation.

"How old was your son?" she asked, her voice soft.

"Five."

She grimaced. "The same age as Brandon." She couldn't imagine what it was like to lose a child, let alone a wife.

"I'm so sorry," she said. Though she meant it from the depths of her heart, the words sounded inadequate, even to her own ears.

Silence stretched between them, and she squirmed with discomfort. She regretted probing into the sheriff's private life, as that only seemed to make him more withdrawn. Now he stared into the crackling fire as if gazing at something that only he could see.

Brandon came over to show her what he'd drawn. He seemed less fearful of the fire, and that was a relief. Grateful for the distraction, she gave the boy her full attention. He held the paper with both hands as if presenting something delicate as a butterfly.

"It's beautiful, Brandon." He had drawn a picture of a black bear, complete with bared teeth. Even at his young age, Brandon showed artistic talent. She must remember to write that on his next report home to his widowed mother.

"I'll hang it on the wall." She looked around for the perfect spot. "How about over there by my desk?"

Brandon shook his head and pointed to the rafter ceiling.

"No one will see it if we put it up there," she said.

Brandon kept pointing, a determined look on his freckled face.

Sophie looked up from her own drawing. "He wants his pa to see it from heaven."

Maddie leaned closer. "Is that why you want me to hang it from a rafter? So your pa can see it?"

Brandon nodded, and Maddie thought her heart would break. It was all she could do to find her voice behind the lump in her throat.

Turning his gaze from the fire, Donovan stared at Brandon with a tender, almost wistful look. Without the harsh lines and firmly set jaw, the sheriff looked years younger than his age, which she guessed was around thirty.

"I know someone else in heaven who would like your picture. My little boy." His voice grew thick. "His name is Jeffrey." He pointed to the crossbar that ran the length of the cabin. "If I hang it from that rafter both your pa and my son will be sure to see it."

Brandon nodded and handed his paper to Donovan, who arranged a pew beneath the rafter to stand on. He then tacked the drawing in place. A draft caused the paper to move back and forth, making the bear look even more menacing.

"There you go," Donovan said, stepping off the pew and sounding more cheerful than he had all day.

Brandon flung his arms around Donovan's waist. Donovan looked startled at first, and then ever so slowly he lifted his hand, holding it in midair for a moment before lowering it to the boy's head. Brandon looked up at him, and Donovan wrapped him in both arms, and they clung to each other as only two people who shared a similar loss knew how to do.

Maddie looked away but only to hide her tears.

Later, she knelt on the floor next to Sophie. Ever the perfectionist, Sophie took meticulous care with her drawing, making every line perfectly straight with the use of a ruler. In contrast Jimmy had spent almost no time on his drawing, choosing instead to fold his paper and shoot it to the rafters, where the wind tossed it about.

"How do you always know what Brandon is thinking?" Maddie asked. "About his pa?"

Sophie carefully outlined her picture of a Christmas tree. "It's easy. I can tell by his face."

"Really?" Obviously, there was more to Sophie than met the eye.

"Yeah. Just like I can tell Jimmy likes me."

"If that's true, why don't you two get along?" Maddie asked

"You're not supposed to let the other person know you like him," Sophie whispered. "At least not at first. That's the rule. Just like the sheriff pretends not to like you."

Maddie's mouth dropped open, but she quickly recovered. Obviously,

Sophie wasn't as perceptive as she seemed, except for perhaps where Brandon was concerned. She leaned closer to Sophie, her voice low. "Adults have different rules. When we like someone, we're not afraid to let the other person know."

Just then Maddie heard something that made her look up. Was that a chuckle she'd heard? Coming from the sheriff? It was hard to tell from where she sat. Donovan stood reading a pupil essay on the wall, his back to her. She couldn't resist joining him to see which paper caught his attention

"I like this one," he said, pointing to a square of cardboard. It was an essay about Joan of Arc written by seven-year-old Benjamin Bond. "I didn't know that Joan was Noah's wife," Donovan said. He then pointed to another essay, and fine lines crinkled around his eyes.

"Jesus couldn't be born until they found a manager," he read, his voice edged with humor.

Maddie felt a warm glow inside. "I do believe everyone could use a manager—don't you agree?" she asked.

He grinned at her before moving to the next essay.

My, my, what a handsome man he was when he smiled. Why had she not noticed that before? She'd always thought of him as a grim-faced man. Is that what grief had done to him?

"What's so funny?" Sophie asked.

Maddie turned and faced the classroom. "We're happy because it's almost Christmas Eve. Like I told you, that's when miracles happen."

If ever she needed a miracle, it was now. They were out of food, and judging by the still-roaring wind, the storm wouldn't let up anytime soon. Her pupils' parents must be half out of their minds.

Donovan held her gaze, her worries mirrored on his face. But she saw something else there, too. Something she couldn't decipher or name. What a complex man: one moment lighthearted, the next so serious.

Just like the sheriff pretends not to like you.

Nothing could be further from the truth, of course. Sophie was an impressionable child given to flights of fancy. She'd simply misinterpreted something she saw or heard. Still, there had been moments. . .

Embarrassed to be caught staring, Maddie quickly lowered her gaze and prayed the sheriff didn't notice her reddening cheeks.

"I think the wind is stopping," he said, his voice strangely hoarse. "I'll take a look outside." He grabbed his duster and left.

❄

Not only had the storm not let up, but it snowed harder than when Donovan had last checked. He pulled up his collar and dug his hands deep into his pockets.

"God would never take away people we care about because He loves us."

Why did Miss Parker's words keep running through his mind? He never blamed God for what happened to his family. True, he'd stopped going to church, and he couldn't remember the last time he'd prayed, but that didn't mean he was angry at God. Or did it?

"God would never take away people we care about. . . ."

Maybe he *had* been angry at God, but who could blame him?

He stood in front of the cabin door with the wind and snow in his face and Jimmy's and Sophie's querulous voices at his back. He wanted to believe in a good and kind and loving God, but he was cold and hungry, and his body ached from sleeping on the hard wood floor. At that moment it was hard to believe in anything.

Chapter 4

Miss Parker's Class

When God said there should be peas on earth,
I don't think He meant us to eat them.
George, age 6

Maddie woke on the morning of Christmas Eve to find the fire almost out. Stuffing her feet in her high button shoes and pulling her woolen cloak around her shoulders, she hurried to add wood to the fire, poking it until flames climbed up the chimney.

It was then that she noticed Jimmy was missing. Thinking he was using the makeshift privy, she called to him. "Jimmy, are you there?"

No answer. She peered behind the slanted pews.

No sign of Jimmy. Alarmed, she swung around and checked the door—unbolted. Cold fear shot down her spine.

"Sheriff, wake up," she shouted. "Jimmy's gone!"

She yanked open the door, and the wind and snow swept in. The storm still raged, and she could barely see outside.

"Jimmy!" she screamed on the top of her lungs, but the wind carried her voice away.

She stumbled outside, blindly grabbing hold of the guide rope Donovan had stretched from the porch to the rear of the cabin. "Jimmy!" The wind hit her full force, but she kept going, the rope digging into her palms.

The rope ended at the lean-to, but it was too dark to see anything. "Jimmy!"

Letting go of the rope, she stepped away from the building and sank into what seemed like a bottomless pit. Her feet struck hard ice, and a pain shot up her shins.

Frantic, she pushed away the chest-high snow, fingers stiff, hands numb with cold. She couldn't move her legs, couldn't see, couldn't breathe. She flailed her arms, trying in vain to reach the guide rope, but it was no good. All she could do was scream at the top of her lungs.

"Jimmy!"

Fear gripped her even harder than the snow. The searing wind cut into her face like icy knives. She gasped for air, and a sob rose from her very depths. *Where is he, God? Help me!*

She felt herself move upward. Was it her imagination? Was this how it felt to go to heaven? She gradually grew conscious of hands beneath her arms, strong, firm, and capable hands. She collapsed into a circle of warmth, her body wracked with sobs.

Clinging to Donovan, she cried, "I can't find Jimmy."

"I'll find him," Donovan shouted in her ear. "Go back inside."

"He'll die out here!"

"I'll find him."

She choked back a cry. No one could stand the cold for long, certainly no child. Donovan scooped her in his arms and held her close as he carried her back to the wooden porch, his boots crunching against the snow.

He set her upright on the steps, but her knees threatened to give way. *If anything happens to Jimmy. . . Oh, God. . .*

Donovan opened the door and pushed her inside. Chilled to the bone, she was unable to fight him.

"Miss Parker, look!" Sophie cried.

Shivering so much her teeth chattered, it took Maddie a moment to make sense of the sight in front of her. It took even longer to believe what she saw. Jimmy stood in the middle of the cabin, his face practically split in two by a wide grin.

Maddie never thought to see a more glorious sight. Tears rolling down her cheeks, she threw her arms around him. "You scared me." She cupped her hands around his face. "You practically scared me to death."

"Eww, you're cold," he said, pulling away.

She wasn't just cold; she was frozen, and snow still clung to her skirt. But none of that mattered, not now.

"Where were you?" Donovan asked. "Why didn't you answer when we called you?"

"I found a cellar." Jimmy pointed to a gaping hole next to Maddie's ironing-board desk. "It leads to a tunnel. I didn't hear you."

Maddie glanced at Donovan, who was blowing on his hands. "But the door was unbolted, I thought. . ."

"I grabbed the hatchet from the porch," Jimmy said. "I used it to pry open the cellar door."

"Jimmy found tin goods!" Sophie's voice was high-pitched with excitement. "There's food. Come and see." She grabbed Maddie's hand and pulled her across the room. "Now we can eat."

Maddie stared through the square hole in the floor. She had known there was a loose floorboard in that spot, but it had never occurred to her it was actually a trapdoor. Sophie held the lantern over the hole, and the light illuminated a shelf of tin goods.

Jimmy brushed past her and climbed down the wooden ladder. "Come on down," he called.

"Miss Parker is cold and wet. She needs to dry off," Donovan said. He slipped off his duster. "Here, put this on. It's dryer than your cloak."

He held the duster for her. She slipped out of her wet garment and slid her arms into the duster's sleeves. The long coat practically buried her, but it felt warm and cozy and so very, very comforting. When she pulled the wool fabric close, she caught a whiff of leather and pine that was as pleasant as it was masculine.

Turning her back, she reached inside to pull off her wet skirt and petticoat, leaving her drawers intact. Donovan took the garments from her, his gaze meeting hers for an instant before turning to spread them in front of the fire to dry.

"Hurry," Jimmy called from below, his voice edged with impatience.

Donovan's eyebrows raised in question. "I'll go below. You stay by the fire."

"And miss all the fun?" she asked, slipping her cold hands into the duster's deep pockets. "Come on. Let's not keep Jimmy waiting any longer."

He gave her a crooked grin. "After you."

She blew on her still-cold hands, turned, and felt for the first rung on the ladder with her foot. The duster was in the way, and she had to take care not to get her shoes caught in the hem. The three children waited for her to descend, Jimmy holding the lantern up high.

The moment Maddie reached the cellar floor, Donovan started down the ladder, the wood creaking beneath his weight.

The cellar had dirt walls and floor, the low ceiling reinforced with wood beams. It smelled dank and musty. Rough wood shelves stretched the length of one wall. Maddie counted a dozen or more cans of food and a package of tack bread. Unbelievable!

She took Brandon's hands and swung him around. "God worked through Jimmy, and now we have something to eat."

Lowering Brandon to the ground, she hugged Sophie and Jimmy and in her excitement threw her arms around Donovan. He looked startled at first but quickly slipped his hands around her waist and hugged her back. Feeling suddenly breathless, she pulled away.

Purposely avoiding his eyes, she studied the cans, reading each label aloud. "Peas, string beans, corn, beets. More peas and—"

"Is that all there is?" Sophie asked, making a face. "Just vegetables?"

"I'm afraid so," Maddie answered.

"If God had worked through me, we would have had roast beef," Sophie grumbled.

Maddie tapped her on the nose. "I think God gave us exactly what He thought we most needed."

"And that includes coffee," Donovan said, holding up a packet of Arbuckles' Ariosa Coffee. When no one else shared his enthusiasm, he shrugged.

"It's either vegetables or nothing," Maddie said. "Take your pick."

When no one moved, Donovan started pulling cans off the shelf. "I don't know about you," he said, heading for the ladder, "but I'm hungry enough to eat a bear."

Chapter 5

Miss Parker's Class

Jesus had twelve opossums, which went out into the world to preach.
The opossum in our backyard just hangs from a tree.
Casey, age 7

M addie insisted everyone wash their hands with soap and water before eating.

"Do we have to?" Jimmy groaned.

"Yes, you have to," Maddie replied. She was dressed again, though the hem of her skirt was still slightly damp. It had just been too difficult to prepare the meal wearing Donovan's oversize duster, the scent of him too distracting.

Hands washed and dried, everyone scrambled to sit on the floor around the pew. They searched the cellar for cutlery and plates with no success, but Brandon found a rusty old can opener that worked just fine.

"Let's say grace," she said. "We have so much to be grateful for."

Ignoring the children's glum faces, she took Brandon's hand, and he took Sophie's. Sophie hesitated before finally offering her hand to Jimmy. He looked about to protest, but Donovan shook his head. Jimmy grabbed hold of the tip of Sophie's pinkie finger.

Donovan took Jimmy's other hand before reaching for Maddie's. Her hand seemed to melt in his, and her heart gave a mad thump.

"Would you like to do the honors, Sheriff?" she asked, looking at him through lowered lashes.

Donovan hesitated as if he was about to decline, but he nonetheless lowered his head. "Our dear heavenly Father," he said, "thank You for bringing us together and for sending us a Christmas miracle. Amen."

Donovan squeezed her fingers, and Maddie quickly pulled away.

"It doesn't look like a miracle." Arms crossed in front, Sophie thrust out her lower lip.

"What? Roast beef and gravy isn't a miracle?" Donovan reached for a can of string beans. "Ah, mashed potatoes—my favorite."

Sophie continued to pout, but Jimmy soon joined in the fun. "Lemon drops!" He reached across the table to grab a handful of corn.

Sophie's mouth dropped open. "I can't eat without a fork or knife." She looked close to tears.

"We don't need forks or knives," Donovan replied. "We have this." He picked up a piece of tack bread and demonstrated how to scoop up food without utensils.

Watching Sophie try to maintain proper table manners under such difficult circumstances, Maddie almost felt sorry for her. In contrast, Jimmy had no qualms about eating with his fingers, much to Sophie's disgust.

Maddie scooped some kernels of corn on tack bread and handed it to Brandon. He ate hungrily, though he refused to eat peas. Soon color returned to his cheeks.

Without silverware or china, it was the crudest meal Maddie had ever encountered, but never had she appreciated one more.

Donovan held up a cracker topped with beets. "I think we should all make a toast to Jimmy."

"What's a toast?" Sophie asked.

"Don't you know anything?" Jimmy said. "It's something you eat in the morning and drink at night."

Maddie cleared her throat. "In this case," she explained, "a toast is our way of thanking Jimmy for helping to bring about a Christmas Eve miracle. God truly worked through him. You see? God does love and take care of His people."

"Amen," Donovan said, his mouth curving upward.

Following Donovan's lead, Maddie held up a piece of hardtack, and Sophie followed suit.

"To Jimmy," Donovan said.

"To Jimmy!" they all echoed, even Sophie.

Jimmy grinned from ear to ear, and Maddie felt her heart swell with thanksgiving. How she had hated this cabin, hated even Maverick. She had counted the days until the end of the school year when her contract was up and she could return to Boston. But at that moment, there was no place she would rather be.

Donovan followed the guide rope around back of the cabin to the lean-to. Morgan nickered and greeted him with a nod of his head. Donovan ran his hand along the horse's neck. "It won't be much longer, buddy." He checked the horse's water and hay supply and stepped outside.

Was it only his imagination, or did the wind seem less fierce than before?

Or maybe he had simply grown used to it. Next to the constant chatter and querulous voices inside the cabin, cannon fire would seem mild. It had stopped snowing, but the sky was still gray, though not as dark.

He headed past the woodpile. His lungs burned from the cold, but it felt good to stretch his legs and clear his brain. He stopped to examine a pine tree, its boughs bent low with snow. This was crazy. No one in their right mind would try to pick out a Christmas tree in this weather.

He remembered the last time he'd traipsed through the woods in search of the perfect tree. His wife, Cynthia, liked her trees short and bushy. He liked his tall, slender, and graceful. Sort of like Miss Parker. He shook his head. Now where had that come from?

He managed a half smile. He could well imagine her reaction if she knew he'd likened her to a Christmas tree. Along with the thought came a whiff of lavender. Was he imagining things? Then he remembered that he'd loaned Miss Parker his duster while her skirt dried. It was a soft, delicate fragrance that brought to mind pleasant, though unwelcome, thoughts.

Visions of her filled his head. The way she looked in the morning, all disheveled with golden locks tumbling down her back. . .the tilt of her head, the sound of her laughter, the way she moved. . . But the strongest memory of all was holding her in his arms.

With this last thought came the guilt, raining down on him like an avalanche. Since Cynthia had died, he hadn't even looked at another woman. At least not in *that* way. Hadn't wanted to. Still didn't want to. Did he?

Cabin fever, that's what he had. He was a large man better suited to the great outdoors. Holing up in the confines of a cabin could make a man like him do strange things. What was he thinking? He'd already done strange things. Like laugh without the usual remorse that followed since Cynthia's death. Much as he wanted to deny it, it felt right to laugh—good even. Just as it had felt right to pray for the first time in God only knew how long.

Thinking of Miss Parker felt right, too. He closed his eyes. *Forgive me, Cynthia. Forgive me.* But it wasn't Cynthia he saw in his mind's eye; it was Miss Parker. *Maddie*, as he now thought of her.

Shivering against the cold, he picked up his pace and circled back to the cabin.

❄

After their Christmas Eve feast, Maddie washed out an empty tin can with water she'd heated by the fire. She longed for a cup of tea, but she would settle for plain hot water.

Donovan had gone outside, presumably for firewood, but he'd been gone a long time. She began to worry. The wind still whistled through the rafters, though not quite as strong.

Cupping her hands around the tin can she used for a cup, she absorbed its warmth before taking a sip. Brandon and Sophie played a game of tabletop ninepins. She used the game to teach her younger pupils the concept of subtraction. If one had nine pins and knocked down five, how many were left?

No math was involved in the current game, just Sophie's endless rules. She had a rule for how close to stand, how to roll the ball, how far apart to place the pins, and where to stand if it wasn't your turn. Brandon accepted every rule with his usual stoic silence.

It was eerie for a child to be so quiet. Maddie wondered what it would take for him to speak again. Recalling how Brandon and Donovan had clung to each other, she blinked back tears. She didn't know if that helped Brandon, but it certainly seemed to help Donovan. He was now more open, more approachable, more fun to be with.

A ball of clay whizzed by her head. She jumped, spilling her heated water.

"Sorry," Jimmy said, slingshot in hand. "That one got away from me."

"What are you trying to do?" Normally, slingshots were banned from the classroom, but the current situation called for leniency, something the school board knew nothing about. Even so, enough was enough. She was just about to confiscate it when Jimmy indicated the ceiling next to a ridgepole.

"See that hole up there?"

Stuffing a ball of wet clay into his slingshot, he took aim and pulled the leather pouch back. The clay shot up, hitting the ceiling with a splat.

Jimmy grinned. "Got it!"

And indeed he had. The clay stuck to the hole separating the vertical support beam from its oak lathing, preventing cold air from coming through.

"Why, Jimmy, that's wonderful." Even Donovan hadn't been able to figure out how to plug the holes in the roof. She felt a surge of guilt. She always knew Jimmy had a fine, curious mind, but she'd been so busy pounding words and figures into him she'd failed to notice his creative problem-solving skills.

"I can't wait to tell your pa how you saved the day." Jimmy's father considered book learning a luxury rather than a necessity, and Maddie had had some lively discussions with him over the matter. Now she was more determined than ever to see that Jimmy got a proper education.

Jimmy spotted another ceiling crack, and while he took careful aim, Maddie gave the door an anxious glance. The cabin seemed different without the sheriff, as if he had taken some vital part of the room with him.

"Let me try," Sophie pleaded.

"It's not for dumb girls," Jimmy said.

Sophie got red in the face. "I'm gonna tell pa that you were using your slingshot in the classroom. So there!"

Maddie sighed. "It would be nice if you let Sophie try it just once."

Jimmy said nothing. Instead, he slung another ball of wet clay upward, hitting his target with a satisfied grin.

Maddie set her tin can down and headed for the door just as it flew open. Startled, she drew back. She couldn't see Donovan for the pine tree he carried. It was so huge he could barely get it through the door.

"A Christmas tree!" Sophie shouted.

Maddie shook her head in wonder. Cutting down a tree in this weather must have been a challenge.

Brandon clapped his hands and jumped up and down.

Donovan stood the tree in a corner and stepped back. The tree was wet and laden with clumps of ice, but it was shaped in a perfect triangle, each bough thick with bright-green needles. The fresh smell of pine filled the room.

"It's perfect," Maddie said.

"We don't have any decorations," Sophie said, frowning.

"You're right." Maddie glanced around. "Wait a minute." She fumbled in her box of supplies. "Found it!"

It was a locket with a broken clasp. She palmed the jewel piece, expecting a surge of pain or hurt or, at the very least, unpleasant memories. Surprised when nothing of the sort came, she draped the chain over an upper branch as if it held no more meaning than a string of cranberries.

Following her lead, Jimmy dug into his trouser pocket and pulled out a penny whistle and penknife, attaching both to a lower branch.

Sophie checked the pockets of her dress and, finding them empty, pulled the blue ribbons off her braids. She then tied each one to a separate branch.

Brandon tugged on his dilapidated angel wings.

"You want to put your wings on the tree?" Maddie asked.

Brandon nodded.

"But those look awful," Sophie said. "They don't even look like wings anymore."

Donovan placed a hand on Sophie's shoulder. "It's okay," he mouthed, with a wink.

Maddie worked the angel wings into the branches. She stepped back. "I do believe that is the most beautiful tree I've ever seen."

"No star."

Never before having heard Brandon speak, it took Maddie a moment to identify the unfamiliar voice as his.

"He talked," Sophie squealed. Even Jimmy looked impressed.

Heart leaping with joy, Maddie smiled at him. "You're right; we don't have a star."

"Yes, we do," Donovan said. He unpinned the star-shaped sheriff's badge from his vest and handed it to Brandon. "Would you like to put this on the tree?"

Brandon turned the badge over in his hands before holding up his arms so Donovan could lift him. Brandon reached for the upper branches and stood the brass star at the very top of the tree, next to the trunk. The badge picked up the light from the fire and appeared to be twinkling.

Maddie lifted her skirt and did a little jig—another rule broken. Teachers were required to remain decorous at all times. Luckily for her, Sophie was too busy gazing up at the tree to notice. "I do believe this is the most magical Christmas Eve ever!"

Nodding in agreement, Donovan set Brandon on the floor.

That night Maddie led the children in singing "Silent Night," and this time Donovan joined in with his rich, bass voice.

Chapter 6

Miss Parker's Class

After Jesus was born,
the sky was filled with heavenly holes.
Charles, age 6

L ater after the children had fallen asleep, Maddie stood in front of the
Christmas tree, thinking of Christmases past. For the most part her
memories were happy ones. At least they had been until last year.

Donovan boiled Arbuckles' in an old coffeepot they'd found in the cellar,
using melted snow. He then poured the brew into two tin cans and handed one
to Maddie.

She blew on the hot liquid and took a sip. The coffee was bitter, but the
warmth was comforting. "Thank you."

She felt relaxed, almost drowsy. What had started like a nightmare had
turned out to be a day filled with blessings. She had much to be thankful for.
God was good.

She set her coffee down and tried to fix her bun. Giving up finally, she
pulled the pins out and flipped her head back and forth, letting the wavy locks
fall below her shoulders.

Donovan's gaze followed her hair down her back before he looked away.
"I think the worst is over. I actually spotted some stars."

"Thank God." Maybe they would be home in time for Christmas, though
the prospect wasn't as appealing as it should have been. Home was a lonely attic
room at Widow Hancock's house.

She glanced at the sleeping children. "Their parents must be frantic with
worry."

"I just hope they stay home and don't try to reach us until it's safe to do so."

She took another sip of coffee. "What time is it?"

He pulled out his pocket watch. "A little after eleven."

"It's almost Christmas Day," she said. Her eyes widened. "Oh, I'm so sorry.
I—"

He brushed off her concern with a shake of his head. "It's hard to escape Christmas when you're around children."

She studied his profile. "Tell me about your family." The flickering flames of the fire turned his eyes to gold, and she wondered why she'd ever thought him cold and aloof.

This time he didn't hesitate. "My wife's name was Cynthia. She was expecting our second child when she died."

"How awful for you." The loss of his family made her own loss seem so insignificant.

His studied her, his face calm. "What about you? What brought you to Maverick? Why did you leave Boston?"

She let out a sigh. "I was left at the altar on my wedding day." She glanced at him, testing his reaction before saying more. "My fiancé ran away with my younger sister."

He grimaced. "That must have been hard for you."

She nodded. "I felt betrayed. To think my own sister. . ." She shrugged. "After learning what you went through, what happened to me doesn't seem that bad."

"Don't say that. You suffered a loss, too."

She gave him a grateful smile. "That's kind of you to say." At the time, no one had considered her feelings. "My parents sided with my sister." That had made things worse. A lot worse.

He frowned. "Why would they do that?"

"My sister was thrown from a horse when she was eight years old and is unable to walk. My parents never thought she'd find a husband. Believe me, they couldn't have been more delighted when she did."

"Even though it meant hurting you?"

"I don't blame my parents," she said, surprising herself.

At first she'd felt hurt and betrayed. Now she felt almost relieved. She'd learned a lot about herself since coming to Maverick. Even the last two days stuck in this cabin had taught her that she was stronger than she'd thought and able to cope with far more difficult situations than being stood up at the altar.

"Aren't you angry at your parents?"

"I was but not now." She tossed a nod in Brandon's direction. "Brandon seems so fragile, and I find myself protective of him. I can't help it. It's what people do. They protect the vulnerable. Just like my parents protected my sister."

"But you don't protect Brandon at the expense of your other pupils," he said.

"No, I would never do that." She glanced at the sleeping child. "You helped him, you know. I think you're the one who got him to talk."

He shook his head. "You're the one who did that. You make him feel safe."

His answer surprised her. "How do you mean, safe?"

"His mother is pretty shook up about her husband's death. Not that I blame her, but I suspect it's affecting Brandon. He never used to be so fearful. I think he feels safe with you."

His words warmed her like nothing else could. A graduate from Miss Benson's School for Young Women, she had learned to teach reading, arithmetic, and other subjects but not how to make a child feel safe. That she'd had to learn on her own.

As for her ex-fiancé, it really was for the best. She knew that now. Philip was critical of her teaching career and disapproved of her joining the women's rights movement. The more she thought about it, the more she realized he found fault with everything she did. Her sister was much more traditional and took pride in her homemaking skills. She was exactly the kind of woman Philip wanted in a wife. The kind of woman that Maddie could never be. . . .

She studied Donovan over the rim of the can. What kind of woman had Cynthia been? What kind of wife would he require?

Surprised—shocked really—at the unexpected turn of her thoughts, she quickly set her coffee down.

"More?" he asked.

"No, thank you."

He regarded her thoughtfully. "You still haven't told me what brought you to Maverick."

"My aunt lives in Houston. After what happened, I decided to visit her. I'd never been outside of Boston, and it seemed like a good idea at the time. I saw the advertisement for a schoolteacher in the newspaper and decided to hop on the train and apply." The former teacher left Maverick following the fire, and there had been no one local to take her place.

Maddie suddenly noticed that her locket had fallen, and she reached among the branches, grasping the delicate chain with the tip of a finger.

Donovan took the locket from her, his hand brushing against hers, and studied the clasp. "I can fix it," he said.

She shook her head. "I don't want you to fix it."

He lifted a brow. "Why not? It's a beautiful locket."

"It was a gift from my fiancé."

He looked surprised. "Then why keep it?"

"I guess we all hold on to things we shouldn't," she said. "Old grudges. Sad thoughts. Painful memories."

He quirked a brow. "And what will you hold on to after we're rescued?"

She smiled, grateful for the opportunity to change the subject. "Let me see."

She tapped a finger on her chin. "You arriving at the cabin all indignant and angry." She tried to imitate him.

He laughed. "Was I really that unpleasant?"

"Not that I blame you." She tilted her head. "What about you? What are you going to remember?"

He didn't even hesitate. "Your expression when you saw that Jimmy was safe."

She shivered at the memory. Even now, the thought of losing any one of her pupils filled her with horror. She pointed at him. "I'll remember the first time I heard you laugh, when you were reading the essays on the wall."

He shook his head. "That was the first time?" Without waiting for her reply he pointed his finger at her. "The look on your face when you first spotted all that food in the cellar."

"You coming in the door with the Christmas tree."

"The look in your eyes when Brandon said his first word."

She laughed. "Is that all you'll remember? How I looked?" No sooner were the words out of her mouth than she flushed. Something like a light passed between them, an awareness perhaps. A sudden realization.

Not knowing what to say or even what to think, she quickly turned toward the tree, her heart pounding so hard it nearly drowned out the sound of the slowly dying wind. The tension that stretched between them was almost unbearable, and she felt profoundly relieved when she finally found her voice.

"I think we should hang the locket from there," she said, pointing to an upper branch.

Without saying a word, he wrapped the broken chain on the branch she indicated and adjusted it so that the tiny little heart hung freely.

He turned to her. "I do believe it's midnight," he said softly. "Merry Christmas, Miss Parker." The formality of his address belied the warmth in his eyes, belied even the easy rapport they had shared only moments earlier.

"Merry Christmas, Sheriff Donovan."

She couldn't be certain what happened next. Did he make the first move? Did she?

However it happened, she was in his arms, and it felt so good. It felt even better when he captured her lips with his own. She moaned in pleasure as shivers of delight raced through her.

He pulled his mouth away and gazed into her eyes. "I apologize for being so—"

"Disagreeable?" she whispered.

"I think I always knew what would happen if I let down my guard around you. I didn't think I was ready to give my heart to anyone else, but I was wrong." He kissed the tip of her nose, his breath warm and sweet. "The question is, are *you* ready?"

For an answer she ran her hands up his chest and around his neck. He pulled her closer, his mouth on hers. Dizzying currents rushed to her head, and she returned his kiss with a hunger that surprised her.

All too soon he pulled away, leaving Maddie dazed, confused, and disoriented, as if suddenly falling out of a soft, warm bed. She then noticed Sophie standing a few feet away, watching them, eyes bright with accusations.

"Teachers aren't supposed to kiss," Sophie said, hands at her waist. "I'm gonna to tell Pa."

Her mouth still burning from the memory of Donovan's lips, Maddie tried to think what to say. The rules were clear regarding a teacher's conduct, and breaking them meant immediate dismissal. Maddie needed the job, and landing another one this late in the school year would be difficult if not altogether impossible.

Before Maddie could speak, Sophie burst into tears. "We're supposed to be home for Christmas. That's the r–r–rule," she sobbed.

Donovan held his arms out, and Sophie ran to him, burying her head in his shirt. "It's good to follow the rules," he said. "But they only help us with the little things. We need God for the big things."

Sophie lifted her head. "Going home is a b–b–big thing."

"And you can be sure God's on the job. It's already stopped snowing. I wouldn't be surprised if we all get to go home for Christmas."

Sophie lifted her head. "Promise?"

Donovan looked at Maddie, and her heart turned over in response. "Promise." Cupping Sophie's face, he dropped a kiss on her forehead.

Sophie's eyes widened in surprise, and for once she didn't check the school rules. Instead she rewarded Donovan with a big, beautiful smile.

"Come on, Sophie," Maddie said, taking her by the hand and leading her back to her makeshift bed. "I'll tuck you in."

"Stay with me," Sophie pleaded, showing a vulnerable side that tugged at Maddie's heart.

She longed to go to Donovan, but she would never leave a child who needed her. "I will."

Maddie covered Brandon with his coat before settling down next to Sophie. "Goodnight, Sheriff," she called softly.

Eyes warm with soft lights, Donovan winked at her. "Good night, Miss Parker."

Chapter 7

Miss Parker's Class

Jesus was born under a star so the three kings could find him.
That's better than being born under a lamppost.
Eddie, age 9

The first thing Maddie noticed when she awoke on Christmas morning was the quiet. No more wind.

She jumped up from her makeshift bed and tiptoed around Brandon and Sophie. Sliding back the bolt, she opened the door to a clear blue sky. The air was still cold, and the sparkling snow nearly blinded her, but it was a glorious, sun-filled day. Still, she suspected her exuberance had little to do with blue skies and everything to do with what had happened at midnight.

She spun around and clapped her hands. "Everyone, wake up. It's Christmas morn, and God has sent us another wonderful gift."

From the "boys' side," Donovan met her gaze with a grin, his brown hair falling across his forehead. "Merry Christmas, everyone," he said, rubbing his hand over his unshaven chin. Maddie felt a warm glow rise inside.

It didn't take long for them to don boots, coats, and gloves. Jimmy was the first to run outside, and Sophie took off after him without checking the rules.

By the time Maddie stepped out on the porch, a full snowball fight was in progress. She was pleasantly surprised to see Jimmy teaching Sophie how to shoot snowballs with his slingshot.

Laughter filled the air, and Maddie thought her heart would burst with joy. How was it possible that in only three days' time the world seemed like a brighter place? As unlikely as it was, five people—all hurting in different ways—had found a safe haven at the cabin in which to begin to heal. Had God planned it that way?

Jimmy and Sophie had teamed up to gleefully bombard the sheriff until he ducked for cover. Even Brandon got in on the act, laughing out loud whenever a snowball hit him.

"Fire!" Donovan yelled. A snowball hit Maddie on her shoulder.

"Why you—" She scooped up a handful of snow and fired back.

Ducking beneath a barrage of snowballs, she quickly slapped together another clump of snow and threw it. Much to her shock, the snowball hit school-board member Mr. Griffin smack in the middle of his forehead just as he stepped out from behind a tree.

Maddie gasped and covered her mouth with her hand.

Sophie shouted "Papa!"

Mr. Griffin trudged through the snow toward the schoolhouse, slipping and sliding and mumbling beneath his breath. He was followed by the other two board members, none of whom looked happy.

"Oh, dear, I look awful," Maddie moaned. The rules were explicit about the importance of a teacher's good grooming. She thought she'd have time to fix her hair before rescuers arrived, and it now tumbled to her shoulders in a mass of unruly curls.

"You look beautiful," Donovan said softly, coming up from behind, though his assurance did nothing to ease her worry.

Mr. Griffin was the first to reach them, disapproval written all over his ruddy face. He was huffing and puffing and could barely manage to speak. He glanced at Donovan before glowering at Maddie.

When he finally was able to find his voice, he practically sputtered. "*Miss Parker*, is this how a schoolteacher behaves in front of her pupils? By throwing snowballs at board members?"

Before Maddie could explain, Sophie tugged on her father's arm. "Papa, Papa."

Griffin glanced down at his daughter, impatience written all over his face. "What is it, child?"

"You won't believe what happened." Showing no sign of being put off by her father's sharp voice, Sophie talked so fast her tongue practically tripped over itself. "We got the door closed before the bear came in—"

Griffin's eyes widened. "Bear? What bear?"

"And Jimmy found a cellar full of food and. . ." On and on she went. "We decorated the Christmas tree, and Brandon talked and. . ."

Griffin placed his hand on his daughter's shoulder. "What's that you said? Brandon talked?" Sophie nodded, and all three school-board members turned to the small boy standing by Maddie's side.

Griffin bent at the waist, his nose practically touching Brandon's. "If that's true, let me hear you say something."

"Let's go home!" Brandon yelled.

Startled, Griffin practically fell backward, and everyone laughed.

"I didn't think you'd get through so fast," Donovan said.

Jake Penman tossed a nod in the direction of the road hidden by the trees. "We hitched a mule team to some logs and plowed through."

"There's a wagon waiting to take us home," Griffin added. "But we have to walk back to the road."

"Couldn't git any closer," Chuck Walters grumbled, blowing on his hands.

Griffin glanced at Maddie. "It appears that everything turned out"—he cleared his throat as if it pained him to say it—"turned out just fine."

"I say we stop jawing and head for home," Penman said. "The missus is roasting a duck, and I ain't wantin' to be late for dinner."

"Wait," Sophie said with a worried frown. "We can't go. The fire is still burning, and rule number four says that we can't leave school until the fire is out."

"Tell you what," Donovan said. "You go on ahead. Miss Parker and I have some unfinished business to attend to. We'll catch up with you shortly."

"Very well," Griffin said, nodding. "You two put out the fire, and we'll meet you on the road."

"We'll do our best," Donovan assured him, his solemn voice belying the mischievous glint in his eyes. It was all Maddie could do to keep from laughing out loud.

Apparently satisfied that everything was under control, Griffin turned. "Come along, Sophie."

The other two board members followed behind with Jimmy and Brandon in tow.

Wasting not a single moment, Donovan quickly led Maddie back to the cabin—and into the warm circle of his arms.

Epilogue

From Miss Stephen's class of 1886

Today we got a new teacher on account of our old teacher Miss Parker breaking the rules and getting married. She didn't have to go to jail or anything because she married Sheriff Donovan. She just has to clean his house.
Sophie, age 11

Margaret Brownley loves hearing from her readers and can be reached through her website. The author of more than twenty novels, she was a 2010 RITA finalist and INSPY nominee and is currently writing western romances for Thomas Nelson. For more love and laughter in the old West, check out Margaret's latest books at www.margaretbrownley.com.

The Christmas Secret

by Wanda E. Brunstetter

Dedication

To Phil and Diane Allen, our special Pennsylvania friends.
We feel blessed to have met you. Thanks for all you do!

Trust in the LORD with all thine heart;
and lean not unto thine own understanding.
PROVERBS 3:5

Chapter 1

Feeling the need for a bit of fresh air, Elizabeth Canning opened her bedroom window and drew in a deep breath, inhaling the earthy, leaf-scented fragrance that she knew even with her eyes closed was like no other season but autumn.

When a chilling wind blew in, rustling the lace curtains and causing her to shiver, she quickly shut the window. It was too cold for the first of November. Did the nippy weather mean they were in for a harsh winter this year, or would they be spared and have only a few bitterly cold days? Whatever the case, she hoped they'd have snow for Christmas. God's sparkling white crystals always added a little something extra to the beauty and atmosphere of the holiday season.

Through the closed window, Elizabeth heard geese honking in the distance, no doubt making their southward journey. She could almost feel their excitement as they flew to warmer territories. It never failed, spring or fall; hearing geese high in the sky stirred a thrill deep in her soul.

When a knock sounded on the door, Elizabeth turned and called, "Come in."

The door opened, and Elizabeth's friend, Helen Warner, entered the room. Her coal-black hair, worn in a chignon at the back of her head and covered with a silver net, stood in sharp contrast to Elizabeth's golden-blond hair, which she wore hanging loosely down her back today. But then, Helen, who'd recently turned twenty, had always been the prim and proper one, often wearing high-neck dresses with perfectly shaped bustles, like the one she wore today. Elizabeth, on the other hand, was the practical type and preferred full-skirted calico dresses, which were more comfortable when one was cleaning or working around the house. She felt rather plain next to Helen, but fortunately their friendship was based on more than the clothes they wore or their differing opinions on some things.

Elizabeth's meticulous friend was outgoing and always seemed to have an air of excitement about her. Maybe Helen's confident demeanor came from being the daughter of an esteemed minister of the largest congregation in Allentown, for she had a certain charisma that glowed like a halo around her. To Elizabeth, it was most invigorating, even though she, herself, was more down-to-earth.

"I thought you were going to help me clean the cabin today, but it doesn't look like you came dressed for work," Elizabeth said.

"I was hoping you'd change your mind and go shopping with me instead." When Helen took a seat on the feather bed, her long, purple stockings peeked out from under the hem of her matching dress.

Elizabeth's brows furrowed. "There's no time for shopping right now. If David and I are to be married on Christmas Eve, then it doesn't give us much time to get the cabin cleaned and ready for the wedding."

Helen's brown eyes narrowed, causing tiny wrinkles to form across her forehead. "It's one thing to have the ceremony in the cabin, since you're only inviting family and close friends, but are you sure you want to live in that dreary little place? It's so small, and far from town."

"It's not that far—only a few miles." Elizabeth took a seat beside her friend. "The cabin has special meaning to me. It was the first home of my mother's parents, and soon after Grandma and Grandpa moved to Easton, Mother married Daddy, and they moved into the cabin to begin their life together. They lived there until. . ." Elizabeth's voice trailed off, and she blinked to hold back tears threatening to spill over. "After Mother died of pneumonia when I was eight years old, Daddy couldn't stand to live there any longer, because everything in the cabin reminded him of her." Elizabeth may have been young, but she remembered how empty and lifeless the cabin had felt once her mother was gone.

"So you moved to town and lived at the Main Street Boardinghouse, right?"

Elizabeth nodded. "We stayed there until I was ten, and then when Daddy got his shoemaking business going well and married Abigail, we moved into the house he had built." She smiled and touched Helen's arm. "Soon after that, I met you."

"So you're used to living in town now, and just because your parents and grandparents lived in the cabin doesn't mean you have to."

"David and I want to begin our life together there." Elizabeth sighed. "Besides, he's just getting started with his carriage-making business and can't afford to have a home built for us here right now."

"I understand that, but can't you continue living with your father and stepmother or even at the hotel David's grandfather owns?"

"I suppose we could, but it wouldn't be the same as having a place of our own to call home."

Helen folded her arms with an undignified grunt. "Humph! That cabin isn't a home; it's a hovel. If David's so poor that he can't offer you more, then maybe you should consider marrying someone else. Maybe someone like Howard Glenstone. I think he's been interested in you for some time."

"I'm not in love with Howard. I love David, and I'd be happy living in the cabin with him for the rest of my life if necessary." It was obvious to Elizabeth that Helen didn't understand or appreciate how the homey little dwelling came to be. It must have taken a lot of hard work, frustration, and long hours for her mother's father to build the cabin for Grandma and the family they'd one day have. How proud Grandpa must have been, knowing he'd built the place with his own two hands.

"I just think a woman as beautiful as you could do much better," Helen said.

Elizabeth bristled. "Are you saying that David's not an attractive man?"

Helen placed her hand on Elizabeth's arm. "I'm not saying that at all. David has very nice features, and with both of you having golden-blond hair and vivid blue eyes, you make a striking couple." She patted the sides of her hair. "Of course, I'd never be attracted to anyone who had the same color hair and eyes as me."

"When you meet the right man and fall in love, you won't care what color his hair and eyes are, because real love isn't based on a person's looks." Elizabeth touched her chest. "It's what's in the heart that counts. While I do think David is quite handsome, the things that drew me to him were his kind, gentle spirit and the fact that he's a fine Christian man."

"He does seem to be all that." Helen smiled at Elizabeth. "I'm sure the two of you will have sweet, even-tempered children with beautiful blond hair and pretty blue eyes."

Elizabeth smiled. "I'm looking forward to becoming a mother. In fact, I'm looking forward to every aspect of being married."

"Including cooking and cleaning?" Helen's nose wrinkled.

"Yes, even that." The springs in the bed squeaked as Elizabeth rose to her feet. "Speaking of cleaning, I should hitch my horse to the buckboard so we can go over to the cabin now."

Helen gestured to her fancy dress. "I suppose I should change into one of your calicos first."

Elizabeth pointed to her wardrobe across the room. "Feel free to wear whichever one you want."

❄

David Stinner had never been one to shirk his duties, but today he was having a hard time staying focused on his work. All he could think about was Elizabeth, and how he couldn't wait to make her his wife. They'd been courting nearly a year and would be married on Christmas Eve. He couldn't think of any better Christmas present for himself than making Elizabeth his bride, and she insisted that getting married to him on her birthday was the best gift she could receive for turning twenty. She was everything he wanted in a wife—sweet-tempered, patient, intelligent, beautiful, and a Christian in every sense of the word. She would make not only a good wife but also a fine mother to the children they might have someday.

"Hey, boss, how come you've been standin' there holdin' that piece of wood for so long?"

David whirled around, surprised to see his helper, Gus Smith, standing behind him. When he'd last seen Gus, he'd been at the back of the shop, cutting a stack of wood.

"I wish you wouldn't sneak up on me like that," David said, shaking his head. "I nearly dropped this piece of oak for the sideboards of Arnold Higgin's bakery wagon."

Gus's bushy dark eyebrows lifted high on his forehead. "Looked to me like you were just standin' there holdin' that piece of wood, and you're nowhere near the body of the bakery wagon you started yesterday."

"I was taking a few minutes to think, that's all."

"Thinkin' about your bride-to-be, I'll bet."

David nodded, his face heating with embarrassment. He hated how easily he blushed.

"Are ya gettin' cold feet?"

"Of course not. I was just thinking about how Elizabeth and her friend, Helen, are going to the cabin to do some cleaning today. I wish I could be there to help them."

"Why can't ya be?"

David glanced across the room, noting the bakery wagon he'd been about to work on. Then there was an emerald-green carriage needing a new set of wheels, a coal-box buggy that was only half built, and the town coach the banker had brought in yesterday for new axles and springs. "I have too much work to do here right now. I promised to have the bakery wagon done by the end of next week, not to mention the other orders we have waiting." Some days could be a bit overwhelming, but David was grateful for the work and good relationships he'd been building with his customers. He was also humbled by their trust in the fine craftsman he was proving himself to be.

"Maybe you can go over to the cabin when you're done workin' today," Gus suggested.

"That's what I'm hoping to do." David leaned the piece of wood against the wall.

Gus moved closer to David. "You still gonna live in the log cabin after you and Elizabeth are married?"

David nodded.

"Wouldn't ya rather live at the hotel your granddaddy owns? It'd be closer to your shop and has a lot more conveniences than the cabin."

"It wouldn't be our own place, and all we'd have is one small room."

"That dinky old cabin ain't much bigger than a hotel room." Gus snorted like an old bull.

"It's big enough for our needs, and once my business grows, I can either add on to the cabin or have a house built for us here in town."

Just then, David's mother rushed into the shop, wearing no shawl around her shoulders, despite the chilly day. "Come quickly, David! Your grandfather fell from a ladder, and he doesn't respond!" Her hazel-colored eyes were wide with fear, and a lock of reddish-brown hair had come loose from the chignon at the back of her head. David figured she must have run all the way here.

"I'll be back as soon as I can," David called to Gus. He grabbed his mother's hand, and they rushed out the door.

Chapter 2

When David and his mother entered the hotel foyer, he was surprised to see his grandfather standing behind the front desk, where the hotel guests were greeted. He appeared to be unhurt. Had Mother made the whole thing up just to get him to come over here? If so, what was the reason? He was about to ask when Mother swooped across the room and rushed to Grandpa's side.

"Papa, are you okay?" She clutched his arm so tightly that David wondered if she would bruise the old man's skin.

After Grandma had died of pneumonia three years ago, Mother had been overprotective of Grandpa. Then when David's father was killed a year later in an accident at the steel mill, she'd almost smothered Grandpa to death.

"I'm fine, Carolyn," Grandpa said, pushing her hand away. "Just had the wind knocked out of me when I fell. If you hadn't rushed out of here so quickly, I'd have told you that."

"But you weren't responding to anything I said. You were just lying on the floor with your eyes closed. That's why I went to get David." She took a deep breath and closed her eyes—no doubt in an effort to calm herself.

Grandpa's gaze shifted to David, who had moved to stand beside his mother. "Were you working at the carriage shop?" he questioned.

David nodded.

"I'm sorry she bothered you for nothing." Grandpa looked at Mother and then back at David. "You know how emotional your mother can be. She probably thought I was dead."

"That's exactly what I thought," Mother said with a catch in her voice.

"Grandpa, what were you doing on the ladder?" David asked.

"I was trying to straighten that." Grandpa motioned to the slightly crooked oil painting hanging above an enormous stone fireplace on the other side of the room. One of the local artists had painted the picture of the hotel soon after it had opened for business nearly thirty years ago.

Mother pursed her lips. "You should have waited for our handyman to do it, Papa."

"Seth's out running an errand right now."

"I realize that, but I'm sure he'll be back soon, and you really should have waited."

Grandpa's face turned red. "Carolyn, please stop telling me what to do. I'm perfectly capable of straightening a painting, and I shouldn't have to call on Seth to do every little thing!"

Mother's chin trembled and tears sprang to her eyes. "You don't have to raise your voice when you speak to me, Papa."

"Sorry," Grandpa mumbled, "but I get tired of you fussing all the time and telling me what to do. I'm not a little boy, and you're not my mother."

"No, I'm just a daughter who's concerned about her father's welfare. Is there a law against that?"

"Of course not, but—"

David cleared his throat real loud. "I'd be happy to straighten the picture for you, and then I need to get back to work."

"There's no need for that," Grandpa was quick to say. "I can climb back on the ladder and finish the job I started." His gaze swung to Mother then back to David. "And since your mother's so worried about me, she can hold the ladder to keep it steady."

Mother planted both hands on her hips and scowled at him. "I will not hold the ladder so you can go back up there! We need to wait until Seth gets here so he can do the job we're paying him to do."

Grandpa opened his mouth as if to say more, but then he clamped it shut and headed for the front door.

"Where are you going?" Mother called to his retreating form.

"Out for a walk. I think a bit of fresh air might do me some good." He glanced over his shoulder at David. "You may as well head back to your shop."

"What about the picture?"

"I've changed my mind. It can wait for Seth."

As Grandpa hurried out the door, David turned to Mother and said, "I hope the rest of your day goes well."

Her forehead creased as she frowned. "I doubt that. When your grandfather returns, he'll probably get involved with something else he shouldn't be doing."

David gave her arm an easy pat and went out the door, smiling to himself. Some things never seemed to change.

❄

"This place is so small," Helen told Elizabeth for the fifth time since they'd begun cleaning the cabin. "I don't see how you're going to live in such cramped quarters."

"We'll be fine. It's just going to be the two of us, so we don't need much room. Besides, we can always add on to the cabin when children come. Even so, I'd hate to change anything that might take away from the quaintness my grandpa created."

Elizabeth picked up a rag and began dusting several pieces of furniture that had been left in the cabin and had belonged to her grandparents. Truthfully she looked forward to living here, away from the noise and hustle-bustle of the city, which seemed to be growing rapidly these days. Even as small as the cabin was, Elizabeth looked around and was almost giddy with excitement, knowing this was going to be her and David's first home, where their life together would soon begin.

"You have no indoor necessary room here, and you'll have to heat water on the stove for washing dishes and bathing." Helen gestured to the floor. "There aren't even any carpets on this drab-looking puncheon floor."

"We'll use the outhouse, just like my parents and grandparents did when they lived here." Elizabeth looked down at the short, thick planks confined by wooden pins. "I can always put some braided throw rugs on the floor."

Helen shrugged and gave an unladylike grunt. "I've finished washing the windows now. What would you like me to do next?"

Elizabeth was about to suggest that Helen go through some boxes of books they'd found earlier, when a knock sounded on the cabin door.

"I wonder who that could be," Helen said.

Elizabeth smiled. "It might be David. When I spoke to him the other day, he said he hoped to come by after he finished working today."

Helen glanced at the simple windup clock on the mantel. "It's only two o'clock. Do you think he'd be done this soon?"

"There's only one way to find out." Elizabeth patted the sides of her hair, smoothed the wrinkles in her dress, and hurried across the room. When she opened the door, she was surprised to see Helen's father, Reverend Warner, standing on the stoop with furrowed brows.

"Is Helen here?" he asked. "She said she might be helping you clean the cabin today."

"Yes, she's here, and we're still cleaning." Elizabeth opened the door wider to bid him enter.

Reverend Warner started toward Helen, and she met him halfway. "Is there something wrong, Father?" she asked with a worried expression.

"I don't believe it's anything serious, but your mother isn't feeling well, and I'd like you to come home. I'm sure she won't be up to fixing supper this evening," he added in a desperate tone.

Helen looked at Elizabeth. "Would you mind if I leave early?"

Elizabeth shook her head. "I'll be fine. You're needed at home more than here right now."

"All right then. I'll return your dress to you soon." Helen wrapped her woolen shawl around her shoulders and followed her father out the door.

As Reverend Warner's buggy wheels rumbled down the dirt road, Elizabeth returned to the job of cleaning, humming softly to herself, enjoying the quiet cabin.

While she worked, childhood memories flooded her mind. Remembering the warmth Mother had brought to this little cabin, Elizabeth could almost smell the homemade bread baking and loved how that smell lingered long after the loaves had cooled on the rack. She longed after so many years to bring those moments alive once again in this cozy cabin she would soon call home.

After Elizabeth finished dusting an old desk's surfaces, she opened each drawer and cleaned the crevices. One of the drawers, however, seemed to be stuck.

Determined to get it opened, she grabbed the brass knob and pulled as hard as she could. It finally gave way. Inside she found some old drawings she assumed had been done by either Mother or her sister, Lovina. Then, to Elizabeth's surprise, she discovered a battered-looking leather journal crammed in the very back of the drawer. Curious as to whom it had belonged to, she lifted it out and opened the cover. Aunt Lovina's name was written there.

Elizabeth smiled. *Mother and her sister grew up in this cabin. Aunt Lovina probably sat right here at this desk to write in her journal.* Elizabeth had never been close to her aunt, who as far as she knew had never married. After Aunt Lovina moved to Easton and opened a boardinghouse, Elizabeth hadn't seen much of her at all. It had always seemed that her aunt preferred keeping to herself. From the few things Elizabeth remembered her mother saying about Aunt Lovina, she'd concluded that the two sisters had never gotten along very well. The last news anyone in the family had heard about her aunt was that she'd sold the boardinghouse and moved, but no one knew where.

Feeling the need for a break and more than a little curious as to what her aunt's journal might say, Elizabeth fixed herself a cup of tea and took a seat on the deacon's bench near the window, placing the journal in her lap.

The first entry was dated June 10, 1856, and included a note about Lovina's sixteenth birthday that day and that she'd received the journal from her parents. Lovina hadn't written much on the first page, other than to say she hoped to write her innermost thoughts in this little book.

As Elizabeth flipped through the pages, she was careful. Some seemed a bit brittle, and the musty odor reminded her that the journal was old and had probably been stuck in the desk for quite a while.

Elizabeth read a few more pages, smiling when she came to a journal entry about a mouse that had gotten into the pantry and eaten the cookies Grandma had made, and frowning when she read how Aunt Lovina and Elizabeth's mother, who was two years younger than Lovina, had argued about who would wash and who would dry the dishes. Their mother had stepped in and settled the dispute.

Elizabeth sighed. She wished she'd known her mother's parents, but they'd both died before she was born.

She turned several more pages and continued to read, until she came to an entry dated April 20, 1860. It read:

My sister, Cassandra, is marrying Charles Canning today, but she's taking a horrible secret with her. Cassandra used to be courted by Raymond Stinner, but when he dropped her suddenly and married Carolyn Flannigan, she quickly turned to Charles and agreed to marry him right away. I wonder what Charles would say if he knew Cassandra was pregnant with Raymond's baby.

Elizabeth's mouth went dry as she stared at the journal entry, trying to piece things together. Raymond Stinner was David's father. Until now, Elizabeth had no idea that he'd courted her mother, much less that she'd been carrying his baby when she married Father. How shocking to learn such a thing about her own mother, whom she'd always held in such high esteem.

But who is that baby? Elizabeth wondered. Her heart began to race. *Could Mother have had a miscarriage, or do I have a brother or sister I don't know about?*

Anxious to learn more, Elizabeth continued turning the pages in her aunt's journal, until she found one that read:

Christmas Eve, 1860: Cassandra's baby was born today. Cassandra had told everyone that the child was due in January, but now she's saying the baby came early. That's just to protect her reputation, of course. She doesn't want anyone to know—especially not Charles—that she was pregnant when they got married. She especially doesn't want him to know that Raymond Stinner is the father of her baby. The little girl weighs six pounds and seems to be quite healthy. Of course the reason for that is because she's not really premature. Cassandra named her baby, Elizabeth. I guess you could say the child is Cassandra's little Christmas secret.

Elizabeth swayed unsteadily as the journal slipped from her fingers and dropped to the floor with a thud. If Raymond Stinner was her real father, that meant she was David's half sister! Stunned, she thought, *No wonder we both have blond hair and blue eyes.*

When the truth of it all set in, she covered her mouth and choked on a sob. "Oh, dear Lord, how can this be? Why did You allow such a terrible thing to happen? I can never marry David now!"

As Elizabeth stared into space, her mind racing, the only thing she could see was her dream of being David's wife and all the wonderful plans they'd made fading further and further away. In a matter of a few minutes, Elizabeth's world had gone from a future filled with hopes and dreams to an unsettling question: *What now?*

Chapter 3

"I got busy workin' and forgot to ask when you first returned to the shop—is your granddaddy okay?" Gus asked David.

David nodded. "He fell off a ladder but wasn't really hurt. Just got the wind knocked out of him, I guess."

"Glad to hear he's all right."

"Grandpa tries to do too much, and Mother worries about him too much."

Gus chuckled. "Guess that's what women do—worry about those they love."

"I suppose Elizabeth will worry about me after we're married." David reached into his jacket pocket and pulled out the gold timepiece that had belonged to his father. "Speaking of Elizabeth, I think I'll head over to the cabin now and see how she's doing."

Gus's forehead wrinkled. "I thought you were gonna work in the shop until the end of the day."

"I can't concentrate on work right now, and I'm sure you can manage on your own for a while."

Gus shrugged. "It's your right to do whatever you want, 'cause you're the boss."

David grinned and thumped the man's shoulder. "I'll see you bright and early tomorrow morning."

When David mounted his horse and guided him in the direction of the cabin, he began to whistle. He could hardly wait to see his bride-to-be and tell her once more how much he loved her.

Elizabeth paced between the deacon bench and the fireplace, pondering what she should do about her aunt's journal. She couldn't let David or her father see it. Something like this would bring shame on both of their families. She would need to call off the wedding, of course, and the sooner the better. If she just knew what to say to David. This was the most difficult thing she had ever been faced with.

She glanced at her satchel full of cleaning supplies. She would put the journal in there for now until she was able to dispose of it properly.

A knock sounded on the cabin door, causing Elizabeth to jump.

"Who is it?" she called, wondering if Helen had returned to help her finish cleaning.

"It's me, David."

Elizabeth's heart pounded so hard she feared her chest would explode. She had to let David in but wasn't ready to call off the wedding or offer an explanation. How could she, when she was still trying to grasp this horrible secret that, less than an hour ago, she hadn't even known existed. She'd have to pretend all was well until she figured out the best way to deal with things.

She whispered a prayer for courage, swiped at the tears on her cheeks, and opened the door. "I—I wasn't sure I'd see you today. I figured you'd be hard at work," she said, unable to make eye contact with David.

He stepped into the room and shut the door. "I said I'd try to come by, remember?"

"Yes, but I. . ." She forced herself to look up at him.

"Is everything all right? Your face looks red, and your eyes are puffy. Have you been crying?" David moved closer and held out his arms. His piercing blue eyes seemed to bore right through her.

Elizabeth wished only to be held in the comfort of his embrace, and have this black cloud of uncertainty go away, but she quickly stepped back. "I–I'm fine. Just hot and sweaty from working so hard, and I—I may have rubbed my eyes when I was dusting."

"I'm sorry you had to work so hard. Where's Helen, anyway? I thought she was going to help you clean the cabin today."

"She was here earlier—until her father came by and said her mother wasn't feeling well. Helen left with him."

"I'm sorry to hear her mother's ill. Sure hope it's nothing serious."

"Me, too." Elizabeth shivered and moved to stand in front of the fireplace, feeling the need of its warmth.

David stepped up beside Elizabeth and, turning her to face him, pressed his forehead to hers.

Her throat tightened. *He's my brother. He's my brother*, she reminded herself. "David, I. . ."

He pulled back slightly, and his mustache tickled as he brushed a kiss across her forehead. "It won't be long now, and you'll be my wife. I can hardly wait for Christmas Eve."

Cheeks burning and heart pounding, Elizabeth moved quickly away, busying herself as she began to dust the desk where she'd discovered the journal. She'd already dusted it thoroughly but needed to put some distance between her and David.

"It's obvious that there's still some work to be done here, so what would you like me to do?" David asked.

Silence filled the room. *Go home. Leave me alone so I can think.*

"Elizabeth, did you hear what I said?" David touched her arm.

She turned to face him but fixed her attention on the buttons of his jacket, unable to look at his handsome face. "I–I've developed a headache, and my stomach is upset. I think I'd better go home and lie down. Besides, it's not proper for us to be here alone together without a chaperone."

"You're right, of course." He retrieved her shawl from the back of the wooden bench and placed it around her shoulders. "I'll follow you home to make sure you get there safely."

"There's no need for that. I'll be fine." Elizabeth grabbed her satchel and hurried out the door.

She was about to climb into her buckboard when David called, "I really would prefer to make sure you get home safely."

"If you wish," she mumbled. The headache she'd mentioned was real and had become worse—no doubt from the time she'd spent crying after she'd found Aunt Lovina's journal. If only she hadn't read those horrible things her aunt had written. If she could just turn back the hands of time.

But if I hadn't read the journal I might have married David—my own brother—and then...

No longer able to deal with her troubling thoughts, Elizabeth gathered up the reins and got the horse moving. She needed to get home so she could retreat to her bedroom and think things through. She needed to pray about this matter and decide how she should break her engagement to David. The most frigid of winters had never made her feel as cold as she did right now.

Chapter 4

Unable to face David, Elizabeth spent the next several days in bed, telling her father and stepmother, Abigail, that she was sick with a stomach virus. Truth be told, her stomach was upset. Food held no appeal, and she'd had to force herself to drink the chamomile tea Abigail had given her. Father had wanted her to see the doctor, but she'd insisted that it was nothing serious and would be fine in a few days.

I can't stay in my room forever, Elizabeth told herself as she climbed out of bed one morning. *I need to break my engagement to David, and I can't put it off any longer. I need to do it today.*

She wrapped the quilt from her bed around her shoulders and plodded across the room to the window. It was a dreary-looking day, full of dark clouds and a blustery wind that caused the branches of the elm tree near the house to brush against her window with an irritating scrape.

Elizabeth shivered and crossed her arms over her chest. It was cold in her room, and she was tempted to crawl back in bed under the warmth of the covers but knew she'd been confined to her room long enough. She'd made a decision before going to sleep last night and needed to follow through with it. She would get dressed, put Aunt Lovina's journal, as well as a few clothes, into a satchel, and go downstairs for a cup of tea and a biscuit. Then she'd head over to the cabin, leave David a note, and stop on her way to the train station to see Helen, whom she'd decided would be her only confidante. She was glad Father had left on a business trip to New York this morning, and since Abigail had gone shopping, she wouldn't have to tell them face-to-face that she was leaving. She was sure they wouldn't have accepted her explanation and feared she may have broken down and told them the truth.

I must never tell them, Elizabeth told herself. *It would bring humiliation on my family, and the shock might be too much for Father when he found out he's not my real father at all.*

Tears sprang to Elizabeth's eyes. Was it possible that Father already knew? Could Mother have told him that she was carrying another man's child when she married him? Oh, surely not. If Father knew this horrible secret, he'd never let on or treated Elizabeth any differently than he would his own flesh-and-blood child.

He'd always been kind, affectionate, and eager to give her whatever she wanted.

If Mother were still alive, I'd go to her and talk about this. But then, Elizabeth thought, *maybe it's good that I'm not able tell her what I read in Aunt Lovina's journal. I'm sure it would be most embarrassing for Mother to learn that I'd discovered her Christmas secret.*

Elizabeth stood before the oval looking glass and studied her reflection. *Do I look more like Mother or my real father?* Elizabeth had always thought she'd gotten her mother's blond hair and her father's blue eyes, but when Robert Stinner was alive, he'd had both blond hair and blue eyes. *Just like David,* she reminded herself.

Elizabeth turned away from the mirror. *Oh, David, I know it's wrong to love you as anything more than a brother, but may God forgive me, I can't seem to help myself.* She nearly choked on the sob rising in her throat. *The only way I can possibly deal with this is to put a safe distance between David and me.*

❄

"How's Elizabeth doing?" David asked when Charles Canning entered his buggy shop. "Is she feeling any better?"

Charles, a tall man with thinning brown hair and pale blue eyes, lifted his broad shoulders in a brief shrug. "She was still in bed when I left home, so I'm not sure how she's feeling this morning."

"I've been worried about her," David said with concern. "I've stopped by your house a couple of times to see how she's doing, but Abigail always says Elizabeth isn't feeling up to company."

Charles nodded. "She's been staying in her room and hasn't taken any of her meals downstairs, although I don't think she's seriously ill."

"When I'm done working for the day, I think I'll stop by there again. I want to be sure she's not any worse." Despite the fact that it had only been a few days since he'd seen Elizabeth, it felt like forever.

"That's a good idea. If she's feeling up to company today, I'm sure she'll be glad to see you."

"So what'd you come by for?" David asked.

"I'm heading out of town on business today, but before I go, I wanted to drop in here and let you know that I need a new carriage. It'll be a wedding present for you and Elizabeth."

David chuckled. "It's not often that a man gets asked to make his own wedding present."

Charles thumped David's shoulder. "That's true, and I wouldn't be asking, but you're the best at what you do. I don't want my daughter riding in a carriage built by anyone else."

David smiled. "I appreciate that, sir, but to tell you the truth, I was planning to give Elizabeth one of my carriages as a combination birthday and wedding present. It's a secret, though. I want to surprise her with it."

"That's fine. I won't ruin your surprise, and I'm sure I can find some other suitable gift to give you and Elizabeth on your special day." Charles started to walk away but turned back around. "Are you sure you and Elizabeth want to live in that old cabin where my first wife, Cassandra, and I got our start?"

David nodded with certainty. "It's what Elizabeth wants, and I think we'll be very happy living there."

"Elizabeth's mother and I were happy there, too. But I wish she had lived long enough for me to give her the house she deserved."

"At least Elizabeth and your second wife have been able to enjoy the fruits of your labor."

"True." Charles's forehead creased. "How long do you think it'll be until you're able to have a home built for you and Elizabeth?"

David shrugged. "I don't know. Hopefully, within the next few years."

"Before children come, I hope. That cabin's too small to raise a family in."

"You did it, sir. You raised Elizabeth there, and from what I understand, your first wife's parents raised two daughters there as well."

Charles nodded. "We managed, but it was crowded, so I hope you and Elizabeth are settled into a roomy home in town before any children come along."

"I understood your concern," David said, "but I promise to take good care of your daughter; of that you can be certain."

Chapter 5

When Elizabeth opened the cabin door and stepped inside, a lump rose in her throat. She'd been looking forward to setting up housekeeping in this special little cabin where her only memories of her mother remained. This would never be her home now. She'd been eagerly waiting to become David's wife, but that was obviously not meant to be.

Elizabeth sank into the wooden chair in front of the desk and buried her face in the palms of her hands. She needed to write David a farewell note and get away from here as quickly as possible, but telling him she was leaving was ever so hard.

She opened the desk drawer and took out a piece of paper. Then, struggling not to cry lest she soil the page, she began writing:

Dear David:

As hard as it is for me to tell you this, I know I must say what's on my heart, and I hope you'll understand. I've come to realize that we're not meant to be together, so I won't be marrying you on Christmas Eve. I'm going away. Please don't try to find me, because I won't change my mind. It's over between us. I pray that God will bring someone else into your life and that you'll find the happiness you deserve.

Fondly,
Elizabeth

Elizabeth folded the note, slipped it into an envelope, and wrote David's name on the outside. Then she placed it on the fireplace mantel next to the set of wooden candlesticks her father had given her mother on their last Christmas together.

Tears blurred Elizabeth's vision as she stared at the envelope. With an ache in her heart she feared would always remain, she slipped quietly out the door. She had one more stop to make before heading to the train station.

❄

"My mother's better now, and it's good to see that you're finally out of bed, too. How are you feeling?" Helen asked when Elizabeth entered the stately house

Helen shared with her parents.

"I'm fine physically, but in here, I'll never be the same." Elizabeth touched her chest and drew in a shuddering breath.

Helen led the way to the kitchen. Then she pulled out a chair at the kitchen table and motioned for Elizabeth to sit down. "You look like you've been crying. What's wrong?"

Elizabeth removed her shawl and draped it over the back of the chair. As she sat, she drew in a couple of deep breaths to help steady her nerves. She had to tell someone the truth about why she was leaving. The secret that lay beneath the pages of her aunt's journal was too much to carry alone. "This is so difficult for me to talk about," she said in a whisper. "Are we alone?"

Helen nodded as she took a seat beside Elizabeth. "Mother's visiting my grandparents today, and Father's attending a deacon's meeting at the church."

With a sense of urgency, Elizabeth leaned forward and clasped her friend's hand. "What I'm about to tell you is a secret, and it must remain so—do you understand?"

Helen nodded. "You've told me secrets before, and I've never betrayed your confidence."

"This secret is different than the ones we shared during our growing-up years. If this secret ever got out, it could ruin several people's lives. It's already ruined mine."

Helen's eyebrows drew together. "What are you talking about?"

"It's a horrible secret that could hurt my father, David's mother, and most of all, David." Tears welled in Elizabeth's eyes as she swallowed against the constriction in her throat. "David can never find out. Do you understand?"

"No, I don't understand. What secret could be so horrible that it would ruin four people's lives?"

Elizabeth reached into her satchel and pulled out the journal. "This belonged to my aunt, Lovina Hess. It was stuck in the back of a drawer, inside the desk I was dusting at the cabin the other day."

"Did something your aunt write upset you?"

"Yes. It's the most horrible secret I could ever imagine." Elizabeth opened the journal to the entry she'd marked with a slip of paper and handed it to Helen. "Read for yourself."

Helen placed the journal on the table, and as she read, her mouth formed an O. "I—I can't believe it! This has to be a mistake."

Elizabeth slowly shook her head. "I wish you were right, but it's not a mistake. Aunt Lovina would have no reason to lie about something so serious." Elizabeth touched the netting that held her long blond curls at the back of her head. "It's no coincidence that David and I have the same color hair and eyes. You mentioned it yourself the other day. And David's father—my real father— he had blond hair and blue eyes, too."

Helen stared at the journal; then turning her gaze to Elizabeth, she said, "Have you spoken to your aunt about this?"

"No." Elizabeth released a lingering sigh. "I don't even know where Aunt Lovina lives anymore."

"What are you going to do?"

"I've written a note and left it in the cabin for David."

Helen's eyes widened. "Did you tell him the truth?"

"Of course not. Revealing my mother's secret would be too humiliating for David and both of our families. I told him in the note that I can't marry him because I've come to realize that we're not meant to be together, and that I'm going away."

Helen handed the journal to Elizabeth. "I feel so terrible for you. I wish there was something I could do to make your pain go away."

"You can't take away the pain I feel. It's something I'll have to deal with on my own. But there is something you can do."

"What? I'll do anything to help."

Elizabeth returned the journal to her satchel. "You must keep my secret and never tell anyone."

"What if David asks me if I know why you broke your engagement?"

"You mustn't tell him."

"But where will you go?"

"I'd rather not say right now. I'll write to you in a few weeks after I'm settled in. But you have to promise not to tell anyone where I've gone. Is that clear?"

Helen gave a quick nod. "David will be so hurt when he reads your note."

"I know, but not nearly as hurt as he'd be if he learned that the woman he planned to marry is really his half sister."

"I—I see what you mean." Helen dabbed at the tears beneath her eyes. "I can't believe how quickly things have changed. When we were at the cabin, you were so happy and looked forward to your wedding. Now you won't even be here to celebrate your birthday on Christmas Eve with your family and friends."

"It's for the best," Elizabeth murmured. Oh, how she wished this was just a bad dream and she could wake up and everything would be as it once was.

"Have you told your father and Abigail that you're leaving?" Helen asked.

"I left a note for Father on the desk in his study. I'm sure he'll see it when he gets home from his business trip in New York."

"What did you tell him?"

"Pretty much the same thing I told David. I also said I would write and let them know where I was when I felt that I could." Elizabeth dabbed at her own set of tears. "I hope Father and Abigail will understand."

"This is too much to comprehend," Helen said. "I wish I knew how to pray about it."

"Pray that David will find someone more suitable to be his wife." Elizabeth pushed back her chair and stood. "You and David have always gotten along well enough. Maybe he'll take an interest in you."

Helen gasped. "Oh no, Elizabeth, I. . ."

Elizabeth turned and rushed out the door. Her heart felt as numb as the cold air that hit her face.

Chapter 6

Elizabeth left Helen's house and hurried down the street. She planned to see if Slim Weaver, the man who ran the livery stable, would give her a ride to the train station. She had to get out of town before she ran into someone she knew. As she neared the Old Corner Store on the southwest corner of Center Square, Howard Glenstone stepped out. He wore a dark-brown suit with a beige bow tie and looked as dapper as ever with the ends of his cocoa-colored hair sticking out from under his top hat.

"It's good to see you, Elizabeth." Howard's handlebar mustache twitched rhythmically as he smiled and gave her a nod. "Where might you be headed on this chilly fall day?" A whiff of Howard's bay rum hair tonic wafted up to her nose.

"I'm. . .uh. . .on my way to the livery stable," she mumbled, refusing to meet his gaze.

"I'm heading to my office, but I'd be glad to give you a ride."

"No thanks. The livery's not far, and I can walk." Knowing she had to hurry or she would miss her train, Elizabeth continued walking at a brisk pace.

"What's your business at the livery stable?" Howard asked as he strode along beside her. "Are you in need of a new horse?"

"I'm sorry, Howard, but I'm in a hurry and really can't talk anymore."

"Oh, I see." He gave her a nod and turned toward his exquisite-looking emerald-green carriage with gold mountings. Howard was not only handsome, but he was also a man of wealth and prestige with many business holdings. He would no doubt make some lucky woman a good husband—just not her. She would forever remain an old maid.

When Elizabeth arrived at the livery stable, she spoke to Slim about giving her a ride to the train station.

"Sure, no problem." Slim offered Elizabeth a toothless grin. "Goin' to Philadelphia to do some shoppin' for your weddin', I'll bet."

Elizabeth made no reply as Slim helped her into the buggy. She didn't feel right about not answering his question, but she couldn't tell him the truth. It wasn't like her to be antisocial. She felt awkward, almost guilty, treating those she'd known since childhood with this silence, but for now, she had no other choice. The fewer questions, the better.

As the horse and buckboard left the livery stable, Elizabeth glanced over her shoulder and caught sight of David's employee, Gus Smith, crossing the street. She wasn't sure if he'd seen her or not but was relieved to see that David wasn't with him. She certainly couldn't deal with seeing him right now.

❉

David urged his horse to move quickly as he headed down the road toward the cabin. He'd stopped by the Cannings' to see Elizabeth, but Abigail, who'd just returned home from shopping, said Elizabeth wasn't there. She thought Elizabeth might have gone to the cabin. But as David approached the cabin, he didn't see any sign of Elizabeth's buckboard. Could she have come on foot? It was worth checking.

David tied his horse to the hitching rail, sprinted to the cabin, and was surprised to find the door ajar. The room was cold, and there was no sign of a fire having been built in the fireplace. He glanced at the mantel and noticed an envelope with his name on it.

He tore it open, and as he read the note, his heart started to pound. *What? Elizabeth isn't going to marry me?* For some reason she thought they couldn't be together. But why? In all the time they'd been courting she'd never given him any indication that she didn't care for him. Until she'd taken ill several days ago, everything had appeared to be fine. Had she been lying all this time, pretending to love him when she didn't? Could there be another man? But if that were so, why hadn't she told him sooner? Why wait until now. . .less than two months before their wedding? And why had Elizabeth come to the cabin to clean and get it ready for them to move into if she wasn't planning to marry him? None of this made any sense.

The only thing David could think to do was to find Elizabeth and hear from her own lips why she'd written the note that had caused all this doubt to suddenly enter his mind.

He stuffed the note in his jacket pocket and hurried out the door. He had to go back to Elizabeth's house. If she wasn't there, he'd speak to Abigail about the note. It couldn't end like this. He had to find out why Elizabeth had changed her mind about marrying him and win her back.

A s Elizabeth sat on the train heading for Coopersburg, she stared out the window at the passing scenery, feeling as gloomy as the gray sky above. She was leaving behind the only home she'd ever known. . .and the only man she'd ever loved enough to marry.

"Are you all right, dear?" the elderly woman sitting beside Elizabeth asked.

Using the corner of her handkerchief, Elizabeth dabbed at the tears wetting her cheeks. "It's nothing, really. I'm just feeling a little weepy right now."

The woman nodded. "I understand. We women are sometimes prone to crying, even when there's nothing to cry about."

Elizabeth gave no reply. She certainly had a good reason to cry but wasn't about to tell this stranger her problems. It was bad enough that she'd told Helen the truth. In another time she might have welcomed a conversation with this kindhearted woman, but instead, she leaned her head against the back of the seat and closed her eyes, trying to calm the knot in her stomach. This was certainly not a journey she'd ever imagined taking. *I do hope Helen keeps my secret. Please, Lord, help me not to be afraid, and lead me down the right path in the days ahead.*

As David urged his horse toward Elizabeth's house, his shop came into view. As he approached the shop, Gus stepped out and motioned him to stop.

David halted his horse. "What is it, Gus?"

"I could use your help putting some wheels on that fancy, plum-colored carriage we got in the other day," Gus said.

"You'll have to manage on your own for a while," David said. "I'm going over to the Cannings' house to talk to Elizabeth right now."

Gus shook his head. "I don't think she's there, boss."

"How do you know?"

"Saw her with Slim Weaver, and it looked like they was headin' toward the train station in his buckboard."

David's heart gave a lurch. Apparently Elizabeth had followed through with her threat to leave town. He certainly hadn't expected her to leave so soon.

David quickly told Gus about the note he'd found in the cabin.

"So she gave ya the mitten, huh?"

"Yes. I'm afraid she has discarded me as her boyfriend," David said with regret.

Gus frowned. "Sorry to hear that. Thought you two was madly in love."

"That's what I thought, but I guess I was wrong." Inside, though, David still had a hard time believing it.

"I've got to go now. I need to find out where Elizabeth has gone!" David clutched the reins so tightly that his fingers ached as he clucked to the horse. Hurrying through the streets of town, he nearly collided with one of the elderly street vendors hawking his goods. As he pulled his horse to the right to dodge the vendor's cart, he heard the man's rhythmic chant: "Scissors to grind! Razors. . .scissors. . .penknives to grind!"

David continued on, until he came to the Cannings' large, gingerbread-trimmed home. He secured his horse to the hitching rail, sprinted up the porch steps, and gave the bellpull a yank.

Several minutes later, Abigail answered the door. "May I help you, David?"

"I went to the cabin, hoping Elizabeth was there, but I found this instead." He pulled the envelope from his pocket and handed it to her.

"What is it?"

"A note from Elizabeth. She left it on the fireplace mantel for me."

Abigail slipped the note from the envelope and gasped when she read it. "This is certainly a shock! I had no idea Elizabeth was planning to leave town or that she had decided to break her engagement." She patted her flushed cheeks and pushed a stray tendril of dark hair into the chignon at the back of her head.

"My helper, Gus, said he saw Elizabeth with the man who owns the livery stable and that it looked like they were heading to the train station. Do you have any idea where she might be going?"

Abigail slowly shook her head. "I wonder if Elizabeth left a note for us somewhere in the house. If she did, it might say." She opened the door wider and bid him in. "If you'd like to take a seat in the parlor, I'll have a look around."

David seated himself on a dark-blue, circular sofa, while Abigail hurried off to another room.

Several minutes later she returned, holding an envelope and wearing a glum expression. "I found a note from Elizabeth on Charles's desk in his study."

David leaped to his feet. "What does it say?"

"Pretty much the same as the note she wrote to you—that she's come to realize she can't marry you and has decided to go away. She also said she was sorry that she won't be here for her birthday or Christmas."

"Did she say where she was going?"

"No, and I dread telling Charles when he gets home from his trip. He's going to be very upset."

"He can't be any more upset than I am. Elizabeth was supposed to be my wife." David frowned. "I don't understand what went wrong. One minute she seemed so happy about marrying me, and the next minute she says she can't marry me at all. It doesn't make a bit of sense."

Abigail sank to the sofa. "Maybe she's not ready for marriage. Maybe she's still too immature and has made herself sick thinking about it."

David flinched. The thought that Elizabeth had made herself sick because she didn't want to get married made him feel guilty. Had he pushed her too hard? Should he have waited another year to propose?

He turned toward the door. "I'd better go. I need to get back to my shop, but before I do, I'm going by Helen's house and see if she knows where Elizabeth went." He hurried out the front door.

❄

A short time later, David entered the Warners' front yard and gave the brass knob a quick pull.

"Is Helen at home?" he asked when Helen's mother, Margaret, answered the door.

"She's in the parlor, practicing the piece she'll be playing for church this Sunday," the petite woman replied.

"May I speak with her? It's of the utmost importance."

Margaret hesitated a moment and finally motioned to the room on her left. "Go on in."

David stepped into the parlor, where Helen sat in front of a spacious organ, pumping her feet as she played and sang, "Sweet Hour of Prayer, sweet hour of prayer, that calls me from a world of care, and bids me at my Father's throne, make all my wants and wishes known!"

When David moved closer to the organ, Helen's head jerked, and she blinked several times, looking up at him like a frightened bird. "Oh my! You startled me, David. I—I didn't know anyone had come in."

"I need to speak to you," he said. "Your mother said that I could come in."

"Wh–what did you wish to speak with me about?" Helen seemed nervous, which was out of character for this usually calm, confident woman.

He reached into his jacket pocket and pulled out Elizabeth's note. "I found this at the cabin."

Helen dropped her gaze to the organ keys.

"It's a note from Elizabeth."

Still no comment.

Why is she acting so strange? She must know something, and I have to find out what it is.

"She called off our wedding and has gone away," he said.

"I'm very sorry, David."

"Did you know about this?" he asked, taking a seat on the bench beside her. She nodded slowly.

"Where is she, Helen? What caused Elizabeth to change her mind about marrying me?"

Helen's shoulders trembled as she lifted them in a brief shrug, refusing to make eye contact with him.

David placed his hand on her shoulder. "Please tell me what you know. I can't bear the thought of losing Elizabeth. I love her so much, and until I found this note, I was sure she loved me, too."

Helen's chin quivered as tears gathered in the corners of her chestnut-colored eyes. "I know this is painful for you, David, but you must accept Elizabeth's decision and get on with your life."

"Get on with my life?" He shook his head vigorously. "How can I accept her decision when I don't understand the reason she called off the wedding?"

Helen said nothing.

Irritation welled in David's soul. Helen was hiding something; he was sure of it. Was she trying to spare his feelings, or had she promised Elizabeth not to tell?

"Is there someone else?" he questioned. "Is Elizabeth in love with another man?"

"No."

"Then what is it? Why couldn't she look me in the eye and tell me that she doesn't love me anymore?"

Helen rose from the bench and moved over to the window. "I can't discuss this with you. I gave Elizabeth my word."

"If you won't tell me why she wrote the note and left town, then at least tell me where she's gone," he said, quickly joining her at the window.

"I—I truly don't know." Helen whirled around and dashed out of the room. David's heart sank. If Helen knew the truth but wouldn't tell him, how was he ever going to get Elizabeth back?

Chapter 8

Elizabeth took a seat in the spindle-backed rocking chair by the fireplace and placed her Bible in her lap. She'd arrived at her grandparents' house in Coopersburg two days ago and had been welcomed with open arms. She was relieved that they'd accepted her excuse for being here and hadn't questioned her about the reason for her breakup with David. All she'd told them was that she'd changed her mind and had come to realize that the two of them weren't meant to be together. Grandma had hugged her and said, "Remember, dear, you're welcome to stay with us for as long as you want."

That could be indefinitely, Elizabeth thought, *because as long as David lives in Allentown, I don't see how I can return. It's hard to think of him as my brother, and I simply can't face him again, knowing the terrible secret that lies between us.*

Forcing her thoughts aside, she opened the Bible. Her gaze came to rest on Proverbs 3:5, a verse she'd underlined some time ago: "Trust in the Lord with all thine heart; and lean not unto thine own understanding."

She was trying to trust God, but it was difficult when her world had been torn apart and there was no hope of her ever marrying David.

Elizabeth heard whispered voices coming from the kitchen, where her grandparents had gone to have a cup of coffee. Her ears perked up when she heard Grandma say, "Elizabeth is so sad. I wish there was something we could do to make her feel better."

"She's obviously hurting over her breakup with David," Grandpa said. "It's going to take her some time to get over it."

I'll never get over it, Elizabeth thought as tears sprang to her eyes. *As long as I live, I'll never forget what David and I once had, and I'll never let myself fall in love with another man.*

❄

Unable to eat, sleep, or work for the past two days, David decided the only thing he could do was to go back to Helen's, hoping he could convince her to tell him something. He needed to know why Elizabeth had broken up with him and where she had gone. He needed to speak with her, and he wouldn't take Helen's no for an answer this time.

When he stepped up to the Warners' front door and rang the bell, Helen answered, wearing an apron splattered with flour over her long, calico dress.

"I need to speak with you. May I please come in?" he asked, praying she wouldn't say no.

She hesitated but finally said, "Father's in the parlor, studying his sermon for this Sunday, and I was in the kitchen making some bread, but I suppose we could speak in there."

"That's fine." David entered the house and followed Helen to the kitchen.

"Would you like a cup of coffee or some tea?" she asked after he'd taken a seat at the table.

He gave a nod. "Coffee sounds good."

She went to the coal-heated stove and picked up the coffeepot.

"Aren't you going to join me?" he asked when she handed him a cup of coffee and moved over to the cupboard next to the stove.

She shook her head. "I have bread dough to knead."

David blew on his coffee then took a sip. The warm liquid felt good as it trickled down his parched throat.

"What did you want to talk to me about?" Helen asked, turning her back to him as she began to work the dough.

"I need to know why Elizabeth left and where she's gone."

Helen whirled around, lifting her flour-covered hands. "I wish you'd stop asking me about this. I promised Elizabeth I wouldn't say anything about what she'd read in her aunt's journal." She gasped and covered her mouth with the back of her hand. "I—I didn't mean to say that. I meant to say. . ."

David leaped to his feet. "What about her aunt's journal? What's it got to do with Elizabeth leaving?"

Helen sucked in her lower lip as her gaze dropped to the floor.

David clasped her arm. "Please, you've got to tell me. I love Elizabeth, and I have the right to know why she called off our wedding."

Helen moaned and flopped into a chair at the table. "I agree, you do have the right to know, but it's going to come as a shock, and it's going to hurt you the way it did Elizabeth when she found out the truth."

"The truth about what?" David took a seat across from Helen and leaned forward, anxious to hear what she had to say. "What could Elizabeth's aunt have written that would have caused Elizabeth to go away?"

David sat in stunned silence as Helen told him about the entry in the journal.

"So as I'm sure you now realize," Helen said in a tone of regret, "Elizabeth is your half sister, which means you can never be married."

David groaned. This was worse than he could have imagined! No wonder

Elizabeth had run away. Learning that she was the illegitimate daughter of David's father had to have been a terrible shock.

"Is Elizabeth sure that what she read is the truth?" he asked, grasping for any ray of hope. "Has she spoken to her aunt about this?"

Helen shook her head. "She doesn't know where her mother's sister is, but I'm sure it has to be true. I mean, why would Elizabeth's aunt write something like that if it wasn't true?"

"What's the aunt's name—do you know?"

"Lovina Hess."

"Where is Elizabeth now?" David asked. "I really must speak to her about this."

"I honestly don't know. I haven't heard anything from her since she left home, and when I spoke to her stepmother the other day, she said she hadn't heard from Elizabeth either."

"Will you let me know if you do hear from her?" he asked as a feeling of desperation gripped him like a vice.

Helen shook her head. "That's not a good idea."

"Why not?"

"It would be too painful for Elizabeth to see you again, and nothing would be gained by hashing this over with her."

Forgetting about the coffee, David rose from his chair. "Thank you for at least telling me about the journal. There's a small measure of comfort in knowing that Elizabeth didn't leave because she's in love with someone else." He turned and walked out the door, a sense of determination welling in his soul. Despite what Helen had said, he would somehow find Elizabeth and try to offer her some comfort. Truth was, he needed comfort right now as well.

Chapter 9

It had been two weeks since Elizabeth had arrived at her grandparents' house, and with each passing day she became more despondent. Even the delicious Thanksgiving meal Grandma fixed for the three of them yesterday had done nothing to lift Elizabeth's spirits. All she could think about was that Christmas was only a month away and she would not be getting married to the man she loved.

She thought about the telegram her grandparents had received from her father the day he'd returned from his business trip and discovered she was gone. His message said he wondered if she may have come here and that he and Abigail missed her and hoped she would come home soon. Elizabeth had sent a reply, letting him know she was here and missed them, too, but that she planned to stay with Grandpa and Grandma for now. She also asked that he not tell anyone where she was—especially David. Then she'd written a letter to Helen, telling her the same.

Dear Lord, please help me, she prayed. *Take away the ache in my heart and the love I feel for a man I can never marry.*

"You've been sitting in that chair, staring at the fire for hours," Grandpa said, touching Elizabeth's shoulder. "Why don't you put on a wrap and take a ride with me and your grandma? The fresh air might do you some good, and since we'll be stopping at a couple of stores, you can do a bit of Christmas shopping." He chuckled. "Your grandma always says she feels better whenever she's able to buy anything new—even if it's for someone other than herself."

"You two go ahead," Elizabeth replied. "I'm not in the mood to do any shopping."

"You're not doing yourself any good by sitting here pining every day. If you miss David so much, then you ought to return to Allentown and marry him."

Unbidden tears sprang to her eyes. She wished it were as easy as Grandpa suggested. "I—I can't. It's over between me and David."

"Are you saying you don't love him anymore?"

She shook her head. "We're not meant for each other, and I'm glad I found out before it was too late."

Grandpa's bushy gray eyebrows furrowed. "I'm not sure why you think that, but if you're in love with the young man, that's all that counts. Your grandma and I don't see eye to eye on everything, but our love for each other is what's kept us together all these years." He gave her shoulder a gentle squeeze. "If you and David had a disagreement, then you ought to resolve it."

She swallowed a couple of times, trying to push down the lump in her throat. "The problem between David and me is not one that can be resolved."

"If you want my advice, the best thing you can do is pray, and ask God to give you some answers."

"I have been praying, but there are no answers for my problem." Unable to talk about it any longer, Elizabeth stood. "I'm tired. I think I'll go upstairs and take a nap." She hurried from the room. There was no way she could explain the situation to Grandpa. It was too humiliating to talk about.

David paced from one end of his shop to the other. In the two weeks since he'd learned why Elizabeth had left town, he hadn't been able to think of much else. He was consumed with the need to speak to Elizabeth's aunt, but no one seemed to know where she was.

His thoughts took him to the day Elizabeth's father had returned from his business trip in New York. David had gone to the Cannings' house, asking if Charles knew where Elizabeth had gone. Charles said he'd received word from her via a telegram, but that she'd asked him not to tell anyone where she was. Feeling more frustrated than ever, David had then asked Charles if he knew where Elizabeth's aunt, Lovina Hess, lived. Charles had looked at him strangely and asked why he would need to know that. Without revealing what Helen had told him about Lovina's journal, David said he had a question he wanted to ask Lovina about something Elizabeth had found in the cabin. To that, Charles said Lovina had once owned a boarding home in Easton, but after she'd sold it and moved, none of the family had heard from her since.

"I wish Father were still alive so I could ask him about this," David murmured as his mind snapped back to the present. Someone had to know if what Lovina wrote was the truth. Had David's father been aware that Elizabeth's mother had been carrying his child? David knew from what Elizabeth told him when they'd begun courting that her maternal grandparents were dead, so he couldn't ask them. He also knew that Lovina was Cassandra's only sibling, so Elizabeth had no other aunts or uncles on her mother's side.

"How come you've been pacin' back and forth liked a caged animal for the last fifteen minutes?" Gus asked, stepping up to David with a curious expression.

David stopped pacing. "I'm pondering a problem."

"What kind of problem? Are you havin' trouble with one of the carriages you've been workin' on?"

"No. I've been wondering where Elizabeth's aunt lives."

Gus's forehead wrinkled. "Why would ya be lookin' for Elizabeth's aunt?"

"I need to talk to her about something she wrote in her journal—a journal Elizabeth found in the log cabin that was supposed to be our home after we got married." David frowned. "The problem is, no one seems to know where Lovina Hess lives."

Gus tipped his head. "Lovina Hess, you say?"

"That's right."

"I know of a woman by that name."

David's eyebrows shot up. "You do?"

Gus gave a nod. "Sure thing. My cousin Rosie's a nurse, and she works for a woman named Lovina Hess who has the palsy and a weak heart. Since Miss Hess can't manage on her own anymore, Rosie's been carin' for her these past five years."

For the first time, hope welled in David's soul. "Where does your cousin live?"

"In Philadelphia. 'Course, the woman she works for might not be Elizabeth's aunt."

"Maybe not. It could just be a coincidence that they have the same name, but I need to find out. Do you have the woman's address?"

"Sure do. Got it off the envelope when Rosie wrote to me some time ago." Gus shrugged. "Don't have it with me, though. It's at home in my dresser drawer."

"Would you get it for me?" David asked.

"I'll bring it to work tomorrow mornin'."

"I can't wait that long. I need it right away." David pointed to the door. "I'd like you to go home now and get that address for me."

Gus made a sweeping gesture of the carriage shop. "We've got work to do here. Can't the address wait till mornin'?"

David shook his head. "The work can wait awhile, and I'll pay you for the time it takes to get to and from your house."

Gus pulled his fingers down the side of his bearded face. "If it's that important to ya, then I'll head over there right now." He grabbed his jacket and hurried out the door.

David lifted a silent prayer. *Thank You, Lord.* Now all he had to do was secure a train ticket to Philadelphia. Hopefully, the woman Gus's cousin worked for was indeed Elizabeth's aunt and he'd have the opportunity to speak with her about the journal.

Chapter 10

As David ascended the steps of the two-story wooden-framed house at the address Gus had given him, his heart started to pound. What if the woman who lived here wasn't Elizabeth's aunt? What if she was but wasn't willing to speak with him? If this was the right Lovina Hess, then he couldn't return home without some answers. He simply had to know if what had been written in the journal was true.

Seeing no bellpull, he rapped on the door a few times and waited. Several minutes later the door opened, and a middle-aged woman with mousy brown hair worn in a tight bun greeted him.

"May I help you, sir?"

"Yes. Well, I hope so. I'm told that Lovina Hess lives here."

The woman gave a nod. "That's correct. I'm her housekeeper, Mrs. Cook."

David shuffled his feet a few times. "Uh. . .if it's all right, I'd like to speak with Lovina."

"Please state your name and the nature of your business."

"I'm sorry. I should have told you that right away." David cleared his throat and loosened his shirt collar, which suddenly felt too tight around his neck. "I'm David Stinner. I make and repair carriages in Allentown."

Mrs. Cook's brown eyes narrowed as she shook her head. "Miss Lovina has no interest in having a carriage made. She's ill and hasn't been able to leave the house in some time."

"I'm not here to sell her a carriage. I've come to speak with Lovina about Elizabeth Canning, whom I believe is her niece."

Mrs. Cook tipped her head and studied David intently. "Miss Lovina has never mentioned a niece, and as I said before, she's ill and isn't up to receiving company right now."

"Please, this is very important, and I promise I won't take up much of her time," he pleaded, in a desperate attempt to make the woman understand.

Mrs. Cook hesitated then finally said, "Very well. I'll see if she's willing to talk to you." She closed the door, leaving David standing on the porch in the cold.

" 'Trust in the Lord with all thine heart; and lean not unto thine own understanding,'" David recited. If ever he needed to trust God, it was now.

Dear Lord, he silently prayed as he paced from one end of the porch to the other, *I hope I haven't come all this way for nothing. I pray that Lovina will speak to me. Help me remember to trust You in all things.*

The front door opened, and David whirled around.

"Lovina will see you, but please don't stay too long. She tires easily these days."

Mrs. Cook held the door open and motioned for David to enter the house. Then she led him up a winding staircase and down a long, dark corridor illuminated by only the small oil lamp she carried. With each step he took, David heard his footsteps echoing on the polished hardwood floor.

As he entered a dimly lit bedroom, a sense of hope welled in his chest. For the first time since this nightmare had begun, he felt closer to finding an answer to the question he sought.

David halted inside the door. A feeling of pity tugged at his heart as he stared at the frail-looking woman lying in the canopied bed across the room. He stood like that for several minutes and then moved slowly toward the foot of the bed. A young woman dressed in a nurse's cap, a long, white skirt, and a striped blouse stood off to one side.

"Is your name Rosie?" he asked.

The nurse nodded. "How'd you know?"

"My employee, Gus Smith, said he was your cousin."

She smiled. "That's right. I wrote to him not long ago."

"May I speak with Lovina alone?" David asked.

Rosie shook her head. "You may say whatever you want, but I shall remain here in the room."

David relented and moved to the right side of the bed, realizing that no matter who else was present, the important thing was having his questions answered.

Lovina, so pale and thin, with straw-colored hair and lifeless brown eyes, looked up at him with a curious expression. "My housekeeper said you know my niece, Elizabeth."

David nodded as excitement coursed through his veins. So this was the right Lovina. "Elizabeth and I were engaged—until she read something in your journal."

Lovina lifted a shaky hand and motioned for him to come near. "I can't hear well and don't know what you said."

David leaned closer; so close he could feel Lovina's warm breath on his face, and repeated what he'd said.

"Journal? What journal?" she rasped.

"Elizabeth found it in an old desk in the cabin where she was born."

Lovina closed her eyes, and for a minute David thought she might have fallen asleep. Slowly she opened them again. "I—I did have a journal once. It was a birthday present from my parents."

"Did you write something in the journal about Elizabeth's mother and my father?"

Lovina blinked. "I don't think I know your father. What's his name?"

"Raymond Stinner."

Lovina's whole body trembled as she gasped and tried to sit up.

Rosie stepped forward and took her hand. "Relax, Miss Lovina. Rest easy against your pillow." She turned to David with a scowl and said, "If she doesn't calm down, I'll have to ask you to leave."

"I'm not trying to upset her," he said. "I just need to know the truth about what she wrote in the journal."

Rosie glanced at the clock on the dresser across the room. "I'll give you five minutes, but that's all."

David leaned a bit closer to Lovina. "I'm Raymond Stinner's son, David. In your journal you wrote that my father and Elizabeth's mother. . . Well, you said that Cassandra was pregnant with Raymond's child when she married Charles Canning. Is it true?"

Lovina's pale cheeks flushed slightly, and she averted his gaze.

"Is my father Elizabeth's real father?" he persisted.

Tears welled in Lovina's eyes as she stared at the canopy above her head, seeming to let her memories take her back in time.

David bit his lip while waiting to hear the answer he sought.

After several minutes had passed, Lovina whispered something.

"What was that?"

"I made it all up. I never should have written that in my journal."

A sense of relief swept over David, quickly replaced with a wave of anger. "But, why? What made you write such a horrible thing if it wasn't true?" he shouted, straightening to his full height.

Lovina whimpered and trembled again.

"Lower your voice," Rosie said, looking sternly at David. "Can't you see how upset she's become?"

"I–I'm sorry." He drew in a deep breath and leaned close to Lovina again. "Please, tell me why you wrote what you did."

Lovina's tears spilled over and trickled onto her cheeks. "I wrote it out of spite and frustration." She sniffed deeply. "I was jealous that my sister had married the only man I'd ever loved."

Stunned by this confession, David drew in a sharp breath. "You. . .you were in love with Charles Canning?"

"Yes, but he only had eyes for Cassandra. My heart was broken when he married her. I—I was angry because they loved each other and I was left out in the cold. . .forever to be an old maid."

"I'm sorry about that, but what does it have to do with Raymond—my father? Why would you have said that he was the father of Cassandra's baby if he wasn't?"

"Raymond had been courting Cassandra, and just when I thought Charles might ask to court me, he turned to her instead."

"So you wrote that Cassandra was pregnant with my father's child, hoping Charles would read it and refuse to marry her?"

"I didn't think anyone would read my journal. I only put my frustrated thoughts on paper in an effort to alleviate my pain. By pretending in my mind that Cassandra only married Charles because she was desperate and needed a husband, I was able to deal with the disappointment I felt because he didn't choose me." Lovina shook her head slowly, as more tears fell. "I—I truly never intended to hurt anyone."

David stood several seconds, staring down at the pathetic, ailing woman. She'd had her heart broken once, and he didn't think he should break it again by telling her what horrible pain the lie in her journal had caused. If he could find out where Elizabeth had gone and tell her the truth about the journal, he was sure she would agree to marry him, and everything would be all right. When he returned to Allentown, his first stop would be to see Helen. Maybe by now she would have heard from Elizabeth. If so he hoped to persuade her to tell him where Elizabeth had gone.

Elizabeth sat at the table in Grandma's kitchen with a cup of tea and the letter she'd just received from Helen.

> *Dear Elizabeth:*
>
> *It was good to finally hear from you and know that you're safe and living with your grandparents.*
>
> *I wanted to tell you that David came here a few weeks ago, asking if I knew why you'd called off the wedding and had left town. He looked so sad and kept begging me to tell him something. I made the mistake of mentioning that you'd found your aunt's journal, and then before I realized what I was saying, I'd told him the whole story.*

He was shocked to hear that his father is actually your father, too, and I hardly knew what to say. Then he said he wanted to know where you were, but of course I didn't tell him because at that time I didn't know myself.

If you want my opinion, I think you ought to see David and talk to him about this. You should give him a chance to express his feelings, because I'm sure he's hurting as much as you are.

Please write again soon.

With love and good wishes,
Helen

Tears pricked the back of Elizabeth's eyes, and her hands shook as she quickly jammed the letter into her skirt pocket. She couldn't believe Helen had betrayed her confidence and told David about Aunt Lovina's journal. It was just a matter of time before Helen would tell David where she was, and then he would come here. She couldn't face him—couldn't discuss the horrible truth about who her real father was.

She pushed back her chair and hurried into the parlor, where Grandma and Grandpa sat on the sofa, reading.

"I appreciate you putting me up these last few weeks, but I can't stay here any longer," she said.

Grandma looked up. "Are you going home for Christmas?"

Elizabeth shook her head. "I need to go someplace where I can be alone. I need time to think and work things through."

"Have we been too intrusive?" Grandma questioned, her dark eyes full of obvious concern. "Because if we have, we can certainly keep quiet about things."

Elizabeth shook her head. "It's not that. I just need to be by myself for a while."

"Where will you go?" Grandma asked.

"I—I don't know. Maybe I can stay in one of the boarding homes here in Coopersburg."

"But that would cost money," Grandma said, "and why pay for a room when you can stay right here?"

"Say, I have an idea," Grandpa spoke up. "Why don't you stay in your cousin Marvin's cabin? He and his wife, Isabelle, are in New Jersey right now, visiting her parents. They won't be back until Christmas, so you'd have two weeks to be alone. Then your grandma and I will join the three of you at the cabin for Christmas dinner."

Elizabeth thought about Grandpa's suggestion and finally nodded. "There's just one thing," she said. "I need you both to promise that you won't tell anyone where I've gone."

Grandma's eyebrows lifted. "Not even your father?"

Elizabeth shook her head.

"I'm sure he and Abigail will want to spend Christmas with you. Do you think it's right not to tell them where you are?" Grandpa asked.

"I wrote them a letter saying I would be spending Christmas with you. Please promise that if David comes here looking for me, you won't tell him where I've gone."

Grandpa looked at Grandma, and when she nodded, he looked at Elizabeth and said, "We won't say a word."

"Thank you." Elizabeth turned toward the stairs. "I'd better go upstairs and pack. I need to leave for the cabin right away."

Chapter 11

As David approached the Warners' house, he quickened his steps. He could hardly wait to tell Helen about his visit with Lovina.

As he stepped onto the porch, the door flew open, and a very surprised-looking Helen stepped out, holding a large red bow and several sprigs of holly. "Oh, you scared me, David! I didn't know anyone was on the porch."

"I just got here."

"Well, if you'll excuse me, I was about to put these decorations on the railing, and then I have some more decorating to do inside." She brushed past him and started down the stairs.

"I need to speak with you," he said, matching her stride.

"I—I really don't have time to talk right now."

"It won't take long, and it's very important."

She halted and turned to face him, lifting her chin a notch. "If this is about Elizabeth, I've already told you more than I should have, and I won't tell you anything else."

"It is about Elizabeth, but I think you need to hear what I have to say." He motioned to the house. "Can we go inside where it's warmer so I can tell you my good news?"

"What's that?"

"I discovered that Elizabeth's aunt Lovina lives in Philadelphia, and I went to see her."

Helen's face blanched. "You went there to ask about the journal, didn't you?"

He nodded. "Can we go inside so I can tell you what she said?"

"Oh, all right." Helen turned, and David followed her up the stairs and into the house, where he was greeted by the pleasant aroma of freshly baked apple pies.

"Let's go in there." Helen motioned to the kitchen. "Mother's in the parlor, visiting with some of her friends from church, and I don't want to disturb them."

David entered the kitchen behind Helen, and after she'd placed her holiday decorations on the counter, they both took seats at the table.

"Tell me what Lovina had to say about the journal," Helen said, slipping her woolen shawl off her shoulders and placing it in her lap.

"She said that what she'd written about my father being Elizabeth's father was a lie," David said. Then he went on to explain the rest of what Lovina had told him.

"Oh my!" Helen drew in a sharp breath and covered her mouth with the palm of her hand. "Elizabeth needs to know about this."

"Yes, she certainly does. She also needs to see the note Lovina signed, admitting that she'd lied, and assuring Elizabeth that Charles Canning is indeed her real father."

Helen's face broke into a wide smile. "That's wonderful, David! Elizabeth will be so relieved to hear this news. I should write to her immediately."

"So you know where she is?" he asked.

Helen's cheeks turned pink as she gave a slow nod. "I got a letter from her a while back."

"And you didn't tell me?" David's voice was edged with the irritation he felt.

"Elizabeth asked me not to tell anyone, and since I'd already broken my promise and told you about the journal, I felt I had to respect her wishes and not tell you where she's been staying."

He leaned forward, resting his elbows on the table. "Things are different now that we know the truth. I feel it's important that I be the one to tell Elizabeth what her aunt had to say."

"I suppose you're right," Helen said with a nod. "She's been staying at her grandparents' house in Coopersburg."

David snapped his fingers. "Of course! Don't know why I didn't think to look for her there."

"Do you have the address?" Helen asked.

"Yes. I went there with Elizabeth several months ago to tell her grandparents that we were engaged."

"When will you leave?"

"As soon as I can secure a train ticket and line out some jobs for Gus to do while I'm gone." David pushed back his chair and stood. "I'm headed over to the shop right now."

Helen smiled. "May God be with you and grant you a safe trip."

❄

Elizabeth had been staying in her cousin's cabin for two days, and despite her desire to be alone, she was lonely and more depressed than ever. Besides missing the sights and sounds of Christmas, being in her cousin's cabin made her think about David and the little cabin they would have shared if they'd been able to get married. Maybe she'd made a mistake leaving Grandpa and Grandma's. She missed Grandpa's cheerful smile and Grandma's tasty cooking. She missed the times she'd spent with them around the fire each evening. At least in her grandparents' house she'd been surrounded by their happiness, making the days a bit more pleasant.

As hard as Elizabeth tried to fight it, the loneliness became heavier, surrounding her like a burdensome piece of clothing. She shivered and tossed another log onto the fire. *If Grandpa were here, he'd be tending the fire, and Grandma would probably be baking.*

With a sigh she took a seat in the rocking chair and pulled a lightweight quilt across her lap. It was cold outside. She could hear the wind whipping through the trees.

Snow could be coming soon, Elizabeth thought. *I wonder if I should go outside and bring in a few more logs for the fire.* Looking up, she noticed a ladybug creeping along the wall as though desperately searching for a warm gap to crawl into until spring. She remembered reading that in some countries they believed a ladybug was a sign of good luck, and although she didn't believe in folklore, this one time she wished it were true.

As she stared into the fire, she thought about Aunt Lovina's journal and how on the day her grandparents had gone Christmas shopping she'd tossed it into the fire. As she'd watched the flames consume the journal, it had done nothing to alleviate her pain.

Elizabeth leaned her head back and closed her eyes, feeling drowsy from the heat of the fire. *I'll just sit here and rest awhile before I go out for more logs.*

Sometime later, Elizabeth was roused from her sleep by the whinny of a horse. She leaped to her feet and raced to the window, surprised to see her cousin, Marvin, helping his wife, Isabelle, down from their carriage. As they walked toward the cabin, Elizabeth opened the door.

"Elizabeth, what are you doing here?" Marvin said, a quizzical expression on his face.

Elizabeth quickly explained, adding that their grandparents had said she would be alone until Marvin and Isabelle returned for Christmas.

"My mother is doing better, and so we decided to come back earlier than planned," Isabelle explained. She smiled up at her handsome, dark-haired husband. "We're looking forward to spending our first Christmas together in this cozy little cabin."

"But if you don't mind sleeping in the loft, you're welcome to stay with us for as long as you want," Marvin quickly added.

Elizabeth glanced out the window. It had begun to snow, and even though she felt like an intruder, she knew she couldn't go anywhere tonight. Besides, where would she go? There was some measure of warmth and solace to be found living under the same roof with family.

"Very well," she said. "I'll stay through Christmas, but then I'll need to find someplace else to go."

Chapter 12

The following afternoon, Elizabeth stared out the cabin window at the swirling snow. "The weather seems to be getting worse," she said to Marvin, who had just thrown another log on the fire.

He joined her at the window. "I believe you're right, so I think I'd better go outside and cut some more wood. We don't want to run out."

"That's a good idea," Isabelle spoke up from her chair across the room, where she sat with some mending in her lap. She blinked her hazel-colored eyes and shivered. "If this weather keeps up, it may be hard to find the woodpile, not to mention that it's awfully cold outside."

Marvin nodded. "I'll get my jacket and head out right now."

"Would you like to sit here by the fire with me?" Isabelle asked Elizabeth after Marvin left. "Or should we go to the kitchen and bake some gingerbread?"

"Gingerbread sounds nice." Elizabeth didn't really feel like doing any baking, but if she kept busy, it might take her mind off the fact that she wouldn't be spending Christmas with David, let alone their whole lives together. She couldn't allow herself to think too hard about how her dreams had been shattered, for fear that she would fall into a black hole of despair and never find her way out.

❄

When David stepped off the train, a blast of cold air hit him full in the face. It had been snowing hard for the last several hours, and the ground was covered with a heavy blanket of white.

Clutching the satchel he'd brought with Lovina's signed confession, as well as the velveteen pouch she'd given him, he trudged toward the livery stable to rent a horse. He hoped the snow didn't get any worse, or he might not be able to see well enough to find his way to the home of Elizabeth's grandparents, on the other side of town.

When David arrived at the Cannings' door sometime later, he was greeted by Elizabeth's grandmother, Mary. "Is Elizabeth here?" he asked. "I need to speak with her."

Mary shook her head. "Elizabeth was here, but she left a few days ago."

"Where'd she go?"

"I really can't say. She asked us not to tell anyone."

David's heart nearly plummeted to his toes. If Mary wouldn't tell him where Elizabeth was, he wouldn't be able to tell her what he'd found out from Lovina.

"I need to speak with Elizabeth," he said. "It's quite urgent."

"My husband and I will be seeing Elizabeth on Christmas, so if you have a message for her, I'll pass it along."

He shook his head determinedly. "I need to tell her myself."

"I don't think so," Mary's husband, Joe, said, stepping up to the door. "Elizabeth obviously doesn't want to talk to you, or she wouldn't have called off the wedding and left home."

David winced, feeling as if he'd been slapped. He didn't need the reminder that the woman he loved had run away without even telling him why.

"There is something Elizabeth doesn't know, and if I could just have the chance to explain. . ."

"Why don't you come inside? You can explain it to us, and then we'll decide," Mary said. She opened the door wider, and David followed her and Joe into the parlor. He spent the next several minutes telling them about Lovina's journal and ended by saying that the lie Elizabeth's aunt had written was the reason Elizabeth broke up with him and came here.

Mary gasped, and Joe's handlebar mustache twitched up and down.

"Elizabeth needs to know the truth about this," Joe said.

"Will you tell me where she is?" David asked, fighting his impatience.

"Elizabeth's staying at a cabin outside of town," Joe replied. "You'll need to go out the main road and follow it north about a mile or so, and then turn left at the fork in the road. The cabin is about a mile down from there."

"Since it's snowing so hard, and it'll be dark soon, you might get lost," Mary said with a look of concern. "Why don't you spend the night here and start out fresh in the morning?"

David shook his head. "Elizabeth and I have been apart too long already, so I'll head for the cabin right now." He bid Mary and Joe good-bye and hurried out the door.

As David headed down the road on the horse he'd rented, his hopes soared. Soon he'd see Elizabeth, and once he'd shown her Lovina's confession, everything would be all right. While he continued on, he allowed the winter scene before him to renew his Christmas spirit. There was something magical about the snow when it came before the holiday. It had a way of bringing out that little-boy feeling he remembered so well in anticipation of a white Christmas.

David's spirits rose a little more, hoping this Christmas would turn out to be all that he and Elizabeth had looked forward to before she'd found the journal.

When he came to the fork in the road that Joe had mentioned, he guided the horse to the left. He'd only gone a short ways when the wind picked up, and the snow came down with such thick flakes that he could barely see. He was quickly losing the light of day, and the horse wasn't cooperating at all. The mare tossed her head from side to side, reared up a couple of times, and finally refused to go.

With a disgruntled groan, David climbed down. He was about to grab the horse's reins when it bolted and ran, knocking him to his knees. As he attempted to get up, his foot slipped on an icy patch of snow. *Crack!* Instant fear gripped him like a vise, and before he could take any action, he fell through the thin ice into a pond that had been obscured by all the snow.

Chapter 13

As David thrashed about, trying to stay afloat, the ice-cold water stung his entire body like needles. He struggled to breathe in.

Think, David. Think. Don't panic.

He looked around frantically, searching for anything he might use to pull himself out. Nothing. Nothing at all.

Think. Pray. Get your thoughts together, and do what you can to get yourself out of here.

Instinctively, David began to bob up and down like a cork. This helped to get his chest and belly high enough so he could eventually fall over on top of the ice. Crawling carefully and quickly to the safety of a snowbank, he stood on shaky legs that were fast growing numb. He paused to thank God that he was safe and unharmed, although thoroughly drenched and shivering badly from the frigid water.

A whinny alerted him that his horse was nearby, and relief rushed through him when he spotted the mare standing beneath some nearby trees.

Grunting, he climbed onto the horse's back and gathered up the reins, thankful that the horse didn't spook. His hands were totally numb, and it was hard holding on to the reins with stiff, ice-covered gloves. David had only two choices. He could either turn around and head back to town or keep going, hoping the cabin where Elizabeth was staying wasn't far from here. The faint smell of woodsmoke in the air was a good sign that he might be closer than he thought.

With faith driving him forward, David urged the horse on until he noticed a flicker of light in the distance. Determination to see Elizabeth gave him the burst of energy he needed to keep going.

A short time later he spotted the cabin; a lantern glowed in the window. As he guided the horse to the hitching rail, he saw Elizabeth with her back facing the window. As he removed his satchel from the saddle horn and climbed down from the horse, his heart skipped a beat at the mere sight of her. Just a few steps and he'd be at the cabin, where warmth and protection from the cold beckoned him. More importantly, he could tell Elizabeth that the dreams they once had were not dead, but very much alive. He was almost to the door when he saw a young man with dark, curly hair step up to Elizabeth and give her a hug.

David's heart sank all the way to his freezing toes. He was too late—Elizabeth had found someone else. He turned toward his horse, ready to admit defeat, but the numbing cold in his limbs won out. He had to get inside where it was warm, or he would surely freeze to death.

With a trembling hand and an ache in his heart worse than the ache in his body from the frigid weather, he rapped on the door.

❄

When a knock sounded on the cabin door, Elizabeth jumped. Who would be calling at this time of day—especially with the weather being so bad?

"I'll see to it," Marvin said, moving toward the door.

Elizabeth stood off to one side, curious to see who it was. When a man stepped inside, wet and shivering badly, she gasped. "David! What are you doing here?"

"I—I came to t–talk to you about y–your aunt's journal." His teeth chattered so badly he could barely talk. "B–but it appears that I'm t–too late."

Elizabeth nodded slowly. "If you know about the journal, then you know that it's too late for us. We can never be married."

He shook his head. "I'm not t–talking about that. I'm talking about h–him." He motioned to Marvin. "I saw him h–hugging you in the w–window. Is he your h–husband, Elizabeth?"

"Certainly not. Marvin's my cousin, and this cabin belongs to him and his wife." She motioned to Isabelle, who had just poked her pretty auburn head out of the kitchen.

Wearing a look of relief, David took a step forward, stumbled, and dropped the leather satchel he'd been carrying.

"Whoa!" Marvin reached out and caught David's arm and led him toward the fireplace. "What happened to you? You're sopping wet and covered with ice and snow."

David explained about his accident.

"The first thing we need to do is get you out of those wet clothes." Marvin pointed to the bedroom near the back of the cabin. "If you'll come with me, you can change into one of my woolen shirts and a pair of trousers."

"B–but I need to speak with Elizabeth."

"First things first." Marvin led the way to the bedroom, and David followed.

Elizabeth flopped into the rocking chair and closed her eyes in defeat. Her grandparents had obviously told David where she was. Apparently she couldn't trust anyone.

David and Marvin returned a short time later, and then Marvin suggested that he and Isabelle go to the kitchen so Elizabeth and David could talk privately.

David pulled a straight-backed chair close to the fire and took a seat. Then he turned to Elizabeth, took her hand in his, and said, "I have some good news."

"Wh–what's that?" she asked, barely able to look at him, fearful that she'd give in to her threatening tears.

"We're not related. Your father is Charles Canning, and my father is Raymond Stinner."

"But my aunt Lovina said in her journal—"

"I know what she said." David gave Elizabeth a heart-melting smile. "I found out that Lovina lives in Philadelphia, and I went there to see her."

"You did?"

He nodded. "Lovina lied. She made the whole thing up because she was in love with Charles Canning, and when he chose your mother instead of her, she was angry and jealous, so she wrote that horrible lie in her journal." David rose from his chair and picked up the satchel he'd dropped on the floor when he'd first come in. He returned to his chair and pulled out a piece of paper. "This is a signed confession from Lovina. She feels horrible about what she wrote and asked me to give you this."

Tears welled in Elizabeth's eyes as she read her aunt's letter of apology, knowing how hard it must have been for her to relive that heartache and admit her mistake. "Oh David, this is a Christmas miracle." Closing her eyes, she silently thanked God for this unexpected turn of events. Instead of being angry with Aunt Lovina, Elizabeth was overwhelmed with appreciation for her aunt's admission to the lie she'd written so long ago.

"You're right—it is a Christmas miracle. It's also an answer to my prayers." David reached into the satchel again and handed Elizabeth a small velveteen pouch.

"What's this?"

"It used to belong to your mother, and your aunt wanted you to have it."

Elizabeth inhaled sharply as she removed a small gold locket from the pouch. "Oh, it's so beautiful."

David stood and gently pulled Elizabeth to her feet. "Elizabeth Canning, will you marry me on Christmas Eve?"

"Oh yes," she said, nearly choking on a sob. "I thank God we're together again, and from now on, there will be no more secrets between us."

Epilogue

On Christmas Eve, snowflakes fell gently outside the window as Elizabeth and David stood in front of the glowing fire inside the small cabin that would soon be their new home. After the blizzard-like weather had abated, they'd left Coopersburg and returned to Allentown to prepare the cabin for their wedding, which was where they'd both wanted to hold the ceremony. David's mother and grandfather, Elizabeth's father and stepmother, and her grandparents and a few close friends, including Helen and her parents, had come here to witness their marriage.

Elizabeth, wearing her mother's ivory-colored wedding gown and gold locket, had never felt more beautiful. *Oh, how I wish Mother could be here to see me get married.*

"And so," Reverend Warner said, pulling Elizabeth's thoughts aside, "what God has joined together, let no man put asunder." He nodded at David. "You may now kiss your bride."

David lowered his head and gave Elizabeth a kiss so sweet she thought she might swoon.

"Happy birthday, Mrs. Stinner. I have a surprise for you," he whispered when the kiss ended and they'd received congratulations from their family and friends.

"What is it?" she asked breathlessly.

His lips curved into a sly smile. "It's a secret. A Christmas secret."

"I thought there would be no more secrets between us."

"This is a good secret." He slipped Elizabeth's shawl over her shoulders and took her hand. "Come with me, and you'll see what it is."

Leaving the warmth of the cabin, David led Elizabeth out the door, where he motioned to the most elegant-looking, mahogany-colored carriage with brass mountings. It was fit for a princess going to a ball.

"I may not be able to give you a beautiful home just yet," David said, "but at least you'll have a handsome carriage to ride in."

Tears welled in her eyes. "I really don't need a beautiful home or a handsome carriage, but I thank you for such a lovely gift." She leaned her head on his shoulder and sighed. "I found all I'll ever need the day I met you, and I'm perfectly happy to live in our little log cabin for as long as necessary." Just minutes after being pronounced husband and wife, Elizabeth didn't think her heart could be any fuller.

David bent down to give her another kiss, this one even sweeter than the last. As they walked hand in hand back inside to their family and friends, a tiny movement caught Elizabeth's eye. She smiled to herself when she spied a ladybug crawling on the wall above the mantel.

Elizabeth was sure that God must be looking down from heaven to bless their marriage. "Maybe someday our own son or daughter will begin their life in this log cabin," she murmured against David's ear. A feeling of contentment enveloped her, and she knew without any doubt that this night was just the beginning of many dreams to come true.

Award-winning, bestselling author, Wanda E. Brunstetter enjoys writing historical as well as Amish-themed novels. Wanda lives in Washington State with her husband, Richard, a retired minister. The Brunstetters have two grown children and six grandchildren.

Christmas
Traps and Trimmings

by Kelly Eileen Hake

For we walk by faith, not by sight.
2 CORINTHIANS 5:7

Chapter 1

October 12, 1811
London, England

Committing fraud, Wilhemina Montrose discovered, consisted of nothing more than the same exaggerated social niceties perpetrated by genteel society daily. One could almost say her entire ladylike life prepared her for this day. Well, her life as a lady, and days of scrupulous scheming. Big plans lurked behind this morning's small talk, after all.

"It's all to be arranged as swiftly as possible." She leaned forward to cultivate an air of confidentiality with her solicitor, carefully placing her left hand on his blotter as though to impress the urgency of her request. In reality, the ambitious and corrupt man before her shared the floor with two other solicitors, obliterating any hope of privacy.

The motion, as intended, drew his eyes to the ludicrously gaudy heirloom engagement ring imprisoning her third finger. His greedy gaze weighed the value of the piece in pounds, then prestige, clearly calculating her rise in worth. As Miss Montrose, heiress to the Montrose fortune, her youth and gender tipped the scales against her, allowing Mr. Gorvin's loyalties to slide toward her cousin. As Miss Montrose, fiancée to that selfsame cousin, bearing the expensive and irrefutable proof of her position, she couldn't be so easily overlooked. Quite simply, Mr. Gorvin couldn't afford it.

He had no way of knowing they'd purloined the ring from the vault earlier that morning, and that it would be returned immediately after this meeting. Just before Mina and Belinda boarded a ship and escaped to the Americas. . .

"Good news, good news," he chortled, all but choking on his glee. "So glad to hear you've given up that nonsense of investing your inheritance and have chosen to leave it in the sensible hands of men."

"It seems I place my faith in the wrong people, as shown by my guardian's continued absence." Mina dropped her hands to her lap and wrung them together while she spoke. This next part was vital to her plans. "Elton didn't have Mr. Carver's direction." She raised her chin in wounded dignity as she continued, "I wish to send a letter informing Mr. Carver that his brief responsibility to me has ended. After his callous shunning I want no possibility the man may someday return to England and claim a connection to me. I'm certain he couldn't have misunderstood your summons after my father's death, so you won't begrudge me the opportunity to write an assessment of what his dereliction has cost him."

"Certainly not," Gorvin blustered, yanking open drawers and rifling through papers and ledgers. He kept up a steady stream of babble as Mina reflected that it would have been very difficult indeed for her guardian to misinterpret a letter that had never been written. She and Belinda—her old nurse, today playing the role of arrogant aunt—held no doubts that Gorvin and Elton conspired to keep Mr. Carver ignorant of her father's passing, thereby keeping her inheritance tied up.

"Here you are." He passed her a scrap of paper bearing the word *Kentucky*. "Letters aside, when you're wed you'll have a family to keep you well occupied."

"Two things can be counted on to keep any lady busy. One is family. The other, of course," Mina widened her eyes guilelessly, "are the shops. After so many months, I'm sadly out of date. I don't want to be a disgrace to the name of my husband." She swallowed hard, visibly distressed. Mr. Gorvin need not know it was the thought of having Elton for a husband that caused the distress, rather than any fashion concerns.

"You'll be a credit to him, I'm sure." A beefy paw reached out as though to pat her hand in consolation. Then, as if thinking better of the impropriety, he reached down to open another drawer. "Besides, shopping is a skill at which every young lady excels. That will be the order of the day?" A book of checks appeared atop the blotter like an offering.

"Her trousseau, of naturally," Aunt Belinda all but snapped at the man. "A pleasure that should be spread over months—selecting fits and fabrics, choosing the perfect accessories, making Mina the bride she was born to be—must now be rushed. Those dressmakers will demand outrageous sums for such a hurry when they should be thanking us for the privilege!" A thump of her cane majestically ended the performance.

"It can't be helped," Mina soothed. "Elton has to travel for business, and the journey will make a fine honeymoon. Such opportunities aren't to be missed. You know he's a head for these things. . . ." She trailed off as Gorvin nodded eagerly.

"Best strike while the iron's hot and all that." His glance appraised the fine fabric and embroidery tracing the ladies' dresses, their lace shawls. Mina bit back a grin as she supposed him to be trying to compromise on a figure that wouldn't insult, but wouldn't be extravagant for their spending spree. "What all will you be purchasing?"

"The usual morning dresses, day dresses, ball gowns, traveling wear, riding habits, boots, dancing slippers, gloves, rib bands, hats to match, of course." Mina paused for breath, smiling as though ecstatic at the idea of perusing shops.

"Shawls, fans, purses, opera glasses—Elton mentioned taking you to the opera," Belinda sniffed. "A gift for your groom. Gifts for your bridesmaids, so we'll need to go to the jewelers. Stockings and such forth." She paused delicately.

"I see." Color leeched from Gorvin's face.

"I beg your pardon." A hesitant overture from the lady at the desk to the left caused them all to turn their heads. "But. . ." Lady Reed, whom Mina had known for over a decade, scowled at her solicitor. A wave of her hand, and the man finally showed enough discretion to leave his desk for a drink of water. She lowered her voice again. "I can't help but hear you're planning to go shopping for your trousseau, my dear?"

"Why, yes." Mina darted an uncertain glance toward Belinda, whose eyebrows had risen toward her hairline as though scandalized by this stranger's presumption.

"You must, absolutely must, take into account what you'll spend at Madam Farnique's. She makes the most stunning creations for the boudoir, delicate like air and bits of lace." The impeccably dressed lady sighed. "Everything she carries is frightfully dear, but worth every shilling. Every married woman knows the men go mad for a woman wearing them. It's the best investment you can make in your marriage."

"Absolutely not. She is to be a proper wife." Belinda's lips thinned into nothing. An observer would consider it compressed rage. Mina knew her beloved companion bit back laughter at their friend's performance.

"I want to be a good wife," Mina murmured. She could feel the heat in her cheeks, and knew she'd turned red. She cast a glance at the book of checks and then a swift glance at Mr. Gorvin, whose ruddy cheeks darkened before he began scribbling a figure.

"Perhaps," Belinda commented dryly, "you'd best double that amount, Mr. Gorvin. I rather doubt any of us wishes to repeat this interview."

❄

December 14, 1811 Appalachian Mountains, Kentucky

Sam Carver cracked through the thin ice shelling his washbasin, plunged his hands inside, and splashed his face with the frigid contents. Scrubbing the grit of too little sleep—and too much desire for more—from his eyes, he reached for a towel to mop up the water running from his beard in haphazard streams.

Winter worked a wonder on the world; slowing time's heartbeat to a creeping crawl. Most sensible animals matched the pace, holing up in their caves and burrows to wait out the slow season. Thing was, man never numbered among sensible creatures, and a trapper couldn't afford to wait.

Not through the season when furs and pelts grew their thickest and most luxurious. Not when he'd invested everything he owned, plus Montrose's generous loan, in John Jacob Astor's Southwest Fur Company. And especially not when failing meant crawling to his smirking older brother back in England and admitting defeat.

Sam snorted at the thought, shoved his feet back into his boots, and stomped them into the dirt floor of his log cabin. A stray rock had been rubbing his heel wrong all morning, and he welcomed the chance to cast his shoes aside during the midday meal. It also gave him the chance to drop off the fresh load of meat and furs he'd gathered that morning. Weather permitting and God willing, this winter would be the making of him.

Grabbing his gun and pack, he opened the door and checked the sky. Just because he'd not been snowed in yet didn't mean he wouldn't be. *Nice weather—storm clouds still a good distance off, not much wind.* He rubbed his hands together in anticipation, keeping warmth in his fingertips.

Even a split-second fumble could cost a man his shot, so it paid to keep flexible. And Sam Carver needed to get paid. No man could be self-made until he repaid his debts. Old Montrose, his father's friend and the uncle Sam would have chosen had he been given the choice of relations, staked his share in Astor's organization when it opened to investors last January.

If the clear skies hold up, I'll have that back room filled twice over before summer. Good thing I threw together that loft during the last cold spell. The added space will keep anything extra out of my way.

The growing beaver and fox population was why he'd chosen this stretch of mountains in Kentucky for the winter. With its range of furs and acceptable availability of supplies—but not convenience, convenience meant too much competition—he was set for a solid season. Next year the area might be too settled, but for here and now, things were the way he liked them. Nice and quiet.

Except. . . Sam cocked his head to the side and his rifle to the ready. The disturbance reaching his ears traveled a ways to meet him, but he shook his head. The sound was still too close. No wheels belonged rolling through his neck of the woods, disturbing any animals taking advantage of the fine day.

There's nothing this way but me for miles, and only fools travel in winter. Sam crept toward the approaching sounds, unwilling to show himself. People inevitably *dropped by* the cabin, but Sam felt no compunction to be sociable with uninvited guests. He kept quiet, cultivating a nonthreatening air around the cabin to lure any wildlife into complacency. The louder people were, the farther he had to travel to hunt.

There. Edging behind a sugar maple, he kept watch as a wagon, drawn by two oxen, lumbered up the road. *Heavy load,* he surmised. Two oxen for a simple wagon was unusual. Then again, so were the two women perched alongside the driver.

"Are you quite certain he's up here?" A faceless crone, hidden beneath a massive bonnet, interrogated the driver.

"Yes, ma'am." A cheery grin revealed the driver's few remaining teeth. "Carver keeps to hisself, but this is the way. None of us ever reckoned he had family to come and visit."

"Well, it is Christmas," came the clipped tones of a young woman who obviously wasn't inclined to satisfy the driver's curiosity. She, too, was hidden behind a hat and scarf.

Sam, despite his trusty double wool-lined leather jacket, froze. These weren't just any women. They were *ladies.* Ladies whose accents made it clear they'd come all the way from Britain, and whose conversation left no doubt their situation was dire.

They've come to visit me. For Christmas. Never mind that Sam couldn't identify the voices. Never mind he'd been thinking mere moments before that only fools traveled in winter. He raced toward the cabin, determined to reach it before they tucked themselves into residence. One thought pounded in time with his steps; *they have to go back!*

Chapter 2

Mina spied the cabin up ahead, only its squared corners and pitched shingle roof delineating it from the trees surrounding it. *As God surely intended trees to remain until sawn into respectable lumber for building.* Everything seemed so much simpler back in England, before the months-long passage had robbed her of far too many meals and an incredible amount of dignity. Mina might have begun the journey full of triumph and hope, but she'd ended the long, perilous path to her guardian in an undesirable mishmash—cold, hungry, dispirited, exhausted, and unsure of her welcome.

She stifled the thought, envisioning it crammed at the very bottom of their heaviest trunk, with the weight of her past and the demands of their future flattening it beyond recognition. Mina prayed for resolve.

She would prevail. She hadn't brought her beloved nurse untold miles over the course of eight harsh weeks only to freeze on an abandoned mountainside. No matter how much patience Mina needed to dredge from her dwindling supply, or honeyed words poured from her sorely chapped lips, she'd use every wile and weapon at her disposal to find Belinda a home before the next storm. Without access to her fortune, goodwill was all she had.

Mina eyed the cabin anew as they pulled to a stop. *I don't have the luxury of taking any perspective but that the cabin is quaintly cozy, Belinda and I belong here, and—most importantly—I must convince Mr. Carver to see things the same way.*

❄

He'd seen their luggage.

Wasn't that always the way of women? To carry the past with them from place to place, passing the accumulation of sorrow, memories, and untold knick-knacks through generations; passing on burdens long extinct in defiance of time?

On the spot, Sam decided *this* was the reason Lot's wife had been turned to salt. She'd been warned to leave all behind, but surely she remembered something she would need, and looked back. It could be no mistake God changed her into the essence of the tears her weakness would eventually have caused. . . .

When I left England, I brought a trunk—one reasonable trunk—to begin a new life. That's all I needed, all I kept, and I'm not taking on any more now, especially not two women lugging half the continent with them. He shouldered his rifle and rounded the corner as the overloaded wagon shuddered to a stop.

"No need to dismount." Sam didn't yell. No need. Even the birds and squirrels were quiet given all the noise the visitors made. Stearns could hear him just fine. The other man sank back onto his haunches on the crowded wagon seat.

"That's kind of you." The young one, perched so precariously on the end of the bench seat that Sam almost marveled she hadn't tumbled off at some point, reached out a gloved hand for his assistance. "But we did engage Mr. Stearns' services for both driving and assisting with our luggage." She tentatively stood, waiting in vain for him to draw near and help her down. Obviously, the lady hadn't realized Sam meant for them to turn back around.

He took a step forward to tell her so, but an ox shifted, and the girl in dark blue lost her uncertain balance after all. Sam barely caught her before the ground did, quickly registering some pertinent facts as he did so.

The mystery girl who'd descended upon his doorstep was a woman, and if startled doe eyes and creamy skin meant what they used to, a very attractive woman. More importantly, she bore no resemblance to himself nor any of his far-flung relations.

The warm surge of relief lasted only so long as it took for him to swoop her right back up onto the plank seat of the wagon. "You misunderstood, miss. I'm afraid you've come to the wrong place and either need to keep going or turn around. Good day."

Sam turned on his heel, scooped up the rifle he'd dropped in favor of the lady, and slowed his steps as she spoke.

"No, Mr. Carver," the sound of his name sliced through his certainty, making him turn. "We've come to the right place, and need to vacate Mr. Stearns' wagon. I see my hopes were unfounded, and my letter did not make an appearance before we—"

"Oh, right!" Stearns scrambled over the side of the wagon, tugging a grubby envelope from his jacket. "Brung your mail."

Sam accepted the thick missive, biting back a groan and raising a brow at the still-seated ladies. His mother wouldn't understand nor forgive his lack of manners, but perhaps his surliness would be enough to drive away this strange duo.

"Would you prefer to read it or converse inside?" The girl's doe eyes held the glint of a riled grizzly as she vigorously rubbed the older woman's gloved hands between her own.

The gesture of tenderness toward her companion trickled toward his conscience like a snowmelt, making Sam aware of the chill in his chest. He thawed, but only enough to not drag out the interview. If he allowed the women inside, he wouldn't be able to oust them. Even if he could ignore the girl, he wouldn't be able to silence his scruples once they'd awakened that much.

"Neither." He stepped forward and thrust the envelope toward her. "Whatever you wrote then or might say now won't change my mind. I don't know you, and I'm not going to wait while you try to talk me into believing you have any right to be here. You don't. Stearns will see you back to town and on your way."

"You may not know me, but you knew my father," she began her explanation, refusing to take the letter. He let it drop onto her lap.

"I know all my relations, miss, and you do not number among them. This is a harsh place for ladies under the best of circumstances. Good day." Clearly these were not the best of circumstances. Whoever she was—and Sam resolutely silenced his own curiosity—she'd barged onto a stranger's land claiming connection. It didn't get much worse.

"She didn't claim to be your relation, you stuffed-up bufflehead." A rasp emerged from the swaths of blankets bundling the old woman. "Miss Montrose said you knew her father."

And for the second time that morning, a name stopped Sam in his tracks. "Montrose?"

❄

Thoughts of patience and honeyed words shattered in the face of this man's callousness. Mina didn't have time to kill her guardian with kindness—not when Belinda would shiver herself into an early grave long before the man showed any measure of consideration. At least he responded to her father's name.

"Yes," she snapped. "Montrose. Upon your sire's death and his own sudden sickness, my father hastily amended his will. You see, Mr. Carver, my father bore the opinion that you would repay his generosity. So he entrusted his most precious possession into your care, in full faith you would do right by his memory." Grim satisfaction trickled through her at the dawning horror her guardian's overgrown beard couldn't conceal.

"You cannot be saying. . ." He gave a hard swallow before attempting to speak again. "I seem to recall something to the effect that my father would take guardianship of Montrose's daughter under such circumstances, but. . ." He gestured curtly, as though blotting out the rest of the equation.

"Yes." She refused to be softened by his obvious shock. Mina had deduced his ignorance long before embarking upon the journey. But ignorance didn't excuse rudeness. "I'm your ward."

So saying, she shuffled to the very edge of the wagon, braced her hand upon the seat, and arched her brow in expectation. When neither man moved to help her down, she almost stomped in frustration. Instead, Mina eyed the ground, gauging the distance and refusing to consider how swiftly the hard-packed earth rushed to meet her when she'd slipped moments ago.

I've crossed an ocean and traveled hundreds of miles via carriage and wagon without male assistance. Now it seems the Lord is asking for a more literal leap of faith. No matter how low the ground, how can I balk after coming this far?

Mina closed her eyes, bent her limbs, and sprang forward. For a second time, strong arms intervened before she hit the ground. But she'd learned from prior experience not to hang limply like a rag doll. Instead, she immediately shoved against the broad chest, wriggling until he dropped her—from a higher distance than she'd realized—onto her feet.

"What did you do that for?" Anger blazed from green eyes, points of light in a face obscured by bushy beard and hat brim.

"Neither you nor Mr. Stearns seemed inclined to help me disembark." She drew in a deep breath. "I'd be obliged if you'd help my companion. Mrs. Banks will need the assistance."

"Not that. I knew why you jumped—foolish thing to do though it was. Why did you fight me?" He reached up and plucked Belinda from the wagon as though she weighed no more than air.

"Because last time you tossed her right back into the wagon," her nurse chided. Even with her boots swinging a hands' span off the ground, Belinda began to lecture. "If you'd spent the last two hours clinging to that seat while splinters burrowed into your palms with every bounce in the road, you wouldn't think jumping such a foolish idea."

"I'll just see to the luggage." Mr. Stearns slumped toward the rear of the wagon, his gait slowed by an odd, almost rolling quality Mina had seen on the docks, as if he were more used to life on ship than on land. His slow progress came to a dead halt all too quickly when Mr. Carver shook his head.

"We'll get these ladies warmed up and rested, but then they'll need to go back." Laughter warmed his voice, but his words chilled Mina afresh. "Women shouldn't winter in the wild."

"There's no place to stay, Mr. Carver, and no stages until spring. No matter the weather, they say they won't risk it."

"I'll hire you to drive them on to the Burnham," he said without sparing her a glance. "The Swan's Wing is a decent enough hotel to hold them through the spring, when they can be sent back to England."

Manners dictated a lady should attempt to be agreeable. Politeness exhorted that one never interrupted. The strongest—and therefore unspoken—rules of society revolved around women tactfully leaving decisions to men. *More links in the chains of convention to break beneath the force of necessity.*

"I am not a parcel to be returned in the post, Mr. Carver." No response to her comment. She found herself irked when the man didn't even acknowledge her objection.

"We cannot reside in a hotel unaccompanied, Mr. Carver." She appealed to the sense of responsibility her father put faith in. "Such arrangements would prove neither safe nor seemly."

"Wilson, the proprietor owes me. I'll send a note, and he'll keep an eye out for you two. Your companion will keep your reputation intact—particularly as far from England as this." He waved away her protests. "Your solicitor should never have sent you, but there should be little damage done upon your return."

"I wasn't sent, and I can't go back." She straightened her spine and locked gazes with him. "I escaped."

Chapter 3

W hat?" Sam gaped after his ward as she looped her companion's arm through hers and they headed into the cabin.

His cabin.

The door swung shut behind them with more force than necessary, but not quite enough to call it slammed. Apparently his new houseguest remained too ladylike to sink that low.

"Escaped." Stearns scratched the back of his head, just underneath his grubby hat. "That's what I heard, leastways. Escaped from *what* is what I'd like to know. For high-born ladies, those two don't seem the sort to quiver in their corsets and flee over nothing. If you don't mind me saying so," he tacked on hastily, correctly interpreting Sam's dark glance.

"You will not speak of their unmentionables to anyone," he ordered. Then he paused. When dealing with Americans, especially former sailors whose tastes might run to the scandalous, he'd found it best to be as clear as possible. "Or any unmentionables whatsoever in their presence." Sam fought a sense of foreboding.

He rubbed his forehead and tried to marshal his thoughts, form a plan of action, but found himself trapped by the notion that henceforth his days would be trussed to the feminine strictures already casting nets. *Ladies arrive, and the conversation of men is reduced to quibbling over the word* corset.

"This will never work," he concluded. "Whatever the trouble, it needn't land them on my doorstep. The ladies need a more fitting place to reside while I work all this out. At the very least, the hotel will give them a more civilized winter than I can provide until spring opens things back up."

"I won't take 'em to the Swan's Wing." Stearns made a revolting hacking noise in the back of his throat and worked his jaw around. "And you don't have a wagon, so that's out."

"Don't be a fool. I said I'd pay you."

"I'm not the fool, here. You say Wilson owes you, but he can't be everywhere at once, and your ward there's a pretty little thing with nothing but a mouthy sack of bones to look after her. Ain't half a miracle she made it across the ocean and all this way without a fellow or worse, a group of 'em, bothering her. Sailors get mighty rough after several trips, and there's not much to keep them in line."

Having said his piece, Stearns hocked a glob of spittle toward the nearest tree, crossed his arms, and squinted as though daring Sam to argue.

"She made it," he pointed out. "And Wilson's hotel is on land with no sailors but you for miles on end, Stearns."

"I still won't do it. My missus took a liking to them, and I won't weather the storm if she finds out I dropped two defenseless ladies off at a hotel. I might've been captain of my own ship, but when winter comes on and I'm land-bound, it's my wife's kingdom." Suddenly, Stearns looked sheepish to have said so much. "Besides, Wilson might up and marry her before you come down off your high perch to check on her again."

"If she marries, she's not my ward." Then Sam groaned as he realized that it would be far too easy for Wilson or another man to force her into something by threatening the older woman. In a matter of minutes he'd noted her Achilles' heel, and he carried no doubt others would, as well. "But if I'm not there, she might be forced into marriage before I could intervene." And that didn't sit well. Any woman deserved protection, and pawning this one off on a hotel owner wouldn't be honoring Sam's debt to her father. "Is there a family or widow I could pay to keep them?"

"To take in one woman? Sure. Two's stretching it, but money could cover that if the house was big enough. But two *ladies?*" Stearns didn't have to shake his head; the disbelief in his tone made it clear that high-born ladies would make more work, help with none of it, and add complaints into the bargain. No sane family would agree to that prospect.

"What am I supposed to do with them, Stearns?"

"You've only got the one choice, Carver." The other man turned toward the wagon and hefted the first trunk into his arms before setting it on the ground. "You've got to keep 'em."

❆

Mina swung open the door, ushered Belinda inside, and shoved it shut with a resounding thud. "If he wants to stand in the frigid air and converse, let him do so. We'll not become blocks of ice." She spent several seconds glowering at the familiar, smooth planks of the back of the door. It eased some of her indignation and allowed her precious time to compose herself so she'd be able to find the good in the situation and highlight it for Belinda.

She closed her eyes, stealing another moment to organize the muddle of impressions assaulting her from that first glimpse of the cabin. Overwhelmingly, she'd noted dimness; partly due to the dismaying fact that even the interior remained armed in bark. Mina let out a breath, drawing air deep in preparation for the conversation to come.

Cedar. The aroma flooded her so powerfully she wondered that she hadn't noticed it before. The scent of smoke, which she'd expected to hit her like a cloud of coal dust, mellowed into the robust spice of the wood. It smelled. . .

warm, inviting. . . . *Such a welcome change from the smoke-filled rooms we've stopped in along the journey here.* . . . With that discovery bolstering her courage, Mina turned to face their new home.

Light flared in the corner where her nurse lit a hanging oil lamp before moving to ignite another atop a nearby table. Mina stoked the flames in the fire, building it up with the help of the wood and kindling piled near the hearth. With the flames leaping and the two lamps burning across the cabin like wide-set eyes, the place didn't seem as dim.

Mina only wished things looked less grim as she studiously ignored the gory pile of who-knew-what creatures slumped atop the table. "It looks like one room, but I think that's a loft overhead."

"We anticipated one room," Belinda reminded, stretching her hands toward the fire and sighing. "Remember that he could have built a dugout. It looked as though the place abuts a hill, so that would've been much simpler for one man to erect."

"Very true." Though living below ground didn't bear thinking about. Mina continued ticking off any and every positive she could think of regarding their new surroundings. "It smells wonderful. I'd thought it made of pine, but the cedar carries through—which will help ward off insects." She winced at the thought that *fewer* insects could be considered one of the highlights of any building.

What more could she say? The place boasted those most excellent necessities; walls, a roof, and a fire, but precious little else. A single bench flanked the table. The opposite corner held a bed of sorts—really more of a pallet. A rough ladder descended off toward the third corner, reaching toward the loft. In its entirety, the room held nothing more. Nor could it measure beyond a dozen feet squared.

"The woodpile outside seemed very healthy, so we'll not freeze. And there's a proper hearth set up for cooking." Her nurse stamped her feet. "The floor's dirt, but hard packed."

"Floors can be covered fairly easily." Mina brightened as she noted darker brown shadows against the walls, and she went to investigate. "There are windows! No glass, but if you move the coverings aside. . ." She did so with great caution, peeping to see Mr. Carver and Mr. Stearns beginning to unload the wagon.

Until relief flooded her, she didn't acknowledge how worried she'd been. *Thank the Lord he didn't turn us out.* She hurried away from the window before they spotted her.

"We can put up waxed paper to let the light in on fine days." If one couldn't alter the dimensions or construction of the place, at least two determined women could work wonders on its inner aspects. "Proper curtains go a long way, and if we strip the walls of bark, it will seem much brighter inside—"

"Also colder." Mr. Carver's voice preceded him through the doorway. "Not to mention that the smell of fresh-cut or exposed red cedar hereabouts is exceptionally powerful. It wouldn't be livable in this place for a solid month if I let you try that."

"Oh!" Mina clapped a hand over her mouth. "I am sorry." She didn't elaborate. Apologizing for planning to redecorate his cabin the first time she set foot inside it was sufficient. Her guardian needn't know she also regretted the infeasibility of those plans. She'd also marked the steel underlying the phrase "if I let you." Obviously, he'd determined to take her in, but he wouldn't allow her to take control.

He and Mr. Stearns carried in the luggage, wedging and stacking it into the space nearest the ladder. Hopefully, it meant his thoughts mirrored their own; the loft should be for exclusive use by the ladies, so they could retreat in peace and sleep in privacy as was decent. At least, it would be decent just as soon as proper stairs could be cobbled together. Ascending a ladder of that sort counted as a minor scandal considering that anyone below would have a view directly up one's skirts!

When they'd brought everything in and Mr. Stearns drove away, Mr. Carver looked at the two of them as though at a loss. Which well he might be, given not only the way they'd descended upon him but also his inconvenient lack of furniture.

Mina had brought the only bench closer to the fire, which bore the added benefit of distance farther from the mess atop the table. Belinda shared it with her, leaving no remaining seats. Because no gentleman would be so far gone as to even think of—

Sinking down onto the bed-like thing facing them, Mr. Carver drew off his hat. The gesture revealed sandy hair a good three shades lighter than his surprisingly red beard. "There's no sense in standing on ceremony just because a lady doesn't approve where a man chooses to sit." He arched a brow, flickering firelight making his shadowed expression imposing. "I built this cabin for trapping, not hosting company or housing unexpected guests. We'll make do with what's at hand. Agreed?"

They nodded. Mina didn't know why Belinda held silent, whether from curiosity or uncertainty. Perhaps she held her peace now so she could win the war later. A contentious woman could never stage an ambush, and she judged that the element of surprise would be needed in any battle fought with this odd guardian.

Chapter 4

A *peculiar girl, this ward of mine.* Sam scrutinized her, struck again by the truth Stearns spoke so readily. *Not a girl. A pretty woman. And one whom I know nothing about.*

"I've been remiss. You already know I'm Samuel Carver. Miss Montrose identified herself and called you Mrs. Banks." A nod confirmed this, enabling him to continue. "Now that we've performed basic introductions, I'd like to hear the particulars of how you came to Kentucky." *And, for pity's sake,* why. He managed to leave the final query unspoken, though it hung heavily in the cedar-scented air between them.

"Your father was to have been my guardian, but he expired suddenly. When my father fell ill, he amended his will and named you to the position. Subsequently. . ." Miss Montrose paused, apparently finding the words difficult to say. "He passed on."

"The man's mind works well enough to understand that much." Mrs. Banks prodded her charge to get on with the tale, prompting Sam to forgive her for dubbing him a *bufflehead* earlier.

"Quite so," Sam said. "What I've not worked out is why he chose me." He didn't bother trying to hide his astonishment. "Why not a relative of your own, or, if it came to that, even my older brother? How is it he chose a guardian on another continent?"

"If you lend one of my relatives an apple, they'll repay you a withered core. As for your brother. . ." Miss Montrose hesitated. "Although Father bore your family in high esteem, I received the impression he considered your brother to be an. . ."

"Arrogant fool who'd tuck you in a country corner and forget your existence?" Sam supplied when she trailed off.

"Extremely busy gentleman whose time was much taken up with the running of his newly inherited estates," she confirmed.

"You grant my brother more leniency than you extend to your own relations, Miss Montrose. Perhaps you don't know him well."

"Or perhaps I know my own relations too well," she riposted. "My father feared I'd be beneath your mighty brother's notice. Though I would say there are worse fates than being ignored."

Sam rested his elbows on his knees and leaned forward. "Unscrupulous relatives prompted what you termed *escape*?"

He retained some faint hope the young miss had lost her temper over some imagined slight and took to the seas in high dudgeon.

If she ran away in a fit of temper, imposing herself upon her unsuspecting guardian, Sam would not shrink from sending her back. Foolish chits, mulish misses, fanciful flights overseas. . .he wanted no part in the sort of poorly scripted melodrama his ward seemed determined to enact before his eyes.

Rather than answer his question, she asked one of her own. "You knew of your father's death?"

"In truth, your father's condolences reached me before the notification from our family's solicitor." The memory jostled loose, sending Sam to his feet. He strode to the opposite wall, retrieved a box from the shelf set into one of the logs, and withdrew a faded, torn letter. "When missives reach me, they're frequently the worse for wear. I could only make out the first third or so. . . ." He unfolded it, suspicions mounting.

Faded script raced across the page as though written by a frantic hand. Blotted in some places, the ink smeared and dribbled by water in others, much of the message ghosted into the parchment. The pertinent portion—at least, what Sam assumed to be the pertinent portion—remained legible along the top.

Dear Samuel,

Although I hope this finds you well, I have to inform you the same cannot be said of your father. His passing shocked all those near him, perhaps myself most of all. We'd not imagined he'd succumb to the fever. Doctors are optimistic in my case, though that will provide little comfort should my letter be the first you receive. As I've always been of more hearty health than James, I hold every confidence of recovery. Nevertheless. . .

Here the lines crawled back into a mist of ink and intention, indecipherable to Sam's eye. At the time, he'd not given it another thought; his father's death preoccupied him. Now, that last word struck him as something along the lines of a warning shot. *Nevertheless. . .*the world might shatter.

Sam passed the note to the women, waiting while they read.

He was not above watching the wary brown eyes of his ward soften at the sight of her father's hand upon the page. She devoured the words as though hungry for explanation, and Sam marked the instant she could go no further. Fresh sorrow darkened her brown gaze to sable. Her lids closed, as though losing part of a letter echoed the loss of its author.

His fists clenched at the sudden depth of her grief and his inability to lessen it. *Why should it matter? I only just met the woman! It shouldn't be my place to comfort her—I'm not equipped for this. She's not mine—she's just visiting.* Somehow, the reminder that he'd be sending her away made him feel worse.

"Nevertheless. . ." The word emerged from low in his chest as Sam offered the only thing he could: a conclusion to the sentence. "The world goes on, and so must we."

"And so she would have," Mrs. Banks burst out, "if her father's solicitor hadn't passed on just after him, leaving that gormless Mr. Gorvin to plant his paws on Mina's money. Or if her nodcock of a cousin hadn't conspired to force her into marriage or an asylum—not that one would've been much different than the other, mind you. Or if you'd been in England to see—"

"That will do." Miss Montrose—Mina, apparently—patted her companion's arm. "Certainly Mr. Carver gets the gist of it."

"Indeed. I surmise that your cousin and greedy sudden-solicitor conspired to withhold your inheritance until they could find a convenient, immoral way to usurp it legally." He caught himself pacing the cabin like a caged creature.

The courtesy title of baron, along with its lands, would have been passed to Montrose's heir. How simple it should be, with his cousin trapped beneath his roof, to seize her fortune. The realization chilled him more thoroughly than any winter frost.

Given enough time, he would have forced Miss Montrose to wed him. Or, should her will prove stronger than his wallet, he'd find an official willing to pronounce her deranged. A locked-away relative is a relative whose finances must be managed by someone competent, after all. By the time he'd reasoned it through, the chill boiled away beneath the heat of Sam's rage. *All because her guardian conveniently resided far away in America and couldn't protect her.*

How terrible for a man to fail at his most important duty, when he hadn't any inkling she'd been entrusted into his care. Sam looked at his ward in a new light, feeling his former ire at her intrusion melt away. "You'll be protected now. Whether you wish to remain in America or travel back to England when the weather permits, I'll arrange for your finances and your personal safety. This Gorvin fellow will be tossed out."

"Thank you."

No prolonged stories of abuse or wailing over the trails of her long journey to America issued forth. A simple thanks for his promised assistance, and his ward fell quiet.

Which left him with one large, unanswered question: "Without access to your inheritance, how did you find me, elude your cousin, and finance your passage to the Americas?"

"Oh." She circled her hand in a dismissive gesture. "We borrowed the heirloom engagement ring and paid a visit to Mr. Gorvin, all aflutter over my upcoming wedding to my cousin." Her finely drawn face scrunched up in distaste. "A waterfall of fribble over the need for a rushed trousseau drowned his suspicions easily enough. He all but leaped at the idea of drawing a check."

Sam scrutinized the pair of women perched before his fire. "Strategists, are you?" Wide, unblinking gazes met his in an attempt to appear guileless. "I'll be sure to remember that."

❄

When she awoke the next morning, Mina had forgotten where she'd slept—another rented room? Worse, one of the infrequent haylofts? Her surroundings, strange and dark, offered little aid and less solace. She might have taken a fright, if it weren't for Belinda's steady snurgling. No matter that her nurse maintained that only men snored and gurgling belonged to infants, Mina believed only Belinda produced this odd combination of sounds.

As an infant she'd found it comforting. Now, as a grown woman wresting the reins of her future from the clutches of her cousin—Mina winced at how dramatic that sounded—she still found her old nurse's snurgling somewhat soothing.

If nothing else, the sound said Mina wasn't alone. Even better, it meant Belinda stayed safe. The older woman need never know it was Cousin Elton's threats against her that prompted Mina's mad scheme to visit the solicitor. If they'd failed, Mina's own actions would trap her into the marriage or brand her as unbalanced. But if she'd not made the attempt, Belinda would have suffered her cousin's next attempt to force Mina's cooperation. . . .

She shook the thoughts away, replacing the memories with a deep breath. Then another. . . *Cedar*. The previous day rushed back in a wave of frustration and relief. *We made it. This is home.*

Sinking back, Mina's recollection melded with what her senses could and couldn't tell her. The stiff bed beneath her was really a slightly raised frame of poles, covered in springy fir branches and blankets—a larger sibling to the one down the ladder. The mysterious Mr. Carver, by turns callous and gallant, had constructed it as soon as their conversation had ended.

Leaving them with instructions to ignore the skin but make a stew of the raccoon on the table. Mina groaned at that remembrance. She'd learned to cook basic meals in preparation of the plan, stew certainly among them. Yet she'd practiced with chicken, beef, venison, and any sort of fowl. Somehow, the prospect of *raccoon* as her first feast seemed an unfair challenge. Particularly considering they'd had to clean and dress it before beginning the actual cooking. . . .

A snurgle-snort interrupted her reluctant reminiscence. Mina held her breath, listening to see if Belinda would awaken. *Not yet.* The snurgles resumed, and she relaxed in near-complete darkness. The brighter light of day barging around the edges of the makeshift blanket they'd tacked over the loft opening to the floor below signaled morning. Otherwise, the floor extended across the cabin, kissing the ceiling in a sharp angle atop the walls. She could stand in the very center—otherwise, the low ceiling rewarded any such ambition with a knock upside the head.

No sounds from below rose above Belinda's sleeping symphony. Easing from the pallet, Mina crept toward the blanket, twitching the corner aside to peer below. The bed empty, fire blazing, no boots in sight. . .it seemed as though Mr. Carver had stepped out. He might be sitting at the table, out of sight, but somehow Mina doubted it. In a cabin so small, surely she'd sense if a man as forceful as her guardian were about.

"What're you about, Missy?" Belinda awoke in a fine mood. In comparatively little time—considering the cramped space and lack of light—they managed to dress. It took some creative contortions and a lot of ducking, but they made it down the ladder without any major mishaps.

Mr. Carver's idea of breakfast left much to be desired, and more to clean up after. A skillet of shriveled bacon, congealing in its own grease, crouched atop the table. The contracted strips looked threatening, as though poised to fling themselves down the throat of any unwary passersby. Alongside it stood a tin pitcher of water, covered with a crisp of ice, and a small plate of dough lumps likely meant to serve as biscuits.

A bowl smeared with the floury remnants of the failed biscuits tilted atop a shelf beside the tin used to bake them. A dirty dish wobbled on top. Mina registered the mess then glanced at Belinda.

A smile scratched deep lines around her friend's lips. "Well, Mina. First we clean, and then we unpack. It should keep us busy for a good long while, by the looks of things."

They knew a brook ran nearby; Mr. Carver had showed them yesterday. With much searching, Belinda unearthed a scrub brush while Mina hunted in vain for something to serve as towels. She ran her hands lightly along the walls, searching for shelves she'd not spotted, when she found a long grove running down to the floor. No logs were cut out for shelving, but. . .

"Here." Mina took Belinda's hand and ran it along the line. "It seems like a door, only there's no latch."

They stared at the wall for a long moment. "I wonder. . ."

Chapter 5

"What have you done?" Sam roared with shock and fury. Less than a day, and they'd destroyed months of painstaking work.

"Isn't it lovely?" Miss Montrose spread her arms wide, pale moonbeams of hair springing from their moorings as though taking part in her enthusiasm. "Would you believe I *found* them? And now Belinda will be more than warm enough through the winter!"

A lesser man than Samuel Carver would bow to the appeal of her exuberance. But a lesser man wouldn't have spent months hunting, trapping, skinning, scraping, packing, preserving, and storing the skins now hanging in every nook and crevice of the cabin. Obviously, Miss Montrose had uncovered the secret door to the old dugout he used as his hideaway store room.

The conniving wench had made a thorough inventory of his goods before pirating them. An orderly row of water-resistant beaver pelts dammed any drafts along the floorline. Directly above, rows of deerskin pranced around the cabin, decoratively topped by the march of fluffier hares. But the true masterwork had to be the fanciful strip of alternating pelts adorning the highest level of the walls.

Here, she'd artistically strung a series of black-and-white-striped skunk skins, plumed tails horizontal, skittering about as though chased by the few precious red fox furs he'd gathered. Whimsical décor didn't raise Sam's spirits, but the destruction of his livelihood sent his better nature plummeting.

Because Miss Montrose showed impressive creativity in displaying the furs without aid of nails. Sam assumed she'd searched for some but had found none on hand. Ruinously expensive, necessitating handwork by a blacksmith, nails had to be special ordered in these parts. So instead she'd diabolically destroyed half the value of the pelts in a plethora of methods.

Ropes stretched across the cabin, bearing larger skins she'd *cut holes in* so they'd string up along the wall. By the looks of it, the smaller pieces remained aloft by means of wedging between the logs, snagging bits of fur along rough patches of bark, and—Sam felt the muscles in his jaws jumping—thick daubing of what looked like mud securing them in place.

"*Found* them," he thundered. "As though all these animals left themselves in neat piles upon my doorstep? This isn't a fairy tale, Miss Montrose, and these pelts don't belong to you."

Her arms lowered to her sides, her smile fading from her face. "They lay underground, behind a concealed doorway. No one made use of them; it seemed as though there'd been no fresh air in the musty place in years. I assumed they'd been abandoned, that the previous owner passed on and you didn't know the hidden treasure of the house when you bought it."

"The owner of the dugout sold me the land with a hole in the hillside, but I built this cabin. Every tree felled, every joist carved, every notch matched and peg hammered were done by my hand. Including," he gritted out, "the spring-touch hidden door to *my* storeroom."

"Oh, dear." Mrs. Banks didn't sound overly concerned. "We debated waiting to make sure, but in the end this idea won out."

"This idea?" Sam waved an arm to encompass the mockery surrounding him. "How, pray tell, did you justify 'this idea'?"

"We wanted," his ward informed him in a very small and stiff voice, "to clean up a bit. You'll notice we put a good bit of our luggage in that back room, and it frees up the cabin a good deal. But mostly we wanted to surprise you as a way to thank you. You were very kind." A pointed pause. "Once you gave us the opportunity to explain our situation, of course."

"Until then, you acted like a *bufflehead*." Mrs. Banks gave voice to the unspoken portion of the statement then fixed him with a glower. "I do hope, Mr. Carver, that despite your current mood, these bouts of buffleheadedness won't prove frequent?"

"Neither of you understands the gravity of your actions. You descend upon my home, commandeer my property, and show the unmitigated gall to insult me? Chide me for *my* conduct?"

Sam stepped toward the nearest wall, reaching for the nearest mutilated deer hide. His fingers curled around the edge, giving a small shake to illustrate his point. The thing flapped on what used to be a wash line, threaded across in a parody of stitches. "In one unthinking stroke, you've sullied months of work." His hand spasmed before releasing its hold. "*Months.*"

"We didn't realize." Miss Montrose, at least, seemed remorseful. "But surely it can be made right, Mr. Carver."

"No, Miss Montrose," he ground out. "Your little decorating whim will cost me. Holes in hides cannot be unmade. I'll never be able to sell these massacred pelts. I'd be a laughingstock if I tried, and I can't advance in the company with nothing to show and no profit made for the better part of a year."

"Oh, but that can be fixed!" She lifted her chin. "As soon as I receive my inheritance, I'll gladly pay you the highest price for your fine work, Mr. Carver.

At worst, my error presents a brief delay to your plans, but surely that's negligible."

"A check can't cover the damage you've done!" Sam drew a breath. "I gave my word to my partners, and you've made a liar of me. The brief delay you speak of means months. In business, time is the one asset that can never be recouped. It's never negligible when a man bears responsibilities to repay."

"Responsibilities?" Her very stillness spoke of a woman riled, her poise a mask to hide the fury she held in check. "You speak of repaying responsibilities to men who've invested with you, Mr. Carver. And who might have been foremost on that list?"

Your father. Her meaning slammed into him with the force of a sledgehammer. With Old Montrose gone, Sam's responsibility transferred to the daughter his friend had left in his care.

The long fingers of loss clutched at his chest, gnarled with knots of guilty sorrow and tipped with angry claws. Sam fought the tightening fist of emotion, focusing on the anger and turning it against the woman who'd brought it all to the fore.

"Don't dismiss your thievery by claiming you're owed anything from my dealings with your father," Sam snapped. "I took you into my house, but it's not yours to do with as you please. The back room was not yours to explore or pillage. My work, my furs, were never yours to use or destroy. No excuses."

"You heard me offer to pay for those goods. You will apologize, Mr. Carver." She spluttered, "Thievery! I never!"

"You did. This afternoon." He sprung the hidden door to gesture at the ravaged storage dugout. "Once full, this now lies empty—" Sam swallowed the word when he caught sight of the stack of trunks, crates, and satchels crowded into his dugout.

His jaw clenched. "You even steal *space*?"

"Bufflehead," came Mrs. Banks' ill-timed pronouncement. "Space isn't something one can take nor steal. It simply is."

"Oh? We'll see if you still feel that way tonight." And Sam stopped listening as Miss Montrose kept a steady stream of protestations and demands for his own apologies.

Fueled by rage, he hauled out now-empty luggage from the soon-to-be empty back room. Uncounted trips up the loft ladder later, the eaves themselves burst with trunks, bandboxes, and crates stacked within each other. By the time Sam finished, the only thing uncovered was the ladies' pallet, with luggage stacked along the cabin walls.

By then Miss Montrose had either lost her voice or showed prudent silence—Sam didn't know which. She edged around the fire, giving him a view of the pièce de résistance of their efforts; his bench.

At least Sam assumed the garish thing squatting alongside his table used to be his bench. Now swathed in a heap of what looked to be every kind of fur, the thing boasted a swaying skirt of raccoon tails. He sank onto it, ignoring the women, and ignoring the traitorous thought that the bench had never felt half so comfortable before.

Some things a man can't approve.

❄

Some things a woman couldn't ignore. That night Mina stared at the ceiling, desperately hoping for sleep. But time stretched on, measured by Belinda's peculiar breathing, until Mina felt forced to face the unvarnished, unsavory truth.

She needed the necessary. Unfortunately, no conceivable contortion produced the chamber pot from beneath the pallet.

When her guardian had hauled their luggage out of the old dugout and banished as many pieces as he possibly could to wedge within the already-small loft, Mina had kept quiet. Stewing over his unreasonable rage and ludicrous accusations that she'd stolen—stolen!—both furs and space did no good. But arguments and recriminations would make things worse. Silence did no harm.

Until now. After prolonged discomfort, Mina wriggled out of the bedclothes and slipped into one of Belinda's dresses. Her own wouldn't fit without proper undergarments to cinch her in, but her nurse's more generously cut items wouldn't require any assistance. That done, Mina swiftly laced her boots and crept down the ladder.

Stealth never numbered amongst her strong suits, but she fancied she'd mastered some level of proficiency since her father's death. Mina's cousin kept a gimlet eye on her fortune, and thus her every move. Anything she accomplished, she managed by balancing secrecy, smiles, and soundless steps. The practice should serve her well this night, since Mina was still bent on proving to Mr. Carver that space couldn't be stolen; and that meant she'd never admit his moving the luggage into the loft presented a problem. A rearrangement would serve to correct the issue in the morning.

Moving slowly, remaining silent, and disturbing as little as possible reigned as Mina's chief goals. Mina refused to even consider the ensuing conversation should she awaken her already-irked guardian while sneaking out in the dead of night.

Some things, she fervently believed, *ought never be explained. Of course, this situation shouldn't even* exist. Casting blame—no matter how rightfully aimed—

brought no comfort or solution beyond her decided course. Sidling past Mr. Carver's sleeping area toward the door, Mina kept her eyes averted.

Her ears, however, readily informed her that her guardian slept soundly and well upon the warm cushion of furs she'd laid atop his bed earlier that day. Snug and silent now, those furs were the one thing he'd not protested earlier. Mina allowed a smug smile, knowing her additions made him more comfortable. *I wonder whether he didn't notice them at first, and then was too tired after hauling all the baggage? For that matter, I wonder whether all men will prove as stubborn, or if his disagreeable tendencies are his alone.*

She couldn't really speculate and wouldn't waste the time to do so. Her cloak provided welcome warmth, a tangible reassurance. Sliding back the bolt proved challenging; it scraped loudly enough to make Mina fear discovery. When no one roused, she eased open the door and darted through, shutting it again quickly.

Cold air knifed through her clothing, stabbing with icy blades where her flesh was exposed to the elements. She halted, senses shivering with something more than the chill of the night. An awareness of something. . .strange.

No sounds layered the darkness as she might have expected. It was eerily windless, and branches didn't sway. No hoots called from their recesses above. As hard as she focused—and Mina focused with absolute determination that no creature should catch her unawares in the dead of night—she made out no skittering nearby. Not so much as a rustle among the trees.

By the time Mina began heading back from the outhouse—thank heaven there was one!—needles of cold pricked about her nose and ears, alternating stings with numbness. Soon she'd be inside, warmed by the fire and protected from any creatures lurking in the darkness.

Though it wasn't, she puzzled, as dark as one would expect. The moon held back its guidance; the stars' glow, shielded by fog, looked as muted as back in London, where a dense miasma of coal dust and fog obscured them. Yet Mina found no difficulty picking her way through the unfamiliar territory. The realization made her clutch her cloak more tightly around herself and seek the dawn on the horizon.

No warm glows in umber or russet. Golden rays didn't peak aloft to light her way. She fought the fanciful notion that the earth somehow swallowed the moon, and its pearly polish worked forth from below. How else to explain this luminous sheen blanketed across the earth? The ghostly glow, coupled with the night's still silence, struck her as alarmingly unnatural.

Mina picked up her pace, eager for the security of the loft and Belinda's snurgles. All about, the glow grew brighter until everything even up to the sky seemed illuminated. Then a great, roaring rumble swept toward her from all sides, freezing her in her place as the earth convulsed.

Chapter 6

The very ground heaved and rocked, shaking so violently Mina fell flat. The noise and motion carried on, emptying her stomach and filling her heart with dread. She might have stayed clutching the ground were it not for one driving thought.

Belinda's in the loft. Oh Lord. The mountain will surely rend in two, collapsing around us, and Belinda is trapped in the least-protected place of all. Please, please, please... Her desperate prayer devolved to the one word as she struggled to her feet, only to be pitched forward again.

Mina crawled, hampered by her nurse's large skirts, until able to stand and stagger forward. She finally made it to the doorway of the cabin. Still unbarred, the door flapped open and shut with great fury, snapping at her hands each time she grabbed for the handle. Finally, she caught it, shoved against the wood.

Powered by the groundswells, the door shoved back with far more force, knocking her to her knees then dragging her forward by dint of her determined clutch to the handle. Once within, Mina let it go, only to have the thing batter her side until strong arms closed around her and jerked her out of the way.

She spied the fallen ladder and reached for it, snagged by her guardian's arms still held fast about her waist. "Let go!"

"Wait, Mina!" Sam tried to argue with her, but she was beyond reason. "There's nothing you can do now."

Mina strained for the ladder as luggage slid around the cabin to block her path and stub her fingers. At the last, the largest trunk came crashing from above mere inches from her outstretched hand. Had Mr. Carver not given her midriff a particularly hard yank, she would have been struck by it.

Winded, she faltered. When her breath came without gasping, Mina realized the severe quaking had lessened to occasional tremors. Up she sprang, snatching the ladder from Sam's hands.

"Belinda!" she shrieked. "Are you all right?" She would have begun up the steps had he not intervened—and Belinda's reddened face popped over the side.

"Don't you go up," Carver ordered. "Mrs. Banks, best you come down at once." He nudged Mina aside, kindly keeping his eyes shut and holding the ladder steady as Belinda climbed down.

Mina enveloped her nurse in her cloak and a tight hug the instant after she touched ground. She found no words to express her worry, her relief, or even her gratitude to Mr. Carver. So after a long moment, she blindly reached out, found his arm, and tugged him close to say, "Thank God. I'm so glad you're all right."

❄

Anyone could see how swiftly the quake laid bare any hidden flaws. Sam surveyed the chaos of his cabin, gaze drawn to Mina as she tended Mrs. Banks. *And exposed secret strength.*

But now wasn't the time to think about that. With the shaking stopped, Sam needed to assess the situation and start making decisions. Middle of the night or not, none of them would manage to sleep again. Too much excitement lingered; too many questions cluttered their thoughts for any hope of rest.

Was it over? What would they find when they left the relative safety of the cabin come morning? Sam's gaze snagged on the loft. Now the riot of doubts and questions swirled more slowly, stabbed into the background by sharp fragments of memory.

The icy whisper a nighttime draft. . .but the vein of chill air, muffled by the plush furs piled atop his pallet, didn't prod him fully awake. The cozy cocoon fashioned by his ward slowed Sam's senses as he blearily sought the source of his discomfort. His makeshift window coverings—not curtains; Sam Carver didn't rig up anything half so fancy as curtains—lay still, no sign of an errant breeze disturbing a loosened corner.

A whitish glow seeping around the edges of the window. . .strangely bright and curiously contrasting against the golden hues thrown by the fire. By the time Sam wrestled his drowsy thoughts and pinned down the source of his unease, that tonight's new moon shed no light at all, it was too late.

The warning roared through his nerves with the first rumbling.

Throwing off the blankets, leaping out of bed, muscles tensed against an invisible threat.

Then, the pandemonium had thwarted Sam's attempt to decipher the danger. Now, those jumbled impressions mocked him as he pieced events together.

The deafening sound rushed toward him as though from all sides, a mass of groaning sod, scraping rocks, and the rumble of rending earth. But the whole thing had rippled from the east, else Sam knew they would have heard the familiar sounds of avalanches from the mountains before the quaking had begun.

A gasping cry from above. . .the women in the loft!

Now, looking back, toward where his ward tucked a shawl around her nurse's shoulders, Sam scarcely believed it had taken that long to remember the women in the loft. Even if it had been a matter of seconds since the sound had started, a larger principle was at stake.

Weren't the women always a man's first thought when danger struck? No matter how sudden their arrival, no matter that the man just woke from a sound sleep, and no matter how used that man might have become to fending for himself? Sam lowered himself onto a nearby trunk and rubbed the back of his neck.

A sudden shriek sent him shooting to his feet, hand on his gun. Mrs. Banks abandoned decorum and her earlier complaints of advanced age to scramble atop the bench. But no one knocked at the door. Nothing large remained in the loft to tumble down. No errant sparks shot from the fireplace to light the ladies' gowns. Mrs. Banks, standing upon the bench—with its new raccoon-tail skirt swaying from her efforts—looked desperately out of place.

"She saw a mouse." Mina pointed toward a new chink beside the fireplace where the creature must have disappeared.

Or have I got it wrong? Sam shook his head and hunkered back down. It could be that his abandonment of polite society and years spent isolated in the wild left him at a disadvantage here. *Maybe polite men think of the women first because usually their caterwauling raises the first alarm?* After all, how often was the trouble itself louder than the upset lady? The vindicating answer came winging back immediately—*not often.*

"'Twas a rat." Mrs. Banks spanned her hands ten inches wide before clambering down. "And make no mistake. The thing gave me a start, though normally I'm not given to missish fits."

"As well I know," Mina soothed. "We don't fault your unsettled nerves tonight, and I can only envy your keen eyes."

"Indeed. When I woke to that apocalyptic clamor then realized you were missing, Mina. . .I feared. . ." Miss Banks trailed off as though unable to find words to describe her horror.

They all fell into silence. The idea that the women were reliving the same moments playing in his head, each from a different view, flitted through Sam's mind before the memories submersed him.

"Mina!" The older woman's unearthly shriek blotted out the cacophony, the single word a freezing terror and a call to action. Sam sprung toward the loft ladder, only to be thrown to the floor as the ground buckled beneath him and then heaved upward.

He had to get them to safety. . . . Sam swallowed his fear, his pride, and focused. The ladder lay on the ground, coated in dust and continuously pelted with detritus from above. They'd never make it down the ladder, even if he could get it up. . . .

He couldn't distinguish whether the furious beating of his blood roared in his ears or if the incredible rumble all around continued as Sam fought his way to his feet only to be pitched against the wall. The older woman continued screaming for his ward. Mina...

"Is she hurt?" He bellowed back to her screeching, no longer standing but crawling toward the ladder. At least he knew his ward didn't lay crumpled on the ground, flung from the loft.

Not yet.

Sickening images of the luggage he'd hefted and shoved in every nook and cranny of those eaves that very afternoon struck him with a fury of guilt and dread. Those trunks, empty of anything to hold them in place, now flew about the cabin, tumbling from above to strike the walls and crash against the floor. Had one—or more—of those pieces of his pride crushed Mina?

Bile surged into his throat at the thought, choking him.

"I don't know!" Mrs. Banks' scream tore through him. "She's not here! Where is she? Mina!" The sound of scrabbling accompanied her calls, and Sam suddenly knew the old woman was trying to reach the edge of the loft. If she made it there, he knew she'd be thrown down in an instant.

"She hasn't fallen!" He yelled, suddenly frantic to know where his ward was. "Stay where you are!" Only then did he notice the front door wildly flapping open and shut, impossible had it been barred.

He headed toward it, dodging winged books from above and smoldering logs from the fireplace. Dust and the rolling put them out before the things set the cabin ablaze, but the smoking missiles held a burning heat, making them even more dangerous should someone step on one.

A muffled shriek of frustration and pain caught his attention as he made out Mina, clinging to the door handle as it dragged her back and forth. She let go, dropping to her hands and knees as the door continued to batter her. Sam pounced forward, grabbing the woman and jerking her out of the door's swing. The warmth of her, alive and muttering breathlessly, gave him the first dose of relief since he'd heard Mrs. Banks's cries.

Until the daft woman started struggling, reaching for the fallen ladder and ordering him to let her go. Obviously, she'd lost any pretense of good sense in her desperation to reach her nurse. Sam's orders that she wait fell on deaf ears. His arguments that she could do nothing were to no avail.

Until he spotted the massive trunk as it came crashing down, intent on Mina's outstretched fingers. Sam wasted no more time on arguments. He simply tightened his grip around her and yanked her back. Blessedly, her fingers remained intact. Even better, she sat, winded, as the groundswells lessened. ....

His ward might be a strange creature who packed up and traveled across a continent without male supervision, thwarted scheming relatives, and set him on his ear by arriving without warning. She might be uppity with terrible taste in wall hangings and no appreciation for how to treat fine furs.

But Mina surprised him with her courage, her loyalty, and her perseverance. More than anything, she'd reached out and grabbed ahold of a part of him that he'd thought long dead when she included him in her exhausted embrace with her beloved nurse. Her words of gratitude were the most simple, heartfelt prayer Sam had ever heard. "I'm so glad you're all right. . . ."

There'd been no warning before the earth lumbered up and began to heave, trying to buck free of the heavy load of humanity. *But the real surprise,* Sam decided as Mina began bustling about their home, *was how shaking up a man's thoughts left room to appreciate what he might have taken for granted.*

Chapter 7

Everything was out of place. Every blessed item she and Belinda had so carefully unpacked earlier that day—or had it been yesterday?—had chosen a new home to settle into. Without her permission.

Mina gradually took in the extent of the damage as she hunted down her books. Rescuing each of her darlings gave her a purpose. Smoothing bent pages, wiping dust from leather covers, closing broken spines allowed her to restore some sense of order and account for the smallest, and most precious, contingent of her belongings. By the time she'd set them in neat piles atop the table, Mina had allowed herself to look wider and see more.

Jars of preserves crouched beneath the table, huddled in gooey broken heaps alongside misplaced fire logs, which sank into the protection of calico sacks of flour lining the far wall. The still-sewn sacks, at least. Those bags of flour, cornmeal, coffee, and sugar already in use had burst open in the frenzy of movement, strewing their precious contents across the far reaches of the cabin. Tumbling trunks had ground loose coffee beans into the hard-packed dirt floor, where their flavor could do no good.

Cloaks, no longer hung on pegs, blanketed unknown odds and ends. The table lamp lay smashed on the floor. Gridirons clattered atop one another as though exhausted from battle. The door hung drunkenly from battered hinges, lopsided even while closed and bolted within its frame. Nothing remained as it had been.

Except the furs she'd hung. Those, oddly enough, clung to the walls as though afraid to climb down or so proud at having weathered the storm they'd never abandon their posts. Mina's peculiar spurt of pride spluttered out as Sam started stacking trunks and crates in corners. She rather thought he appreciated the tenacity with which the embellishments held to the cabin walls about as much as he'd welcomed Belinda's frenzied reaction to the mouse. Namely, not much.

He'd looked so thunderstruck by the older woman's revulsion, Mina wondered whether he'd noticed its cause. Not the mouse itself, but that the chimney had shifted enough to allow the creature inside. *Should I mention it? Will he take it as an insult to his construction of the cabin he built?*

A slight snurgle interrupted her thoughts. Mina cast a glance toward the raccoon-skirted bench, where Belinda's chin met her chest in fitful slumber. Her head tilted slightly to the left, leaving her mouth askew to emit the undignified noise.

"Let's put her to bed." Sam's solid warmth reached her side at the same time as his voice. An unfamiliar smile softened his jaw as he looked at her nurse and then gestured to his own pallet. "No one goes into the loft until I'm certain it's safe."

"She'd be mortified by the idea of sleeping in a man's bed, but I doubt she'll notice." Mina grinned her agreement.

A soft shake to her shoulder brought the older woman around enough to loop her arm around Mina's neck and shuffle the few steps to the bed. A satisfied sigh dissolved into the deeper sounds of sleep as Belinda burrowed into the soft furs.

"Does she always make that sound when she sleeps?" Sam's whisper made Mina clap both hands over her mouth to stifle whoops of laughter. His shoulders shook with his own mirth.

"Oh," she hissed once she got her breath back, "as though you've not heard her sleeping before. For shame, Mr. Carver!"

"I never did," he swore. "Sleep finds me the moment my head hits the pillow, Miss Montrose, and it takes more than that to awaken me. Though the quake counts as a first." They both sobered at the reminder of what had awakened him that night.

"A first for all of us then." With no immediate danger, Belinda not needing reassurance, and the distraction of Sam's laughter now gone, exhaustion swathed Mina like a too-large cloak.

"Why don't you tuck in for a little while?" He nodded toward Belinda. "Sunrise is a couple hours off. No sense in the two of us knocking into each other in this mess until then."

Oddly enough, the idea of bumbling around the cabin with him, putting things to rights and working together, held a certain appeal. Her guardian, Mina couldn't help but notice, now that things were winding down, cut a fine figure in boots, breeches, and his shirtsleeves. Those strong arms had pulled her out of the doorway and drawn her away from danger several times that night. When he wasn't growling at her about furs, Sam Carver's fiercely protective streak made her feel. . .safe. Cared for.

"Oh, I couldn't possibly sleep now, not when—" *we're getting along so well!* A sudden yawn overtook her protest and had him steering her toward the corner, where the warm mound of furs concealed her nurse. From the sound of it, the pallet made for cozy sleeping arrangements. And she was dreadfully tired.

With Sam watching over them, Mina could actually rest for the first time since her papa had passed on. She drifted toward the bed without further argument, lest her own yawns make a liar of her.

❄

Sam no longer knew what to make of the seemingly serene woman sleeping in his bed. The snoring lady alongside her, he understood perfectly, but Mina Montrose posed more of a mystery than the day she first appeared. When she'd arrived, admittedly before he'd even spoken to her, he'd pegged her for an imposter. Then she'd started talking, and his perception deteriorated further until he accepted Miss Montrose as his—one could only pray temporary—ward. One with grand plans. And the luggage to match.

Baggage. Sam snorted at the sheer volume of paraphernalia Mina lugged along—and the trouble it caused. *Come to think of it, didn't Grandmother used to call impertinent women* baggage?

A smile broke out at the memory. *She did, and she would say it of Mina. Any woman bold enough to con a solicitor out of some of her inheritance certainly qualifies as impertinent.* His smile faded. *And desperate.*

But most of all, brave. Brave enough to refuse her cousin's insistence that she marry him. Brave enough to escape his clutches and seek her own way before it was too late. And brave enough to make a home in the wilderness with a stranger turned guardian. *Perhaps desperation gave her that bravery.*

But it didn't give her the courage to make it through tonight, or the endurance to keep a smile on her face until her nurse slept soundly. Loyalty and love give her strength.

Tying off the final fire iron, Sam looked at his makeshift grate with grudging approval. Planting fire irons into the dirt floor like metal flowers and then binding them tight to the pot pegs above the mantel didn't make for a pretty sight, but that wasn't the point. They just needed to keep long, flaming logs from flying about the cabin during future quakes, until either they could be certain there'd be no more groundswells or Sam found a more permanent solution. He hoped for the former.

Sam looked around at the cabin, strewn with luggage, sacks, jars, pots and pans, dishes. . .more than the place should hold. And it made him wonder all over again. *For a woman so determined to escape England, why did she bring all of her past with her?*

The contradiction of it was enough to make his head throb and his eyes ache. Mere days before, everything on this mountainside marched in order. Now, with every corner thrown into chaos, precious little made sense, and the cause couldn't even be pinpointed when so much had shifted. Between the women's intrusion into his life and the quake, Sam didn't know which disturbed him more.

The thin streams of daylight sliding around his crooked window coverings offered little illumination on the subject but proclaimed they'd made it through the night without any other major upsets. Sam stretched, rolling the kinks from his neck as he walked to the window and lifted a corner of the cover.

A glance outside confirmed what his ears already told him. No squirrels rushed about; no birds flew overhead. Even the wind itself seemed to have deserted the mountainside, leaving only the sun's rays brave enough to venture toward the cabin's perch.

Every sound in nature shared a wealth of meaning behind its music, and the silence outside screamed a warning.

It's not over. The conviction hit Sam like a punch to the gut. Stricken, he looked at the sleeping women and considered his options. *If the next quake is stronger, it might bring the cabin down.* But outdoors presented still more peril with the trees and rocks from the mountainside that could come plummeting down.

Even if Sam would consider leaving the women to check the paths, tall trees toppled more easily than squared, notched cabins. Precious few clearings dotted the mountains bristling with forests of oak, chestnut, cedar, and white pine. No. He couldn't risk leading the women through a maze of branches and rocks.

Decision made, Sam sprang into action. First, he pulled down the loft ladder and laid it flat on the ground, where it couldn't fall and strike the women. With the fireplace already secured and the loft emptied from the first upheaval that left the smaller items littering the cabin. Basically, everything.

The plan formed as Sam started working. The trunks and crates needed to be weighed down; the smaller items easily broken or thrown about needed to be contained. *Easy enough.*

Into one satchel he tucked the few remaining unbroken jars of preserves. He figured he could be forgiven for saving his favorite food first. Dry goods prone to burst seams or spilling became prime targets for plunking into crates. Besides, staples like flour, cornmeal, sugar, and—most important—coffee held value and filled immediate needs. Like his stomach, which grumbled that he'd been awake far too long with no breakfast.

There's far more than I laid up for winter. Guess some of that luggage held foodstuffs. At least I won't be needing to go down to the mercantile. He hefted the pots, a cast-iron skillet, newly dented biscuit tins, and a Dutch oven into a trunk.

Wonder what shape the mercantile's in.

He'd have to find out later. While he worked, Sam came across an assortment of things the women must have brought. Crocks of butter, vinegar, baking powder, honey, and even a bottle of white wine with a note tied onto it: *That you may toast your success when you arrive in the Americas. Do write and tell me how you get on. Your co-conspirator, Lady Reed.* A crate full of straw and oiled eggs held broken, oozing casualties. Sam closed the lid.

He carried that one outside, before anything could seep through and begin to rot. A series of soft thuds greeted his return before Sam's eyes adjusted to the dimmer interior of the cabin. Mina stood at the table, packing her books into a large chest she'd obviously dragged away from the wall.

"Belinda's still sleeping," she whispered when he drew near. "I heard you moving about, and I see what you're doing. It's a waste of my breath to argue against superstition, because the sailors blamed everything on having women on board, too. But I'd never imagined an educated man would think like that— it wasn't my fault. Sending me away won't stop the quakes."

"Sending you. . ." Understanding robbed him of words. Sam shook his head, and then he realized she couldn't see him shaking his head. He clamped his hands on his ward's shoulders and turned her to face him, fully prepared to blister her ears over her foolish, insulting assumptions. Tears pooled in her eyes before following shimmering paths down her cheeks. *She's crying. Mina didn't even let her tears fall when she read the letter from her father. But now she's crying.* Sam's anger fled, only to return a hundredfold with no target but himself for being such a. . .bufflehead.

"No one's blaming you." His hands shifted from her shoulders to her arms, rubbing warmth into them. "I'm not sending you away. I don't want you to go." *Not anymore.* A sudden thought halted him. Sam peered at her. "Unless you want to?"

"No." The sniffled syllable sounded sweet to him. Until her brows drew together and she scowled up at him. "I've been trying to make a home here. *You're* the one determined to undo it!"

Chapter 8

Mina pursed her lips, and she brandished a book. The man dared to look surprised! "Don't deny it, Mr. Carver. It was understandable that you weren't pleased with my arrival. An undesirable reaction, but an understandable one. But your unreasonable rage over the furs, the petulant display regarding the storage area and moving the luggage, and now. . .this?"

"This isn't what you think—"

"Look around you!" she hissed and gestured widely, using *A Compendium of Cures* to extend her reach. "Repacking my belongings? I'm neither blind nor foolish, although I am stymied as to why a forceful man such as yourself felt the need to wait until I lay asleep before evicting me."

Instead of righteous ire swelling her accusation to a grand end, the creeping sense of betrayal broke Mina's voice on that last statement. *I lied, Lord. Forgive me for being unwilling to admit as much to Sam. I told him I'm not blind or foolish, but I'm both. How could I have slept, feeling cared for and protected, when he wanted me gone?* Tears threatened, but she blinked them back, hating that he'd already seen her cry that day. *I've tried so hard to keep my faith and push forward. Where do I go now, God? Am I never to have a home? To belong?*

"You are foolish and obviously not blind, but you might just as well be." His exasperation cut through her self-sorrow in an instant. "I never understood that verse in second Corinthians about how we're to walk by faith, not by sight, until now. Have you no faith in me, Mina?" Sam still kept hold of her other arm, his gaze searching hers as though her answer mattered to him.

"I should." She blinked. "You saved me earlier, took care of Belinda. . . ." Mina closed her eyes. "But you don't want us, and I'm upset that I let myself forget it this morning."

"You're right." His agreement felt the way she imagined one of those trunks crushing her might have—all weight and no mercy.

"I see." She took a deep breath and placed the book in the chest, reaching for another before he gave an exasperated sound.

"You're right. . .you should have some faith in me." He grabbed two entire stacks and dumped them, chock-a-block, into the chest before shutting it. That he managed to shut it on her haphazardly crammed darlings spoke volumes as to how much he wanted her to hear what he had to say. "You're also right that I didn't want you when you and Mrs. Banks arrived."

This time Mina held her tongue and waited for him to finish.

"You're even right in calling my reaction to the trunks in the back room *petulant*. But I'm not sending you away. Strange though it sounds, you belong here. And I'm not undoing your efforts to make the place homey." He pointed toward the fireplace, where he'd rigged some sort of fence across the hearth. "I'm weighing down the trunks and containing the smaller items so they won't fly about again. Your things are worse than worthless if any of them hurt you or Mrs. Banks."

Mina blinked back fresh tears and gave him a tremulous smile. "In that case, I forgive you for shoving my books."

"And since you were trying to make our cabin a home, I forgive you for hanging my furs." He cast a wary glance at the walls. Mina knew how much that cost him.

Almost as if the earth itself knew how unnatural Sam's concession was, the quakes chose that moment to start anew. The first groundswell sent her reeling toward the chest of books, but Sam caught her, holding her tight and turning her away from its sharp corners. "I've got you, Mina. Don't worry."

And with his arms around her to hold her steady, she didn't.

Four mornings after the massive quake and its smaller sibling, Sam still found changes in the landscape. Other, lesser disturbances shook them at irregular intervals, but as these proved short-lived and lesser in intensity, Sam felt the deepest danger passed. If birds sang, he could venture forth.

Marks of the upset scored the terrain at every turn. Mighty trees stirred loose from the ground lay on their sides, tangled roots drooping in defeat. Collapsed branches blocked passes, and, worse, lay caught in the canopy of their peers waiting to fall the fatal distance. Boulders stacked atop one another for centuries tumbled down destructive paths to lay like so many giant scattered marbles. Streams changed course or dried up, their sources now blocked or altered by shifting mud and rock.

But worst were the blights Sam never thought to imagine. The small hill to the west, now sunken into itself as though its insides had leaked out. A narrow fissure in the forest floor, mouth opened in a yawn. A previously clear, fresh stream that ran from the east now carried the putrid smell of spoiled egg. Plants nearest the water began to brown, some evergreens taking a sickly yellow cast.

He trudged back to the cabin, eager for the comforting warmth and reassurance that Mina and Mrs. Banks remained safe. Before he even reached the door, he came upon Mina sitting outside, staring at a piece of foolscap that she held up against the sun.

As he drew closer, he recognized it as the letter from her father. Clearly, Mina was trying to decipher the faded portion. Just as clearly, Sam could see from her furrowed brow she hadn't met with success.

"Drat." She huffed, pushed back an errant lock of hair, and changed her angle. With her eyes squinted and nose scrunched in concentration, Mina bore an unlikely resemblance to a badger.

But a very cute badger.

A corner of his mouth quirked upward at the observation, but Sam stealthily slipped into the cabin. Spotting Mina reminded him of something he intended to follow up on. With Christmas a mere four days away, Sam needed to get to work.

Making a beeline for the book chest, he pulled out the volume he'd thumbed through a couple of nights ago. Flipping through the pages, he found what he sought. Fancifully entitled "A Liquor to Wash Old Deeds," the receipt promised to "revive lost writing" with the use of six galls, bruised, steeped in white wine for two days, and brushed atop the paper. White wine they had, courtesy of Mina's friend, Lady Reed, who'd apparently helped her and Mrs. Banks the day they'd defrauded the corrupt solicitor. But. . .

"Mrs. Banks, are you in possession of galls?" he asked as best he could, not being entirely certain what a gall might be.

"I've got bottom, nerve, and cheek." The old woman's response made him smother a laugh, until he spotted the twinkle in her eye. Then he didn't bother to hold it back. "But I've never liked the term *gall*. Sounds bitter and bad."

"Spirit, Mrs. Banks." He tweaked her mobcap. "You're spirited. However, I refer to galls mentioned in this. . . ." Sam passed her the book, waiting for her to read the description.

"I see." She carefully shut the book and peered up at him. "I suspect, young man, if you wanted to read your letter so much I'd think you would have done something about it long ago."

"It's for Mina," Sam explained. "Since it's from her father, about her future. . . A Christmas surprise, if I can manage it."

"Keep it up, Mr. Carver." She passed him the book with a sage nod. "Soon enough no one will call you a bufflehead."

"No one did before you, Mrs. Banks." He chuckled. The old woman's approval sat warm in his chest. "Now, the galls?"

"Oak galls. Those round knobs that grow on the trees."

"Thank you. We've plenty of oak around these parts. I'll go hunt a few of them down. And then we'll see what comes of it."

"Looks like something interesting from where I'm sitting," she laughed after him. "I hope you're ready for what's revealed once Montrose's words come creeping back to life."

"It's not the words that are important," he called over his shoulder as he headed out the door. "It's Mina."

❄

"Happy Christmas," Mina smiled and passed Sam the package she'd been working on for the past week. She and Belinda already exchanged their customary Christmas letters—each of them still had every letter, going back to when Mina had begun to write.

"Socks!" Sam pulled two out of the gift wrap and flapped them in the air as though utterly surprised. "Just what I need. How did you know?"

Laughing at his antics, Mina shook her head. "How did you not? You've sat across from me as I knitted those every night!"

"Ssssh," he cautioned. "This is a time to celebrate the miracles wrought by love. Last night we read from Luke. During Christmas, we remember the gift of His Son coming to earth, born as a man to later die for our sins. Angels sang, the Star of Bethlehem shone to mark the occasion, and great kings traveled to pay homage to the miraculous newborn with presents."

"They didn't arrive until Christ was older, and not in Bethlehem any longer," Belinda pointed out. "No one likes to mention it, but after the trip to the Americas, I think it bears recognition. Traveling a great distance takes time, commitment, and belief in what you're journeying toward. A years-long trip makes far more of an impression than one short enough for the Magi to reach Christ at the manger, if you ask me."

"I'd agree with that." Sam pulled out a small wooden box. "And sometimes, the wait makes something even more meaningful."

"What's this?" Mina accepted the box with curiosity.

"Usually, you open the present before you ask that." Belinda's chuckle softened her joke. "Otherwise, it's an empty box."

Opening the lid, Mina found a bottle of ink and a tapered brush. Her brow furrowed, no more enlightened than before she'd opened it. "Thank you," she murmured, fingering the brush. "I'm not sure what. . ."

"Fetch the letter from your father," Sam instructed, anticipation brightening his face. His excitement spread easily.

"Here." She tried to pass it to him, but he shook his head.

"Now we'll see if an old recipe can make a small Christmas miracle of our own. Lay the letter flat, and then use the brush." He mimed painting. "Try a little

147

on the faded parts, and wait."

"Do you mean. . . ?" Mina's breath caught. In the next moment, she spread the letter flat against the top of the box, uncorked the bottle, and dipped the brush inside, wiping excess fluid on the lip of the bottle. Brush in hand, she stopped.

"Whether or not this works, thank you." She reached out her free hand to clasp Sam's. "I wanted to say it now, before it mattered either way. Just knowing that you went to the trouble to think of this, and to try to make it work, is the best gift you could have given me." When his warm hand clasped hers in a firm, strong grip, Mina drew the strength to put brush to paper.

At first, the paper merely looked damp. Then, as though pulled forth from unseen depths, pen strokes appeared across the surface of the paper. So faint Mina feared at first she imagined them, the words gathered strength until they lay legible. So she could read her father's reasons for making Sam her guardian.

How desperate I was to understand Papa's reasons when I arrived. Mina laid down the brush, gathering her thoughts. *I think I understand now. He chose Sam for his good heart, inner strength, and strong will to protect others. Papa chose well.*

No longer searching for answers, Mina picked up the letter, savoring the words connecting her to her father's final thoughts on her future. She skimmed the oft-read portion above, until *I hold every confidence of recovery. Nevertheless. . .*

My daughter will require protection. When a woman is gifted with beauty, fortune, and wit, it follows she'll be plagued by men attempting to claim one or more of these. Elton, for one, will do his best to control her fortune but will more likely succeed in driving her witless.

My heir, you see, is a twiddlepoop. But even a titled twiddlepoop, left unchecked, can be dangerous when desperate. So, in the (hopefully unlikely) event of my demise, Mina needs a guardian. Your father can no longer serve as such, which leaves you, Sam. You're far enough away you won't meet my daughter yet, but perhaps that's best. I've a sneaking suspicion that if and when you and Mina do meet, sparks will fly. Perhaps one will catch flame so long as no overprotective father hovers in the middle?

With high hopes and better plans,
Montrose

The letter made her laugh, made her gasp, and even made her blush. Mina could feel the heat rising to her cheeks at the implication that her father had hoped she and Sam might be more than guardian and ward. But most of all. . .

"It sounds just like him." She smiled and passed the letter—written to Sam, after all—back to its rightful owner. He had freed the words trapped within the page, but the true gift was freeing her from the prison of her final doubts. *I was right to come here.*

Mina watched as Sam read, seeing a faint smile, no doubt at the part where Papa predicted Elton would drive her witless, and then she grinned with him when he reached the "twiddlepoop" comment. He glanced at her and then continued reading.

The slight nod Mina took as acceptance of guardianship. When Sam's eyebrows shot toward his hairline, she bit her lip and thought he'd reached the sparks part. *Heaven help me, I can't look. Now he must be reading the part about a spark catching flame, and father having high hopes and better plans.*

"Sounds just like him." Sam's agreement got her to look up. Only then did she recognize his even tone for the trap it was. His eyes seared through her, making her blush even harder.

"His keen sense of humor comes through," she ventured.

"Twiddlepoop," Belinda snorted from where she read the letter.

"Yes." Mina almost sagged with relief at the distraction. "Papa always called Elton the twiddlepoop."

"Who's talking about Elton?" her nurse muttered.

"I didn't mean his sense of humor." Sam's intensity didn't lessen as his gaze snagged hers. "Strategizing runs strong in your family, Mina."

"Yes," she admitted. "I didn't know Papa had hatched any hopes regarding the two of us, but. . ." Somehow, the appropriate apology withered, wordless, on her lips. *I hope he's right* couldn't be confessed. So Mina just let it trail off into nothing.

"Strategizing isn't a bad thing." He stepped toward her. "Not when the Montroses seem particularly gifted in it."

"Oh." Her breath fled as Sam's meaning sank in. "You mean, you think Papa's plans, er, hopes, might be worth considering?"

"I was considering them before I knew he'd planned them."

"When I arrived, I'd hoped to make a home. After the quakes, when you said I belonged, I knew it wasn't the place that mattered. It's the people." She met his gaze, lowered her voice, and amended, "The person."

"Having already opened one present this Christmas, it seems I've become a greedy man. Some gifts are given only when asked for, and there's one I desire more than any other. Wilhelmina Montrose," Sam sank down on one knee to finish, "would you do me the honor of becoming my wife?"

"We've not known each other long," she cautioned and then paused to consider. "My heavenly and earthly fathers seem to have conspired to put me in your care, and my heart agrees. Yes, Samuel Carver. I'll gladly be your bride."

Belinda's cheers let Mina know she approved.

"But I don't know where the pastor lives in these parts," she said.

"We don't have one," Sam acknowledged. "But until we can reach a proper priest in spring, Mr. Stearns *is* a captain. . . ."

Epilogue

Dearest Lady Reed,

I can scarcely believe that it's been a full half year since you sat across the solicitor's office, pretending to be a stranger and helping me fool Mr. Gorvin so that I could begin my great adventure.

Do you know, when the scriptures speak of charity, of love, as the virtue that "Beareth all things, believeth all things, hopeth all things, endureth all things," I think it must also mean such love is God's gift to strengthen us so we can bear, endure, and still hope. How else to explain the inconceivable events after I'd arrived in America and found my guardian?

Surely even your great imagination would be astonished to hear that two days after I'd found Mr. Carver's mountain cabin, a series of devastating groundswells threatened our lives.

Love saw us through those harrowing quakes, which I think shook us closer together. Incredible as it may seem, we were wed by a sea captain on dry land on Christmas Day! And you might not believe such a short union as ours would already be blessed with a coming child.

Nevertheless. . .

All my love,
Wilhelmina Carver

Author's Note

T he quake depicted in this story was the first of the sequence of New Madrid Earthquakes, a series of three major quakes that took place December 16, 1811, January 23, 1812, and February 7, 1812. By far the largest-known quakes east of the Rocky Mountains, historians and geologists conservatively rank them as probable 7.7 on the Richter scale—seismographs not having been invented yet in 1811.

The incident depicted in this novella, the quake on December 16, 1811, occurred at roughly 2:15 a.m. and was followed by a large aftershock at approximately 7:00 a.m. The more specific details, such as shifting chimneys, the eerie stillness and the strange luminescence, the rushing rumbling roar preceding the shaking, clear streams giving off the odor of eggs and poisoning wildlife, are pulled from firsthand Kentucky eyewitness accounts in journals of the period.

While no single account mentions all such details, they are each accurate and compiled to give a more complete picture of the experience and devastation of the quakes.

Kelly Eileen Hake is a reader favorite of Barbour Publishing's Heartsong Presents book club, where she released several of her first books. A credentialed secondary English teacher in California with an MA in writing popular fiction, she is known for her own style of witty, heartwarming historical romance.

A Star in the Night

by Liz Johnson

Dedication

For Judy and Ann, first readers and faithful friends.
Thank you for your encouragement, kindness, and example of joy.

Chapter 1

Although it had not yet snowed that morning, Cora Sinclair sniffed the air for any sign of a coming storm. Despite the frigid breeze, oh, how she wished it would snow now. How she wished the pure white flakes would cover the ground stained with the blood of thousands. At least until Christmas.

Pulling her cloak tighter around her shoulders, she ventured a swift glance at the white columns and brick walls of Carnton. Unable to control her emotions, tears filled her eyes, and she shuddered as memories of the last two days in the grand house flooded through her.

"Has it really only been two days?" She spoke to herself, as no servants could be spared to walk the half mile with her to her home.

While the sun rose, illuminating the barren trees and scarred earth, Cora could not help but envision the soldiers who had marched over this very land. Her gaze darted around the grassy fields, looking for signs of any soldiers still there.

The silence turned eerie, and more shivers ran down her arms.

There! What was that shadow in the tall grass?

Fear rooted her feet in place as the shadow moved.

Surely it wasn't a Union soldier who'd lost his regiment, interested in taking a woman as a prisoner. Was it?

Why had she been so swift to assure Mrs. McGavock that she could safely find her way back to the cabin she shared with her grandfather? Why hadn't she waited until someone could be spared to join her?

Cora tried to swallow but found the lump in her throat was actually her wildly beating heart. A strangled sob tore from her as the shadow moved again. And again.

She tripped over her feet as she backed away, falling hard on her hip. Closing her eyes, clutching the lapels of her cloak, and pulling her shoulders up to her ears, she waited as the rustling grass drew near. When the movement stopped, she squinted at the bright red fur and round eyes of a little fox several yards away.

Jumping to her feet, she threw decorum aside, picked up her skirts, and ran toward the small cluster of trees that hid a wooden cabin just off the Harpeth River.

Her breath came in ragged gasps as she reached the outer ring of sycamore trees, and she leaned heavily on a sturdy trunk until her breathing returned to normal. Dark auburn waves had escaped the knot at the nape of her neck, and she pushed them behind her ears, her hands growing damp from the streams of tears down her cheeks.

Suddenly the swelling sunlight shimmered off a piece of gold.

Her mind had to be playing tricks on her again. She blinked several times, but the soldier didn't vanish. In his Union-blue frock, and covered with branches up to his waist, he sat perfectly still against the base of a tree. His right arm hung at an odd angle, the fabric there more purple than the deep blue of the rest of his coat.

She took a tentative step toward him. "Are you—are you. . . ?" She didn't know what she was going to ask, but he let out a low, pain-filled groan, effectively halting her words and the hand she reached out.

Cora jumped back, snatching her hand to her chest. As she concentrated on his shoulders, they rose and fell in a shallow rhythm.

"Papa!" she yelled. But she was much too far away for her words to carry to her grandfather.

Racing over the uneven earth between giant trees, she finally reached the clearing dominated by the one-story log cabin. She nearly crashed into the front door when the handle did not unlatch on her first attempt. After yanking on the rope again, the lever on the inside of the door rose, and it swung open.

"Pa–papa." She swallowed, trying to catch her breath as the old man with silver hair slowly pushed himself from the rocking chair in front of the fireplace. He still held the family Bible open. "Please. There's a soldier in the grove. We have to help him."

❄

Cora didn't realize how much the fire in the stone hearth warmed the cabin until she stepped back into the freezing cold, her teeth chattering. Stepping next to her grandfather, she leaned into him as a coughing fit seized his body. That same cough had kept him from accompanying her to Carnton when the fighting finally finished and Mattie ran to their home asking for help with the wounded.

Papa waved off her look of concern and trudged against the wind as she led him toward the fallen man.

When they reached the soldier, he hadn't moved, but his shoulders continued to rise and fall. Papa quickly laid one of the blankets he'd brought with him on the ground. "Help me roll him onto this."

Together they pulled the brush off of him and then gently laid him on his side. Rolling him onto the blanket seemed the only option, as he was much too big to lift. He never stirred as they situated him in the middle of the makeshift travois, or as Papa slipped one of the blankets under his arms and covered him with the third.

"Take that corner," he said, and Cora bent to pick up the edge of the blankets at her feet.

It took them several tugs to get the blanket moving, but once it began sliding over the roots and foliage, they continued at a steady pace all the way back to the cabin.

They dropped the blankets next to the fire, and the soldier moaned but made no other movement until Papa rolled him onto his side. Just as the discoloration of his overcoat suggested, the telltale round hole from a minié ball marred his right shoulder.

"Boil water, and get some clean cloths," Papa directed. "We need to take it out."

Cora carried her teapot to the corner of the room near the door and filled it from the large tub of creek water there. Then she slid the pot onto the cast-iron stove, which Papa had added to the cabin just a couple of years before the war began. While she waited for the water to begin bubbling, she hastened to the bedroom, rummaging through the single trunk at the foot of the bed. Her hand finally landed on soft, white cotton, and she removed a pair of much-used petticoats. She had outgrown them more than a year before, and had been saving them in case she needed to mend her only other pair.

Heat rose in her cheeks as she realized that her underthings would soon be tied around a man to whom she had never even been introduced. Staring into his face, she tried to perceive the kind of man he might be and how he had come to be in their woods. Was he a deserter? Or had he simply lost his way and been separated from his regiment?

Mud-caked curls clung to his temples, and dark lashes convulsed, but his eyes never opened. Unruly whiskers covered his cheeks and chin, but he was not altogether unattractive. The slope of his broad shoulders and quirk of his colorless lips made her heart beat unusually fast, and her stomach filled with a sensation she could not name. Certainly it was only concern for his well-being. Someone cared about this man and waited for his return.

Was he married? Was his wife waiting at home for him, terrified of reading his name listed among the missing or dead?

Just the thought forced her to put her mind on the task at hand. She ripped the cloth in her hands into even strips, as Papa struggled to remove the man's coat.

"Let me help you."

Papa looked up and smiled as they rolled him to his stomach. "Will you pull on that cuff?"

Soon they had stripped away his outer clothes and piled them on top of the satchel he had carried, leaving only his undershirt and the red stain that covered nearly the whole of his back. Papa sliced the saturated fabric with his knife, until they could clearly see the man's injury.

Cora bit down on her lower lip to keep from crying out at the sight, and she blinked several times in order to rein in her emotions.

Papa's hand shook as he held the knife over the wound, and she reached out. "I'll do it, if you like." Her eyes pleaded with him to refuse her offer, but he did not. He simply handed her the blade.

"Good. I'll hold him down. You cut out the minié ball." Papa leaned down on the man's shoulders, pressing him into the floor.

She pinched her eyes closed as she poured steaming water over the weapon and into a basin.

"God, give me a steady hand," she whispered as she touched the point to the jagged opening. Blood immediately bubbled from the hole, and she gulped another breath as she pressed in deeper until metal met metal. The tip of the blade scratched and prodded at the foreign object, and the soldier cried out.

Cora jumped at his agony but didn't stop digging until the projectile poked out of its aperture. She snatched the minié ball away then pressed on the seeping wound with one of the strips from her petticoat.

Papa's knee cracked as he stood and walked toward the cabinet near the kitchen table. He pulled out a glass decanter and swiftly returned to her side. "We have to make sure it's clean, or he'll develop a fever."

She agreed, nodded, and pulled back the cloth as Papa poured the amber liquid into the injury. The muscles in the man's back bunched and quivered, and he let out several groans, but still he did not open his eyes.

By the time they had bandaged the wound and cleaned up after the surgery, the sun had set, and the only light in the room came from the flickering fire.

When another coughing fit took hold of Papa, Cora put her hand under his elbow and helped him toward the bedroom. "Why don't you go to sleep? I'll stay up and make sure that he doesn't take a turn for the worse." She looked over her shoulder at the sleeping man, a pang of fear eating at her stomach.

How could she possibly lose another man to the wounds of this battle? Already the faces of the men haunted her dreams.

"Thank you," Papa mumbled as he pressed a kiss to the top of her head. Despite his stooped shoulders, he still stood nearly a head taller than her. "Call me if there's any change."

"I will."

Papa left the door to the bedroom mostly open as Cora walked past their patient to the jumbled pile of clothes on the floor. Folding them piece by piece, she cringed when she held up the long jacket, covered in blood and grime from the floor of the surrounding forest. As she folded it, a piece of paper fell from an interior pocket. She bent to pick it up, surprised that there was no envelope or address on what was clearly a letter.

Many men carried them into battle. Letters to send to their loved ones if they didn't make it home, but this one was simply folded in half.

Glancing into the handsome features of the man before her, she opened the page filled with long, even pen strokes. What secrets hid beneath his long, brown lashes? Was he dreaming of the woman to whom this letter belonged?

Her stomach clenched at the idea of reading another woman's post, but she pressed on. How would she know where to address it if he did not survive?

My dearest Bess,

If you're reading this, then you know that I won't be coming home. I cannot express to you how sorry I am to leave you and our son on your own. But I trust that God will hold you close during these difficult days. I have loved you with my whole heart and will eagerly await the moment when we can meet again in glory.

The closing words swam before Cora's eyes, and she had to stuff the letter back into the jacket pocket before it made her cry any harder.

Every letter just like it—and the reason for them—had made her sick to her stomach as she'd passed water and tea to the soldiers crowding the house and yard at Carnton. If only she could share that pain and grief with someone.

But who could understand? Papa needed her to be strong. And the McGavock family would be consumed with caring for the wounded for months.

The faces of those wounded men and the women who waited for them to return were memories she had to carry on her own.

Straightening her shoulders, she brushed her fingertips over her eyelids and cleared her throat. As she set the captain's folded uniform at the foot of his pallet, she shot him one more glance.

But this time, something had changed.

His stunning brown eyes stared back at her, sending her stomach to her toes.

Chapter 2

Jedediah Harrington's shoulder burned like it rested in the fireplace. The pain that had almost certainly woken him also indicated that something else was amiss. As he opened his eyes, he remained still, taking in his surroundings and trying to place the room.

It wasn't an overly large room, but it felt as though families had grown and loved each other in this place. It looked like a home ought to, with a gentle blaze below the stone mantel at his back and a kitchen table and benches on the far side of the room. Even at the distance and with only the light from the fire, he could see that the corners of the furniture had been rounded by years of use. The only other place to sit was an equally worn wooden rocking chair.

Twisting slightly against wooden floorboards, he looked around until he spotted the skirts of a young woman near the foot of his bed. When his eyes made it to her face—all smooth lines, soft freckles and pink lips—she glanced up at the same moment and immediately darted to the other side of the rocking chair, holding it carefully between them.

"My papa is in the other room." She stretched her finger over his head, but Jed didn't have the strength to follow her movement again. Did he look like he was a danger to her? Certainly she thought so.

He managed a small nod, immediately regretting the way it made his head swim. Resting his ear against the thick blanket spread below him, he opened his mouth but found that he had no voice.

The woman took a tentative step around the chair, keeping one hand on it, probably to use as a weapon if he made a wrong move. "Do you need some water?"

Again he tried to speak. Again he met with the same outcome, so he offered an almost imperceptible nod, trying to limit the pounding behind his eyes. All but her lower half disappeared to the far side of the room, and water rang against the bottom of a tin cup.

He tried to swallow, his tongue like a desert, so he waited until she returned.

"Drink this," she whispered as she knelt by his head. The tin cup she pressed to his lips tasted of metal, but the water tasted like rain in a drought. He tried to guzzle the entire contents of the cup, but she pulled it back every few swallows. "Not so fast. You'll spill all over."

162

Finally it was empty, and she stood and took several small steps away, as though their nearness had been too intimate for two people who had never been introduced. He immediately missed the sweet scent of lavender and gentle touch of her hand.

He cleared his throat and closed his eyes for a long moment. "My na—" His voice cracked, and he had to try again. "My name is Jedediah Harrington. Nearly everyone calls me Jed."

She squinted as though uncertain if she would believe him. After a long pause, she whispered, "Cora Sinclair."

The fractured grin he offered must have broken through at least one of her reserves, as she brought a hand to the high neckline at her throat but responded with a faint smile of her own.

"How did I end up here? Where are we?"

"I found you in the woods not far from here, so my grandfather and I brought you to our home. I removed a bullet from your shoulder and patched it up the best that I could."

Suddenly the memories crashed through his mind. "I was shot by Confederate scouts. We're about a mile from Franklin. There was a skirmish." She confirmed his memory only with a quick motion of her head. "I was headed to Ft. Granger when I stumbled on the troops. I was just trying to get around them, and someone shot me off my horse. They took my weapons." But had they taken the War Department missives he had been carrying to General Schofield?

His gaze darted around the room looking for his gear, for he knew that the leather satchel that had been hanging over his shoulder and across his chest no longer rested there.

"Where are my things?"

Cora glanced over her shoulder to a pile of neatly folded clothes on the floor near the door to the bedroom she had indicated earlier. "It's all there. Your coat and vest and shirt." She blinked long, fair eyelashes before continuing. "And your bag also."

The missives could be of little use to General Schofield or anyone else at Fort Granger in the aftermath of the unexpected skirmish, but he could not afford for them to fall into enemy hands either.

Could he trust her to keep him safe until he could return to Washington? What if she had already called rebel troops to come and get him?

But if her intent was to turn him over, why hadn't she left him to freeze?

Oh, and it had been bitter there beneath that tree. He had been there for at least three nights, blacking out for long stretches of time. But he'd never forget the cold. Somehow he'd pulled branches and leaves over himself, in an attempt to retain any heat still in his body, and it must have worked.

"Why did you bring me here?"

Lines appeared on her forehead, and she tilted her head to the side, escaped strands of her rippling hair falling over her shoulder. "I couldn't leave you outside to die, could I?"

"I'm an officer in the Federal army. You're from Tennessee." He looked toward the ceiling, letting his gaze settle on the rough-hewn rafters. "Most would have."

When he looked back, her face turned gentle, her blue eyes compassionate, and she sank into the rocking chair. "This is not my war. I have no stake in it."

"No brothers? What about your father? A beau?" A sad smile tugged at the corners of her mouth, and remorse pinched his stomach when he realized he was the cause of her sorrowed expression.

"My father died when I was very young, and my mother also. I was their only child, and I was raised by my grandfather and grandmother—she died last year. He's all I have now." Her gaze jumped to the bedroom door then returned to meet Jed's. "I haven't lost anyone I love, and the men here aren't fighting to preserve my way of life."

Her hand fluttered to the corners of the room, and he understood. She had never owned slaves, never owned a plantation or probably even concerned herself with politics. This war wasn't her choice.

But could she really be as harmless as she seemed? Nashville had been under Northern control for several years, but nearly twenty miles south, this battle in Franklin only served as a reminder that many pledged their allegiance to their homeland, not to those in power.

She leaned closer. "You have nothing to fear from my grandfather or me," she said, as though reading his mind. "You will be safe as long as you're here."

An unexpected chill swept his body, and Jed cringed as the muscles in his shoulder contracted, piercing the wound with fire again. He closed his eyes against the throbbing pain, Cora's pretty face appearing on the back of his eyelids. He wouldn't soon forget her tenderness or compassion.

Suddenly Cora's cool hand rested on his cheek, her eyes studying his face. "You should rest," she whispered.

Doubts about her honesty seeped into his mind, and he wanted nothing more than to walk out of the cabin and return to his home, to Bess. If only he could push himself off the floor, put his coat back on, pick up his bag, and leave. But wishing did not give him the strength to do so, and he shivered again.

"Let me check your wound again." She leaned over his back and rolled back the blanket covering his shoulders. She inhaled sharply as she jumped to her feet, quickly returning with fresh bandages in hand.

He could not refrain from flinching when an icy, wet cloth touched his bare skin.

"I'm sorry. I should have warned you." The cloth swiped like hot coals over his back. "You're bleeding again."

"Of course." He bit down on his bottom lip to keep from letting on how much pain even her gentle touch caused. It seemed like hours before she firmly pressed another bandage in place and secured it with a piece of cloth already wrapped around his chest.

As she pulled the cover back over his shoulders, he asked, "May I have another blanket?"

"Are you cold?"

"Yes."

She spread another blanket over the layer already in place and then knelt beside his head, putting her palms on his cheeks and forehead. "You're very warm. You shouldn't feel cold."

"I do." A yawn caught him unaware, making him stutter. "So very cold." He closed his eyes, and the pressure building at his temples begged him to succumb to a long night of sleep in front of a fire and free of the outdoor temperatures he'd suffered.

"Let me get you more water before you go to sleep."

She scurried across the room, but he could not even ward off slumber until her return, as he sank into the darkness of oblivion.

Chapter 3

"How is he?"

Cora glanced up from where she knelt by the captain as her grandfather carried in an armful of logs for the fire. "The same." She pressed her palm to the cheek of the man on the floor. But his eyes didn't move, and his face remained unchanged. "I made him drink more water, but he won't eat."

Papa unloaded the logs onto the pile next to the hearth, tossing a few of the smaller ones onto the already-radiating fire. "How does the wound look?"

Jed's muscles twitched as Cora peeled back the sodden bandage. Even though she'd washed it and changed the bandage several times, the ragged flesh and pungent odor made her cringe every time.

"Do you think it's getting any better?" She couldn't keep the hopeful lilt out of her voice.

His hands on his hips and leaning clear forward, Papa shook his head. "It's hard to tell. Truth be told, I'm more concerned about that fever."

"I gave him some ginger tea." She held up a half-empty teacup. "Well, as much as he would take. But it doesn't seem to be helping."

Still deep in sleep, Jed's legs jerked. Cora shot her grandfather a helpless look and sighed.

"Keep pouring the tea down, but make sure it's not too warm." Papa sat on one of the benches along the table, his eyebrows drawn tight and usual smile a distant memory. "I don't know that there's anything else we can do for him."

Cora's stomach lurched, and she knew it to be true. The captain had suffered a fitful sleep for nearly two days, never fully waking up. She had done everything she knew to do. He needed a doctor. And she knew exactly where one could be found.

Certainly there were still surgeons tending to the wounded at Carnton. If the thick, black smoke rising over the tree line was any indication, all of the fires there burned day and night, for boiling water and cleaning surgical instruments. For the men. Those wounded soldiers.

They were in so much pain, and the chloroform administered by the doctors only numbed the injured. But the fires hadn't blocked out the metallic smell of artillery fire still lingering in the air mixed with the sharp odor of unwashed bodies.

Her stomach jumped again, bile rising in the back of her throat as the memories of the injured men leaped to mind.

She didn't want to go back there. Ever.

She didn't want to see those men still recovering. Or have to again cross the field where so many soldiers had marched toward the Union line in Franklin.

"It's getting late." Papa dragged her from her thoughts. "Will you sleep in your bed tonight? You need to get some rest. I can stay by him."

Cora's gaze shifted to the single doorway on the far side of the room then back to her patient. "No. I'll stay up with him. If there's a change, I want to be here." She dipped a clean rag in a basin of cool water, using it to bathe Captain Harrington's face. Above his dark eyebrows, past his ear, and under his broad chin. *My, but he is handsome.* "Just in case."

"All right. Good night then." Papa walked past her and bent down to kiss the top of her head before disappearing into the dark bedroom. She heard him unsnap his suspenders and the rustle of cotton as he hung up his shirt. With the door all the way open, his rhythmic snoring soon echoed through the cabin as it did every night.

After cleaning and rebandaging the wound on the captain's back one last time, Cora crawled to her rocking chair. Fighting sleep and the haunting dreams that waited just behind closed eyes, she picked up her mending, one ear always listening for a sound from the mat at her feet. Her eyelids drooped as she pushed the floor with her toe, the crackling of the fire and squeaking of the chair her only companions as her mending dropped to her lap.

The clock on the mantel chimed twice, jerking Cora from unwelcome images dancing through her dream. Wrapping her arms around her stomach, she curled as tightly as she could, trying to erase the faces of the men at Carnton who would never return to their loved loves. Uninvited tears leaked down her cheeks, and she swiped her knuckles across them, her heart broken for the families who'd lost their husbands and fathers, brothers and sons.

She shivered despite the heat from the smoldering embers.

Tossing another log on the fire before kneeling next to the captain, she brushed his hair from his forehead. Heat radiated off him stronger than ever before, while barely discernible chills made his teeth click together.

She pressed her hands to Jed's cheeks. She barely knew him, yet she was responsible for him. Even though she'd never met the other woman, Cora owed it to Bess to make sure Jed returned home.

He needed a doctor and medication, but taking him to Carnton could mean a fate worse than the one he faced on her floor. The Confederate troops at the main house wouldn't look kindly on a Yankee. Even if he was an injured officer. If taken captive, the captain could spend the rest of the war—possibly the rest of his life—behind bars.

"I wouldn't wish that on anyone," she whispered to the shadowed face. "What if you were sent to a prison, and I had no way of finding Bess to tell her what happened? Oh, Captain. You have to wake up." A single tear slipped down Cora's cheek, as she sent up a silent prayer for his healing.

❄

The air smelled of frying ham, the meat sizzling not far from where Jed lay, still on the floor. For the first time in days his stomach rumbled, a not-altogether-unpleasant sensation for a man who had thought his life was coming to a slow and painful end.

When he twitched his shoulders, pain eased through his back, rolling through the muscles like gentle waves on the beach. Heaving a sigh of relief that it no longer burned like an unquenchable fire, he ventured to open an eye and lifted his hand to wipe the beads of sweat from his forehead.

Suddenly a pan crashed to the floor, and a familiar voice hollered, "You're awake!"

In a flurry of skirts, Cora knelt beside him, her cool fingers paradise on his cheek. "I supp–ose I am." His voice cracked with disuse, but she ignored him as her soprano filled the room.

"I was so worried. Your fever just kept getting worse and worse last night. I tried to give you ginger tea, but you wouldn't drink much of it. This morning I thought you might be getting better, but I couldn't be certain." As they locked eyes, her hands ran over his face and down his neck before she jerked back, her cheeks tinged pink and gaze dropping to the floor. "How do you feel?"

Jed barely suppressed a grin at her familiar actions. He couldn't blame her. She'd clearly been watching over him for days, and he had no objections to a pretty gal touching him like that. "Better." He wheezed, and she rose to her feet like a doe in the morning light. When she returned with a cup of water in hand, she lowered herself just as gracefully.

"Drink."

He did as ordered, gulping greedily as she held tin to his lips. When the water was gone, he rested his head back on the mat, taking several deep breaths. A sharp aroma mixed with the woodsy scent of the fire and spicy lye soap that had certainly been used to clean the blankets on which he slept.

"Is something burning?"

Cora's eyes grew round as she scrambled to her feet, all sense of grace abandoned. She muttered to herself as a skillet sizzled and clanked against the small cast-iron stove in the corner next to table.

"I've ruined dinner." She sighed to no one in particular just as the hinge on the front door lifted and her grandfather stepped inside.

"Well, well. It's good to see that you're awake finally," the old man said. He squatted near Jed's feet, eyeing him with equal parts suspicion and interest. "How do you feel?"

Jed twisted to get a better view of the wrinkled features, not sure if there was more to the question than what the other man had said. "Better, sir. I appreciate your hospitality. You and Miss Sinclair have been more than kind."

Nodding thoughtfully, the man slapped his own thigh as he stood. "Well, if you're going to stay here awhile, you might as well call me Horace."

"Very well. Will you call me Jed, then?"

Horace nodded, putting his fists on his hips. "Do you feel well enough to sit up, Jed?"

"I'm not sure. Shall we give it a try?"

Maneuvering Jed into a seated position turned into quite the ordeal even with Cora and her grandfather at each of his elbows. By the time he leaned against the log wall, cool gusts of wind seeping through cracks in the chinking between the old logs, he needed to lie down again. But he fought the drowsiness as Cora handed him a bowl filled with a thin broth. As he tried to lift the spoon to his mouth, it clattered back into the bowl.

Immediately by his side, Cora offered him a gentle smile. "May I help you?" She didn't hold out her hand for the bowl or even move to take it back, but her posture indicated immediate help should he ask for it.

"I can do it." Making a fist with his right hand several times, he stretched and practiced the movements. Forearms crying for mercy after days of disuse, on the third try he managed to get a half spoonful of brown liquid to his mouth. It tasted better than any feast at his mother's table in Maryland ever had.

After finishing more than half of his evening meal, he set the bowl aside and leaned his head back as the old man opened the big Bible and read aloud the story of Ruth and Boaz.

Cora's eyes remained firmly on the red fabric in her hands, her needle never slowing. Maybe it was the fresh log on the fire or just Jed's imagination, but Cora's cheeks seemed to glow with extra color when Mr. Sinclair reached the end of the story.

Had Cora slept at the foot of his bed like Ruth had with Boaz?

What a foolish thought to have about a woman he'd barely met. He hadn't thought to be married since the war began, but if he had a wife as kind and pretty as Cora, perhaps he might think on it more. But there was no use. He would be moving along shortly. Mrs. Puckett wouldn't hold his room at the boardinghouse for long. And first there would be a stop at the farm in rural Maryland, tucked between rolling green hills.

Bess would be there, and she deserved an explanation, even if he had none to give.

When the Bible was safely stored on the kitchen armoire, Mr. Sinclair excused himself to look in on their only remaining livestock. "When the Army of Tennessee came through and took our horse and chickens back in sixty-two, we couldn't pay them to take that hog off our hands." He laughed.

His exit seemed Cora's cue to put away her sewing. As she walked past him toward the bedroom, she stopped but did not turn to face him. "Papa will help you lie down to sleep tonight." She took another step then thought better of it. "You should put an address on your letter to Bess in case you ever need to mail it."

His eyebrows pulled tightly together. "Did you read that letter? You had no right." He hadn't even read it.

"It fell out of the pocket of your jacket as I was folding it." Her head dipped low. "And a wife has a right to know if her husband isn't coming home."

Jed nodded slowly. "I agree. That's why I'm taking it to her."

Her gaze sought his, blue eyes reflecting the flickering flames. "I don't understand."

"Bess is my sister. Her husband and I were on an assignment together." The lump in his throat refused to be cleared, so his words sounded like a bullfrog. "And he won't be returning to her."

If only they hadn't been separated. If only Grant hadn't run into those scouts. If only.

Cora blinked several times, biting on her lips so hard that they disappeared. "I am sorry for your sister. And for you, as well."

"Thank you." Jed sighed quietly. "If you're sad for anyone, it should be my nephew, Matthew. He'll never know his father, who was a good man. Grant took good care of my sister, and he was shaping up to be a good father to that little one."

"Do you have a letter like that for your wife?"

"My wife?" She nodded, as though encouraging his memory. "I'm not married."

"There must be someone waiting for you."

He shook his head. "Just Bess and my parents."

Her hand shot to her cheek, covering something that looked like relief.

"They deserve letters, too, I think." With that she bolted from the room, disappearing into the bedroom and closing the door softly.

If she'd given him a chance, he'd have told her. He had letters for them. Letters in envelopes, addressed to his childhood home. But he wouldn't need to have them sent yet.

Chapter 4

The cold December days passed quickly, but still Jed didn't move from the floor. He tried to stand on several occasions, always refusing Cora's help. And each attempt left him weak and defeated. While his color improved, his scowl grew deeper with every passing day. And it was that attitude that concerned Cora most.

Three days after his fever broke, she approached his pallet carrying a plate of stew. "Will you let me help you to the table?"

"I can take care of it myself." As if to prove his point, he pressed his palms against the floor. He didn't budge. But his face twisted in pain.

"You're too weak." She set the plate down, crossed her arms, and shook her head. "You were seriously ill for four days and faced the elements unprotected for at least two. And you lost a lot of blood. It's going to take you some time to regain your strength. Please, won't you let someone help you, Captain?"

He cocked his head to the side, closing one eye almost all the way. The corner of his glower crept upward, his face slowly transforming. "Captain?"

The skin at her throat burned instantly, and she covered her cheeks before the red stain became obvious to him. He trapped her in his gaze like the rabbits Papa snared near the riverbanks. She could not escape without telling him the truth. "Yes—well—it is your rank. . .and I just thought that. . .it seemed too. . . I wasn't certain that it was proper. . ." Breaking eye contact, she stared at her brown boots. "I hardly knew you, but I had to call you something."

His laugh surprised her, rich with mirth, the opposite of the scowl that had taken up residence.

"Don't your men call you Captain?"

"Of course. I've just never had anyone as pretty as you call me that before."

Her cheeks burned stronger, and she wrinkled her nose against the telltale sign of her discomfort. "Well, should I have called you Mr. Harrington?"

She peeked up to see one of his shoulders rise and fall. "Call me whatever you like. But Jed is fine."

"Miz Sinclair! You home, Miz Sinclair?"

Cora's head snapped to the narrow gap where the wooden planks of the front door missed meeting the frame. "I'll—I'll be right there." She spun back to Jed, her eyes like saucers. "Quick. You must hide," she whispered. "No one can know you're here. Since Papa is out checking his traps, you must let me help you."

He nodded quickly as she wrapped an arm around his waist, careful to avoid the bandages still tied in place. Her shoulders tingled where his arm rested across them. She'd cleaned his wound, washed his face, and combed his hair, yet none of that had made her stomach churn as this informal pose did.

"Where to?"

His question pulled her back to the urgent present. "The bedroom?"

On shaking legs and leaning heavily on Cora, Jed shuffled across the room. His eyes closed tightly, but his feet never stopped moving. Just as she stepped away from his side, her visitor knocked loudly. "Miz Sinclair?"

She practically pushed Jed to sit on the bed, and then she raced back into the main room, closing the bedroom door on him. Nearly missing his folded uniform and leather bag, she caught a glimpse of it just before answering the knock. Scooping them into her grandmother's trunk, she could hardly breathe for rushing when she swung the door open on a familiar face from Carnton.

"Mattie! What brings you all the way down here?" The cold December wind had her quickly motioning the petite woman inside and helping her off with her damp shawl.

"Missus Carrie sent me to check on you. To make sure you made it home fine." Mattie rubbed her dark hands together. "And she wanted me to check on your papa. Is he feelin' better?"

Of all the things to ask! With a house full of wounded soldiers, Carrie McGavock, the mistress of Carnton, wanted to check on her and Papa. Mrs. McGavock's kindness had always made her a favorite of Cora's. And Mattie was an extension of that same gentle spirit.

"Oh, yes. He's doing much better. Please thank Mrs. McGavock for her kindness."

Mattie turned her back toward the fire, thawing from the freezing rain. "I thought I saw 'im checking 'is traps when I was walking up."

Cora smiled. "Yes. He wanted to make sure they didn't freeze before he cleaned them." Mattie's eyes drifted to the pallet on the floor at her feet, but she seemed to stop herself before asking a personal question. Quicky Cora piped up, "Would you like a cup of tea before you go back?"

Mattie shook her head. "Missus Carrie needs me back right away. But she said I should ask if you have any blankets or cloth for bandages."

"Then there are still wounded men there?"

"Oh yes. They're packed into every room in the house, 'cept the sitting room."

"From both sides?"

"Not many Yanks left." Mattie pulled her shawl from her shoulders, holding it in front of the fire. "They left without their wounded, so them that could be moved were taken prisoner."

Cora's stare shot to the bedroom door before she could stop it, and a chill that had nothing to do with the howling wind shook her shoulders. If anyone knew there was a wounded Union officer in her home, Jed would be headed to the same prison as those other poor souls.

Of course, Mattie and even Mrs. McGavock wouldn't tell Jed's secret, their compassion stronger than most. But what if one of them had an accidental slip of the tongue? Cora couldn't live with herself if she endangered his life.

"Those poor men." Cora sighed.

Mattie offered a half smile. "Maybe the war will end soon."

Cora had nothing to offer in return. They'd all hoped the war would end soon. They'd been hoping that for years. Even as isolated as she and Papa were, nearly a mile from Carnton and that much farther from the rest of the town, they'd hoped and prayed for an end to the bloodshed. The men dying on these fields weren't her brothers, but they were someone's kin, and they haunted her as if they were her own.

"I should be getting back." Mattie's view dropped again to the pallet at her feet. "Can you spare some blankets and such?"

Cora's knees rattled. She couldn't give Mattie the quilts spread out on the floor. Some of them held bloodstains from the captain's wound. If anyone looked closely at them, they'd know she was hiding something.

"Let me just check the bedroom." Her legs could barely hold her as she stumbled toward the closed door and slipped into the room. But it was empty. She spun around, expecting to spy Jed in every corner. He was nowhere to be seen.

She'd have to find him later. After Mattie left.

Grabbing the only extra bedcover from her mattress and the last pieces of her old petticoats, she hurried back into the main room. Mattie had tied her wrap tightly about her shoulders and hugged the items that Cora handed to her.

"Thank you, Miz Sinclair."

"You're quite welcome, Mattie. Be safe."

Mattie smiled and disappeared out the door in a flourish, leaving Cora to find her missing soldier.

❄

Jed wasn't sure he'd ever be able to move again. His head spun, and all of his limbs shook with the effort it had taken to crawl beneath the bed. He couldn't risk being seen by anyone, even a house slave from the next home over. He just needed to get back to Washington and his assignment there as a special courier for the quartermaster general.

He'd just have to make his legs move long enough to get back there.

When Cora said farewell to the other woman, Jed forced himself to roll from his side to his stomach. Using one hand, he pushed against the wooden bed frame until he was all but free of the quilt, which hung to the floor.

"Jed!" Cora's footsteps stopped the moment she entered the room. "What are you doing on the floor? Where did you go?"

Pushing himself to his knees, Jed rested an arm on top of the mattress as he drew several quick breaths. Cora stooped next to him, her hands reaching out but not touching him. Her dark blue eyes unblinking, she simply stared at him.

"I've put you and Horace in danger just being here." He looked away, through a clean glass window toward the grove of trees where he'd been injured. "I have to go back to Washington."

She stood to her full height. "You're in no shape to travel." Placing her hands on her hips, she imitated a stance his mother had often taken when he was a boy. "Besides, we have no means of transportation. Our horse was taken two years ago. How could you possibly make it hundreds of miles on foot?"

"If the rebels knew that you were hiding me, you could be imprisoned. . .or worse." His eyes swept back to hers, and he very slowly pushed himself to his feet. "You've been so kind to me, but I can't put you at risk. I have a job to do back in Washington. The War Department will want to know where I am."

Cora crossed her arms over her chest. "You can't leave. It's not safe for you"—she motioned to the great beyond—"out there. And you don't have the strength."

Could she see the way his legs trembled beneath Horace's ill-fitting trousers?

It didn't matter. He didn't have a choice. They'd already been far kinder than they should have been to a Union soldier. He wouldn't jeopardize them any longer. Neither would he argue the point with Cora, whose eyes flashed with something akin to fire.

So he stayed through the afternoon, eating more at noon than his stomach wanted, but he would need the energy from rabbit stew. As he sat on the table bench next to Horace and scraped at a piece of wood with his knife, the sun began to set.

Supper was a quiet affair. Cora mentioned Mattie's visit and looked as though she might say something about his intent to leave but bit her tongue instead.

The wind howled past the cabin later that night as the fire dimmed to embers. Horace had been snoring for at least thirty minutes. Jed could only assume that Cora had also succumbed to sleep after a long day.

Pushing himself off his mat, he sat up and rolled to his knees. Groaning as he stood, he walked over to his uniform and slipped the stained and ripped fabric back into place. He reached into his leather bag and pulled a letter from the other papers. The sound as the paper tore in his hands seemed to echo even above the wind, and he whipped around to make sure Cora hadn't heard and come to investigate. The room remained still as he scribbled a short note and left it on the table next to Horace's spare set of clothes.

As he settled the strap of his bag across his chest, Jed glanced over his shoulder once more as he opened the door, the wind wailing as though it were crying. A quick glance around the room did not calm the sensation that he left something behind, his stomach a knot as his gaze landed on the bedroom door. He could not stay with Cora, so he stepped into the frigid winds of the night.

Chapter 5

C ora awoke with a start, at once feeling something was amiss. Papa continued to snore in the bed on the opposite side of the room, so she donned her shawl over her white cotton nightgown and tiptoed into the main room. Jed's pallet lay empty, his uniform gone.

Her stomach churned, and the hair on her arms stood on end. She didn't even have to read the note on the table to know where he'd gone. But she read his messily written words nonetheless.

Dear Horace and Cora,

Thank you for your kindness. I will be forever beholden to you. I must return to my duties in this war now, but I pray that God will protect you both. I hope our paths will cross again.

Sincerely,
Jed Harrington

Cora smiled at the scrap of paper in her hand. He hadn't mentioned his rank or regiment, or even which side of the war he fought for. Still protecting them, even if they didn't need it. No one else would ever see this note. She rolled the paper in her hand and clasped it under her chin.

Not even Papa.

As she stood at the window and wondered how far Jed had gotten during the night, her stomach plummeted. The night was full of dangers: wild animals and rebel forces, not to mention a river that ran much higher and faster than she'd ever seen it before. Jed had still been so weak when he left. Would he ever make it back to Washington?

"You fool," she whispered to the window just as gentle white flakes peppered the floor of the clearing.

"I hope you're not talking to me."

Cora jumped at her grandfather's voice, nearly dropping Jed's note. Clutching it in both hands at her waist, she offered Papa a weak smile. "Of course not." She nodded toward the trousers and shirt folded neatly on the table. "The captain is gone."

"Gone? But he could barely walk yesterday."

She nodded and looked through the snow and trees, hoping to see his form making its way back to them. "After Mattie's visit, he told me he wanted to leave. He was afraid he put us in danger. Afraid there might be a visit from one of the Southern soldiers, who wouldn't take kindly to us caring for an officer from Washington."

Papa grumbled something under his breath as he turned back to their room.

Cora couldn't seem to move her feet. Eyes alert, she held her breath for long intervals as she waited for Jed to return.

But he didn't.

Not while she made biscuits for breakfast. Or while she heated water on the stove to wash their clothes that afternoon. Not even as they ate their evening meal.

Cora couldn't taste the potatoes she'd grown that summer in her own garden as she put them in her mouth. Every time the wind rustled the leaves outside their door, her head spun to see if it might mean the captain's return.

It never did.

As Papa opened the family Bible later that night, Cora picked up her knitting, something she could do and still keep watch. When the fire was so low that he could no longer read by its light, Papa stood.

"I need to find more firewood tomorrow."

"Why?" Cora's attention jumped at her grandfather's unexpected announcement. "We had plenty stored up. It should have gotten us through the winter."

He nodded grimly. "When the river rose, it flooded our woodpile. Only the logs on the very top are dry enough for us to use."

Her heart sank, and tears jumped to her eyes. "But we worked so hard to gather enough to last the whole winter."

Cupping her cheek with his weathered hand, he tilted her face up to look into his eyes. "Don't worry. God will provide for us. Didn't you hear what I read tonight?"

Oh, she hadn't been paying any attention for worry over Jed's safety.

"I'll be leaving early," he said. "I'll have to look farther away from the river. Those trees close by will be as wet as our pile."

"Be careful," she pleaded. "There might still be soldiers out there." Her mind didn't conjure an image of soldiers seeking help but the bodies of those at Carnton who they could not help.

Cora had to look away, the back of her eyes burning as she blinked quickly. She didn't want to remember the faces she'd seen. But it didn't seem to matter. She saw them every night in her dreams.

"What's wrong, Cora-girl?" Papa placed his large hand on her shoulder, but still she could not look him in the eye. "Why are you so sad?"

She wiggled her head back and forth, biting her lips against the longing to tell him the whole truth. How she wanted to tell him of the memories and faces that caused her anxiety to bubble like water in her teapot. But he had enough concerns with replenishing the firewood and helping them survive the winter and the war.

She could not give her burdens to him, so she patted his hand and whispered, "Please don't concern yourself with me."

Papa rubbed her shoulder again. "If you're certain."

"I am."

He took to bed, but Cora could not drag herself out of her rocking chair to follow him. She tried to focus on the steady rhythm of his breathing after he fell asleep and the clacking of her needles. Tried to wipe the terrible images from her mind. But as her chin fell to her chest and her eyes closed of their own accord, the faces she mourned played across her mind.

"Jed!" Cora screamed, waking herself from the nightmare where the captain's face joined the others. Tears trickled down her cheeks, and she swiped at them, rubbing her eyes with her fingertips, trying to press that terrible image from her mind.

It was good that he had left. She might have fallen in love with him, ending up one of those women left to wonder if her love would return.

The sun had just broken the plain of the horizon line as she set aside her yarn and pushed herself from the chair, refusing to give her body opportunity to fall back asleep. Wrapping her arm around her waist as she walked toward the window, she shivered against the chill seeping through the wall, where beams of light broke through breaks in the chinking.

Then as if she were still asleep, Jed's form materialized between two trees in the distance. She smiled to herself, as though this were her mind's way of apologizing for that awful dream. But the figure continued walking and then stumbled, barely catching himself on the trunk of a tree. He pushed himself up again, favoring his left arm. The side on which Jed had been shot.

Cora was in the yard, racing toward the figure, before she fully recognized that he was more than her imagination.

"Jed! Jed. . ." She fell to the ground where he had tripped, resting her hands on either side of his ice-cold face. "You're freezing. Let me help you inside."

For once he didn't object, silently allowing her to wrap her arm around his waist as she pulled his arm around her shoulders. They stumbled at the threshold, slipping through the doorway, which she'd left wide open. She led him inside, and he collapsed to the floor in front of the fire.

Immediately she knelt at his side, helping him take off his sodden coat and soaking boots. "What were you thinking? You could have died out there." She shook her head and glared at him as she hurried to pour him a cup of chicory root that Papa had left on the stove before leaving that morning.

He pulled a blanket from the pile on her grandmother's trunk and hugged it around himself, leaning toward the fire. "I–I'm sor–ry." His teeth chattered, and his entire body shook. "I shouldn't have left."

Handing him the steaming tea cup, she muttered, "That's the smartest thing you've ever said to me."

Sipping the hot drink, he sighed. "You were right. I didn't have the strength to make it very far, and I ran into rebel scouts near Franklin. The town is still a terrible mess, but I was able to hide in a barn until nightfall, and then I came right back here." He looked away from her, clearly ashamed, but she couldn't be certain if it was caused by his leaving or having to return. "Should I not have returned?"

She glanced down and realized that her arms were crossed, one hip stuck out in a pose not unlike one her grandmother had often struck. Lowering her hands to her sides, she shrugged. "I never asked you to leave."

"I'm sorry."

"Very well. You may stay. As long as you promise not to leave until at least Christmas."

His face turned thoughtful. "Another two weeks here?" She nodded, and he took a long sip of the bitter coffee substitute. "Agreed."

Chapter 6

In the days that followed, Jed's health improved rapidly, his strength return-ing in waves every day. Each evening he fell soundly asleep after working steadily alongside Cora and Horace to take care of their home. As the snow melted and daytime temperatures rose, they all spent much of their days collect-ing firewood to replace what had been ruined by the flood.

When all the trees were picked bare as high as they could reach, the two men felled one of the sycamores farthest from the cabin, dragging it in parts to the yard.

The ring of the ax splitting new firewood didn't seem out of the ordinary to Cora as she cut thick slices of bread to complement their lunch.

"The way that boy's going, we'll have enough heat to last two winters." Papa chuckled to himself as he plunged the dipper into the barrel of drinking water, sipping right from the ladle.

Cora spun around, knife still in hand, and glared through the window. Jed stood next to the stump in the yard, resting his forearm on the long ax handle as he gently rotated his shoulders and stretched his back. Marching to the door, she flung it open and pointed her knife at him. "What in heaven's name are you doing?"

Jed had stripped off the red-checked shirt he'd borrowed from her grandfather and even rolled up the sleeves of his white undershirt. He swiped an arm across his forehead and quirked one eyebrow. "Whatever it is that I'm doing, I'm sure there's no need for violence."

"What does that mean?"

He nodded toward her hand, the corner of his mouth lifting in an ever-so-slight grin. "I don't know. You're the one holding a knife."

Cora looked at the blade then back at Jed before realizing he was teasing her. "All right then." Lowering her hand to her side, she put her other fist on her hip. "You know you shouldn't be out here chopping wood."

"I know. There are several cracks in the chinking that need to be fixed. Horace said we could start that tomorrow."

She glanced over her shoulder at Papa. "Did you ask him to daub the cracks?" Jed began to speak, but she cut him off. "Oh, it doesn't matter. You're working far too hard for someone who could barely walk five days ago."

"I feel good." As if to prove his point, he picked up a piece of the tree, centered it on the stump, and split it evenly with one slice of the tool, barely favoring his left arm. "This is good for me. Well, this and all your good cooking."

His attempt at flattery would get him nowhere, but she wasn't going to argue with the fool either. If he wanted to injure himself again, that was his choice. No matter the nagging concern that forced her to look back at him once more before returning to the meal preparations. Or was it the way his handsome features glistened under the midday sun?

Certainly she felt only concern for him, as someone who had been under her care. The way her heart fluttered at the sight of him hard at work was nothing more than a natural apprehension. Wasn't it?

The long hours of labor and so many late nights caring for Jed finally caught up with Cora that afternoon as she washed the dishes. She yawned loudly and often, battling the heaviness of her eyelids. Finally conceding to rest her eyes for a moment, she dropped into her rocking chair and had just dozed off when Jed stomped his boots clean just on the other side of the door.

Through one eye, she glared at him as he stepped into the home. When he looked over and caught her gaze, his smile fell. "Were you resting?"

She shook her head, fighting the desire to succumb to sleep once again. "Not quite."

He fastened a button below his chin. He'd put the red cotton shirt back on over his undershirt, although his cheeks still glowed from the exertion. "Don't let me keep you from whatever you were doing. I just needed. . ." His voice cut off as he lowered himself to a seat at the table. A wry grin spread across his face. "Well, I guess you were right. I don't have as much stamina as I thought."

She opened her mouth to say she'd told him so but bit her tongue instead. Pulling her knitting from her basket, she asked, "Where's Papa?"

"He was just going to finish stacking the wood that I cut and then go down into the cellar to bring up more smoked ham."

They'd been alone many times, but Jed was nearly fully healed, and her stomach fluttered uncomfortably. She pressed her hand to it while consciously averting her gaze. She knew his features by now. Knew the way his hair fell across his forehead and his hands curled into fists. Knew that gleam so often in his eye that meant he was teasing her.

But sitting alone with him as he pulled out the fair scrap of sycamore he'd been carving for days felt strange and new, and not even a distant relative of the concern she'd felt for his wellbeing. And not altogether unwelcome.

Slamming her eyes closed against the curious feelings brewing within, she was soon lulled by the consistent rasping of knife against wood and gentle motion of her chair.

Jed flinched as the knife in his hand scraped his thumb, nearly drawing blood. He had to focus on the little figure emerging from the lumber, despite the way the sun shone through the window, turning Cora's hair to the color of honey. He admired the graceful lines of her cheek as her face was turned away from him, yet he couldn't make out the words she mumbled.

"Hmm?" He leaned toward her, still unable to see her face.

She took a deep breath, nearly a sob. "Just hold on. Hold on. The doctor will see you soon."

Jed jumped to his feet, moving silently across the room. When he reached her side, she swung her face toward him, her eyes closed and silver trails slipping down her cheeks. And then she wailed so loudly that he leaped back, nearly tripping on his own boots.

He'd heard that terrible sound before. The night that he'd tried to leave for Washington—he'd thought it was the wind.

Her breath hitched, and more tears streamed down her face, but still she didn't wake.

What if she woke up and was angry that he'd been there? He shot a glance toward the door. But what if she awoke and was frightened to be alone?

Considering all the nights that she'd stayed by his side as his fever raged in front of this same stone hearth, he owed her at least the same. So he pulled over the bench and sat right next to her as her gentle features twisted in pain and something akin to fear.

Utterly helpless, he did the only thing he could think to do. He slipped his hand into hers and squeezed gently. Her fingers were long and soft, the opposite of his callused, chapped hands. But she clung to him, clenching his hand with each stuttering breath.

The longer she clutched his hand, the easier her breathing became. Her tears dried, and the pinched features of fear relaxed until she slept, finally at peace with the world inside her own mind.

Jed lost track of time as he whispered prayers of serenity over her, hunched so close that his lips brushed her hair. When Horace opened the door, Jed jumped enough to jolt Cora from her rest as well. Her eyes darted between Jed's face and her two hands, still clinging to his. Hopping to her feet, she dropped his hand and pressed her palms to her face. Her eyes open wide, she just stared at him before shaking her head slowly.

"I'm so embarrassed," she whispered. Without warning, she bolted, disappearing behind the bedroom door, refusing to emerge even to join them for supper.

Jed sat across the table from Horace that evening, his eyes staring only at his plate, focused on the memory of the way Cora's cheeks had burned with embarrassment. He'd wanted to scoop her into his arms and hold her until she confided what made her cry in her sleep. But he hadn't done it. For propriety's sake and her composure, he'd stayed rooted to the floor.

His stomach fell, and he set down his fork. If her pride got in the way, she might never let him close enough again to learn what was really going on in her head.

"Was she crying in her sleep?"

Jed jerked his head up to look the other man in the eyes. Nodding slowly, he said, "Yes, sir."

Horace rested his chin against his chest, his shoulders sloping to his elbows, the furrows above his eyes growing deep. "I don't know what to do. It's every night since she came back from Carnton—since she came back from tending to those men."

"Those men?"

White hair bobbing, Horace mumbled, "She went to Carnton after the battle. The house had been turned into a hospital, and Carrie McGavock sent word that Cora should go help if she could." The old man's hands shook as he folded them on the table next to his plate. "Her grandmother would have known what to do now, but all I can do is stay awake at night listening to her sobbing and pray that God will give her rest."

"I understand." Jed's eyebrows pulled together. "Have you tried touching her arm or holding her hand?"

"She won't let me near." The sadness in Horace's eyes was a punch to the gut for Jed. "It's like she can feel that I'm close by, and she thrashes out like a trapped raccoon."

Jed swallowed the fear that he might hurt the old man's feelings and pushed forward in the hopes of helping Cora. "She let me hold her hand today."

"I know."

"I'll hold it again tonight." He glanced over his shoulder at the bedroom, longing to give her some semblance of peace in her sleeping hours.

Objections crossed Horace's face as clearly as if he'd spoken them aloud. It was improper. Her reputation could be ruined. What if she awoke while Jed was there and was even more embarrassed? "I don't think that's a good idea."

"Sir, I realize there are a lot of reasons why I shouldn't, but if it could help your granddaughter rest peacefully. . .even for one night. . .would it be worth it?"

Horace heaved a loud sigh, the love for his only grandchild filling his eyes with compassion. "I suppose so."

That night, after the chores were done and the cabin was closed up tightly, Jed waited on his pallet until a new cry joined the wind whistling between the logs. He knocked softly on the door of the bedroom and waited until Horace let him in, and then he sat on the floor between the two beds and reached for Cora's hand.

She wrapped her fingers around his, her breaths slowing to a steady rhythm until she finally rested.

Chapter 7

"You attended West Point, but did you graduate?"

Jed laughed at her. "Of course I graduated. It was my dream to be a soldier, and I wasn't going to squander it."

"Why a soldier?" Cora picked up another handful of kindling, filling in larger cracks between the cabin logs.

As Jed stirred his bucket of mud and straw, which he would use to fill the smaller spaces and seal the openings, his eyes shifted down, his eyebrows drawn tightly together. "My father wanted me to run the farm—"

"In Maryland?"

"Yes, but my great-grandfather fought with George Washington, and I grew up hearing stories of those battles. Those men at Valley Forge were my childhood heroes, so when I entered the academy my only regret was that I wouldn't have a noble war to fight as they had."

Cora pressed another piece of wood into place, keeping her gaze on Jed's face. "And now that you have a war?"

Jed shook his head, his hand never stopping, lest the mud harden beyond use. "It's not romantic, but it is noble to fight for what you believe in."

"What about the farm? What will your father do?"

"Grant and Bess were going to farm it." A painful expression seared through his eyes. "Now, I suppose he'll give it to my nephew. I'm a lifelong soldier." Suddenly a yawn cracked Jed's jaw. Leaning against the rough timber of the outside of the cabin, his eyelids drooped.

"Are you not sleeping well?" Cora asked as she pressed the last pieces into place. "You look terrible."

Jed grinned at her. "*I* look terrible? If you're not careful, you'll look worse." He stirred the sloppy mess, moving as though he would pitch it at her.

She ducked and screamed. "Don't you dare!"

Taking a menacing step toward her, he waved the stick of muck in her direction. "Oh, wouldn't I? I'll show you what terrible looks like!"

She shrieked and ran from him, picking her skirts nearly up to her knees as she bolted around the side of the house. His breathing loud and close behind her, she knew she couldn't outrun him. He had returned to almost full health and strength, so she hid around the corner of the cabin. When he rounded the building, still growling and waving the muddy stick, she jumped out and screamed.

He plunged to his backside in an instant, his bucket flying and covering him in the sticky daubing. Cora fell to her knees beside him, laughing harder than she could ever remember.

With his forearm Jed swiped at the black streaks that covered his forehead. "This is awful." His face remained stoic, but the lilt in his voice gave away his good humor.

"Just don't waste any of it," Cora managed between fits of laughter. "You still have to fill in the cracks between the kindling."

"Thanks for the reminder," he grumbled, his hand shooting out to wipe a black stripe down her cheek, his smile suddenly matching her own. "Now we look alike."

She grimaced as she poked the mark on her face and then inspected her finger, her eyes squinting and nose wrinkling at the dark coating. "I suppose I deserved that." He nodded mutely before they both broke out in laughter again.

When her stomach hurt too much to continue, Cora pushed herself up, taking in the sticky mess before her. "Do you think you can salvage any of that and finish fixing the wall?"

"I think so."

"Good. Then clean up. It's almost Christmas, and we still don't have a tree." She looked off to the eastern sun, her lips pulling into a straight line. "My mother always had a tree. She came over from England and said the Royal family had a tree every year. When I was young, she read an article about them putting decorations on their trees, so we've been doing that almost my whole life."

"What else did you do to celebrate Christmas with your parents?"

Her gaze turned wistful, still not turning back to him. "My mother had a beautiful voice, so she often sang Christmas songs as we baked sweet breads."

"What did you sing?"

"Oh, anything that came to mind. But 'Joy to the World!' was her favorite, and we would sing it over and over." Cora bit her lip, her smile growing. "Mama and I would spend weeks baking on her brand-new step-top stove. No matter how cold the outdoors, we were warm as fresh pie in front of that fire. And oh, the pies we made!" Turning back to Jed, she didn't try to hide her pleasure at the memories flowing forth. "When the pies were done my father always tried to steal a bite of the peach, but it wasn't for him. Mama bundled me up in a cloak that covered me to my toes and wrapped scarves around my head. And then we carried baskets full of sweets to our neighbors, stopping at each house on our street to wish them a happy Christmas." She swallowed hard. "I do miss them sometimes."

Jed's deep, brown gaze turned soft, his eyes never wavering from hers. "What happened to your parents?"

Cora shook her head. She didn't want to talk about it right now. She only wanted to think on the happy memories, the times of laughter and joy.

Jed's hand reached for hers, familiar like she'd dreamed of it fitting so perfectly into his own. When he squeezed gently, she sighed. "They died of yellow fever when I was twelve, so my grandparents took me in." Jed pressed her hand again and opened his mouth to speak, but she cut him off before he could respond. "It's not as painful now as it was once. I just wish I wasn't such a burden on Papa."

"A burden? But you take care of this whole house."

She waved off the flattery. "He worries about me." She pursed her lips and looked over Jed's shoulder. "He doesn't say that, but I know it's true. He worries about what will happen when he's gone. Who will take care of me?"

Jed squared his shoulders and spoke with a boldness unusual even for him. "Did you never have a beau? There must have been men who wanted to marry you."

Heat threatened to burn her cheeks again, but she forced herself to respond to his question. "I was barely sixteen when the young men at church in town began leaving to fight." She could offer him only half of a smile. It wasn't as though she had never wanted to marry. It simply wasn't an option now. The man that she could love and respect would be fighting until the war ended. Just like Jed, who would soon be returning to Washington.

And if she loved him, she'd become one of those women with a broken heart. One of the ones left behind. One who might never know the fate of her beloved. That was a worry she could never manage, one she could not carry on her own.

Pain filled her stomach, but she forced a happy expression and spun away. "Get yourself cleaned up. We have a tree to find."

By the time Jed washed his hair with the thick soap Horace had loaned him, changed his clothes, and caught up with Cora, who was stuffing a burlap bag into the bottom of her sewing basket, all trace of her sadness had vanished. She'd tried to cover it at the time, but he knew he'd upset her by asking about a beau. He'd just been unable to stop the question from rolling out, even if he didn't want to admit why it mattered.

"Are you ready?" she asked. He nodded, his stomach rolling at the bright smile she offered. "Good. Get the ax. We have quite a trip to make before it gets dark."

"Why do we have to go so far?"

She laughed at him over her shoulder as she trotted away from the river headed west. "There aren't many fir trees in this area, so Papa planted a small grove of them, but he didn't want them to be too close to the river. He said it was bad for them to be in ground that is too wet."

They trudged through the groves of sycamore and towering oak trees, both shivering with each step, despite the sun high in the sky.

"Are we almost there?"

Cora didn't bother answering his question. She simply led the way between two trees that had blocked the view of a cluster of twelve or fifteen small firs, their tops about even with his shoulder. Jed squinted at them, not sure if his eyes played tricks as to their color. "Are they. . .that is, they look blue."

She nodded enthusiastically, as she ran up to one on the right side. "They are. They're called concolors and appear to be both blue and green. And just wait until you cut it down."

Jed did as he was told, swinging the ax at the base of the young tree until it split and toppled to its side. As he leaned over it, he caught the scent to which he knew Cora had been referring. "It smells like oranges."

"I know." She laughed. "Isn't it wonderful?"

He agreed and joined in her Christmastime merriment as he hooked his arm around a branch to drag it back home. As Cora prattled away about the corn they could pop and string around their beautiful tree, Jed's mind continued drifting to what would take place later that night. Long after the popcorn was wound around the tree, he would sit on the floor next to her and hold her hand until morning came.

But he couldn't be there for her forever. After all, Christmas was a week away, and then he would leave. He had to go back to his post in Washington, but he didn't want to leave her alone with her nightmares.

Just as he started to speak, his heart heavy with her internal agony, large flakes of snow began to drop before their eyes. Cora held out her mittened hand as though she could catch the white flecks before they melted. "Don't you just love snow? It feels like it washes away everything wrong with this world. Like it could cover every ugly thing."

Jed stepped toward her, putting his hand on her shoulder, but she didn't turn toward him. "What is it that you want to be covered?"

She shook her head, hunching her shoulders away from his touch. "I saw a lot of things that I can't seem to forget."

"Is that what you dream about at night?"

She whirled toward him, her face a mask of vulnerability and pain. "How did you know?"

"I hear you sometimes." He swallowed the lump in the back of his throat telling him not to tell her the whole truth, took a breath, and pushed forward. "And I hold your hand while you're sleeping."

Her knitted mitten covered her mouth as tears welled up in her eyes. She blinked twice but couldn't seem to stop the quivering of her chin. "I'm mortified," she cried as she turned and ran.

Thankful he had the strength to catch her, Jed dropped the tree and chased her several steps, finally wrapping his hand around her wrist just firmly enough to stop her. "Please, don't be ashamed. Tell me what it is you dream that makes you cry so hard."

She shook her head, her gaze on his hand, still clinging to hers. "I can't tell you."

"Why not?" He tucked a snow-flecked strand of her hair behind her ear, leaving his hand on her cheek and wishing that he could protect her from all the awful things of the world. "Have you forgotten that I've been in this war for four years? I've seen terrible things, too."

Her chin rose until she looked into his face, if not quite into his eyes, tear tracks still marring her apple cheeks. "There were so many men. The uninjured soldiers kept bringing the wounded into the house until they filled every room. I brought them water and blankets and passed out supplies. And I was fine. The blood didn't bother me until they brought in Danny Pa–car." Her voice hiccupped on the last word, and Jed did the only thing he could. He pulled her into his embrace, tucking her head under his chin. She nuzzled into the shoulder of his wooly coat.

"What happened to Danny?"

She hiccupped again, her shoulders shaking under his hands. "His arm was gone."

Jed smoothed her hair with one hand while rubbing circles on her back with the other, his cheek resting on top of her head. "Was he the only one with a missing limb?"

"Nooo. . .but he was the youngest. He couldn't have been more than fourteen." The damp spot on his coat swelled as she sniffed softly. "When I was wiping the dirt off his face, it felt like a brick in my stomach. He was someone's son. They all were. Even the ones being buried behind the house were some-one's family."

190

"Oh, honey," he murmured into her ear. "I am sorry."

Her arms slipped around his waist until she held him as tight as he hugged her. "After that, every drop of blood was another mom or wife or daughter who would never see the man she loved again. I couldn't stop thinking about those faces until it made me physically ill."

"And now? Is that what you see when you dream?"

She nodded into his shoulder, rubbing her cheek against his arm.

"I am sorry that you've seen such terrible things." Resting his ear atop her head, he inhaled the lavender and rosemary scent of her hair. "Do you know that in the Good Book it says to cast all your care upon Him; for He careth for you?"

"Ye–es."

"Do you think you could try to do that? Could you give these memories and nightmares to God?"

Her breath caught loudly as she drew in a breath. "I'm not sure."

He didn't have easy answers, so he whispered a prayer over her. "Heavenly Father, please give Cora peace. Help her to cast these terrible memories upon You. Take them far from her mind. And please give comfort to the families of those men who won't be returning home. We pray in Your name. Amen."

Long after his prayer ended, they stood among the trees holding each other as snow covered the ground all around them. Finally, when her grip on him loosened, she leaned back just far enough to look into his face. "Thank you, Captain."

He meant to say that he was happy to help. He meant to offer another gentle word of comfort. He meant to give her a soft hug and then let go.

He did none of those things.

Instead he took one look into her sapphire eyes and leaned down until there was just a breath between their lips. He waited for a moment, giving her ample opportunity to pull away.

She didn't.

When their lips finally met, Jed's heart pounded so hard that he was certain she could feel it. She tasted like the sweet peach preserves they'd eaten together at lunch—a meal he wanted to share with her for the rest of his life.

The unexpected thought crashed through him, turning his stomach to stone. He'd fallen in love with the woman in his arms, but he could not take her home with him.

Chapter 8

Cora's hands moved automatically, drawing the needle and thread through the thick blue wool. Each stitch blended with the rest of the frock, but she didn't pay attention. Her ears stayed attuned to the sound of Jed's ax breaking apart the last of their renewed firewood supply. When the consistent rhythm stopped, she quickly bundled her project into a sack and tucked it into her sewing box.

A voice in her head asked why she even bothered. She was in no danger of Jed returning to the house as long as Papa was still in the cellar. After all, Jed had made certain that they hadn't spent any time alone since their kiss.

Her stomach danced at just the memory of the strength in his arms and the compassion in his voice as he'd spoken that prayer over her. Being in his arms had been everything she dreamed of, sharing her first kiss with the man she loved. But her love wasn't enough to make him stay, and a band around her heart constricted with that certainty.

She'd fallen in love with a man and become her own worst nightmare, the woman left behind to wonder.

When the front door opened, she wiped a wayward tear from her cheek, hunching over her knitting.

"Where's Jed?" Papa asked as he set down the items he'd brought up from storage.

"I suppose where he usually is lately." Her tone sharper than she meant, she quickly offered a softer follow up. "I'm sure he's whittling somewhere by himself. He's been doing that a lot."

Papa walked over to the fireplace, clapping and rubbing his hands in front of the flames. "Is everything all right between you two? I haven't seen you spending much time together lately."

"I'm sure everything is fine." That same voice in her head gnawed on those words.

If that's really the truth, then why is your heart breaking?

Papa shoved his hands into the pockets of his trousers so hard that his suspenders pulled taut over his white shirt, a sure-tell sign that he was about to broach a subject with which he was uncomfortable. "Your dreams seem to be getting better."

Cora glanced into his dear, weatherworn face. "They are."

"Did something happen to help?"

Her eyes drifted to the corner of the room, filled almost entirely by the tree now adorned with strings of popcorn and bright-red bows made of ribbon, gifts from her mother. "I suppose talking with Jed helped."

One of Papa's furry eyebrows lifted in an arch. "When did you talk with him?"

"A few days ago."

Papa nodded in a way that indicated he understood a lot more than he let on. "What did he say?"

Eyes still on her sewing, she said, "I'd rather not speak of it right now."

Papa knelt by her chair, resting both of his hands on her arm. "Why won't you let me in? Why won't you tell me what burden it is that you carry?"

Tears blurred her vision. "I can't."

Christmas morning dawned bright, the sun sparkling off the thin layer of fresh snow blanketing the front yard. Cora stood by the window, enjoying the simple beauty for nearly thirty minutes, her mind recounting the promise she'd forced Jed to make. He'd said he would stay until Christmas, and she knew he would not stay even a moment more. This would be their last day together.

Even if he had been distant since their kiss, she would miss his presence in their little home. His voice sometimes filled the whole room, and his laugh forced her to join in.

"Merry Christmas, sweetheart."

She turned into Papa's embrace, holding him close. "You, too."

Boots thudded against the outside door frame, and Jed stepped into the room, his cheeks rosy from the cool morning. "The chores are done," he announced.

"Merry Christmas, Jed." Papa shook the other man's hand with a firm grip. "Thank you."

"My pleasure. What's for breakfast?"

Both men turned to Cora, whose face must've turned as pink as Jed's. "Oh my! I haven't even started it." She motioned to the rocking chair. "Sit down. It'll be ready shortly."

She broke several eggs into the cast-iron skillet and cooked them until they stopped wiggling. Then she added thick pieces of ham, which sizzled when they hit the pan. While warming several biscuits from the day before, she set the table with the last of her orange marmalade.

Cora barely tasted the food as she ate, but Jed and Papa enjoyed it immensely if their mumbles of appreciation between bites were any indication. "Just like your grandmother used to make," Papa sighed at one point.

The morning meal finished quickly, and as Cora washed the plates, Jed pulled the bench near her chair. Papa handed him the Bible. "Start in Luke, chapter two."

Jed did as he was told, beginning just as Cora settled into her seat. "'And it came to pass in those days, that there went out a decree from Caesar Augustus that all the world should be taxed.'" In a clear timbre Jed read the story of Mary and Joseph's journey to Bethlehem and the birth of the Messiah, and the angels and shepherds who were there that first Christmas night.

When he had finished, Jed set the heavy book on the bench beside him, and Papa prayed over them. He prayed for an end to the war and a peace to come again. He prayed for their safety inside the little cabin, but when he asked God to protect Jed when he returned to Washington, Cora bit on her lip to keep from letting a sob escape.

Papa was the first to give his gifts, a beautiful knitted shawl for Cora and an old knife he said he'd intended to give to his only son. But now it seemed fitting that Jed take it with him.

Next Jed handed them each a small parcel wrapped in paper and twine. "Open them at the same time," he urged.

"You didn't have to do this." As Cora's fingers opened the paper, a perfectly carved wooden angel fell into her hands, the feathers of its wide wings and cherubic features etched with precise detail. "Oh my." Her thumbs ran across the smooth edges, her mouth hanging open in awe.

"This is remarkable craftsmanship." At Papa's words Cora glanced over to see a manger resting in his palm. Even at a distance, she could see the lines of straw Jed had so meticulously fashioned into the soft wood.

Jed's smile carried all the joy of a gift appreciated, and Cora warmed into it. "Thank you. These are beautiful."

"Well, I meant to make a star, too." He ran his fingers through his hair. "I just ran out of time. Lots of wood to cut." He chuckled, the first time in days.

"Well, now it's my turn." She handed a small paper-wrapped parcel to her grandfather, who thanked her profusely when he opened it to reveal a blue shirt. "For Sunday services when they resume, I thought."

"It's very nice. Thank you."

"And for the captain." Cora stretched to pass him a substantially larger burlap bag.

A line formed between his eyebrows as he reached into the carrier, recognition lighting his eyes only when he pulled the folded pile of cloth into the light. "My uniform." He flipped the frock over, his smile growing at the clean material.

His finger traced the small stitches around the mended hole. "You fixed it."

"Good as new, I think. Do you like it?"

He caught her eye, his smile nearly making her forget that the uniform meant that he would be leaving. Tonight.

❄

That night Jed stood with Cora so close to the door of the cabin that firelight illuminated them through the window, flashing on the polished brass buttons of his blue frock. He held both of her hands gently in his, looking anywhere but into her eyes. He hadn't made any secret about having to return to Washington, and he'd kept his promise to stay through Christmas. They'd both known this was coming, yet somehow he felt as though he was letting her down and betraying the affection growing in his own heart.

"I have to go tonight. It's safer for me to travel in the darkness."

She nodded. "I know."

He squeezed her hands, offering a subtle smile. "Thank you again for mending my uniform."

"You're welcome, Captain." Her head turned so that she could look in the direction of the grove of fir trees, near where they'd shared their kiss. "Thank you for all you've done. For the firewood and—and. . .well, for helping me put my worries into God's hands." Her voice cracked on the last word as tears spilled down her cheeks.

"Please don't cry." He brushed away one of the tears with his thumb. Forcing out a strained sigh, he closed his eyes to the pain flickering across her face.

"I'm sorry," she whispered, lips drawn tight.

As her tears made their trek near the corner of her mouth, he physically fought the urge to kiss them away. Wrestling the impulse to pull her tight and relive that moment in the forest that he'd taken such caution not to repeat for fear that this night would be harder than it had to be, he latched back onto her hands and took a small step back.

"I care for you, Cora. I truly do." He shook his head, as he butchered his attempt to explain his mounting love for her without breaking her heart further. "The truth is that I care about you far too much to leave you to wonder whether I'm ever coming back. I won't let you be one of those women in your nightmares." He hung his head, even though she still refused to look at him. "I don't know how much longer this war will last, and I can't promise you that I'll be able to return."

Suddenly her head whipped back toward him, her eyes locking with his. "Then don't go!"

"I would stay if I could. You know that, right?"

Her eyes filled with another batch of tears, and she nodded.

"You're going to meet someone. . ." Jed had to stop to clear his throat, unable to get out the words he needed to say. "You're going to meet an amazing man and have a wonderful family. Any man would be lucky to love you."

I certainly was.

Her eyes turned dark, brooding like the sea, the firelight transforming her features into shifting shadows. She'd probably never been to Maryland, but as he let go of her hands and stepped into the woods, he knew he could never be home without her.

Chapter 9

December 24, 1865

Cora inhaled the sweet scent of fresh snow as she traipsed across the wide field in front of Carnton, holding out her mittens to catch the flakes before they melted. Her breath curled into a cloud floating above the frozen earth. The ground before her had long since been washed clean by the summer rains and leveled by Mr. McGavock's plow. Someone just passing through might never know that this land had once been marred by the shells of the Union army.

Not all of Franklin had returned to normal more than a year after the battle, but almost a mile from the hub of the fighting Cora's little world had resumed as it once had before the war. Before the nightmares.

Before the captain.

As she entered the stand of trees, her eye instantly caught the small stones laid out in the shape of a cross at the base of the tree where she'd first seen him. She knelt by them and wiped each rock clean of the light dusting of snow.

As she'd done every day for a year, she whispered a prayer for Jedediah Harrington, wherever he might be, giving all of her concern for him to the only One who could take away her anxiety.

"This year could have been miserable," she whispered so quietly that the morning birds continued to sing. "But I will continue to cast my cares upon You, for You careth for me. And for Jed, too."

As she stood and resumed a steady gait back toward the cabin, a slow smile curved her lips. The war had ended in April according to the newspapers, and still there was no word from Jed, but she would wait until there was. He'd made no promise to ever return, but deep in her heart, Cora knew that if he was able, he would come back to her.

So she hoped. And she continued to pray.

As she entered the clearing, the snow began falling in earnest, and she could barely make out the figure of her grandfather walking along the side of the cabin.

"Papa!"

He turned and waved. "I'm going to get some water. Did Carrie like her new dress?"

"Very much! I'm going to start dinner. Hurry back." He waved again, resuming the path toward the small inlet from the river.

It wasn't until Cora reached the front door that she spotted six wooden stars on the windowsill. Running the last few steps to them, she snatched one, turning it over and over in her hands as though it would reveal what she hoped to be true. Her stomach in knots, she spun on the spot.

"Jed?" Her voice barely a whisper, she tried again. "Jed!"

And then he was there, stepping out from behind a tree, marching across the yard. Unable to wait for him to reach her, she sprinted toward him, throwing her arms about his neck when they met. His embrace nearly stole her breath, or was it the way her heart doubled its speed?

"I have missed you," he whispered into her ear. His smile wavered as he put his hands on her waist and pushed her a half step away, his gaze running from her head to her toes as though confirming she was truly in front of him.

She blushed but didn't dare look away from the face she'd longed to see all these months.

"I'm not too late, am I?" The tone of his voice turned serious.

"No. I haven't even started dinner yet."

His laughter, so rich and familiar, covered her like a second cloak. "Not for dinner. For you."

"For me?"

His face pinched in serious concentration. "When I left, I told you to find a good man. Have you found someone else? Are you married? Am I too late?"

Her mirth as deep as the conviction in his voice, she laughed heartily. "No! Of course not. How could I marry someone else when I have been in love with you for more than a year?"

The relief that crossed his face brought a boyish grin with it as he swooped down and kissed her soundly, his arms wrapping about her shoulders as he made her forget everything but them. Her toes curled, and she tried to smile as joy bubbled deep in her stomach. He had been more than worth the wait.

When he finally pulled back, his smile only radiated brighter. "I wanted to ask you to wait. Do you know how much I wanted you to wait for me? But I just couldn't put you through that."

"I know." She brushed the snow from his whiskers before cupping his cheek with her hand.

"And then I couldn't stop thinking about you. About your sweet smile and beautiful eyes. About getting home to you."

"But your home is in Maryland."

Pressing both of his hands to her cheeks, he laughed. "My home is wherever you are, so I returned as soon as I could."

"Did you see Bess?"

His smile dimmed. "Yes. I delivered her letter on my way to Washington and stopped again on my way back here. That letter broke her heart, but I believe she's beginning to find hope again. Matthew is walking now, and she chases after him. A neighbor that we grew up with asked if he could court her, so there may be a wedding on the farm soon."

"What else did you think about while you were away?"

He grinned like a cat who had stolen a bowl of milk. "About how I owed you a star to add to your set. So I just kept carving them for you."

She tossed a glance over her shoulder at the row of stars leaning against the window. "They're beautiful. Thank you."

"I have about a dozen more in my saddlebags."

"A dozen?"

"I told you. I couldn't think of anything but you." The intensity in his gaze deepened.

"I'm so glad you're here in time for Christmas! But I don't have a gift for you."

"You've already given me the best gift I could ask for." He leaned in to briefly press his lips against hers.

She dove back into his arms, wrapping hers around his back. But as soon as she tucked her face into his shoulder, she realized something was different. "Where's your uniform?"

"I resigned from the War Department."

"But your job? It was your dream."

The corner of his mouth tilted up. "You're my new dream."

Tilting back to look into his face, she bit her bottom lip to keep from smiling. "How long can you stay this time?"

He pressed his lips to hers quickly and passionately, the kiss fueled by the same fervor she'd carried in her heart for a year.

"Forever."

Liz Johnson holds a degree in public relations from Northern Arizona University, in Flagstaff, and works as a full-time marketing specialist for a major Christian publisher in Nashville, Tennessee.

The Courting Quilt

by Jane Kirkpatrick

Dedication

To my husband, Jerry, who stitches well.

Chapter 1

Twenty-five, twenty-six, twenty-seven. Well, that last one is just half a button, so I won't count it, Lacy," Mary Bishop told her dog. At the sound of her name, the little spaniel's tail wagged on the log store's puncheon floor. In her window box, spring daffodils nodded sleepy heads to the season in the Willamette Valley of the young state of Oregon. A March sunrise flirted between big pines and firs to light the small window of Mary's Dry Goods and Mercantile. It was home even without Dale, though these weary, rainy months after Christmas always made her sad, missing him more than ever.

Mary kept counting buttons. She planned to give at least fifty buttons to the Widow Mason down the road. She'd tell the mother of eight that these were old buttons, not in fashion anymore, and some were broken, couldn't she see? Mary hoped the widow could "take these out-of-date buttons off my hands." The widow wasn't one for charity, so Mary had devised what she thought was the perfect plan. She was always planning. Dale, God rest his soul, often chuckled at Mary's many plans, but weren't they here on earth to implement what God planned for each one? That's what she'd told him. He'd reminded her to let God handle the details. Mary sighed. How she missed that man!

"Thirty, thirty-one, thirty-two. . ." The bell over the door jangled, and Mary looked up. She must have unlocked the door out of habit, for it was way too early for customers. *Oh no. Laird Lawson.* Lacy's ears perked, and the dog rose then scampered toward the counter, away from the intruder, her little nails making skidding sounds on the pine floor.

"Good morning, Mrs. Bishop," the old rancher greeted her. He frowned at the sight of the dog scurrying but added cheerfully, "Always good to see a woman up before dawn, ready for her day."

She nodded to him but didn't hold his gaze. He'd read more into any gesture of familiarity, and she'd be a half hour diverting his attention from his latest advice, probably about how dogs didn't belong inside commercial establishments or log homes, for that matter. Even worse, he'd begin to tell her that her wares were out of date and she needed a man to sell farm equipment successfully. He had a tendency since Dale's death to think she needed a man's help and had assumed the role of advising others on their purchases. Sometimes Mary thought her prematurely white hair led Mr. Lawson to assume she was older and more frail and needed his assistance more than she did. What she needed were sales! Mary's husband had been older by several years, and they had no young children running about, so she supposed people made assumptions about her age and abilities. She might look more "grandmotherly" than not with that pale hair and being a bit on the plump side. Yet she'd just reached thirty, and she'd had white hair since the age of twelve when she'd been struck by lightning.

Mary took a deep breath. She mustn't let her financial problems drain her of good manners. "And a fine day to you, too, Mr. Lawson."

"Ah Mary, isn't it time you called me Laird? 'Twas my father who was Mr. Lawson."

"And I've known many a Mary," she corrected. "But I'm Mrs. Bishop still to friends."

"Well now, Mary, you're of an age where familiarity isn't such a bad thing, is it?" He waggled his finger at her, and she noticed there was no dirt beneath his nails. It was a good feature of the man, his attention to cleanliness despite living in that log cabin in the woods without a wife to tend him—not that he hadn't tried his best to get a woman to do just that. She'd heard he'd asked the Presbyterian mission in the East to send him a possible wife, just as the Reverend Spaulding had done. But Mr. Lawson wasn't a Presbyterian or a reverend, so he had to recruit a new wife on his own. Mary feared that she had become his latest target.

"What can I help you with this morning, Mr. Lawson, to get you on your way to what I'm sure is a busy day ahead for you?"

"Oh, I have time before I head over to Smith's store."

"Smith's *store*? It's opened?" Her competition was already stiff with Cooley & Company in the heart of Brownsville.

"Brand-new clapboard establishment."

"I wasn't aware we needed larger, more modern establishments," Mary said. She wasn't that far from the heart of the town, but she was across the river, and her sales had been off. She'd thought it was the winter doldrums when people stayed at home in their cabins and sat by the fire to sew, read, or mend harnesses. Cooley & Company was well established, having bought out the original Brownsville store. Now this Smith had arrived to make it a three-way competition for customers.

"Mary, a woman alone can hardly expect to keep men customers in this old log store. I guess Smith figured a growing place needed a modern establishment."

"Smith," Mary said beneath her breath. "One can hope his wares will be as common as his name."

"Didn't mean to be the bearer of bad tidings." He cleared his throat. "I need this list filled." He handed her a page torn from a ledger book. "I can help you pull things," he said. "Make it go faster. I know you keep your molasses on the top shelf."

"No, no. That's my job," Mary assured him. She wiped her hands on her apron, smelled the lavender she put into the soap when she washed, and remembered Dale again. He'd loved the scent of lavender. "I'm not so old and decrepit that I can't fulfill my duties to the good citizens of Brownsville," she told Laird. "Why don't you tend to your other business and come back in about an hour?" She didn't want to be stuck with him hovering over her as she put lantern oil, salt, cone sugar, safety matches (she imported them from Sweden), seeds, needles, molasses, and a dozen other items into the wooden box he'd brought in for her to fill. "It shouldn't take too long," she said cheerfully. "I thank you for your business."

He nodded then sauntered out, his eyes scanning the room as he left.

Checking on my inventory, she thought. He always had suggestions for new things she should be carrying or ways to display her wares, but she liked to keep it the way she and Dale had arranged it.

She returned to finish counting her buttons. The act of counting and the idea of giving them away brought comfort to her restless soul. "Give and ye shall receive" scripture told her. "Fifty. Just right." The ivory, shell, and tin buttons looked festive through the clear, thin apothecary glass jar. She decided not to tie a ribbon around it so it would look more like a leaving, something left behind, and not an actual gift. The widow could likely use the jar later for something else if she wished. When little Jennifer came in for her hard candy, Mary planned to send the buttons home with her with a note asking that the widow "take them off her hands." She set the jar on the plank counter.

Now she tended to Mr. Lawson's order so if he came back early she'd already have his bill posted and wouldn't have him in her store when other customers came in. As she worked, she kept Dale's spirit with her, letting the logs wrap their thick round arms around her for comfort. She checked off each of the items on Mr. Lawson's list and then set the box aside, finished. She noted that he hadn't ordered any large, more expensive items like a new axhead or a scythe. She supposed he was buying the more costly equipment at Cooley's or the new Smith store. He did request a needle case, and she happened to have an ivory one. She hoped he'd not think it too expensive.

Once again the door bell jangled. *Back already?* Mary lifted her eyes but not to Laird Lawson. Instead, it was a man wearing top boots, his pants tucked neatly inside, and a leather vest over a shirt with a collar. He stared at her with one brown and one blue eye. His smile would smooth wrinkles from a well-worn dress.

She brushed her hands on her apron. She rarely saw top boots in these parts. Men here mostly wore brogans to resist the snow and mud. And those eyes. . . "May I help you?" Mary asked.

"You may not," the man said. "But the proprietor of this fine establishment can." He looked around. "I love cat-and-clay chimneys and puncheon floors." His eyes gazed at the ceiling. Mary wondered what he thought of the cobwebs she hadn't broomed away.

"My husband and I built this store together," she said. "Found the logs, dragged them with horses and prayers, and with our neighbors raised it up."

"It's a fine store," he said, and then turned back to face her and added, "My name is Richard Taylor, of the New England Taylors, at your service." He swept his bowler hat from a head of hair as yellow as sunflowers. Soft curls nestled at his neck, but he was otherwise clean-shaven with close-cropped sideburns. The curl behind his ear reminded her of a small child's just before a first haircut. He stood erect in his pants and vest, though his collar looked to need starching. A well-portioned man. *Good confirmation*, Dale would say if he were here and the man a horse. Mary blinked. *What am I thinking?*

"I represent the Barbour Brothers," he continued. "Thomas, Robert, and Samuel, formerly of Ireland and now of Patterson, New Jersey, where last year they built a flax mill and where they produce this fine, fine line of thread." He carried a leather case and set it on the counter, pushing the jar of buttons aside. He reached into the satchel and then stopped. "But I'm ahead of myself. Will you secure your husband so I may make his day as well as yours and not repeat myself nor waste the time of such busy folks?"

"I'm the owner of this store, my husband being deceased. Mrs. Bishop." She introduced herself. She noticed the softening of his eyes at the mention of Dale's death, eyes that warmed like late-night coal ready for stoking.

"Ah, my mistake, my terrible mistake." He lowered his eyes to where he saw Lacy staring up at him. "Will your mistress forgive me?" he said, his hands out as if pleading. Lacy's tail began to wag. "Your dog has a forgiving heart," he said as he looked at Mary. He gave her one of those puppy-dog looks that follow a broken cup just knocked off of the table.

His expression of exaggerated remorse made Mary smile. "At least you didn't ask to see my son, the owner," she said fluffing the white bun at the nape of her neck. *Now why did I bring up my age and draw attention to my white hair?*

"The thought never crossed my mind," he said. "But I surely meant no disrespect by suggesting you weren't capable of being the owner. I rarely see female proprietors. Here, let me show you what I've brought that will delight you." His eyes stopped at the button jar. "I see you have a fine selection of shell and ivory."

"Those are for a friend," she said, "who cuts all the buttons off her children's clothing before running the shirts and pants through the labor-saving washer device her husband gave her for Christmas shortly before he died. The ringer breaks the buttons, you see. Then she sews them back on before Sunday church."

"What people do for love," he mused. "And what a generous spirit you have to cut down some of her time. How many children does she have?" Mary held up eight fingers. "Ah," he said. He looked at her as though he might say something further, but instead he took from his leather bag a large cone of thread and tore off the white paper protecting it, revealing the most brilliant ruby color Mary had ever seen. "Named Rosa Red," he said. "Names are important, don't you think? A name sets your mind free to imagine. It's yours for a pittance; I assure you."

If Dale had been here, he'd have kept any smile from his face and begun to bargain. But Mary was taken by that red thread or maybe by this man's savory voice, his stunning eyes. She held the cone in her hand, fingered the smooth flax. It was beautiful. She could see her quilting customers liking this brilliant color. "I'll take three spools."

"Three?" Mr. Taylor blinked those colorful eyes. "Well, that's wonderful indeed, but wouldn't you like to look at the other colors first? Maybe you'll want one of each, Mrs. Bishop."

"Please. Call me Mary," she said. She felt her face grow warm with her boldness, giving a stranger her given name. "But I'm partial to red."

"Why thank you. And you must call me Richard, if you please. You must be quite a seamstress," he said, digging for what Mary supposed was his order form. Firm arms flexed beneath his white cotton shirt as he pushed things around in the satchel. "Such a good eye for quality."

"For my customers," Mary said. "I don't actually sew myself except for buttons, of course."

Richard's hand stopped, and he looked at her. "A woman who doesn't sew? Rare indeed"—he looked around—"without a maid."

"I've no maid," she said. She found herself moving from his brown eye to his blue, wondering at the unusual coloring. "My husband taught me to sew on buttons." She didn't tell him that as a child growing up in Prairie du Chien, Wisconsin, servants in their estate overlooking the Wisconsin River did such mundane things for her. Her mother had died when Mary was born, and the servants and her indulgent father had been her family, until Dale. Dale had been a little shocked when he'd realized she had few domestic skills, though she assured him she was "quite trainable." He set about doing that as they made the wagon trip west, their marriage beginning a new and glorious chapter of her life and a new skill at button sewing.

"A man after my own heart," Mr. Taylor said. He stepped back as if surveying this unusual creature. "I do adore a woman who sews," he continued, "but then, finding one who services those who do is almost as good. . .for a salesman like me." He unfurled another cone of thread and then dug deeper into his bag, taking out pyramids of deep blue, sunflower yellow, and of course, snowy white. These would be samples. She'd have to order and wait for them to arrive, but Mary knew that. "Let me show you other necessities for the seamstresses of the region." He set out ivory thread barrels carved with delicate flowers. "Chinese," he said. "Look at these bead containers, netting rollers, and ratchets, and of course if you buy the cones, you'll want these ivory thread winders for the skeins and hanks. I can make quite a good deal for you on all this." He showed her several more items and then a catalog with even more choices.

He was a good salesman, Mary decided. Earnest with a few rough edges but honest, she thought, not monitoring every word for its sales affect. And he made her smile, telling stories of his travels and even one of tangled thread when he tangled a skein of yarn he showed her. He created distinctive yet respectful images of the Barbour brothers and the proprietors he'd met in the valley. He appeared to be a good observer of humanity and kindly disposed toward people.

"They're lovely," Mary said finally as she fingered the ivory winders that looked as delicate as snowflakes. She wondered just how much they might cost, but instead of asking, she returned to the thread cones. "I don't really need the white cone." She had to show some discipline, after all. She wasn't sure she needed any thread at all, now that she considered. Though the war in the East had been over for a time, people still weren't buying much. And with Smith's store open, she'd have even more competition for people wanting Rosa Red thread.

"I'll throw the white in if you take one of each of the spools," he said, "and of course three of the red, as you indicated earlier. I can telegraph the order to the Barbours, and it will be here within two weeks. You'll find them and me, their agent, quite reliable and most professional." He snapped his top boot heels together and bowed at his waist.

She tapped her index finger to her lips. "I. . .I'm sorry. I really have no need for so much Rosa Red. I'm not sure what I was thinking," Mary said. "If I invest at all in something new, it would be my plan—" She stopped herself. "My husband used to say that my optimism sometimes bordered on lunacy."

"It sometimes takes lunacy to spread ones wares wide and far. The Barbours weren't sure that sending me west was a good investment, but here I am. Lunacy in person."

Mary smiled. "And I'm sure you will sell far and wide, Mr. Taylor—"

"Richard," he corrected.

"But—"

"The quality will attract new customers for you, provide reasons for them to come to your store. From wide and far, they'll arrive."

Wide and far. Mary stared at Richard Taylor, whose dual-colored eyes looked anxious as he awaited her final order. Could *he* be the detail God provided? Why, he might be just the man to implement her plan to expand her sagging sales *wide and far.* Doing so could mean her very survival. *Is this what I should do?* she prayed. Richard Taylor might just have provided her the sustenance she needed sandwiched between two other stores. She breathed a prayer of thanks and asked the newcomer to take a cup of tea with her. Lunacy or faith reigned. She'd soon find out which.

Chapter 2

Richard Taylor chastised himself. Why hadn't he just taken the woman's original order of three spools of red? Why did he have to push for just a little more? And then he'd said she was "almost as good" as someone who sewed? One should never insult a woman or worse a woman in a position to buy one's products. He needed this sale. Life hadn't been all that easy since he'd come west following the war. His few sales had at least convinced the Barbour Brothers to give him a little more time before they recalled him and gave him his walking papers. Stores were few and far between in this region, and other salesmen already covered the high population cities like Portland and Salem and many of those stores—even Cooley & Company down the street—traveled to San Francisco to fill their orders. He hoped to make inroads at the smaller establishments in the territory with his charm and his steady horse and good products. It was his philosophy that every product needed, first, to be of great quality and, second, to have a story. If the product had quality, people could buy it anywhere; if he had a good story to go with it, they'd look forward to buying it from him. He hadn't convinced Cooley & Company or Smith of many sales; he hoped for more from this lovely older woman.

"I assure you the quality is of the best," he told her as he followed her into the back room of the log store. "I sold several spools at the Aurora Colony north of here. They're known for their fine tailoring, I'm told. Dr. Keil himself made the purchase for the colony store and the outsider's establishment. They have quite a grand selection."

I'm a wreck, he thought, praising her competition that wasn't all that far down the road.

"A woman who knows the needs of her neighbors surely makes wise choices," Richard said, in an effort to recover. "Perhaps the three spools of thread will be just what they need."

"Perhaps," she said.

Something had changed in her demeanor, Richard noticed. He wondered what he'd said or done. She'd been sweet, almost flirtatious, when he'd first showed her the Rosa Red, asking to call her by her given name. Now she was looking all, well, professional. He wondered how old she was. Her skin was the shade of sunrise, all pink and smooth. A few lines marked her eyes, but her white hair reminded him of his dear old mother, God rest her soul.

"Mr. Taylor," Mary said. "Are you declining my invitation to tea?"

She'd invited him to tea? He'd been so busy chastising himself he hadn't heard her. Maybe his hearing was going, a sad state for a man of only twenty-seven years.

"There's a proposition I'd like to discuss with you before I finalize my purchases."

"Tea? Why yes, certainly. Tea would be good."

Praise God and his mother's prayers. She was inviting him into her private quarters to discuss business.

Mary Bishop led him through a storage area into a small back room of the log store, where she swung a pot hung over the coals at the fireplace. It was a cozy room with Ocean Waves—the quilt pattern he noted on the bed just beyond a screen. A checkered tablecloth matched pillows on the four chairs set around the square table.

Mary Bishop left the door to the store open so she could hear the bell jangle, he imagined, or for modesty's sake. The little dog lay in the doorway between the two rooms, head on paws stretched out. Richard didn't see many animals inside the stores he sold to. He kind of liked the comfort the little rust-and-white spaniel brought.

"I realize this may be somewhat presumptuous on my part," Mary said as she set the tea cozy and pot of loose tea on the table. "For a while now, I've had this idea but haven't known how to implement it. I'm not sure if your employers, the Barbour Brothers, will allow it, but I do think you have the means and ability to do what I'm thinking."

"It's nothing. . .illegal you'd be asking of me now, is it?" *There I go again!* Richard thought. *Why can't I just wait things out!*

Mary frowned. "Oh no, nothing illegal at all. It was your working for more than one employer at a time that I wondered over. Let me explain."

She used her apron to pick up the handle of the hot pot and poured steaming water over the tea leaves in his mug. "We'll let that steep a bit," she told him, putting the pot back. She sat across from him at the table, brushed at absent crumbs, her eyes on the tablecloth. She had the most graceful hands.

"Here's what I've been thinking," she continued. "I do a fair business in this store, but I'm dependent upon people coming to me for their purchases. Where I came from, back in Wisconsin, my father ran a store. The Indians and local people bought there, but when my father decided to service outposts, taking his wares up the streams to the Indians and others living along the creeks and rivers, his business improved. He no longer needed to wait for people to come to him; he went to them."

"Very resourceful," Richard said. And it was.

She stood to finish the tea, straining it, dumping the tea leaves into a separate tin possibly to be used again. *She's a frugal one.* "It may be a little strong for you," she said. "Dale, my husband, always resisted tepid."

"Never liked tepid myself," he assured her. Her smile lit her face, those violet-blue eyes. They stared at each other for a moment until she looked away. This woman certainly wasn't tepid! Had he embarrassed her?

"So where was I?" she said.

"Your story of your resourceful father." Richard took a sip. He longed to wipe his nose but had forgotten his handkerchief, so he sniffed.

She sat back down and took a drink of her tea. The moisture from the cup brought a fine mist to her upper lip. She was quite a lovely woman, he decided. Perfectly arched brown eyebrows. Luminescent skin lacking blemishes or brown spots, which was rare for someone of her age, which must be close to forty, maybe even fifty with such pure white hair. She combed it folded softly over her ears into a thick bun at the back of her neck. He'd seen lovely ivory combs holding the bun when he'd followed her into the back room.

"My father taught me to look for other options in business, that one always had to be either the very best at something, be the biggest, or provide added value for one's customers," Mary told him. "He chose the latter of those three, and that's what I want to do, too. So here's my plan. What if you were to not only visit local establishments to sell your thread, but were to also sell to individual homes along the way, showing skeins or hanks, offering new thread barrels? I could make up more convenient skeins from the thread I purchase from you, which you could sell. Along with books of cloth, thimbles, lace, ribbon—the sorts of things women are always needing but must wait for until they come in to town or send their fathers or husbands in here, never being certain if what their men bring home will really be what they wanted."

He was impressed with her idea. "We might want to include a few pots and pans," Richard said, expanding on it. "But always the latest items a woman might need, indeed."

"Can you sharpen scissors?"

"I'll learn."

"You'd have to be exclusive to my establishment, though you could continue to take orders for the Barbour Brothers' threads sold in their spools and deliver them to other stores around. But sales to individual homes, those would come from my store."

"I'd need a cart for my horse to pull."

"That could be arranged," Mary told him. "And you'd earn a percentage from what you sold, the amount to be deducted from the cost of the cart until it was paid for, assuming you'd want to own the cart eventually."

Richard thought about that. "To begin with, I'd take the percentage in cash," he said. "I've no need for a cart until we see how this works."

"Very good," Mary said. "Does fifteen percent sound fair?"

"Indeed it does," he said. More than fair. He'd make her pleased she'd trusted in him. "And I see no problem with the Barbours. I'll still be taking orders for their thread and even making it possible for them to sell more." He reached out his hand to shake hers, hesitated, and then said, "Ought we sign something officially?"

"I don't think that's necessary," Mary Bishop said. "My husband always said a contract was only as good as the man—or woman—who signed it."

"I think I would have liked your husband," he told her. "What can I do to assist?"

"First, we need to decide on the thread order and get that Rosa Red sent out," she told him. "Then I'll show you the cart."

He retrieved order forms from the front, the little dog tagging along beside him, her nails clicking on the floor. Mary read the papers at the table, sipping tea. He smelled lavender stronger than the tea leaves coming from her person, a pleasant scent indeed.

They'd just finished up the order when the doorbell dangled. Mary lifted her eyes to the outside door.

"Mary," the man called out. "Is my order ready?"

"Yes indeed, Mr. Lawson," she told him as she rose. The man cast his eyes through the open door to the private area, where Richard sat. He caught Richard's gaze.

"I see you have company," he said. "I can come back later."

His words held scorn, and Richard hoped his presence didn't tarnish Mary's reputation.

"We're doing business," she said.

"And I was just about to leave," Richard said as he stepped through the door and reached for the man's hand and introduced himself. "May I carry the box to your wagon for you?" he asked.

"Carry my box? No. I can handle it myself," Mr. Lawson scoffed.

For some reason, the man appeared annoyed as he hoisted the box from the floor. Perhaps that's what caused his abrupt movements, which sent his elbow against Richard's sample bag, which then slid on its hard leather toward the jar of buttons sitting on the pine slab counter. Richard's leather bag flopped open, and out spilled the cones of thread that rolled like peeled logs against the button jar, sending it flying.

The dog barked.

Richard reached for the cones.

Mary grabbed for the jar.

But her hand gripped too tightly. The jar shattered within her palm, sending buttons and shards of glass to the floor and blood pouring from Mary's hand.

"Ah, Mary, I'm so sorry," Lawson said tossing his box to the floor inches from Richard's boots. "Such a clumsy man." *Was he speaking of himself?*

Richard grabbed a linen towel and held Mary's injured palm. Worried that he might be forcing glass into her palm but wanting to slow the bleeding, he pressed with the towel.

"You've cut yourself, and it's all my fault," Lawson said.

"It was my spools of thread," Richard said. "I'm so sorry."

"Let me take care of you," Lawson ordered. He literally pushed Richard out of the way, grabbing at Mary's hand. "Mr. Taylor is it? You'd best run and get the doctor while I bandage this up."

"I have no idea where the doctor is," Richard said, still pressing the towel to Mary's palm. "You go."

"Ach!" the old rancher said, disgusted. "I need to take care of Mary. I've caused this."

"I can take care of myself," Mary said. She jerked her hand from Richard's and Lawson's pull and scurried around as though to find her hat or shawl.

Richard would rather have been holding Mary's hand than running for the doctor, but clearly she didn't need two men arguing about how to take care of her. His mother would be rolling his eyes at his lack of manners. He stepped back.

"I'll go at once," Richard said, deciding he could ask after the doctor's location from someone on the ferry. He picked up Lacy and put her in the back room, away from the glass, then headed out the door, hoping to catch the ferry on this side of the river. That was how things happened with him, he thought as he caught the ferryman's eye. His life was made up of splinters of bad following anything good.

❄

"You'll need help now, Mary. Don't be so proud you can't accept it," Laird told her after the doctor left.

"I'll do just fine," she said. The stitches hurt more than she cared to admit, and halfway through the surgery she'd wondered if maybe she should have accepted the second dose of laudanum to numb the pain. The stitches ran across her palm, making her right hand stiff as if frozen. For how long, she didn't know. "The good Lord gave me two hands, Mr. Lawson. I'm sure I'll do fine."

"I can help," Richard said, and when she started to protest, he added, "To proceed on our business arrangement."

"What would that be?" Laird turned, becoming instantly proprietary. Mary needed to stop that yeast from rising.

"My business arrangements are private, Mr. Lawson," she said. To Richard she said, "Yes, you can assist, Mr. Taylor. And Mr. Lawson, what you can do to be of assistance is please deliver these buttons to the Widow Mason. That is, if you truly want to help," she said.

"Of course I do, Mary. Mrs. Bishop," he corrected. "Anything at all." Mary thought she heard him mumbling under his breath something about "all those children scampering about." Glumly, Laird left, taking the buttons that Richard had carefully sorted from glass and washed.

Richard's presence calmed her for some reason, even though Mary wished she could lick her wounds in private. She'd told him he ought to telegraph the order, then return tomorrow to begin setting up the cart.

"I need to rest now," Mary said.

"Agreed," he said. He smiled shyly, adding, "Just one more thing." He grabbed the broom and swept again to make sure no glass remained caught on the puncheon floor and then wiped the pine with a damp cloth. Mary wasn't sure she'd ever seen a man on his knees with a wash rag. No, she was sure of it; she never had. When he finished, she opened the door to the back room, and Lacy came bounding out, sniffing at Mary's bandage then lifting her front paws onto Richard's top boots as he stood.

"It's all fine." He patted the dog then looked at Mary. "Except for your mistress. I'll put the sign on the door saying you're closed today if you'd like. Or if you trust me, I could come back and begin putting things together and help your customers, too. It might give me a better idea of your stock."

Mary sighed. She couldn't afford to put things on hold. "Yes. I will need help at least for a time. There's a cart and harness in the shed out back. It's covered, fortunately." For the past year, she'd been working on the cart herself, making drawers for buttons and needles, allowing shelves for books of cloth. She had the heavy, round, scissors sharpener attached to the bottom that could be removed and set up outside a patron's home. Mary was glad the roads would be drying up soon and her new partner wouldn't get bogged down in the mud. She'd be bogged down in this store, though. She couldn't even sweep the floor with one hand, could she?

She heard a familiar patter on the shake roof, and Mary looked up, holding her right hand above her waist with her left to keep it from throbbing, which it did when she forgot and put it at her side. She guessed she'd have to use that sling for a while.

"I could have sworn we had sun, and now it's pouring," Richard said.

"It'll let up soon, and we'll have our sun breaks," she told him. "Little gifts to remind us that there is always sunshine after a rain." And soon her hand would heal, too, but not soon enough. She'd need his sales more than ever now with a doctor bill she hadn't anticipated. Laird would insist on paying it, but that would obligate her to him—and she wanted that less than a bill. Or worse, he'd come by more often offering to "help her out" if she didn't let him pay. She'd have to find a way to deal with that.

"I'll make a big circle around the region and keep track of purchases our customers make so we can follow up the next time I swing by," Richard said. Mary liked that he already said "our" customers. "Tug their memories about what they might be running out of since they didn't buy it last time."

"That's a wonderful idea," Mary told him. She sat on the plank chair Dale had made.

"Let's put the sling on," Richard said.

"Well, all right." She knew it would help. His long fingers—musician's hands—lifted her wounded palm, and she felt the tenderness of his care like sunlight kissing the rain. He slipped the cloth triangle around her neck, and she could feel his breath on her cheek. Her steady heart took flight. "I'm. . .I'm. . . thank you. And for your good idea of keeping ledgers for each customer to anticipate what they might need."

He beamed. "I clerked for the army. North," he said. "Keeping track's easy for me. By the way, I got a good look at the Smith's store. Smells of fresh lumber all right, and shelves are already stocked." Mary frowned. "But you've a much better supply of sewing things," he said. "I'll put the order in and return, and if you're up to it, we can choose what bolts of cotton you want to put into the cart for sales. You know who's out there and what they'll be interested in. And don't you worry over the doctor bill. My thread sent your jar careening; I'll take a smaller percentage from the cart sales until that bill is paid."

Mary nodded and headed into the back room, listening for the door to close when Richard left. She lay down on the rope mattress, Lacy beside her. She could rest with this plan in place, and she didn't mind accepting his suggestion as a way to pay for the doctor. That would take Laird out of the equation. *Thank You, God,* she prayed as she slipped off to sleep, *for tending to details even if gleaned from the shards of a broken jar.*

216

Chapter 3

There's Nelia Williams and her spinster sister, Ruthie. Nelia's a fine seamstress," Mary told Richard, "but I don't think Ruthie sews much. She's great with horses, though, and works leather in the winter." Four days had passed, and in the interim Mary had rested her hand on a pillow while Richard tended the store, loading the cart during sun breaks and letting Laird Lawson know all was under control each time he came by talking about the busy activity at Smith's new store, raving about the pickle barrel and the little potbelly stove Smith installed instead of the sooty old cat-and-clay fireplace that warmed Mary's logs or the big brick one at Cooley & Company. Mary put on her best face for Laird, assuring him that competition was the American way and good for business. The town's fathers suggested that with the sawmill and Moyer's Sash & Door Factory open now, she ought to abandon the old log store and build a new clapboard one. Modernize, they advised; find a better location, they offered; look more prosperous, they concluded. Now Mr. Smith had done just that.

But she and Dale had built this cabin together, chinking the logs themselves using pine needles, dried grass, and clay from the bank of the Calapooia River flowing beside them. Together she and her husband had served the good people of Brownsville. They'd done so for five years until Dale had taken sick with smallpox and died.

Many in the region had succumbed to the epidemic in 1863, and Mary thought it a miracle that she had not. But after Dale died, she'd wished for months that she'd gone with him. Being surrounded by the logs squared at the end by his hands, watching the sunlight filter through the isinglass windows he'd made himself kept Dale close to her heart. Why, she'd even used the froe to split logs into boards for shingles and door planks. They'd put their sweat and soul into the log home and business. She couldn't imagine ever leaving it.

"What is Miss William's preference, wool or cotton?" Richard asked.

"Nelia tends to use wool for quilts and such, so we'll need a heavy thread for them with good, thick needles even though she can sew twelve stitches to the inch, or so they've told me."

Richard whistled. "That's mighty fine stitching," he said. "Maybe we should carry eyeglasses. They might have eyestrain from such detailed work. Or maybe something for headaches."

"I believe you're right, Mr. Taylor," Mary said. She wondered how he'd finesse them into buying eyeglasses without offending them. Everyone knew eyeglasses were for the elderly or weak. Mary pushed her own eyeglasses up on her nose. She'd worn glasses since she was a child. "Cotton, too, though. Good cotton material," Mary continued. She liked talking with Richard about her inventory. He nodded enthusiastically and smiled at her often without carrying any obligation the way Laird's smiles did. They might carry something else, but Mary didn't want to think of that. She was in business with this man, nothing more.

Richard made notes in a ledger book.

"What about quilt patterns?" he said. "I know you're not a quilter, but—"

"I have patterns here," she said and rose to find them. "I know the women exchange block patterns, but these are new," she told him. "It's a Bible quilt-block book. The squares have names like Garden of Eden, Jacob's Ladder, Job's Tear. Oh, and look at this one, Storm at Sea. It'll require a sharp scissors to get those curves right."

Richard said, "Even though the design has no rounded curves, it looks like it does from the placement and size of the triangles."

"Really?" Mary said. "There aren't any curved pieces?" She was amazed, but then she had a hard time even seeing the squares in the pattern until Richard ran his finger around the edges of the triangular pieces, his hand over her fingers as he traced the pieces making the curved design. Mary felt a tingle at her wound, though his hand covered her left one, not the wounded palm. The tingling wasn't unpleasant, more of a surprise. She let his hand linger, felt the slightest callous and the greater warmth of his hand over hers.

She cleared her throat, pulled her hand out. "Storm at Sea. Quite turbulent," she said as she tried to figure what to do with her hand. Why was she so fidgety all of a sudden?

"Bessie Thompson, over by Amelia, she'll buy thread," Mary said collecting her wits. "Abigail Schultz outside of Lebanon will. Her father's the blacksmith there. She looks after him. She's a widow, like me. Oh, and Matilda Kaliska. Now there's a seamstress! Her wedding dresses of satin and silk could win over New York if she had a way to get them there. Maybe when the train comes to Brownsville, the world will widen for Matilda." Mary told him of several more women who came into her store—or used to—that she thought would be amenable to having a handsome man bring wares right to their cabins.

"You leave it to me," Richard said. "I'll convince them to reach beyond scraps for quilts, to invest in good cotton with whole colors and pieces made with a mix of Hoyle's Wave or brown serpentine stripes. You have a good selection, Mary. Better than at either Smith's or Cooley & Company."

"Thank you." Her face grew warm at the compliment. "I've done as well as I could, but someone who knows material and thread as you do will expand on that. I do believe our partnership is off to a very good start."

"We're off to a very good start indeed," he told her. She wondered if the twinkle in his eye emphasized only a business transaction. Foolishly, she hoped it didn't.

❄

Mary's hand throbbed, and she found even dressing took more time and energy than she'd ever imagined. Richard had performed a number of tasks that eased her day, and with him gone, she was truly discovering how difficult it was to have the use of only one hand. Even if Richard was successful with his outlying sales, a venture he'd been off on for more than two weeks now, she had to do something to bring customers into the store and perhaps have a little help as well. Brushing off her one dress because she needed help washing clothes could only go on for so long.

Flower seeds had arrived, but she needed a way to let people know they were here. Richard loved a woman who sewed. She wondered if he liked a woman who gardened? "That's so silly of me," Mary told the dog. "Why worry about what Mr. Taylor likes one whit? But he did look flummoxed after he traced the quilt block with my fingers." The thought renewed the tingling in her palm. "Maybe he felt too. . .oh, for heaven's sake." She was acting like a schoolgirl.

Mary moved her thoughts back to work. She wished they had a newspaper in town so she could place an advertisement. She decided to post a notice at the church. Surely the growing of flowers was an act of faith. One planted a seed unseen beneath the sod and waited for it to grow and bloom. It was a metaphor of hope. She'd have to close the store while she went to speak to the pastor, missing customers who might be coming in. Her log-cabin store was the first commercial establishment on this side of the river. When ferry passengers approached, she hoped they'd come in before crossing over to the other establishments. But today, she had to take the risk and close up so she could talk to the Presbyterian pastor. Besides, she wanted to survey the competition.

With her left hand, she turned the key, and Lacy trotted beside her as she boarded the ferry, crossed the Calapooia, and headed toward the church.

"Good morning, Pastor Blaine," she said when she found him setting out flowers in window boxes. "Lovely day, isn't it?"

"Indeed it is. April's my favorite time." He pulled on his bushy mustache, which hung like a lazy caterpillar over his lip. "Love to see the daffodils popping up."

"That's the very reason I stopped by," Mary said. "I want to place a sign to let the good people of Brownsville know that I have newly arrived flower seeds," she said.

"Do you now? Well, that's interesting, as Mr. Smith just asked the same thing of me."

"He did? Mr. Smith is a Presbyterian?"

"You didn't see him in church on Sunday last?"

"I guess I didn't recognize him," she said.

"Well he's got access to nurseries in the East with actual starts of marigolds and daisies not to mention a dozen more varieties."

"Actual starts. When will they arrive, do you know?"

"Already have, and I can tell you that the ladies of the congregation are quite excited about it."

"I imagine they are."

"Surprised me. Most of the time people get sent seeds from home. Makes them feel well, like they have a little of what they left behind planted in their yards. But things change." He pontificated now. "There's a time to weep and—"

"A time to laugh," Mary finished though she didn't feel much like laughing. Instead she walked away. Smith had starts, the pastor said. The blooms would be much further along than on any plants produced by customers planting Mary's seeds.

She walked to Smith's store to see what he did have. She wished she hadn't. The scent of new lumber filled her head as she slowly turned around, her eyes taking in the rich wares finely displayed. Maybe there was something to a clapboard establishment without the logs to remind one of earlier days. This was progress; even she could see that. Near the window were petunias and dahlias growing inside squash halves as though they'd been started a month ago. The seeds may have come from back East, but it was clear Mr. Smith had planted them and had gotten them going right here in Brownsville. His customers wouldn't care; they'd just be pleased to see them nearly ready to line their paths and fill their window boxes.

But of greatest interest was Smith's inventory of furniture! Bedsteads and lamps and harvest tables with carved legs stately stood next to parlor tables and copper-lined tobacco stands. People wouldn't have to imagine what a new dresser would look like when they perused a catalog; they'd be able to see what their purchase would look like, maybe even buy it right off the store floor! She didn't see much in the way of cloth books or thread, so perhaps she'd be all right, especially with Richard selling far and wide.

A few customers nodded to Mary, the women asking about her hand while looking a little guilty that they were enjoying this newest establishment. Why, Smith was even serving cinnamon rolls. He'd attract women with his flowers and the men with his food. What did that leave her?

Mary had no answer to that question as she rode the ferry across the Calapooia to her comforting log store.

"I told people to come back in a little bit," Jennifer Mason told Mary. The child waited outside on the log bench, her short legs swinging and bobbing her braids at the same time.

"Thank you for that," Mary said as she pulled the heavy iron key from the leather cord around her neck. She fumbled with her left hand, and Jennifer jumped up to assist. "My ma is sure happy for those buttons you sent over," Jennifer said. "And the molasses, too. I thought I'd come by to save Mr. Lawson the trouble of delivering your leavings." The child was missing her two front teeth, so *Lawson* came out as *Lawthon*. "I'm not so sure he likes children."

"Oh, he just hasn't been around them much," Mary said.

"You haven't either, but you don't frown when the baby smacks her messy hand on your forehead."

The image and Jennifer's toothless words made Mary smile. "It's something new to him. Give him a little time," Mary said. "Thanks for your help with the key. And for advising customers to return. I knew that might happen when I closed." The thought reminded her of Smith's foray into flowers, and she got addled all over again.

"Ma told me I'm to help you while your hand is so bad."

Mary looked at the wiry child and wondered if she could even drag a bag of rice from the storeroom, let alone lift it to fill the pottery. "Tell your mama that's very kind, but I'm doing fine."

"I know I don't look strong, but I am." The girl flexed her thin arms, showing a bump little larger than a mosquito bite beneath thin calico. "And Ma says you give a gift when you let people help you."

"But can you drag a fifty-pound sack of rice or flour from the back room?" Mary asked.

The girl stood thoughtful. "No, ma'am. But I can carry it here a bucket at a time. I can keep it filled just fine."

"How old are you, Jennifer?"

"Eight and a half. How old are you?"

"Thirty," Mary said.

"That's a lot of miles," Jennifer said without smiling.

"Indeed it is."

"Tell your Mama I accept her offer of your help, Jennifer. You've a fine mind and just the right amount of muscle."

"I can start by getting rid of that old hard candy, Mrs. Bishop." Mary smiled at the child's *Mithus Bithop* as she handed her the striped candy the girl pointed at. She and Jennifer would fill a wooden box lined with cheesecloth they could fold over to keep the spiders from dropping in the rice, and that would free up the large stoneware pot for pickles. She could serve pickles with the best of them. When Richard Taylor returned, she'd have him build a bin with a cover for the rice. Or maybe with her direction, she and Jennifer could build it together. She had no idea whether Richard Taylor knew one end of a hammer from the other, but he did know his needles and thread. Right now, that was a detail and a gift from heaven.

Chapter 4

After Richard's first circular route, he reported back about his sales. They were excellent! Mary could barely contain her glee at his success. At least she thought her heart started beating faster with the ledger results and not when his top boots first stepped through the door.

"It's your doing," he said. "You carry the right materials. That brass stencil you added at the last minute, the one for inking calling cards, it sold right away. We'll need to get a few more of those ordered in." They sat at Mary's table, tasting of tea.

"I'm just so surprised that you're in need of additional whole-color cloth," Mary said. "So many of the women quilt from their scraps using popular dress prints. I expected you to sell Prussian blues, the double pinks, and everyday calicos and ginghams, but solid red and some of silk? That chintz? And so much wool. Those are expensive European imports," Mary reminded him. "I'm just stunned that we need to order more. How did you do it?"

"Just my charm," he said. He grinned at her, and Mary felt a familiar flutter inside her stomach. She hoped she was just hungry. She needed to be hungry and not anything else. He showed absolutely no interest in her, she realized; and she didn't need to embarrass herself by allowing her feelings to ride on a fast horse only to take a tumble later.

They worked well together, and Mary loved his stories of his encounters with her neighbors. A few new families had moved into the region, and he brought them to life. His stories captured the essence of the men and women populating this new state. John Carpenter's wife, Adele, for example, sported a snaggletooth, but she made a black bean soup that he'd "crawl across glass to get another bowl of." Richard continued, "She bought up the cast-iron pot with the glass lid you had only one of. Seemed happy indeed to have a new pot for that soup."

Richard's left eye, the blue one, drooped just a bit. He looked tired. They'd reloaded the cart, and soon he'd be heading out. Mary offered him supper before he returned to his boarding room, and he accepted. He continued to tell stories as she prepared the grouse Laird had brought by.

"You're a superb cook, Mary," Richard said. "If things go sour with the store, you could always open up a boardinghouse."

Mary frowned.

"Oh, I didn't mean they will. My mother, rest her soul, always said my foot was attracted more to my mouth than my shoes. I'm sure the mercantile will do well." He stuffed dressing into his mouth, shaking his head.

Mary guessed that at least he was sensitive to a sour look on her face and did his best to recover.

"I almost had a request for corn seed," Richard told her. "But instead Mrs. Miner—yes, she's new—and her family told me that she'd brought just a half cup of corn seed with her from Iowa. She planted the seeds carefully only to discover that her rooster had come along behind her and gobbled up each seed."

"Oh," Mary said. "How awfully discouraging to have brought those seeds all that way and then lose them to the rooster."

"Not for Mrs. Miner. When she realized it, she killed the rooster, cleaned out his crop of the corn seeds, and kept on planting. They had the rooster for supper."

Mary laughed. She'd missed laughing with a man across her table. "Mrs. Miner is a major gardener!"

After supper they shared a coffee, and Richard saved his last stories about the women who bought cloth. "Your selection is the best of any stores in the region. You should just specialize in selling fine fabrics."

"The competition is stiff. Cooley & Company sells to farmers, and Smith is obviously targeting the household furnishing market along with his flower seeds." She heard the grumble in her own voice and didn't like it. "But I can't afford to limit myself to women's things; it's the men who come in and authorize the sales."

"Women who quilt will figure out a way to get their menfolk to buy," he assured her. "They'll keep at it through thick and thin, those women. Making things for the families while indulging in beauty for its own sake. I love a committed quilter," he added.

Mary sighed inwardly. A committed quilter she was not.

❄

Weeks passed, and Mary found herself remembering looks and words of Richard Taylor. She daydreamed about what a favorite color of his might be or when his birthday was. At first she felt disloyal to Dale, but she thought that Richard and Dale would have been friends if Dale had lived, and that eased her fears. She told herself she simply looked forward to Richard's return and his stories. But then she ordered a new face powder and tried a rose scent for her soaps because he'd mentioned once liking wild yellow roses.

They ended each restocking of the cart with a dinner and sitting outside the log cabin, watching the sun set.

"Nelia Williams, now there's a seamstress," Richard said. They sat outside the store on the bench on a hot July evening. The cart was loaded, and tomorrow Richard would leave again.

"Didn't I tell you that?" Mary chided. She'd almost lost count of the number of trips he'd made, and Mary admitted to herself that she was sad at the prospect of his leaving. She liked cooking supper for him before he headed to the boardinghouse, and she enjoyed his early-morning arrival where he was willing to take Lacy for a walk while Mary cooked up bacon and eggs and fried eggplant for their shared breakfast.

"Miss Williams and her sister, Ruthie, are working on a quilt together, Adam and Eve. Quite a production. Ruthie said they'll appliqué Eve in pink and give her a hoopskirt for modesty."

"Oh, for heaven's sake," Mary said.

"Apparently so."

They laughed.

"But they also took the Bible quilt-block pattern book, so I suspect they'll be working on a new quilt now." He sipped a sarsaparilla. "The wedding-dress maker. . .what was her name?"

"Matilda Kaliska?"

Richard nodded, and Mary was secretly pleased he hadn't been able to remember Matilda's name.

"That's the one. Cute as a button, and she does know her silks. Wanted taffeta, too. I told her we'd bring that on the next run. And Bessie Thompson bought a pair of glasses. Did I tell you that?"

"Did she?"

"I told her you'd said she made the finest stitches in the West and marveled at that close work."

"And that made her want to buy glasses?"

"Well, I told her I was personally partial to a woman confident enough to wear glasses so she could excel at her God-given talents."

Mary adjusted her spectacles on her nose. She wondered if he could see her blush, and then she scoffed at herself.

"What?" he said.

"Oh, nothing. It's just such a perfect salesman thing to say," she said. "And it worked."

"It did." But then he turned to look directly at Mary. "It worked because it's true. I do admire a woman who takes advantage of such things as glasses, knowing it will help her, and not letting wags talk her out of it because it might not be in fashion. A woman like you, Mary. I admire a woman like you."

"Oh," Mary said, and she found that flutter starting in her stomach, tingling at the healed stitches in her palm and making her breath come just a little shorter than she liked. "Well. Yes. My father made me admirable by insisting I wear glasses as a child."

"But as a grown woman you've continued because you knew it was a good thing. You chose for yourself, which is what admirable women do."

His tone and his gaze unnerved Mary, made her think he spoke of something more than glasses.

"Yes, Mary, you remind me of my mother in that way."

The mention of his mother brought her to reality. *He sees me as an older woman.* At least it was nice to know he admired his mother, but it was time she stopped daydreaming about Richard Taylor, making up stories that could only have disappointing endings.

"It's time I turned in," she said, standing.

"Must you?" He sounded disappointed. "I hope I didn't say anything to offend you. I'm terrible that way, my mother always said."

"Yes, your foot not fitting your mouth. But you're fine, Mr. Taylor. Your mother would be proud. Come along, Lacy. You enjoy the sunset. We'll get you sent off in the morning."

❄

As the months went by, and despite her admonition to not think of Richard as other than a business partner, Mary still found she anticipated Richard's return not just for his stories. It was pleasant to have a man around to talk with about politics, business, and the weather. She'd missed the presence of a deep, male voice, the way Richard devoured her food, making pleasing sounds as he consumed her blue kidney potato pie. She liked the sound of boots stomping on the doorstep and looked forward to September when oysters came available, as she hoped to soothe his palate with her oyster pie. She was just being. . . neighborly, that was all—though dreams of Richard Taylor eased into her sleep.

His skills as a salesman were unequaled, and Mary felt quite proud of herself for having gone into partnership with the man all those months before. She'd counted up her figures for the summer months and had expected things to slack off come autumn, but they'd continued to sell well from the cart. Her in-store sales had increased, as well, and little Jennifer had proven to be of fine help even after Mary got the use of her hand back.

In September while she spoke with the Knight brothers, who would bring oysters from the Willapa Bay area of Washington Territory, she was surprised by the arrival of the Williams sisters at the store. Both Nelia and Ruthie swirled in with their hoopskirts bouncing long after they'd stopped walking. Mary was pleased the walls of her log cabin store were smooth as taffeta and didn't catch the fabric of skirts as wide as wagons that hugged the edges as the women pushed through the door.

"How good to see you," Mary told them as she sent the Knight brothers on their way. "Mr. Taylor tells me you've been stitching up a storm."

"Oh, we have, we have." Nelia giggled.

"I certainly appreciate your business," Mary said. "What with the new store and Cooleys, too, it hasn't been an easy year, but your purchases have helped immensely."

"Well, Mr. Taylor—Richard—has made buying so easy," Ruthie said. She wore her hair in a tight bun usually, but this day curls floated out from behind her black bonnet. "And because of him, Nelia and I have found working to-gether on a project to be much more fun than each of us staying in our own lane, so to speak."

"Yes," Nelia added. "For the first time since Papa died, we've found something we both love. Ruthie always did the outside work, while I was the inside girl."

"We thought we'd come by and see what you had for wedding-dress material," Ruthie said.

"Oh, how wonderful," Mary said. "One of you is getting married?"

"Well, it's not official yet," Ruthie said, leaning in toward Mary. She whispered, "But one can't be too prepared now, can one? A wedding dress can take a long time to make. And then we have our quilt to finish, of course."

"Adam and Eve?" Mary asked.

"Oh, we finished that one. No, this is a special one, from the Bible quilt book we purchased. Job's Tears."

"Oh, right. I remember Mr. Taylor saying you'd bought that book."

"We are each making the blocks and so hoping ours will meet the test."

"Test?"

"Oh, it's nothing official." Ruthie chastised her sister. "We just have a surmising,"

"A surmising?" Mary asked. "I'm not sure I know what that means."

"Oh, silly me. We can't say any m-o-o-ore," Nelia sang out. "Let's just look at that silk and satin you have in stock, Mrs. Bishop. We can't wait for Richard—Mr. Taylor—to come back around in three weeks!"

Mary thought about the odd conversation after they left, but Jennifer's arrival and their walk to the garden to get her digging potatoes put the Williams sisters from her mind. It wasn't until a week or so later, when Matilda Kaliska came in, that she recalled the earlier visit by the sisters. Matilda, too, looked at wedding silks, but then she was a seamstress who specialized in wedding dresses.

"I hope to blend a deep purple taffeta with a lighter purple silk," Matilda said. "I'm going to cover the buttons. There'll be two dozen down the back, and I'll ruche the bodice. It'll be two pieces, the jacket and then a pleated back plate below the bustle on the skirt."

"It sounds lovely," Mary said. "Who is the lucky bride?"

Matilda blushed. "Oh, I can't say," she said. "It's a secret, but of course the bride-to-be hopes she meets the test." *Test. That word again.*

"Is there some sort of contest about?" Mary said.

"Contest? Oh no, nothing like that. I shouldn't have said anything. I need to pick up additional material for a quilt I'm making, too. Richard—Mr. Taylor— needs to come every week to keep me in supplies," she said, wagging her finger at Mary in a kindhearted way.

"I didn't know that you quilted, too. What pattern are you working on?" Mary asked as they walked toward the bolts of cloth on the shelf near the back of the store. Mary had decided to move her best sale items to the back so that customers had to walk all the way through the stoneware, furniture, and lanterns to reach them, thus being exposed to other products along the way.

"Storm at Sea," she said. "It's a Bible quilt block."

"Yes, I know." Mary's heart fluttered at the memory of Richard holding her hand over that troubling sea. "I could get you the book of—"

"Richard—Mr. Taylor—mentioned that he'd sold it, and then he drew the pattern on a piece of butcher paper from memory. His skill of recall is fabulous, and he so enjoys quilting. So many men discount the intricacies of a seamstress. He said he'd order in a book for me, but his sketch was sufficient to get me started. I've nearly completed it using Rosa Red thread. I just adore the feel of that flax thread—don't you? Oh, that's right, you don't quilt, do you? Richard— Mr. Taylor—mentioned that."

He'd talked about her? But it was her lack of something that was the focus of the conversation. Mary's heart sank.

Matilda bought two yards of plaid wool along with the purple taffeta and said she'd get whatever else she needed when "Richard—Mr. Taylor" came by next. "But Mary, I can't thank you enough for hiring him. His visits have brought such a delight to Mama and to me. And I believe I will take him up on his suggestion that I consider opening a shop in Brownsville proper. Of course I'd buy all my materials from you, Mary. Richard—Mr. Taylor—said it would be only right since it's your store that gave me the confidence to branch out."

Richard—Mr. Taylor—had apparently acquired a spread-out name, as each of his customers Mary encountered referred to him with both his informal and then formal titles. Well, Richard—Mr. Taylor—was like that, Mary supposed. It was part of his charm, and she should be grateful; her business was in the black for the first time since Dale's death.

But she wasn't grateful at that moment; she was envious, not a helpful emotion to harbor at all.

Chapter 5

Why Bessie, it's so good to see you," Mary told the woman, who
sported new glasses.

"It's good to see you, too, Mary. Now that I can." She adjusted
her spectacles. "I had no idea what all I'd been missing not being able to see,
don't you know?"

"And still you made the most endearing quilts," Mary said. "Even without
glasses."

"Oh, but they'll be better than ever now. That's what Richard—Mr. Taylor—
told me. In fact, that's why I'm here. I'm so hoping I can meet the test of a truly
fine quilter."

"What test would that be?" Mary asked. Though she didn't know why, her
stomach hurt in anticipation of what Bessie might tell her about this infamous
test. . .and Richard's part in it.

"Well, I shouldn't say, really, but Richard—Mr. Taylor—has as much as said
that if he can find a woman who is truly devoted to her quilting; who stitches
patterns to give away, showing her generous spirit; who also serves her family,
using scrap pieces quilted to keep them warm and to demonstrate her love for
them; and who quilts with color and design to honor the gift of creativity given
by our Creator; well, that's the kind of woman who meets his test for a bride."

"Bride?"

"Yes. Bride. I took it to mean that he'll marry a woman who meets his test
and that he was too shy to simply come out and ask me, at least not before the
quilt blocks are finished. And surely, I do meet his test, don't you know? What
with my glasses to help me see better. I know he wanted that for me, to improve
my skills, so surely, well. . ." She lowered her eyes and fluttered her lashes to
Mary's stunned stare.

"And what quilt pattern would you be working on to meet the test?" Mary
asked.

"It's from the Bible quilt-blocks book. Richard drew patterns from
memory—he's so gifted. He suggested Road to Jerusalem, and I adore it. It's not
unlike Road to California, but it has so much more spiritual meaning behind it,
don't you know? Who wants to go to California anyway? I'll write my signature

on the blocks, but I plan to give it away as a sign of my generosity. The new owner will know whose work it is. Richard loves a generous woman."

"Does he now?"

"Solids mean a woman has the means to purchase whole cloth new and not just piece a quilt top together from her father's old pants or mama's aprons. Besides, a good solid red will set off my colored "roads" to Jerusalem just perfectly. And I get to use that Rosa Red, don't you know?"

Mary did not know. What she did know was that Richard—Mr. Taylor from now on to her—had somehow suggested to her best customers that if they created the kind of quilt he wanted that he'd request their hand in marriage. His behavior was. . .appalling, outrageous. Worse, terrifying, because it meant that once he actually chose one of the women who met his spurious test, the sales to the other customers would drop. The good news of the past summer with increased sales would become the worst news she could have. There'd be few customers wanting cloth and fabric doo-dads once word of his scheme got out. She may as well close down the store now.

After Bessie left, Laird Lawson interrupted Mary's anger and growing self-pity by shyly entering the store, hat in hand. "Mrs. Bishop," he said, "I wonder if you could, that is, if you'd be so kind as to help me find the proper gift, proper birthday present, for a woman friend of mine."

Oh, good grief, now he wants to buy me a birthday present? How did he even know my birthday was next week?

"Mr. Lawson, it's really not necessary."

"Oh, but it is," he said. "I find her company to be quite pleasant. . .when the babies are put to bed. And the other children quite well mannered. She's a good cook, too, Mrs. Mason is."

"Oh, you're looking for a present for Widow Mason," Mary breathed.

"Yes, of course."

Mary recovered quickly. "Would you like something in personal wear such as jewelry? Or store-bought clothing? Or—"

"Something practical," he told her. "Say Geer's Improved Cherry Stoner," he pointed to the object.

"Mr. Lawson, are you hoping to impress the widow? Because if you are, then buying something she might never buy for herself even if she could afford it will tell her more than if you bring her an improved cherry stoner."

"But she's a woman who is both practical and. . .lovely," he said. Color rose past his muttonchop sideburns up to his eyes.

"That she is. So let's consider something both practical and lovely." She moved toward the window and removed a fashionable hat. "Every woman needs new felt, and one that complements her face with a dash of style is even better."

He tested the felt thicknesses with his fingers then picked up another hat and surveyed the lining, even sniffed the white silk flowers that adorned the edges of the hat Mary handed to him next, hoping he'd buy it. She was grateful she'd had Jennifer dust the hats after school yesterday. "And this hatpin, with the cherub on the end, I like it best of all of these." Mary took the long pin from behind the glass case.

"It would honor her role as a mother," he said turning the metal piece in his hands.

"It would indeed."

"I'll take them both," he said and waited while Mary wrapped the hatbox and placed the hatpin, all eighteen inches of it, in a velvet pocket bag. "I hope you don't mind my not coming in as much to check on how things are going," Laird said. "But this is all because of you, Mrs. Bishop." He put his own hat back on then lifted the hatbox. "If you hadn't asked me to deliver those buttons and all the things since, I might never have discovered what a fine woman Mrs. Mason is."

"I'm glad for you, Mr. Lawson. Very glad indeed."

"I'm glad for me, too," he said and smiled like a schoolboy.

And Mary was pleased for him despite the fact that after he left she shut the door, turned the CLOSED sign out, and walked to her back room. This temporary lull of romance couldn't take away the sour taste of what Richard Taylor was doing to her customers. What was she to do? She couldn't allow this charade to continue; her own integrity was at stake with her partner proposing such "tests." But she also didn't know how she'd manage the loss of sales that would surely follow the revelation of what he'd done. Worst of all, it was clear that Richard Taylor loved quilting and the women who quilted, which left her without a stitch of a chance to sew him to her side. "What am I to do?" she prayed. "This isn't the kind of detail I thought I'd ever have to manage again," she said, "this. . .this. . .falling in love." Lacy whined, and Mary picked the little dog up, cuddling at her neck. Then she lay down on her bed and wept.

❄

"What's wrong?" Mr. Taylor said. "You've barely spoken a word to me since I got back, and I do so miss our evening chat over your sumptuous meals. Those tomato figs are beyond description, as good as anything created by the chef at the Astoria in New York." He kissed his fingertips and blew them toward her. She didn't smile. "Haven't the sales been good? Hasn't our association been successful? I thought you enjoyed our time together. I know I do."

"Do you? Even though I don't quilt and couldn't possibly meet your test?"

She nearly spit the word *test*.

"Mary, what is it?"

"I am absolutely torn, Mr. Taylor, absolutely torn." She held a handkerchief and found as she pulled it through her damp palm that the wound was still sensitive even after seven months. If she hadn't cut herself, maybe she would have come to her senses and taken the cart on her own, hiring someone to work the store while she was gone. Maybe she'd have been more attentive to how charm could also be deceptive. Maybe he didn't even know of his bifurcated ways.

"About what? What are you torn about?" He motioned for her to sit on the bench outside the store.

"You're deluding my customers into thinking that if they create the very best quilt block they'll have met your 'test', and you'll marry one of them. Only they don't know that there are other women carrying on with the same 'surmising', as the Williams sisters put it."

"Ruthie and Nelia?"

"And Bessie and Matilda. I have no idea how many more. The others just haven't come into the store to add to their supplies or maybe to gloat a bit and tell me of their good fortune."

"Why would they gloat to you?" he asked. "You're not a quilter nor in the market for marriage, are you?"

His words wounded deeper than she'd thought.

"I'm still a young woman," she whispered. "Barely thirty."

"But. . .you seem wise, the kind of wise that comes with age. And you're devoted to your deceased husband. I just thought. . .and your hair—"

"Has been white since I was twelve," she snapped, "not that it's any matter to you nor this discussion. Wise," she scoffed. "Not wise enough to see through you."

"But I didn't, that is, I never meant to deceive them. It's true I love a woman who sews beautifully. I love the stitching like tiny commas in a grand manuscript. Quilt patterns are like. . .engineering feats, getting color to create movement, taking your eyes to places they wouldn't otherwise go."

"And taking Bessie's eyes to places they wouldn't have gone either."

"What?"

"You convinced her to buy glasses suggesting. . .well, you know."

"Now Mary, that's not true. I told her she could sew even better if she could see, and that's the truth. The rest have been truthful things said, too. I mean, they love being inspired. That's all it is, just inspiration for their creativity."

"They see it as something more, Mr. Taylor. And when they find out, there'll be—oh—"

Perhaps he did intend to marry one of them. At least *all* of the women wouldn't be upset with him and with her for hiring him in the first place if he actually chose a woman. Still, they'd be distressed because they all thought they were special to him. "And do you intend to marry one of the quilters who meets your test?" she asked. Her heart pounded as she feared his answer.

"Well, I hadn't really thought they'd take it that way. I only meant to inspire. Maybe I can back off, start finding flaws in their work. I hadn't thought that—" He looked at Mary. "I never intended to hurt you or your log cabin store in any way. I only wanted to be successful," he finished, as though speaking to himself.

Mary didn't like the idea of his now finding fault with a customer's skill, and she told him so. "There's nothing worse than demeaning a potential buyer."

"I know, I know." He tugged at the yellow curl at the back of his neck. "A terrible predicament I've put us in, isn't it?"

"It is indeed. We'll just have to think of a way to save the store and their dignity," Mary said. "But we may not be able to save you from a marriage you never intended."

"Maybe I'll just have to choose," he said.

Mary swallowed. "Maybe you will."

❄

Mary wasn't really angry with Richard anymore. She didn't envy him his current circuit, but maybe he'd come up with a plan after seeing each of them again, seeing them with new eyes. And Mary had to accept that her moments of camaraderie with Richard Taylor would have to end. Once winter came and the circuit could naturally be closed down until spring, it would be the ideal time for Mr. Taylor to move on. She'd miss him—that was certain—but his attention had been a good reminder for her of what she and Dale had had. Love grew like a vine, but it had to have good roots planted in healthy soil. She didn't really know much about Richard Taylor's soil or his soul.

A light snow fell, putting her into the mood for Christmas. A November bazaar was planned at the Presbyterian church, where there'd be sleigh rides and sledding outdoors if they had enough snow. Inside, the women of Brownsville would bring their wares for sale and maybe just a little flaunting. The kids would bob for apples. It would be a festive time.

Mary busied herself with preparing for the event. She and Jennifer walked to the hills to saw branches of mistletoe from the trees and hang the clusters beneath the fir shed to dry so they could be wrapped into wreaths. She'd ordered in sleigh bells and holiday candles with white stripes on red and a peppermint candy so strong it scented the entire store and lodged itself into the logs as well. Mary also ordered in more red material since so much had been used through the year, and with the great interest in quilts, Mary made sure she had plenty of cotton batting and enough cheaper cloth for backing. At least they might all finish their quilts before running Richard out of town.

When Richard Taylor returned, he said little about what had happened, but he had new orders from her customers. "I told them they'd have to come into town to get these." He handed the lists to Mary. "Circuits only for spring, summer, and fall, I told them."

"And did they, that is, are you. . . ?"

"Engaged? No. I think I've dodged that bullet at least for this season. I've told them I knew they'd need just a little more time to create the perfect quilt and suggested they might want to make a quilt for the pastor's wife as a gesture of confidence in her husband, each making a block and signing it." He looked sad to Mary, and she saw genuine remorse in the lines of his face. "I thought if I diverted them from, well, marriage thoughts to spiritual ones, they might surmise something other than their upcoming engagement."

"I hope you've ducked a bullet," Mary said. "And if you have, I have, too, since we're in this skirmish together."

"There are other things I'd rather be in with you," Richard Taylor said, "but I'll take what I can get." He smiled, and Mary thought again that he just didn't realize the power of his words to touch a woman's heart.

❄

The Christmas bazaar was held right after Thanksgiving, and Jennifer helped Mary take seasonal items to the church, things Mary donated that they'd sell along with fruitcakes and pies, saddles and harnesses, and dolls and wooden trains made for the children by the good citizens of the region. A portion of each sale went to the widows and orphans fund, so people tended to be generous in their purchases. Holly garlands spirited the hallway and led visitors into the sanctuary, where chairs had been lined around the walls so the children could play games. Presbyterians didn't dance, but they had lively games with music. And of course, the Christmas items for sale brought people out to browse, drink apple cider, and catch up on the news.

Mary was dressed in her almost-best dress, a wide, red velvet skirt and jacket with white rabbit trim that looped like a garland around the skirt and formed a soft collar at the jacket's neck. She'd lost weight these past months since she'd worn the dress last year. *Maybe it was having the use of only one hand for so long*, she thought. She could eat or work, one or the other, but not both, and that could account for the slenderizing of her waist, as she always had work to do.

Richard stood with the men, looking dapper with his top boots. Mary noticed that a few of the younger men had latched on to that look by sporting new top boots, too. Smith must have ordered in several pairs because Cooley didn't carry such; he relied on catalog orders he'd fill when he went to San Francisco in a week. Or at least Cooley hadn't. Maybe Smith had changed Cooley's routines, too, just as he'd changed Mary's.

Mary stood behind her table with her wares, nodding to people or calling them by name. Off to the side sat a group of women with their embroidery hoops, stitching or appliquéing quilt blocks as they chatted. Mary saw Nelia in that group. Ruthie chatted with the saddle maker. Matilda and Bessie and even Abigail, the blacksmith's daughter all the way from Lebanon, were chatting at the punch table, and then they moved slowly back to the sewing circle.

The pastor announced the juniper tree game, and young boys and girls not yet in their twenties lined up to play. They'd all sing together as they stood in a circle:

> "Oh sister Mary how happy we'd be
> The night we sat under the juniper tree.
> The juniper tree, heigho, heigho!
> Take my hat off it will keep your head warm,
> Take a sweet kiss, it will do you no harm.
> The juniper tree, heigho, heigho,
> The juniper tree, heigho, heigho!"

When the song ended, each boy attempted to grab a girl and kiss her. Mary had laughed when she and Dale first saw the game played. "It would be better if the Presbyterians would just let them dance," Dale had whispered to her. But the next time, the two of them had joined the children, and Dale had kissed her right there in front of everyone.

"Mrs. Bishop." Jennifer pulled on her sleeve. "Mr. Taylor wants you."

"Does he?" Mary looked over at Richard. He wasn't watching the commotion in the center circle; he was staring at her.

"What makes you think he wants something from me?" Mary asked.

"The game has your name in it," Jennifer said. "And that's how Mr. Lawson looks at my ma," Jennifer added.

"Oh."

Just then the Widow Mason signaled Jennifer to join her and her brothers and sisters clustered around their mother. . .and Mr. Lawson.

Mary watched as Laird Lawson signaled to the musicians to wait before beginning another juniper tree game. He cleared his throat. "This is a fine evening to make a special announcement." He looked younger than he had in years, and Mary could see just what love did to a person: gave them back new life. "I'm pleased to tell you folks that the Widow Mason, Elizabeth Jane to me, has agreed to be my wife, and Pastor Blaine here has agreed to marry us."

Applause and cheers rang out. The musicians played a short ditty of joy. "And we won't be calling her the Widow Mason anymore—now will we, fellows?" Murmurs of approval followed his proclamation.

Mary thought the evening would end on this sweet note, but Nelia Williams stood up, quilt block in her hand. "What do you mean you're going to meet the test?" Her voice carried above the crowd as she shouted at Abigail, who Mary saw held a block with the exact same border and set block color as Nelia's. Ruthie came to stand beside her sister.

"Test? Who else has a test?" This from Matilda, the wedding-dress maker. She stood, too. "If there is anyone who can claim to be the finest seamstress in the region, it has to be, well, me. I don't mean to brag, but most of you would agree, wouldn't you?" She scanned the crowd to nods of heads. At Richard Taylor's spot in the room, Matilda stopped. "Why don't you tell them, Richard—Mr. Taylor. Go ahead."

"What's he got to tell you?" Bessie said. "If anything, it's me who should do the talking here. Look at my block. The stitches are perfection. Better than perfection with my glasses. Some of you girls would do well to wear glasses, too. Richard likes a woman who has the courage to wear glasses."

"You know Richard, too?" Matilda stared at Bessie. "And you, Abigail and Nelia and Ruthie?"

"I know him," Ruthie said, "But I'm not having an interest in marrying him. He didn't promise me like he did Nelia."

Matilda gasped. She turned to Richard. "You promised me!"

"Is that why our set blocks are all the same color?" Bessie said.

"Oh boy," said Laird. "Let's just have a little music."

The musicians started up, and Mary hurried to Nelia and Bessie, Matilda and Abigail. Ruthie stood beside her sister, Nelia, where tears made tracks through her powder makeup, saying, "There must be some mistake. He said he liked my quilt block best."

"He may have said he liked yours well enough, but did he say you met the test?" Matilda asked. Her voice rose so high the musicians stopped once again.

"No. But I was certain—"

"So was I." This from Bessie. Each held material in her hand, and by this time, the men of the party had pushed Richard toward the small circle of women, clapping him on the back and saying, "Prepare to meet your Maker."

Then they darted to the side far enough to be away from any thrown dishes but close enough to hear.

"You. . .didn't you say ours were the best quilt blocks? Didn't you say that?" Nelia said.

"I—I may have implied that, but you see, I love them all," Richard said. "Just as I am so fond of each of you. I never meant my conversations about what I'd want in a wife to mean that, well, that if I saw some of those features in you that it would mean I was ready for marriage." Sweat beaded on Richard's face, and Mary actually felt sorry for him having to face this line of women who obviously cared deeply about him and who were very, very disappointed.

"I can't believe you'd let us all believe you were interested in us," Matilda said. "You're. . .you're despicable."

"I am," he said. He hung his head.

Bessie chose that moment to throw her quilt with hoop around it at him, the hoop thumping his forehead before he could dodge it. Her aim was perfect, and she said so. "Because you got me to wear glasses," she said. "Now look at me!"

"You look wonderful in the glasses," Mary said, deciding to enter in to the fray. "You really do. And your quilting will only get better because of them. And you, Matilda, didn't you say you now had the confidence to open your own tailoring shop in Brownsville?"

"Well, yes. I could make it as a businesswoman," she said. "But that's beside—"

"Indeed, you could."

"But I'm not sure I'll buy material or thread from you, Mary Bishop. You should face some consequence for sending this. . .this. . .rapscallion—"

"Cad—"

"Rogue—"

"Knave above knaves," finished Abigail.

"But each of you gained, too," Mary said, "from this rascal's hand. Bessie, you can see better. Ruthie and Nelia, didn't you tell me that the two of you had worked on something together for the first time since your Papa had died? And Abigail, we haven't talked about this at all, but I bet if we did, you'd tell me of something good that's come of Richard's circuit sales from my old log store. There's always something good to come from the bad."

"Well, I did finish up a bunch of blocks I'd had stacked beside my bed for years," Abigail said. "And took them to the circle in Lebanon, where I quilted and had a fine afternoon with the women. My father's not always the best company, so it was good to be out and about and have a reason to tell him he'd have to heat up his own dinner 'cause I had an appointment. I'd just rather have had an appointment with Mr. Taylor there, at an altar."

"Wouldn't we all!" the women said in unison. And then as one, the remaining women tossed their quilt pieces at Richard; some with hoops and some without, colorful designs and with only the red-set pieces the same for each quilt, all stitched with Rosa Red. Richard tried to dodge, then to catch them, but ended up pulling them from his face and shoulders to fold them into his arms like a man carrying linens to the wash tub for his wife.

There was nothing Mary could do to stop them, and they gathered their fathers and brothers, who had brought them, pulled on their heavy shawls, and headed out into the night, a fierce group now defined by a common foe.

"Not the perfect sort of finale," Laird said to Mary. "But not the worst it could have been either. No need for an undertaker, at least."

Mary sighed as the music started up again. "Thank goodness something wonderful happened tonight for the two of you."

"And maybe for you, too, Mary," Elizabeth Mason said. Her glance moved past Mary, and when Mary turned, Richard Taylor stood, his face red, his arms filled with partially finished quilts and blocks of color that took him on the Road to Jerusalem and through a Storm at Sea, and with moisture in his eyes to match Job's Tears.

"What's that one?" Mary asked, pointing to the block Abigail had thrown at him.

"Robbing Peter to Pay Paul."

His answer so surprised Mary that she laughed. "Really? There's a quilt block with that name?"

"From the Bible quilt-block book," Richard said. "I guess it's better than Walls of Jericho because that would have been a premonition of my walls of charm come tumbling down." He took her elbow and moved her back toward her table. "I'm so sorry, Mary. I hope Matilda will change her mind about buying material at your store and that the others will see it was me and not you that brought this disaster their way."

"We can hope," Mary said. "But I suspect this is the time for you to make your escape."

"May I at least help you take your unsold items back to the mercantile? And I don't know what to do with all these quilt blocks in various stages of finishing."

"Bring them back. I'll think of something."

They put the items in the cart that Richard had brought to the bazaar. He led his horse, and Mary walked beside him. It wasn't snowing anymore, and Richard pointed to the moon. "Moon breaks?" he asked. "Like sun breaks in the daytime?"

"I guess," she said. She was aware of his closeness and wondered if he was. Better if he wasn't. She couldn't quilt; she didn't want to, and that's who Richard Taylor was drawn to. But her association with Richard wasn't all lost. The cart sales had been effective, and by next spring, perhaps the women would be willing to buy from her cart store again. . .with her as the saleswoman instead of a man. Yes, that could work. She'd just have to buy a mule.

Back at the cabin, Richard stoked the fire as Lacy scampered off the bed she'd been lying on while her mistress had been at the bazaar. Mary pulled her rabbit-trimmed bonnet from her head, pulled off her gloves, and then lifted her hair with her fingers. Richard watched her.

"You have the loveliest hands," he said.

"Do I?" Her heart fluttered again. *It mustn't!*

"I noticed them the very first time we met, even before the terrible accident that cut your palm. May I?" He reached for her hand and turned over her palm. He ran his fingers along the scar. "It's healed well," he said.

"But it's quite sensitive to cold," she said. She didn't pull her hand away.

"And to heat?"

"Yes, that, too."

He folded his hand over her fingers, cupping them in his own. "Mary. I made a terrible mistake—"

"Yes, you did. Those women will be some weeks if not months recovering from your—"

"No, the mistake I made was in thinking of you as an older woman, one set in her ways and devoted to her deceased husband."

"I am," she said. "Both older and adoring of my Dale."

"But you are also a woman willing to try new things like the circuit cart sales, like trusting a stranger to give him a chance, like making a way for the Laird Lawsons and Elizabeth Masons of the world to come together. And your wisdom and gentle spirit found the good things in each of my errors with the women. You reminded them of the eyeglasses, the changed relationships, the business opportunities. They'll come to see that new things await them. And what kind of a husband would a man who chooses a woman by her stitching skills really make?"

Mary chuckled. "Well, in my house, he'd probably face frustration unending as I'd never meet his test," she said.

"Nor would you need to. Because I can do all the stitching necessary for both of us."

"Both of us?" Mary's voice cracked.

"Indeed. I adore the wisdom of your age"—he corrected quickly—"and I'm not all that much younger than you, I'd guess. And I adore your hands; your fine mind; your faithful, giving heart." Mary swallowed. "Those are much more important details in the quilt of life than how many stitches you might make to the inch."

"What are you saying to me, Mr. Taylor?"

"I'm asking for the winter to see if I can redeem myself in your eyes and that in the spring you might accept my offer of marriage."

"I've met your test?"

"You met it a long time ago; now you'll have to see if I can meet any test you might have for me."

"I'm not the testing kind," Mary said, and then with boldness she added, "Just love me, Richard Taylor. That's what I'm used to, and that's all I ask."

"Ah, that I do. And this old log store and your dog and even the rain that marks the season. I just hope you can forgive me for my. . .troubling charm."

He kissed her then, and Mary felt a flutter in her stomach that wasn't hunger, at least not the kind that would be satisfied with food. She opened her eyes to see the candle glow against the peeled logs, this place of such comfort. It would continue to be whether by spring they found they'd made their way together or not. It had served her well, this log cabin; it would again, and this Christmas there'd be a man to help trim the tree they'd go out and cut together.

Richard blinked over his one blue eye and one brown. "I have an idea," he said as he stepped back but still held her hand. His voice shook a little.

"Will I wish I hadn't heard of it?" Mary asked, but she smiled.

"I'm going to stitch those blocks together, Mrs. Bishop, and have the most amazing courting quilt when I'm finished. I'll give it to you in the spring, if you'll have it, as a wedding gift."

Mary thought for a moment. Would she want a quilt made up of blocks stitched by women who'd hoped Richard Taylor would seek their hand in marriage and be reminded of it as they slept beneath it? Yes, she would.

"What woman wouldn't want a quilt stitched by her husband-to-be?" Mary said. "But I'd want something more."

"Name it," he said.

"You'll have to sew on buttons when they come off my dresses or your shirts, too. I may know how to do it, but I never really liked to!"

"Agreed," he said and kissed her again. "I'm partial to Rosa Red regardless of the button color."

"That's just fine," Mary said. "It will always remind me that Rosa Red brought me you."

She saw God in Richard's words, a loving God who stitched her life with colorful flax. Red thread through ivory buttons? It was a detail she could live with.

The following spring, Richard finished the quilt, and he and Mary were married in the Presbyterian church in Brownsville. They kept the log store that Mary and Dale had built, rechinking the logs tightly. Mary took up the circuit route soon after leaving Richard to manage the store until she announced they'd have to change the log cabin after all—they'd need another room for their growing family. Regardless of whether the infant was a boy or girl, Richard promised to teach their baby how to sew.

 Award-winning author, Jane Kirkpatrick is well known for her authentically portrayed historical fiction. She is also an acclaimed speaker and teacher with lively presentation style. She and her husband live in Oregon and, until recently, lived and worked on a remote homestead for over 25 years.

Under His Wings

by Liz Tolsma

Dedication

To Doug.
Thank you for encouraging me to follow my dream and for
loving me and supporting me as it came true. Always and forever yours.

Chapter 1

Camp Twelve, Wisconsin, 1875

Adie O'Connell pictured the farm in her mind as if she'd dropped in a thousand times before. In a way she had. The little log cabin would be snug and cozy, with tight chinking and real wood floors. At one end there would be a big stone fireplace and, at the other, a loft with a ladder leading to it. She'd have a red barn, milk cow, a chestnut mare, and lots of laying hens. In the garden she'd plant tomatoes, sweet corn, pole beans, and peas.

"Howdy, Miss Adie."

She jumped a mile, scolding herself for daydreaming again. She'd been knee-deep in her fantasy and had walked right over to Derek Owens. He leered at her as tobacco juice ran down his dirty brown beard. His perpetual habit of tobacco use had stained his teeth. The husky lumberjack spit a stream onto the floor then raked his gaze over her slender form.

"Got anything for me this morning?" Derek wiped the back of his huge hand across his mouth. A few of the men seated near him at the large U-shaped table in the mess hall tittered, though no one dared to speak. Cookie, busy in the kitchen, ruled the roost around here and tolerated no talking in his dining room.

Drawing herself to her full five-foot-three-inch height, Adie raised her chin and thumped a bowl of sausages on the wood plank table. "Here's your breakfast. Enjoy." She hoped her curt reply hid her nerves. If she let him know how much he flustered her, he would come on stronger. She'd learned that much in the years she'd worked in lumber camps.

She scurried toward the kitchen to retrieve more food for the hungry throng, not glancing back at Derek.

Cookie met her near the big woodstove, a plate of flapjacks in his hand. "Sure you don't want me to deliver these sweat pads for you? Don't want Owens giving you more trouble."

She took the dish from the slight man with only wisps of white hair left on his head. His huge gray apron hung past his knees.

"I can handle him." She smiled, loving this man who looked out for her.

Cookie wielded his spatula. "You let me know. I can give him whatnot, and he won't bother you."

"I don't doubt it." She chuckled as she pushed the swinging café doors open with her shoulder.

She paid better attention to where Derek was when she stepped into the dining room this time. She walked a wide arc around him and set the plate of pancakes on the far side of the table, not bothering to push them his way.

Derek winked at her, sending a shiver down her spine. "Hey, Adie, I sure could use some of what you got down there."

Her hands shook, and she wiped them on her white apron, hoping to conceal their trembling. "Boys, please pass Mr. Owens some pancakes and maple syrup."

Derek sneered. "Why don't you bring it down here yourself?"

One of the jacks pounded his fist on the table. "Enough, Owens. Treat Miss O'Connell like a lady, and leave her alone."

Adie recognized the tall, lean man with eyes the color of the syrup. Everyone called him "Preacher Man" because he didn't cuss, didn't carouse, didn't womanize, and wanted to go to seminary. The moniker stuck. In fact, in the two weeks he'd been in the logging camp, she couldn't recall hearing his given name.

Derek hefted his bulk from the long bench and stood, leaning on his knuckles on the table. "What you going to do to make me?"

She feared Preacher Man's interference would make matters worse. She had enough experience following her father to the camps in the past seven years to know men like Derek Owens didn't cater to being told what to do. He might escalate his advances to spite the man.

Preacher Man rose to his feet, a head taller than Derek. "I'm asking you to be a gentleman and mind your manners. Remember what your mama taught you."

Wrong answer.

"I'll teach you what I do to a mongrel like you."

Adie knew fisticuffs would ensue, so she retreated to the safety of the kitchen, desiring not to land in the middle of the melee. If only Preacher Man had kept his mouth shut.

❄

Noah Mitchell steeled himself for the blow to come. He'd heightened Derek's wrath by opening his mouth to protect Adie and diffuse the situation. In the end, he'd made a mess of things.

He wouldn't fight back, but he'd turn the other cheek as the Lord commanded. He came here to earn money to go to seminary. Several winters of work might pass before he saved enough, but he would go. In the meantime, he wanted to be a Christian example to the rough, heathen men in the camp.

Around him, the lumberjacks cheered on Derek, their champion. Hoots and hollers echoed off the mess hall's log walls. Roars of approval swelled around Noah as Derek faced him. He swallowed hard, wishing the bully would get it over with. He closed his eyes. He could smell Derek's fetid breath. He locked his knees and braced himself for the pain.

Why had he made an enemy of such a man?

All at once the room fell silent. Men muttered, and he heard them shuffle to their seats.

Someone clapped him on the back in greeting. "Morning, Preacher Man."

Noah dared to open one eye.

Quinn O'Connell stood beside him, his jade-green eyes sparkling, a grin spreading across his face. Old enough to have fathered most of these men, nevertheless he was as broad as any jack and as strong.

Quinn's wild, unkempt hair made him appear a bit rough around the edges, but Noah hadn't been fooled. Quinn held a fierce love for his daughter and all that concerned her. The man had a soft heart.

Quinn commanded respect too, as evidenced by the scurrying of the men around them.

"What's going on? When I came in, Owens looked about to kill you." Quinn spoke softly as he and Noah took their seats next to each other on the rough benches.

"He may have if you hadn't arrived." He sat down, his knees suddenly weak.

"Did he bother my daughter again?"

Noah shrugged, not wanting to see a fight break out between Owens and Quinn. The older man wouldn't stand a chance. "I took care of it. He'll leave her be from now on."

Adie's father growled. "I'll make sure he keeps his distance."

"Please, don't."

"I won't hurt him. Not now, anyway." Quinn spun around in his seat and clomped to the other end of the long table.

Noah could do nothing more than watch the older man confront the burly lumberjack. Owens spat then nodded. He may have acquiesced for now, but Noah didn't miss the fire burning in his dark eyes.

Quinn made it halfway back to his place at the table when Adie appeared from the kitchen, a steaming coffeepot in her slender hand. Noah watched, entranced, as she sashayed over to her father, stood on her tiptoes, and planted a peck on his hairy cheek.

The seasoned woodsman squeezed her and whispered in her ear. The way she gazed at him caused Noah's heart to beat faster than two jacks' sawing.

He'd better watch out. If Quinn knew how Adie affected him, Quinn would send him to the floor instead of Derek Owens. Make no mistake—the man was possessive of his daughter. He tolerated no coarse talk about her and shot dangerous looks at anyone who dared to come within ten feet of her.

Noah couldn't help but stare at the beautiful young woman. Locks of curly red hair fell about her face as she poured coffee. Her eyes, described by her father as the color of the hills of Ireland, danced in delight as Quinn teased her. Noah would give every penny of his seminary savings if she would smile at him with those full, red lips.

No, he needed a long walk in the crisp November predawn. He jumped from his spot at the table, ashamed of himself. He had no right to be thinking about Adie O'Connell in such a way.

"Thank you."

He turned and stared into her amazing green eyes.

She smiled her smile at him. "I appreciate the way you stepped in with Derek, but you didn't need to. He's not a problem for me."

"You're, uh, welcome." A smattering a red freckles crossed the bridge of her upturned nose. He couldn't bear the thought of Owens laying a hand on her. "But don't underestimate him."

Quinn stepped beside his daughter. "He won't hurt her."

Noah peered at Owens from the corner of his eye. The man scowled, and he didn't need to step into the Wisconsin winter to notice a chill in the air.

Noah and Quinn pulled the crosscut saw between them in an easy rhythm. Around them the music of other saws rang, punctuated by the staccato hammering of axes. The towering white pine they worked to fell had already been notched by an axe on one side. Now they labored at sawing it on the opposite side, a little above the gash. Wedges were inserted from time to time to cause the tree to fall.

"I appreciate the way you took care of Adie." Quinn wiped the back of his arm across his forehead. Temperatures may be below freezing, but the men worked up a sweat.

"My pleasure." And Noah meant it.

"I hate what this life is doing to her. I've dragged her from camp to camp in the winter and from odd job to odd job in the summer for the past seven years. It's not been easy. She's done her share of man's work without complaining, but I know she's not fond of it. She'd like to settle down, live in one spot again, but I can't. Since Claire passed, I can't stay in one place. She held our family together and helped me be a good father. Without her, I've been lost." He ran a hand through his tousled brown hair.

"Adie loves you. I can see it in the way she looks at you. She doesn't hold any of this against you."

The lines around Quinn's green eyes softened. "Adie's a good girl, especially to put up with the likes of me."

"She does more than put up with you."

Quinn shrugged. "We'd best get back to work. If I rest these old bones too long, I'll never get going again."

The men put their hands to the crosscut saw once more, working in silence. In a short amount of time they had almost completed their chore. The pine would soon fall.

Then a loud crack split the air.

A long, vertical fracture appeared, traversing the trunk and ruining the lumber. Worse, it destabilized the tree. If the jacks couldn't wedge it hastily, it would fall. And no one could predict where.

Quinn and Noah, along with other men, worked frantically, driving in wedges. The tree groaned.

"She's going, boys!" Quinn shouted.

Men scattered.

The tree leaned.

Noah watched it descend to earth.

"Quinn!"

Chapter 2

A die plunged her hands into the hot dishwater. She hated this part of her job. Stacks of tin plates and cups surrounded her, topped by a load of greasy pans. When she completed this chore, a mound of potatoes waited to be peeled. The loggers called them murphies, which made no sense whatsoever. Over the years she had come to understand the jacks' lingo but refused to speak it.

Her hands stilled in the water as she wondered about the big, tall man who came to her defense. No doubt, he was a gentleman with perfect manners. They called him Preacher Man. Daddy told her he wanted to go to seminary someday. She didn't know his name. No one called him anything else, not even her father.

He sure was handsome—broad and strong, with brown eyes that made you think of things that caused Adie to blush. He talked like a preacher. Where did he come from?

She sighed. Her pile of dishes had not grown one inch smaller. The cup in her hand went into the rinse water.

She longed for a view of the majestic pines just beyond the log walls of the camp kitchen. Having something beautiful to look at would make her work seem to go faster. She could stand here and gaze at the snow sparkling in the sunlight.

A commotion clamored in the dining hall, jarring her back to reality.

A shout came from outside the swinging doors. "Bring him in here. Lay him on the table. Be careful. He's bad off."

Men yelled back and forth to each other.

Adie's heart rolled over.

An accident. There had been an accident.

Please, Daddy, be all right. Be safe.

She swiped her shaking hands on her apron as she hustled to see who had been injured. With every breath, she prayed she wouldn't find her father on the table.

A large crowd gathered around the wounded lumberjack. The flannel-covered backs of tall, brawny men blocked her view. Adie couldn't see who they'd brought in. She searched the sea of hats, the various sizes, shapes, and colors

252

making it possible to distinguish the wearer. She spied Preacher Man and Derek Owens. Where was her father's dark-blue felt cap? He would be in here with the men, wouldn't he?

It doesn't mean anything that I can't find Daddy. Maybe he stayed outside with the horses. Maybe he had run to fetch the camp boss, who acted as physician. Willing her stomach to cease its jumping, she stepped into the crowd.

The noise around her ceased.

The men parted.

Her father lay, unmoving, on the table.

Everything around her became hazy. Through a narrow tunnel of light, she spied her father's pale face. Blood coursed from his temple, but his chest still rose and fell. She rushed to his side.

"Daddy."

His eyes remained closed. He lay still. So still.

Too still.

"Daddy?"

She rubbed his cold hand.

No, God, You can't do this to me again. You can't take him from me, too. Do You hear me?

She turned and found herself staring into Preacher Man's warm, brown eyes. They filled with unshed tears.

"The tree split and fell. The trunk clipped him. I yelled, but he couldn't get out of the way quickly enough. I'm so sorry."

He reached out to her, but she shoved his hands aside. "He's not dead. Look, he's still breathing. Why are you standing there? Run and get Mr. Larsen. Help my father." Why was no one doing anything?

"Someone went for him, but there's not much anyone can do."

Adie stamped her foot in frustration. "Don't say that. Nothing is going to happen to him. Now do something. Anything! Boil water, or tear sheets for bandages or whatever you can think to do."

A moan sounded from beside her. She turned back. Her father's eyelids flickered.

She leaned over the man who had always been there for her and stroked his whiskered cheek. "Shh, everything's going to be all right. You'll be fine."

He parted his lips, but no sound escaped.

"Don't try to talk. Save your energy. You're going to need it when you get back to work in a few days."

Her father's mouth moved again, and this time he croaked out a word. "Noah."

Preacher Man leaned in. So his name was Noah.

"I'm right here, but Adie's right. Conserve your strength. Whatever you have to tell me can wait."

Daddy moved his head from side to side, wincing. "No." He took a shallow breath. "Take care of her."

Noah's big hand covered her father's. "I will. I promise."

She didn't like the direction of the conversation. Everyone talked like her father was dying. "Why would you say that, Daddy? You're not going anywhere. We'll be together like we always have been. Come spring you'll hire on and help someone with their planting. But it will be the two of us, looking out for each other, like you said it would be, forever."

Daddy gave her hand a small squeeze. "I love you, Adie."

The lines in her father's face softened, and his hand went limp. His eyes stared blankly.

"No! Daddy, no!"

Strong arms enveloped her and kept her from falling to the floor. Noah whispered in her ear. "I'm so sorry."

She couldn't speak, couldn't think, couldn't breathe.

She was utterly alone.

❄

Little light filtered through the cracks in the chinking of the cabin. A frigid wind blew, and ice built up on the inside of the walls.

But nothing compared to the chill in Adie's heart. When Mama had died seven years ago, she hadn't thought anything worse could happen. Well, it had. Both her parents were gone. She closed her eyes to shut out the reality of her father dying. Maybe, just maybe, when she opened them she would find this had been an awful nightmare. She would wake up, and everything would be the way it should be.

But when she did, nothing had changed. Outside, men continued to chisel her father's grave from the frozen earth. Sawing and hammering came from the blacksmith's shop next door as the jack-of-all-trades smithy constructed the coffin.

Her father's smiling eyes looked down on her from a photograph in a wood frame. Adie took the daguerreotype from the crude shelf above the stone fireplace. His hair was slicked back. She ran her finger over the glass above his image. Her mother sat beside him, prim and proper, a cameo at her delicate throat. Every chance he got, Daddy reminded Adie what a wonderful person her mother had been. He'd never stopped loving her. His grief over her death caused him to sell their farm. They became nomads, working wherever work could be had.

She couldn't blame him for wanting to escape the memories inhabiting their little log cabin. Right now she wanted to run as far from this place as her legs could carry her and never look back. Of course, it was impossible. Winter had settled into the Wisconsin Northwoods. No one would come or go for a long time.

And Adie had nowhere to go anyway. What could one woman do alone?

She sighed and replaced the picture on the shelf. Her numb mind couldn't make such decisions now. At this moment she needed to focus on getting through the next few minutes and hours. She'd worry about the future when it happened.

The cold of the room seeped into her bones, and she shivered. Without kicking off her high-button shoes, she slid under her brightly colored patchwork quilt. With frozen fingers, she traced the stitching. Her mother had sewn this quilt for her bed under the eaves in the attic. She had allowed Adie to do some of the work. Together they had chatted away the hours.

Her memories took her to the day she and her father had packed their belongings and moved from their home. They'd left so much behind, but Adie had insisted she take the quilt. Since that day it had traveled with them from place to place. Some nights it covered her in cabins such as this one, some nights in haylofts, some nights on a blanket of pine needles beneath the stars.

Always her father had been nearby. Not tonight.

Tonight she would be alone.

At last she permitted herself to grieve for all she had lost. She cried and cried until her pillow was soaked and her body exhausted.

❄

Work stopped for only a brief time after the accident. Trees needed to be harvested, after all. The lumber company didn't want work to slack off, even because of a tragedy.

Noah sawed trees with Butch, his new partner, pulled from the swamper crew cutting limbs from trunks. Usually, the steady back-and-forth motion of the two-man crosscut saw soothed him. Now he couldn't keep his attention on his task. Despite the danger it posed for him, his thoughts returned time and again to Adie. His heart ached for her. Quinn had told him they had no other living kin, and Noah imagined how alone she must feel. He wanted to comfort her.

She'd felt so good, so right in his arms when he'd caught her. A wren weighed more than she did. But she was soft and warm and curved in the right places. He longed to hold her forever, to shield her from more pain.

The saw caught in the tree, and worked paused. Noah closed his eyes for a moment and erased his thoughts. He had no right dreaming about Adie like that. Her father had died a few hours ago. And he had to take care of her.

Butch yanked on the saw, and their rhythmic work started again. Noah's promise to Quinn came to mind. Even before the accident, he'd been concerned for his daughter's well-being if something should happen to him. His anxiety deepened when Derek Owens began making advances toward her.

Without her father there to watch out for her, she became a prime target for Owens and women-thirsty jacks like him. Unfortunately, there were too many unprincipled men in a logging camp. They wouldn't see another woman all winter long, so they'd try to take advantage of the one in their midst.

Noah wanted to see her protected. The thought of her falling into the clutches of someone like Owens disgusted him. She made clear her distaste for the man's suggestions.

Early on, Noah and Quinn had formed an unlikely friendship. Quinn was the only lumberjack who didn't ridicule Noah for his beliefs, the only one who listened to anything Noah had to say. So when Quinn asked Noah to make sure no harm came to Adie if anything happened to him, Noah had agreed to it without much thought. Right before he passed away, Quinn had reminded him of his promise.

He shook his head and wiped his forehead with the back of his sleeve, his plaid flannel shirt and woolen long johns damp with perspiration. His nerves were as jagged as the saw blade.

He stepped back to watch Butch hammer a wedge into the saw cut with the back of his axe. The tree creaked and moaned, then leaned. *Tiiiimberrrr.*

It plummeted to the earth with a crash.

No problems. Not like this morning.

Noah groaned. He had an obligation to the one man who didn't laugh at him or put him down. He knew he needed to keep his promise to Quinn. But how? What might be the best way of going about it? Noah felt inadequate.

Adie needed someone to watch out for her and to keep her reputation from being sullied by men like Derek Owens. A logging camp was no place for a woman alone. But what could he do?

Chapter 3

After work halted at nightfall, and with a hearty dinner behind him, Noah knocked on the back door of the wanigan, the company store, where Mr. Larsen slept.

"Come in."

Noah entered the boss's small and sparsely furnished lean-to. A narrow but neatly made bed occupied one wall, a colorful quilt tossed over it. Mr. Larsen sat in a straight-back chair at a long table on the opposite wall. That left little space for even as simple a task as turning around. Noah could just step inside and still have room to close the door behind him.

Mr. Larsen looked up from the books and papers spread over his desk, his glasses on the very tip of his hawk-like nose. He was probably somewhere around forty, but his importance in the camp made him seem much older. He nodded in Noah's direction. "Mitchell. Have a seat." He motioned to the bed.

Noah sat, the corn husks in the mattress rustling as he settled into position.

"I'm sorry about O'Connell. What exactly happened?"

Noah shifted, those horrible images of Quinn's accident repeating themselves in his mind. The eardrum-busting crack of the tree. The men rushing to insert wedges, racing to control the fall of the pine. The sight of the tree leaning directly over Quinn. The look of surprise, horror, fear on the man's face. The icy cold that shot through his own veins.

"It's like I told you. The tree split. Why? I don't know. We tried to wedge it to no avail. I yelled to Quinn, but it was too late." Noah closed his eyes and took a couple of quick deep breaths, trying to dissolve the lump in his throat. "He did nothing wrong. None of us did. The Lord called him home today. That's all."

"I'm sorry, Mitchell. I know you two got along real well."

"Thank you, sir." Noah cleared his throat and twisted the end of his mustache. "But I didn't come about that. Well, maybe in a way it is. I have a problem. I was wondering if I could ask your advice."

Larsen removed his spectacles and placed them on the desk. "What is it? Owens bothering you? You know, he's done nothing illegal. There's not much I can do about him. You two'll have to work it out yourselves."

The man sounded exasperated. Noah wondered how many others had complained about Owens.

"No, sir, it's nothing like that." He shifted, the mattress crunching beneath him. "In a way it is, though. I mean, it does involve Owens. Sort of."

Larsen tapped his fingers on his desk. He was getting impatient.

"Sir, what is going to happen to Miss O'Connell? Quinn's daughter."

"Happen to her? What do you mean?"

"She's a beautiful young woman. Some of the men have made advances toward her. Inappropriate advances." He wished he could halt the progress of the heat up his neck and into his face.

The boss leaned forward and rubbed his chin. "Go on."

"Quinn always watched out for her. Protected her. When he was around, none of the men dared to even look at Miss O'Connell. Without him here, I'm afraid of what some of them might do. She's vulnerable." A vision of Adie, her slender white hands grasping a sweating water pitcher, a red curl falling across her pink cheek, crossed his mind. "She needs someone to watch out for her."

"And you propose to do the job, Mitchell?"

"I promised Quinn several times I would take care of his daughter should something happen to him. I didn't ever think. . ."

Larsen slapped his knee. "No one ever does. And you're right. Miss O'Connell needs a protector. All the women I've ever run across in a logging camp have been married. And matronly. Never had one young and single like she is. O'Connell was a good worker and a leader. He kept the men in line, and they respected him. That's why I allowed him to bring her along. But now—well, what she needs is a husband."

Noah didn't like the way Larsen looked directly at him. His mother had that same I-have-a-chore-for-you-that-you-won't-like kind of look. One that usually meant he was about to muck out stalls.

He swallowed. "A husband?"

"If someone married her, she would come under the protection of her husband. While the men here might be wild and some would say uncouth, they wouldn't dare touch a married woman."

"Who?"

Larsen laughed. Actually laughed. The crinkles around his eyes deepened. "Seems to me, Mitchell, if you made the promise to O'Connell, it ought to be you."

Noah stood so quickly the room spun. "Me? Marry Miss O'Connell?"

"She is beautiful. Maybe a bit spirited for a quiet man like yourself, but you could do worse. Much worse."

The world tilted, and Noah reached for the rough lumber wall to steady himself. Him? Marry Adie? Couldn't he just treat her like his sister? That's what he'd had in mind when he'd promised to protect her. Not marry her. That hadn't come to mind at all when Quinn asked.

His plans did not include a wife. A spouse would change his future. With someone else to support, he would never be able to save enough money for seminary. Later, maybe, there might be room for a wife, but not now. He needed to scrimp and save every last penny to pay tuition, not have it frittered away by a woman buying lace, ribbons, and other frippery. He hadn't seen any of that on Adie, but his sisters liked those sorts of things.

He would have to give up so much to marry her.

Yet his loss couldn't compare to Adie's. He had a choice in the matter. She didn't choose to be brought to this camp, didn't choose to lose both her parents, didn't choose to be stranded, alone, and defenseless. The apostle Paul commanded Christians to care for orphans, and he supposed she fit that category. And her father told him she knew the Lord.

"Mitchell? You all right? You need a drink of water?"

Larsen's voice pierced his thoughts. For a moment the room was so silent he could hear nothing but the sputtering of the oil lamp.

Noah shook his head, clearing his mind.

He trembled at the thought of what the Lord wanted him to do. His life was about to change forever.

"I'll marry her, sir. If she'll have me."

❄

Adie stared at the mountain of dishes that awaited her this morning.

This morning, like so many other mornings, yet so different. In one day her father had laughed with her, died, and been buried.

Everything was different.

Everything was the same.

Cookie had told her she didn't need to come to work today. If she didn't work, though, what was there to do?

She scrubbed the egg pan, telling herself her tears came from the ache in her knuckles, not from the pain in her heart.

A soft knock sounded at the swinging door. "Miss O'Connell?"

She recognized Preacher Man's—Noah's—soothing tenor voice.

She swiped away her tears with the back of her hand. "Yes."

He came through the swinging door, tall, lean, but somehow soft. Maybe it was the look of compassion in his golden-brown eyes. "I'd like to speak with you, if you have a few minutes." He shuffled his weight from one booted foot to the other.

"Just a few. I need to wash all of those." She tilted her head toward the pile of dishes.

He held the café door open for her and gestured for her to sit on one of the benches in the mess hall while he stood, then paced, rolling one end of his mustache between his fingers.

He stopped in front of her and looked straight into her eyes. "I'd like to extend my sympathies to you on the loss of your father."

She dug her ragged fingernails into the edge of the wooden bench, willing herself not to cry. After last night, she thought she had cried all the tears in the world. But today, if she let herself give in to the grief, she knew she would weep and weep and never stop.

"Thank you, Mister. . ."

"Mitchell. Noah Mitchell. Please call me Noah."

"Thank you, Noah."

"He and I were felling the tree together yesterday. I don't know why it happened. He did nothing wrong. But he loved you very much."

She bit her lip. She couldn't speak, so she nodded. He was sweet and thoughtful, but she didn't want to talk about this.

He resumed his pacing, and she relaxed her grip on the bench. Without warning, he spun around.

"He was always concerned about you. Wanted to make sure nothing happened to you. He loved you very much and felt bad about dragging you all over the state, never giving you a place to call home."

She couldn't take any more. She rose and touched his upper arm, surprised by the firmness of the muscles. For a moment she forgot what they were speaking about. Then it rushed back.

"Mr. Mitchell—Noah—I want to thank you for your sentiments." She didn't know how many more words she'd be able to force through the narrow opening in her throat. "But truly, I need to finish the dishes and start peeling potatoes for supper. Cookie will be upset with me for wasting so much time."

She started toward the door, but he caught her by her wrist. Though his grip was firm, he didn't hurt her. She paused and turned, her face so close to his she could feel his rapid, warm breath on her cheek. "Mr. Mitchell, please."

"Miss O'Connell, I promised your father that I would be the one to take care of you if anything happened to him. For some reason he felt I could be trusted with his most treasured possession."

His eyes turned dark, and she couldn't tell what he thought.

"A lumber camp is no place for a beautiful young woman all alone. There are men who. . .who would do things."

"I assure you, Mr. Mitchell, that I can hold my own with the jacks. They don't frighten me in the least." Well, none of them but a certain Derek Owens.

The man disgusted her and yes even caused her to tremble. But her father was always there to keep him in line.

Her father. Who wasn't here any longer.

Noah touched a curl that had strayed from her pins. The hairs on her arms stood up straight. This big room must be cold without the ovens going. She took a step back, and he released her wrist.

"I don't think you understand. Some men might try to take, well, advantage of you." A blush heightened the ruddy look of his face. "You need someone to take care of you, to protect you. A husband."

"A what? A husband? You have to be kidding me." Where did he get such a ludicrous suggestion? "I have no need of a husband. Besides, who would I marry? One of those ill-mannered jacks you mentioned?"

Noah turned, walked to the end of the table, gripped the edge, and then faced her. For some reason she held her breath. He put his hand over his heart and pressed his chest. "Me. You could marry me."

Chapter 4

Y ou? You want me to marry you?" Adie's eyes widened. "What kind of crazy idea is that?"

Noah wondered the same thing. "It's not all that wild. Look, these men aren't going to see another woman until March or April. Some of them might try..."

Her calm voice belied the touch of fervor behind her words. "I've been in logging camps around jacks much longer than you have. Don't try to tell me what they're like. I can take care of myself."

Noah thumped himself down on the bench by the table. "I realize the idea might take some getting used to. I wasn't fond of it when Mr. Larsen mentioned it. But it's wise. If you came under my protection, as my wife, the men wouldn't dare touch you."

"This wasn't your idea? Mr. Larsen suggested it?"

"It's not that... I mean, you know, I wanted to. But I just didn't..." He was tangling himself like a dog in a leash.

She sat next to him, rubbing her hands together. "I appreciate the thought. But I'm not going to marry you. Or anyone else. I'll be fine. You'll see." She touched his arm, sending the words in his brain scrambling.

"It would be in name only. The marriage that is." Noah hated the schoolgirl blush heating his face. "If that makes a difference."

"I know you made a promise to my father, to take care of me." Her eyes sparkled with unshed tears, even as she lifted her chin. "And you're the kind of man who would never break a promise. You're noble. If it makes you feel better, I hereby release you from your vow."

Before Noah could say a word, she rose from his side and made her way to the kitchen, her skirts swishing at her ankles.

He sat there for a while running the palm of his hand over the rough wood of the bench, still warm from her body. While the idea of marrying her had sounded insane when Mr. Larsen first spoke of it, Noah knew now he had no other way of protecting her.

❄

Cookie took one look at Adie when she returned to the kitchen and put down the potato he'd been peeling, but not his paring knife. "I seen Preacher Man out there talking to you. He giving you trouble?"

She cleared the tears from her eyes with her fingertips. "No. He, well, he proposed to me, for my own protection. If I was his wife, none of the men would bother me anymore."

"And? Are you gonna marry him?"

"No. Of course not. I have you to take care of me, don't I?" She pointed to his hand, holding the knife.

This light jesting always brought a smile to Cookie's face, but not now. "Might not be such a bad idea. I seen how Owens treats you. You can't be too careful around him. I'd think on it again if I were you."

She didn't want to think about it. Or talk about it, for that matter. "I'll finish the dishes and then help with the potatoes."

"Preacher Man wouldn't make a bad husband. He works real hard. I ain't never heard him cuss or talk coarse or nothing. Later on you might regret passing him up."

She was pretty sure she wouldn't. All she wanted was a small piece of the world to call her own, a simple log cabin, a simple life.

She stuck her hands in the cooling water and got back to her dishes. She knew her father had watched over her. The jacks respected him.

She sloshed water all over the counter, the floor, and herself, not caring about the mess. Until Derek Owens came along, she'd never had problems with any of the men. There was the time a year or two ago when a jack slapped her backside as she came around with the coffeepot, but she'd steered clear of him from then on and had no more trouble. She'd do that for the rest of the winter, and once the thaw came and the logs were downriver at the mill, she'd leave. Perhaps she'd go to Green Bay or even Milwaukee, hire on as a maid there, and save her money. If she were careful, someday she'd have enough for her own farm.

She reached for another dish to wash and with relief realized she'd reached the end of the pile. Her present state of mind had helped her get through the chore at a rapid pace.

After wiping down the counters, she headed outside to dump the dirty dishwater and to pump more. The bright sun shining off the white snow hurt her eyes but did nothing to warm the air. A chill wind blew through the clearing.

Quiet permeated the camp. Even the blacksmith's anvil remained still today. The jacks wouldn't return from the woods for hours yet, not until dark began to fall. They ate their lunch outside. Sometimes they worked at a great distance from the camp, and coming in to eat would take too much time from their jobs.

Each evening she'd waited with anticipation for her father to file into the mess hall for supper. He'd smile at her. The gesture comforted her. Someone in the world loved her.

The longing ache in her heart ripped open again. She missed Daddy. Her throat constricted. She dropped the dishwater pan on the snow and covered her face. Her breath came in gasps.

God, how could You do this to me? How could You take both Mama and Daddy from me? How could You? I'm all alone now. Do You hear me, God?

A boot crunching in the snow answered her.

A moment later, a rough hand slipped behind her neck. She ripped her hands from her eyes. Derek Owens leered at her from mere inches away. She backed up a few steps until she bumped into the log walls of the mess building. He came right after her, placed one hand on either side of her, palms against the wall, wrists against her shoulders.

He had her hemmed in.

"I've been waiting for this chance, Adie. You're a hard one to catch, but I knew I'd get you sooner or later."

Her palms began to sweat. Her heart thumped in panic. "What are you doing here in the middle of the morning?"

"I volunteered to tell Cookie we shot a deer. He needs to come skin it so we can have some good eatin' tonight. What a bonus to find you here by yourself." He touched her cheek with his rough hand.

She recoiled at his touch, trying to think of a way to escape. Maybe if she slipped under his arms and ran faster than she ever had, she could get back safely inside.

Derek spat a stream of tobacco juice into the snow, wiping his mouth on his shoulder. He leaned in, planting a hard, heavy kiss on Adie's mouth. The sickeningly sweet, pungent scent of the cheap corn liquor he loved to drink flavored his breath, to nauseating effect. Bile rose in her throat when his cracked, dry lips scraped hers.

She couldn't scream. She tried to plant her arms on his chest and push him away, but he grabbed her wrists, pinning them against the log wall. All blood flow to her hands ceased.

The blows her high-buttoned shoes landed on his shins didn't bother him. He leaned in harder. She couldn't draw a breath. The world spun. Bright colors flashed behind her eyes.

Then two hands grabbed Derek around his neck and pulled him off her. She gulped air. Noah tightened his grip on Derek, his thumbs on the shorter man's windpipe. "You'd better leave your filthy hands off this lady."

Adie wilted against the building in relief.

Noah shook him. "Stay away from her. Do you understand?"

The big man fell to his knees.

"Do you understand?"

Derek nodded. Noah released his grip and gave the jack a kick.

But then Derek stood and spun, fists balled, lunging at the slender man, who darted to the side moments before those huge fists would have connected with his stomach.

Fear jerked her legs from under her. She slumped in the snow.

The giant took another step toward Noah. Before he could strike, Mr. Larsen emerged from the wanigan. "Ah, Owens, perfect. Cookie mentioned he needed more wood chopped. Since you're free, you can take care of that. Get your axe. The woodpile's behind the kitchen."

Mr. Larsen stood with his hands on his hips. Derek searched a moment before locating his ax next to Adie. She didn't want to think about what he would have done if he'd remembered it. She'd been so afraid for Noah she hadn't noticed it beside her.

"Come on, Owens, let's go." Mr. Larsen still stood in the store doorway.

Derek surveyed Noah and Adie. Her skin felt like it crawled with ants. "This ain't over. My pa was a weak-willed man who let my ma beat up on him. I'm not like him. Not at all. I always get what I want. Watch and see if I don't."

Chapter 5

After Derek left, followed by Mr. Larsen, Noah helped Adie to her feet. Her heart trembled at his touch, along with the rest of her body. He wrapped his arms around her.

She wished she could clean the taste of Derek—with his tobacco and booze—out of her mouth.

"Can't you see you're not safe here? You need someone to protect you. You need me." He paused for a moment then tightened his embrace. "You have to marry me."

His hold warmed her. She stopped shivering, yet she couldn't bring herself to admit he was right. "You did protect me today, even though we aren't married. Derek took me by surprise and had me pinned before I could react, but Daddy taught me to fight for myself. Look, you came to my rescue at the precise moment I needed you. We don't have to be married for you to watch out for me." Relief mingled with disappointment at those words.

"I saw Owens coming through the woods as I went to join the other loggers. For a while I kept going, but God gave me this feeling that things weren't right. Part of me knew I had to go after him. If I hadn't been late today, I wouldn't have seen him. There's no telling what he would have done if I hadn't stopped him. If he surprises you again—and he will—you won't be able to protect yourself."

She tried to ignore the truth in his words but couldn't. All the labor in the camp had made her strong but hadn't made her grow or put on weight. She'd only be able to fend off Derek if she had the element of surprise on her side.

"I'll be careful. Next time I'll pay better attention."

Noah shook his head and released his hold on her.

If only Daddy were here to give her some advice. Of course, if Daddy were here she wouldn't be in this pickle. Adie didn't know what to do. How could she marry a stranger? Cookie encouraged her to do so, but what did he know about marriage and a woman's heart?

Stepping to the side and looking up, she examined Noah. A slight smile curled his lips, and something about him that she couldn't pinpoint exuded warmth and kindness.

Her father had told her Noah came to the camp this winter to earn money for seminary. He wanted to be a preacher. All the preachers Adie knew rode the circuit. They didn't settle down. Unless he wanted to be a big-city preacher. That kind lived in fancy brick houses, not in cozy log cabins. Either way, she'd be forced to give up her dream forever. She'd never have her quiet, peaceful life.

Noah reached out to her. He stopped before he touched her. "Adie?"

She turned her back to him, thinking of Derek. Her arms tingled where he'd squashed her wrists. The crush of his weight against her hadn't fully eased. What could she do to defend herself? He had well over a hundred pounds on her. If he came back for more like he promised, would it end as well as it had today? She knew the answers to her own questions.

Noah was right. She was alone. Defenseless. A lumber camp was no place for a young woman. Women worked in other camps. Much older women, married women. Or the other kind, the kind she didn't want to be, but the kind she'd end up as if Derek had his way. She'd be easy prey then for any man in the camp.

She didn't have another choice.

She turned toward Noah, staying out of arm's reach. "I'll marry you."

Noah stared at Adie as she stood by his side in her simple brown gown. He'd never seen her in anything other than her faded work clothes, covered with an apron. This must be her Sunday best.

Mr. Larsen, who served as justice of the peace among his other duties, intoned the words of the marriage ceremony. Noah didn't hear a word.

She clasped her hands in front of her so tightly her knuckles turned white. "Do you, Noah Bradford Mitchell, take this woman. . ."

Did he? Yes, this was the right thing to do, the thing the Lord would have him do. He may never lead a congregation as their pastor, but he would serve the Lord this way.

He'd insisted the blacksmith fashion crude rings for them. Derek Owens and the others needed a visual reminder that Adie was his wife and that they had to stay away.

They said the appropriate words at the appropriate times, and so they were married.

By the time Adie returned to her little cabin after supper dishes that evening, Noah had built up the fire, and warmth enveloped the small space.

Noah. Her husband. How strange that sounded. How odd to see him in this place.

She studied him as he stirred the logs, muscles rippling under his lumber shirt. He had a strong profile with a regal-looking nose and the indefinable quality of compassion about him. And he was good-looking.

Adie heard her mother's voice in her head. "Handsome is as handsome does." So far, this applied to Noah inside and out.

She warned herself not to lose her heart to this man. God had a way of taking from her all the people she loved. Caring about another person led to heartbreak in the end. She'd have to exercise caution so she didn't come to feel for him.

He noticed her and placed the poker on the mantel, next to the daguerreotype of her parents. A picture of another couple with several children had joined it. She furrowed her brows.

"Those are my parents and sisters. While I waited for you, I brought my things from the bunkhouse. I won't get in your way, but I'd like to have my picture there, too."

"I don't mind." And she didn't, until she spied his quilt on Daddy's bed. When she'd changed her clothes after the ceremony, she'd folded her father's quilt, the one from the bed he and Mama shared, and placed it in the small trunk at the foot of her bed. Noah's red star coverlet looked strange there, out of place. At least he'd kept the sheet hanging between the two rope beds.

"You are bothered. I can tell."

She shook her head, unwilling to speak the lie.

"Come on, sit down. It's been an unusual day. I made a pot of black lead." He poured them each a cup of coffee.

He sat across from her. "This is strange to both of us. We need time to get to know each other and feel comfortable together. I'll keep my promise and not, well. . .you know. But I want us to be friends. Life will be easier if we can get along."

"Thank you." She sent him a small smile to let him know she appreciated his kindness. "I'd like for us to get along." But not too well or too close. "Tell me about all those sisters of yours."

She'd picked a good topic. While she sipped her coffee, he told her about each of his sisters, their personalities, their likes and dislikes, and the families of the ones who were married. In spite of her heart's warning, she laughed when he told her how he'd teased them, pulling boyish pranks like snakes in beds and frogs in lunch pails.

"Of course, they got even with me. I remember one piece of pumpkin pie complete with a dollop of Pa's shaving cream instead of whipped cream."

She laughed, surprising herself. She shouldn't be merry so soon after her father's death, but it did warm her heart.

He leaned back in his chair and took a swig of his coffee. "Now it's your turn.

What about your family? I know you don't have any siblings, but do you have cousins? Aunts and uncles?"

"I don't have any family." The ache in her chest returned full force and then some. She wanted this conversation to end. Scraping her chair back, she stood. "It's been an exhausting day. I'm going to retire. Good night."

He opened his mouth as if to question her but slammed it shut. "Good night, Adie. Sleep well."

As she closed the sheet that served as a curtain, the one separating her from her husband, she remembered how her parents said good night. Such a tender look would pass between them. Her father would take her mother in his arms, hold her close, whisper into her hair, and kiss her for a long time.

The memories brought tears to her eyes. The knowledge that she would never have that kind of relationship sent them streaming down her face.

Noah thunked his forehead with the palm of his hand. How could he be so stupid, bringing up her family like that? They had been having a good time, getting along. She laughed in all the right places and put him at ease. Then he had to go and mention her family, right after her father passed away. What a *dummkopf*. He knew she didn't have any family; Quinn had told him more than once.

From now on he would need to choose his words with care. He knew he had to protect her from the uncouth men in the logging camp. He didn't realize he'd have to protect her from himself.

Chapter 6

Adie washed, dressed, and left the cabin the next morning before Noah woke. He marveled at the long hours she worked. At four, Cookie woke them with his call, "Daylight in the swamp," and they were at the mess hall by four-thirty. He never thought about how early Cookie and his assistant rose to have the meal ready.

Anticipation swelled in him when he thought about her. His wife. To care for and watch over. The task almost overwhelmed him. She'd be part of his life from now until he died.

On the short walk to the mess hall, he met some former bunkmates. Roger, the one with a spotty beard, clapped him on the back. "So, Preacher Man, you enjoy your wedding night?"

He tried to convince himself that the wind made his cheeks burn.

"How lucky to have a woman to keep you warm. Wish I had one."

He let them believe he and Adie had a true marriage, to keep them from bothering her.

As they entered the mess hall, he spied her bringing pancakes from the kitchen. The men broke Cookie's absolute silence rule as she came with the sweat pads. "Morning, Mrs. Mitchell," they chorused. An invisible brush painted her cheeks pale pink. My, she was beautiful. Part of him came to life when he gazed at her.

She sashayed to his side, and a red curl, escaped from its pins, bounced along. "Good morning."

He grinned like a kid with a peppermint stick.

A jack at the far end of the room shouted, "Come on. Kiss her already."

The men pounded on the table. "Kiss her! Kiss her!"

Cookie emerged from the kitchen, glaring at those who broke his no-talking rule. Noah asked Adie the question with his eyes. She nodded. He rose and wrapped his arms around her. Their first—and probably their last—kiss happened in front of a crowd. He bent and placed his lips against hers. They were warm, soft, and tasted like syrup. She leaned into him. Everything faded but the whoosh of blood in his ears.

The men cheered, and they parted after a too-short time. Cookie raised his voice. "Enough. If you want breakfast, you'd best be quiet."

As if doused with ice water, they hushed. Noah, awash in embarrassment, shoveled pancakes on his plate and drowned them in butter. Adie returned to the kitchen, a rush of cold air filling the void beside him. He missed her.

He remembered the promise he made last night. He had to round up his stampeding emotions before he hurt her.

Only the scrape of forks against tin plates made noise. But the stares of the men dug into him, like his mother's when he'd been up to something.

He hurried, wondering which dish Adie had prepared—sweat pads, cackleberries, or doorknobs. Ma would scoff at his jack lingo and tell him to speak proper English.

With his stomach satisfied, he went to find her. He had to see her. Sometimes she came with Cookie when he brought pots of steaming soup, but not always.

"Where you going, Preacher Man?" Derek, stationed in front of the kitchen door, spat the words. No one could mistake the challenge in his voice and tone. He might be sober at breakfast, but liquor was sure to make him feel bulletproof by sundown. Bulletproof enough to challenge Noah with more than words. Best to set Derek straight now, in front of everybody.

Noah leaned around his rival, placing his left hand on the table. The hand with the crude ring. "I'm going to see my *wife*."

Derek spoke through clenched teeth, his chaw bulging in his cheek. "You made a mistake. I'd wager the marriage ain't real. Hope you don't regret it, 'cause things ain't over between us."

❄

Back in the kitchen, Adie tried to concentrate on frying bacon. Not that concentrating on anything was easy, considering Noah's kiss. She knew they had to put on a show for the jacks, but, against her will, she wished the kiss could have been real.

Noah's gentleness proved such a contrast to her vile encounter with Derek. The pleasant aroma of shaving cream clung to his face, making her want to draw closer. His lips, which she felt certain had never spat tobacco juice or touched a drop of strong drink, felt full and luxurious—yet unmistakably manly. When they broke away from each other, she'd sensed he hadn't been unaffected. Had she seen a flicker of longing, of what could be?

No. You can't think these things. This is a marriage of convenience. That's all.

The sound of the door opening completed her journey back to reality. She turned to see Noah. Instead of the soft look he'd worn after their kiss, the angles of his face were hard. He bore the stance of a rabid dog straining to be let loose.

All fantasies evaporated. "What's wrong?"

"Stay away from Owens."

"Why?"

"Have Cookie bring out the platters. Or I'll serve. And don't go outside for water. Cookie can."

"He won't hurt me."

"Was I wrong about him coming after you?"

Every ounce of her hated admitting defeat. She didn't want anyone to know she was afraid. "I'll be careful. I promise."

He touched her upper arm. The heat of his hand soaked through her cotton sleeve and made her shiver. "Come with Cookie when he brings lunch. I don't want you alone."

The old man piped up from the big griddle across the room. "Don't worry none. I got my eye on her."

Adie laughed. Now two men observed her every move. Soon they'd be escorting her to the outhouse.

Noah touched her cheek then stepped back. "Don't go out alone. Cookie can walk with you wherever you need to go."

She couldn't suppress her giggle.

"What's so funny?"

"We've been married less than a day, and already we're thinking the same thoughts. Mama and Daddy finished each other's sentences." She warned her heart not to get attached. She'd had enough heartache.

Compassion filled Noah's eyes. "See you later."

"You be careful, too."

She couldn't bear another loss.

❄

Adie had two Dutch ovens from tonight's stew to wash, and then she'd be finished. She longed to return to the cabin. How would she and Noah spend their evening? She recalled Mama darned socks or mended petticoats while Daddy whittled, their cabin snug against the bitter winds. Daddy had done a great job with the chinking. Not a finger of cold had seeped through.

That was all she wanted. Not a big house with so many rooms you got lost, but a cozy cabin with a loft. She'd slept in their cabin's loft before Daddy had started wandering. In the summer, rain pattered on the roof inches from her head. In the winter, frost covered the windowpanes and hoary nails in the eaves.

Her daydreams took her so far from Camp Twelve that she jumped out of her skin like a snake when two hands grabbed her around the waist. She yelped and spun around, planting her foot in the man's belly.

She'd expected Derek. Instead she found Noah, doubled over, clutching his midsection, groaning.

She covered her mouth in horror. "I'm so sorry. Please forgive me."

Cookie rushed to Noah's side. "You gotta watch out for that gal. She's tiny, but she's got a mean punch."

Noah nodded but didn't speak. She pulled over Cookie's bean-snapping chair. "I'm sorry. I know I hurt you, but did I do permanent damage? Do you want some water?"

He waved her away. "I'm fine."

"I thought you were Derek. I was daydreaming, and you scared my heart right out of me. Forgive me? Please?"

She put on her best I-won't-do-it-again face, the one her father couldn't resist.

"Your father taught you to fight well. Next time I'll be noisier."

He hadn't forgiven her. He must be upset. But if she thought about it, he shouldn't have come from behind her. What had he been thinking?

"What are you doing here?"

"I came to see you home. I don't want you out alone, even a short distance."

She repented of the bad things she'd thought. "I'm almost done."

She hurried through the rest of the pots. Before long, she and Noah entered their cabin. A toasty room greeted her.

A book, papers, a pen, and an inkwell littered the tiny table. Curiosity overcame her, and she went for a peek. She sat in the chair, her feet grateful to rest.

The book was a Bible, its leather cover worn. Guilty about snooping, she didn't read the papers.

Noah sat opposite her. "It's a letter to my mother. I can't send it until spring. More than likely, we'll be home before it arrives. But Ma said to tell her all about camp life. I write a little every night."

"Did you write about our marriage?"

"Yes. Would you like to read it?"

She was afraid of what he might have said. "No. Will you tell her I kicked you?"

Noah guffawed, the sound as rich as pound cake. Maybe his laugh meant he wasn't as angry anymore. "Only if you want me to."

"We'd better skip that."

"Would you like to write something?"

A sudden shyness stole up on her. "I wouldn't know what to say."

"You'll love my mother. And she'll love you." He embraced her hand with his own. Unbidden tears welled in her eyes. Oh, to have a mother again.

He removed his hand, leaving her bereft. Her reaction caught her off-guard.

He opened his Bible. "I'd like to read."

She stood. "I'll leave you alone."

He motioned for her to sit. "I'd like to have devotions with you."

She perched on the edge of her chair, tentative. Daddy had read his to himself. She hadn't read the Bible in ages. Her mother's sat in the bottom of her trunk. She didn't understand how God could take Mama from the daughter who desperately needed her.

"I'm going through the Psalms. I'm up to 103. Is that all right?"

She nodded, and he began. She didn't hear most of the passage until he said, "Like as a father pitieth his children, so the Lord pitieth them that fear him."

Did the Lord pity her? Did He love her? She didn't think so. Otherwise He wouldn't have left her without parents and married to a man she didn't know.

He finished reading and she stood suddenly, knocking over her chair, hurrying from the room.

Chapter 7

As it often did, the rhythm of the crosscut saw grinding through the sweet pine carried Noah's thoughts far away. In the past weeks, they'd wandered to Adie.

Butch, his partner, broke the tempo, wiping his sweaty forehead and stretching his muscles. "What's eating at you, Preacher Man? Your eyebrows are scrunched."

Noah made an effort to smooth them. "Nothing."

"There can't be trouble with your wife already. You've been married less than a month."

If Quinn were here—and if he weren't Adie's father—he'd let the words flow like water. But Butch wouldn't understand. On the surface, things with Adie sailed smoothly. Noah anticipated the evenings, when they sat and chatted.

But when talk turned personal, things changed. She withdrew. Most of the time she fled before prayer.

Why couldn't he break through her defenses? They'd be together forever. He wanted to know her. Why couldn't he get close? What caused her to shut herself away?

Butch wouldn't understand.

"No trouble. I couldn't ask for a better wife."

"You sure couldn't. You landed a beauty, with her curves and the way she swings her hips."

Noah's breakfast hardened in his stomach. "That's no way to talk about a woman, especially not my wife. Let's get back to work."

Butch picked up his end of the saw and shrugged. "Sure wish I had a woman like that."

The lump in Noah's gut grew. Were others speaking the same things about his wife?

❄

Adie inhaled, enjoying the soft, cool air after the heat of the stoves. Her boots crunched on the snow as She and Noah walked home one evening. The stars in the inky-black sky danced for them. Not a breath of wind blew. Temperatures were almost balmy.

"Do you mind if we take a walk?" She had a question to ask him, but her nerves acted up. Perhaps it would be easier if she couldn't see him.

Noah, wearing his lumberjack coat with a bright-red scarf, strode beside her. "Let's stay around the clearing. We don't need problems with Owens." He sounded troubled.

They strolled in silence, their feet breaking the sheen of ice before sinking into soft snow. All the while, she contemplated how to phrase the question. Her future loomed in front of her. She knew it wouldn't be what she wanted, but she desired to know what it would be.

Without warning, she stumbled into a hole in the snow left by another's foot. Noah reached to steady her and then offered his arm. She wrapped her fingers around his elbow. Now her heart tripped.

When the tip of her nose stung from the cold, she decided she had to ask. No better way, she supposed, than to come out with it.

"Where is your seminary? Will we go there right away in the spring?"

The footfalls beside her paused, and she stopped too. She could almost hear him holding his breath.

Very softly, so quiet she almost missed his answer, he said, "I won't be going. I'm not going to be a pastor."

Did he speak those words? "Why not?"

"Things have changed." He didn't elaborate, and she chose not to press him.

Her hopes for the upcoming years brightened. His father farmed, and perhaps Noah would, too. "We could homestead somewhere. Minnesota or Iowa."

"No, I'm not going to farm."

"Cattle ranching? One of the farmers Daddy and I worked for last summer headed west." The desert and mountains were dry, but there had to be trees along the rivers for their cabin.

"Maybe I'll try my hand at banking. Bankers lead a settled life. We'll go to my parents' home while I look for a job. I think Madison or even Milwaukee."

A banker? In the city? His voice fell flat, devoid of enthusiasm, not like when he spoke about pastoring. Banking wasn't his dream. What had changed that he couldn't or didn't want to go to seminary?

Her. That's what.

They had married. Now the lumber company fed and housed them. When spring came, that would disappear. He'd be financially responsible for her. The money he'd saved for seminary would be used to provide food and shelter for her.

All her energy drained away. She withdrew her hand from his elbow. "I'm tired. Let's go home."

What could she do? Her best course of action might be to have the marriage annulled as soon as the thaw came. Then he'd be free.

It could be her Christmas gift to him.

The moon rose and cast its pale light across Noah's face. Lines radiated from his eyes and etched paths around his pinched mouth. He'd given up everything to marry and protect her. She hadn't realized that. Her husband was the most unselfish man she'd ever met. Her heart swelled even as it broke into thousands of tiny pieces.

Noah walked beside his wife, gulping lungfuls of mid-December air. Adie's question started him thinking. He hated contemplating the future.

Since he was little, he'd loathed farming. The smells from the cows and pigs had caused him to upchuck more than once. He'd been ashamed of being so weak, but he was powerless against it. As the only boy, he'd had no choice but to help his Pa. He'd had to do his share of the chores.

When he was fifteen or sixteen, a guest pastor spoke at church. He'd never forget the passage the reverend preached on. "Lift up your eyes, and look on the fields; for they are white already to harvest." God had stirred his soul, and Noah had known he'd found his calling.

Or he thought he had. Now he needed a new profession. One that didn't require an education he had no means to finance. Banking sounded dreary and dull. He hated the idea of being surrounded by money all day. But he had to find work because he had a wife.

Adie finished the dishes early a few nights later. She swept the floors and insisted Cookie retire. Noah hadn't arrived, but she decided not to wait for him. What could happen between here and the cabin? She wouldn't be out of screaming range of her husband.

She slipped on her long, blue wool coat and snuffed out the lights. In the depths of winter, the nights were dark and long.

Jack Frost worked hard. A frigid blast met her as she stepped outside, the weather far different from a few nights ago. Fat snowflakes whirled around her, a storm in the making. Lowering her head, she pushed forward.

She hadn't progressed more than a few feet when she ran into a hard, solid object. A man. "Noah, I'm sorry I didn't wait. We finished early, and I started home. But I'm glad you're here."

"I'm glad you're here, too." Derek sneered.

Chilled to the bone, Adie attempted to sidestep the tree-trunk frame of the man in her path. He shifted behind her, grabbed her wrists, and held them both in his huge hand. With his other hand, he covered her mouth. Pressing forward, he pinned her against the mess hall wall, his hand still over her mouth. His rancid breath passed across her neck.

She struggled against his weight.

He crushed her.

She gasped.

He spit tobacco into the snow then wiped his beard across her back. Her stomach heaved, but she refused to vomit.

"You listen up good. I aim to have you. You tell your old man that he needs to be on watch. One day, I'm gonna come for him."

Chapter 8

The snow drifted through the air.

Adie no longer thought it pretty as Derek crushed her against the rough logs.

His lips stung her neck.

She detested him.

He backed away.

She crumpled to the ground. The crunching of his boots faded.

Then she heaved.

She sat and trembled for a while before Noah arrived.

"Adie? Adie!" He rushed to her side, wrapping her in his arms. He felt so wonderful, so secure, that once her stomach was empty she cried.

He lifted her as if she were a child and carried her to the cabin. He tucked her in bed, folding the quilt around her. All the time, she sobbed, unable to stop her tears.

With the coverlet over her, he removed her high-button shoes. His respect for her modesty touched her. She wept harder. He sat beside her, holding her hand, stroking her hair.

A while passed before she'd exhausted her store of tears.

He touched her forehead. "You don't have a fever. Do you still feel ill?"

She shook her head. Though her stomach had quit heaving, it rolled whenever Derek's words echoed in her mind.

"Did you eat something that didn't agree with you?"

She didn't want to alarm him or make him worry, but she had to tell him. He needed to know.

"Derek threatened us."

❄

Owens. Hot anger and cold fear blasted through Noah as he stood over Adie. "What did he do to you?" He became aware of a bruise darkening her forehead. *Dear God, don't let him have touched her.*

She sat and steadied herself. Regret coursed through him. He shouldn't have been so harsh. He knelt beside her. "I'm sorry. It's just that if he. . .I couldn't stand it."

"No. No. He didn't hurt me." The black-and-blue mark on her face belied that. "Cookie and I got the dishes done ahead of time, and I wanted to get home, so I left without you. I walked smack into Derek."

She closed her eyes and took a deep breath. "He told me you needed to watch out for him, that he was coming for you. When he was finished with you, then he could have me all to himself. I think he was threatening to kill you."

She might be right. He wasn't afraid for himself, however. His concern lay with her. Their marriage had done nothing to halt Derek's advances. Instead, it emboldened him.

Quinn had entrusted Noah with his beautiful, beloved daughter. She'd had two run-ins with the louse. He'd failed to protect her. What if Owens didn't back off next time?

The picture of Owens with his hands on her blinded him with rage. She'd become important to him. A sense of comfort and a feeling of home had filled him as he'd watched her mend his shirts and darn his socks, shadows from the flickering firelight dancing across her freckle-spotted face. The gesture was personal and intimate.

She stared at him, her pupils wide in her emerald eyes.

He held her hand, rubbing small circles over the back of it. "Don't worry about me."

"But Derek can't get to me unless he gets rid of you. Our marriage was a mistake. Now you're in more danger than me."

He remembered the emotions streaming through him when he'd discovered her in the snow, sick and sobbing. Her tears felled him. He was as helpless to stop his feelings as he was to stop a toppling pine.

He studied her. Her sunset-colored hair, her sparkling eyes, her proud chin, her soft cheeks, her gentle hands—all mesmerized him.

Far more than that, her lively, charming disposition and caring spirit captured him. She adored Cookie and worked hard to make the older man's burden lighter.

What were these strange, tingling feelings coursing through his soul?

She cupped her hand over his whiskered cheek. "Please be careful, Noah. I couldn't stand it if I lost you, too."

In that instant he identified his feelings.

He loved her.

❄

Noah ambled with Adie through the freshly fallen snow on the way back to their cabin the following night, her arm looped through his. They were joined, connected, and it felt right. He hadn't expected love to happen, but it had. You can't put water back in the pump.

He'd walked her to the mess hall this morning, not leaving until Cookie had arrived. Before breakfast, he'd reported last night's incident to Mr. Larsen. His boss had claimed he could do nothing.

Nothing.

No one had witnessed last night's exchange. Derek would deny it. Mr. Larsen warned him to be extra vigilant the next few days.

He kept his eye on Owens during work, barely caging his rage. He stayed in the dining hall after supper, helping her, and now walking her home.

His newly discovered love grew. He wanted to learn everything about her. Maybe she would trust him enough someday to open up. He wanted to woo her.

When he'd hung up her coat last night after she'd slept, he'd tucked her mittens into her pockets. A crinkling had come from one, and he'd felt a piece of paper. Had Owens slipped her a threatening note? He'd retrieved it. Before him, sketched in pencil, had been a little log cabin. She must have drawn it herself. He'd held his breath as he stared at the beautiful likeness. The proportions had been perfect, the details amazing. She'd included knots in the trunks and traced each chimney rock.

He twirled his mustache as they walked along, wanting to ask her about it, but she yawned. "I'm so tired. You must be exhausted, doing my chores after logging all day."

He stifled a yawn and chuckled. "Guess I am. Maybe we should have devotions and head for bed." The drawing could wait.

Once at the chilly cabin, they settled in for Bible reading. He chose Psalm 91. He wanted to reassure Adie—and himself—that the Lord watched over them.

"'He that dwelleth in the secret place of the most High shall abide under the shadow of the Almighty. I will say of the Lord, He is my refuge and my fortress: my God; in him will I trust. Surely he shall deliver thee from the snare of the fowler, and from the noisome pestilence. He shall cover thee with his feathers, and under his wings shalt thou trust: his truth shall be thy shield and buckler.'"

He peered at her. Tears ran in rivulets down her pale cheeks. He bolted from his chair, flying to her side, grasping her hands. "What's the matter? Did Derek threaten you again?"

❄

Adie shook her head, unable to turn off her tears for the second night in a row.

She'd never been one to cry, but the words Noah read tonight probed all her pain. Ever since Mama had died, and then Daddy, she'd had difficulty reconciling the idea of a loving God with the things happening in her life. Why did He leave her alone in the world? Why did He allow Derek to threaten her and force her to marry a man she'd spoken less than a dozen words to? In this passage, God spoke to her. After all these years, He had a message for her.

"Read it again."

He returned to his chair and traced his finger over the page. "'And under his wings shalt thou trust.'" She stopped him.

"Under his wings." The concept drew her back to sunny childhood days. Daddy had bought Mama laying hens as a birthday surprise. At first they hadn't collected many eggs. They'd allowed some to hatch to increase their flock. She'd loved to watch the fluffy chicks scurry about the coop. When she'd bend to scoop some into her apron, they'd scatter and dart under the hens' wings. Their mothers protected them from Adie's chubby, too-tight grasp.

Was God like that? Did He protect her like the hens protected their chicks? Another memory bombarded her—their log cabin, alone in the Big Woods. No matter how fierce the winter winds had howled, her family had remained snug and secure.

"Is that what God is like? Like the walls of a log cabin keeping out the snow and the predators?"

His eyes shone in the lamplight like melted chocolate. "Yes, I suppose He's as dependable as these four walls. That's a beautiful idea. So perfect. We need to trust with a childlike trust that God will protect us."

She wanted to believe him more than she had wanted to believe in fairy princesses and handsome knights when she was young. "If only I could."

❄

Noah lay in bed and stared into the darkness. Adie had yet to open up to him, but after tonight he held out hope that perhaps he'd thawed the tiniest bit of her barrier. To get her to confide in him might take a long, long time. Noah would wait. Love demanded patience. One wrong word might send her skittering away forever.

His plan to win her heart would commence, though. And he knew the perfect Christmas gift for his wife.

Chapter 9

Adie turned the bread dough, dug in the heels of her hands, stretched away, gave it a quarter turn, and dug in again. She loved to knead. The rocking lulled her, pulling her into her dreams. She imagined firelit shadows on a log wall and a family, happy, laughing, loving. Turning the dough, the dream changed, new shapes appearing.

Two heads, bent over a book, one lean body much taller.

The dreams faded, and her musings wandered to Noah. Gentleness tinged his touch when he'd tended to her after the run-in with Derek. His arm around her ill body had lent her peace and comfort. It had been right that he was there. She'd seen Daddy embrace Mama much the same way when she'd felt sick or had been upset.

When he'd scooped her up and carried her home, his beating heart had knocked against her ribs. They connected. They shared the same fear and pain and formed a marriage union. That circumstance linked them forever.

Adie rounded the dough and patted it. Smooth as a baby's bottom. She divided it into four pieces, shaped them into loaves, set them in pans, covered them with towels, and pushed them to the back of the counter to rise.

She wiped her flour-coated hands on her big apron.

After Noah had laid her in bed the other night, he'd clucked over her like a mother hen.

There appeared that hen image again. This time Noah was the hen, removing her shoes, tucking her into bed, watching over her, protecting her. If she had both God and Noah shielding her, then why did Derek continue to bother her? If God took care of her like He said He did in that psalm, why did she find herself in this situation?

She turned toward the pantry to get flour for pies. Distracted by her contemplations, she rammed into a body. She jumped.

Derek!

Gnarled fingers clasped her forearms. "Whoa, there!"

It was Cookie. She told her heart it could start beating again.

"You're 'bout as skittish as that colt I bought for my Jane one year. He'd eye her, watching, wary, and when she'd get close to him, he'd back up in his stall so far I was afraid he'd kick himself a hole in the wall and take off for the pasture."

"I'm sorry. Did I hurt you?"

The wizened man released his grip and examined himself. "Looks like I'm pretty much in one piece. When you're my age, that's a mighty good thing to say."

She giggled. Cookie had a way of turning on the sunshine. He watched out for her, too. Between him and Noah and God, Derek shouldn't be a problem.

But he was.

"Now you've gone and gotten sad looking. What's troubling you?"

Would he understand everything happening inside her soul? "I have so many things whipping around my brain, I wouldn't know where to start." Her life felt like river rapids, running over rocks, redirecting course at a moment's notice.

"Things been changing for you an awful lot. That's enough to upset anyone. But you want to know a secret?"

She brightened and leaned near so he could whisper in her ear. She loved secrets. As a schoolgirl, her classmates had confided their deepest and darkest desires because they knew she'd never tell. "Go ahead."

"Noah loves you."

She hopped back. Did Cookie murmur those three words? "Noah loves me?"

"Hush now, gal—it's supposed to be a secret."

"How do you know this? Did he tell you?"

"Nope. He didn't have to. I just looked at him looking at you. He can't help himself. He's got it worse'n a cat's got fleas."

"That's such a lovely, romantic picture, Cookie."

He tipped his head and shrugged. "My Jane seemed to think I was pretty romantic. Anyways, only a man crazy in love would do dishes without being hounded. And I seen the way he puts his hand on your back when you two leave. Yup. He sure does love you."

Cookie must have been touched in the head, perhaps even a mite senile. Noah didn't love her. Theirs was a marriage of convenience. At his suggestion.

He couldn't love her.

Cookie continued toward the stove and his simmering soup while she continued to the pantry. As she loaded the apples in her apron, she considered the old man's words. She had married the kindest, most thoughtful man. He took his promises and obligations seriously. The look in his cinnamon-brown eyes caused a giggle to slide up her throat. Maybe a bit of truth hid in Cookie's words.

And Noah gave up his one dream for her. He didn't speak of it much, but when he did she caught the pain that flashed in his face. He wanted to be a preacher. And he'd be a good one. He answered her few questions with care and listened to her thoughts as though they were profound.

Put all together, did that mean he loved her? She dumped the apples on the big scarred farmer's table in the middle of the room. She'd forgotten the flour. Before she could retrace her steps, Cookie interrupted with a wave of his wooden spoon. "I got you a Christmas present."

Her heart skidded. She didn't have anything for him. "What is it?"

"Now, if I up and told you, it'd ruin the secret."

She could keep secrets, but she detested not being told one. Cookie knew that. "That's not fair. Please tell me."

"Nope. You gotta guess."

The worst punishment. "I hate guessing."

"Then I won't tell you." He turned his attention to the beef soup.

She gave an exaggerated sigh. "A palace of gold?"

"Be reasonable, gal."

"Okay, a new apron."

"Better guess. But not right."

The man downright relished teasing her. "A china doll with eyes that open and shut."

"Now where'd I get that? The wanigan don't have none."

"I guessed three times. Now you have to tell me."

"Who made up that rule? I'm not telling you."

Men were the most infuriating creatures God made. She took two steps toward the pantry.

"I'm giving you Christmas Eve supper off so you and Noah can spend it together, without them other men there. Maybe he'll even tell you he loves you himself."

Christmas Eve. Tomorrow night. The night she planned to give Noah her gift. "I can't leave you to do the cooking and dishes yourself. That's too much."

"It'll be soup and cold sandwiches. The men'll have their Christmas goose the next day." He took the empty water pail and exited through the back door, ending the conversation.

Daddy had always made Christmas a nice celebration for them. Before they came to the camp in the late fall, he'd hide away a few sticks of peppermint candy and some small item—hair combs, fabric for a new dress, the photograph of him and Mama that sat on the mantel.

This year she dreaded it. Knowing Noah loved her would make it a hundred times more difficult to set him free.

❄

Noah and Adie hung their coats on the peg driven into the log near the door before rubbing their hands together in front of the fire. Even though the walk between the mess hall and their tiny home took three minutes at the most, with the temperature plummeting below zero tonight, their fingers froze in that short time.

Noah cast a glance at his wife. She turned away and studied her red hands as if they fascinated her. Several times this evening, while they'd done dishes and swept the floor, she'd also glanced his way. She peeked at him again, a quizzical look slanting her auburn brow.

"What is it? Do I have crumbs in my mustache?" He twirled the end.

Ribbons of pink streaked her cheeks.

She shook her head. "I was thinking."

"About what?"

She paused. "Nothing." With a swish of her skirts, she twirled toward the table and sat down. "What is this? Where did you find it?"

Adie held the log cabin drawing in her hand. He'd neglected to put it away before he went to fetch her. The few minutes each day he had here without his wife he spent whittling and fashioning her gift. He'd finished it tonight, imagining the look in her green eyes when he presented it to her.

"I wasn't snooping. The night of your encounter with Derek, I stuck your mittens in your coat pocket. The paper crackled, and I was afraid I'd wrinkled it, so I took it out to see. It's beautiful. It's so realistic it could almost be a photograph. Did you draw it?"

She nodded. "My parents and I lived there. I never wanted to leave. Every night I dream of returning. I drew this picture a summer or two ago, so I would never forget."

He couldn't wait to give her the replica he'd made. If he hoped before she'd be pleased, now he knew without a doubt that she'd love it. He almost reached under his bed to give it to her now, but then decided against it. Tomorrow, Christmas Eve, he'd hand it to her. Perhaps in her eyes he'd spy the same love he felt.

Chapter 10

Adie's ham, baked in apple cider in the kitchen's oven, sat on the tiny table in the cabin. The mashed sweet potatoes, smothered in butter, were whipped up fluffy. At the center of the table, on top of her mother's special violet-dotted tablecloth, stood a three-layer spice cake, slathered in buttercream frosting.

She sat in her chair, its curved arms smooth from years of use. Tonight she didn't mend or knit but twisted her fingers as she thought about giving Noah his Christmas gift, the gift of freedom. If he did love her, he wouldn't be happy. She'd have to convince him it was for the best.

And it was.

An inexplicable sadness settled over her. She'd miss him. She'd come to care for him. He'd been so good to her—how couldn't she? When she left in the spring, she'd be alone, nowhere to go, no one to go there with, only God and His promise to keep her under His wings. That would have to be enough.

Tonight she'd taken her time to look her finest, sweeping up her curls and putting on her best dress, her wedding gown. She smoothed the brown poplin against her lap.

The door swung open, and Noah arrived in a blizzard of snow and sleet. "That storm is something." He stomped the snow from his boots and unwound his muffler.

She ran to assist him. "Warm yourself by the fire, and I'll pour the coffee."

He looked at the table. "Is this your surprise?"

She tugged at her sleeves. "Do you like it?"

He stopped in front of the fireplace and rubbed his hands together. "You made all of it?"

She nodded.

"I say we hurry and pray so we can eat."

He liked it. Now if only he'd eat slowly, prolonging the time before she told him the rest.

An hour later, he wiped the ends of his mustache with his napkin and leaned back. "That was the best meal I've had in a long time. Almost as good as Ma's."

Though better than his mother's would have been nice, she accepted the compliment. She wanted to enjoy the evening, but anxiety was about to burn a hole through her stomach. Maybe it was best to just say it.

She wished she didn't have to hurt him. She felt his pain as her own.

"Adie, what's wrong? You look distressed."

She couldn't hide it any longer. "I have to tell you something."

He sat forward. "What? I'm not going to like it, am I?"

"It's my Christmas gift."

"Why are you upset? I'm sure I'll love it."

"I appreciate how you stepped forward to take care of me. That cost you your dream. I don't want to steal that. I'm giving you your freedom. Come spring, I'm leaving. Alone. We'll have our marriage annulled."

Mama would've told him to shut his mouth 'cause he'd catch nothing but flies. "What are you saying?"

"In the end, you'll be happy. It's for the best."

He stood, towering over her, his words firm. "No, it's not." He lowered his voice. "*I* made the decision to marry you—voluntarily. I knew the cost."

She peered back, not intimidated. "I won't stand in the way of what you want."

"What if I want you?"

He didn't know what he said. Adie shook her head. "My mind is made up."

He stomped to the door and grabbed his jacket from the hook.

"Where are you going? It's storming, and the temperature's dropping. You'll freeze to death."

"And that wouldn't bother you much, would it?"

Tears blurred her last glimpse of him.

Noah walked into the storm, not knowing where he was going and not caring. How could she do that? Just say she would leave him in the spring. He loved her. He thought she at least liked him.

He'd been mistaken.

Her rejection smarted worse than the snow pellets stinging his face. Tears filled the corners of his eyes.

He walked a few more minutes, blinded by his hurt, wondering what he'd done wrong. Had he said something that had driven her away? He had to think of a way to convince her she was his dream. He wanted her to stay.

Lost in his thoughts, he never heard anyone approach. Rough hands grabbed him from behind and dragged him into the snow. Rock-hard fists slammed into his face and belly. "I always get what I want." A blow with each word.

Owens.

Noah fought back. He landed several punches to the side of Owens' head. He connected hard, injuring his hand. The heavier man wasn't fazed. The strikes kept coming. He tasted blood.

Then Owens knocked him on the temple. Hard. His ears rang. Dots danced in his vision.

His last thoughts were of Adie.

❄

Adie must have paced a mile or more between the door and the table. She had done it all wrong, springing the news on Noah like that. On the most blessed of days, too.

Now, because of her, he'd been gone a long time. Frigid air seeped under the door. She feared for him. If anything happened to him, she'd be to blame.

Lord, cover Noah with Your feathers. Keep him warm and safe under Your wings. She needed to find him.

A few minutes later, wrapped in as many layers as she could manage, she grasped the knob to open the door. She pulled, and someone pushed and then stumbled into the room.

"Mr. Larsen." At least she thought that's who was under the floppy hat.

"Where are you going on a night like this, Adie?"

"Noah and I had a disagreement. He walked out and has been gone too long. I'm worried."

He handed her a bulging envelope. "I came to deliver this. You stay here." He raised his lantern. "I'll look for him."

"But. . ."

"Stay put. It's too cold for you. He couldn't have gone far. I'll find him."

Before she mounted another protest, he left. She unwrapped herself and tried to settle in front of the fire. She had no heart to clear the table.

"What ifs" assailed her. What if he didn't come back because he was so angry? What if the storm worsened and he couldn't find the cabin? What if he never came back?

She didn't want to lose him. She crumpled with the thought. Without him, life would be empty. By her own actions, she'd lost another person she loved.

Loved.

She sat up with a start. She loved him. Why hadn't she realized it before?

Her mind had closed itself to the possibility of love, but her heart hadn't. Without even knowing, she'd fallen in love with her husband.

And sent him away.

She needed to make things right. Again she pleaded with the Lord to bring him home.

As she finished her prayer, something—or someone—crashed into the door. "Open up."

She let in Mr. Larsen, who dragged Noah with him. "Found him in the snow. He's taken a pretty good beating, and he's cold. Get some coffee while I settle him in bed."

Mr. Larsen peeled off Noah's shirt. She turned to coax the fire to life but glanced over her shoulder from time to time. She'd never seen her husband like this. Her pulse throbbed wildly in her neck, and her legs trembled. His arms, though thin, bulged with muscles. Dark, curly hair covered his chest, and his flat stomach caved inward.

Heat suffused her.

She brought the coffee, and Mr. Larsen rose. "He's bruised, and I suspect his ribs are cracked, but he should be fine."

"Thank you for saving his life."

Mr. Larsen nodded. "Now I need to take care of Owens."

A rush of alarm swept over her. In all her concern about her husband, she'd shut Derek from her mind. He might be out there. He might come after them.

"Do you think he'll. . . ?"

Mr. Larsen patted her back. "I found him in the snow about fifty yards from Noah. Don't know what happened to him, whether your husband landed a good blow to his head or he drank himself to his grave. Either way, he'll never bother you again."

She wilted in relief. Here in this cabin they were safe, snug, secure.

Chicks under God's wings.

After Mr. Larsen left, she checked Noah, brushing a sandy lock from his brow.

"Did you hear that? I'm safe. But I didn't think it would be this hard to let you go."

He stirred and opened his eyes. "Adie?"

"Right here." She ceased breathing for a moment as she realized she was right where she wanted to be.

"I love you."

Her heart asked if this could all be a dream. No, Cookie had been right. He did love her. "I know."

"Please don't leave me."

She didn't want to. But no reason remained for the marriage. "Derek's dead. I'll be safe. I won't let you give up your dream."

"You're my dream."

She couldn't reply.

"Your present is in the top of my chest. Get it."

"You don't have to give me anything." Especially after the disaster her gift had turned out to be.

"I want to."

She'd upset him enough for one night and didn't want to distress him further. Going to his chest, she discovered a package clumsily wrapped in brown paper.

"Open it."

She wondered what could be inside the strange, lumpy parcel. Her hands shook as she tugged away the paper. She pulled out a miniature cabin and gasped. Turning it, she inspected it from every angle, not able to believe what she saw.

"It's perfect. Just like my drawing, like the log cabin from my childhood."

"Do you like it?"

"I love it." She sat facing him on the edge of the bed. "Thank you." Her supple lips brushed his.

❄

Her touch ignited him. He embraced her and, ignoring the pain it caused, drew her close, claiming her kisses. She reciprocated. When they parted some minutes later, they were both breathless.

Something changed in Adie. She shone. The words burst from him. "I love you."

She began to cry. "Don't say that."

He saw the truth in her face, in the soft curve of her pink lips. "I know you love me."

"Nothing's changed. No matter how we feel about each other, I won't allow you to trade what you've always wanted for me."

He moaned in pain as he struggled to sit. "You're the most stubborn woman God ever put on this earth."

She giggled through the tears. "Daddy told me that all the time." She went to sit at the table. Her eyebrows creased as she picked up a large envelope.

The parcel caught Noah's curiosity, too. "What's that?"

"I don't know. Mr. Larsen brought it. That's when he offered to look for you."

She unfolded the flap. Her eyes grew as large as tree trunks, and her hands shook as she withdrew a sheet of paper and read it. Then she laughed.

"What's inside?"

She came and handed him the envelope. "This is for you."

He gasped when he saw the number of bills inside. Why would she give him all this money? Where had it come from?

"The note says Daddy saved it to buy me a farm, like I'd always wanted. Use it for seminary. Don't give that up."

He couldn't take Quinn's final gift from her. Not deserving, he held out the envelope. "I won't take it. You can't give up that for me."

She picked up the miniature log cottage. "I won't be giving up anything. I'll always have this, wherever we go. Whether we live in a palace or a hovel, or even a little log cabin, it will be home. Because you'll be there."

Would she give it all up for him? Them? "Are you sure?"

"I love you. God protected you for a reason and gave us both our dreams."

His heart pattered in disbelief. God had blessed him beyond measure and graced both him and Adie with everything they'd ever wanted. His throat clogged, but he squeezed out the words. "I love you, too. Marry me."

She swept her fingertips across his temple, and he pressed her hand to his cheek. "We're already married."

"I want to be married the way two people should be."

A soft pink touched her cheeks. "I do."

He drew her close. "Merry Christmas, Adie."

"Merry Christmas, my love."

Liz Tolsma has lived in Wisconsin most of her life, and she now resides next to a farm field with her husband, son, and two daughters. Add a dog and a cat to that mix and there's always something going on at their house. She's spent time teaching second grade, writing advertising for a real estate company, and working as a church secretary, but she always dreamed of becoming an author. When not busy putting words to paper, she enjoys reading, walking, working in her large perennial garden, kayaking, and camping with her family. She'd love to have you visit her at www.liztolsma.com or at www.liztolsma.blogspot.com.
Soli Deo Gloria

The Dogtrot Christmas

by Michelle Ule

Chapter 1

B alanced on top of the sticky pine cabin wall, Molly Faires clung to the end of the log roof beam while Jamie fought to place it.

"Easy now. I think I've got it. Get down and out of the way." Jamie didn't take his eyes off the log as Molly scrambled down the unchinked walls to the ground.

Molly tucked a strand of blond hair back into her sunbonnet as she watched her brother wrestle the log toward the notches.

"Is it lined up?" he called.

"Almost there." She held her breath. This was the first one. If the two of them could set the beams, they wouldn't need to bother the neighbors for more help. Once they got the beams secure, Jamie could build a single roof covering the two small cabins and the breezeway in between: a "dogtrot" cabin.

When his straw hat blew off in the direction of the flourishing vegetable patch, Jamie stayed on focus, inching the heavy log into place. But then a swallow flit too close; he jerked and lost his hold. "It's going. Watch out!"

Molly sprinted a dozen yards north to where she'd tied the young'un, Andy, to a loblolly pine stump already trying to sprout again.

The log shuddered down the side of the western cabin wall, landed on end, and fell forward with a mighty thud into the stump-studded yard. Belle, the yellow dog who had followed them all the way from Tennessee, hightailed it to the woods.

Molly hugged the toddler to her side while she gauged Jamie's reaction. All around her the forest seemed to wait, too: the bobwhites in midcall and the mourning doves worrying in the underbrush.

From his perch on the cabin wall, Jamie snickered.

Molly bit her lip in hope.

He slapped his thighs, threw back his head, and laughed with a crescendo that exploded the world back into action.

Molly's shoulders relaxed in relief. He hadn't laughed since his wife, Sarah, had died in childbirth on the trail from Tennessee fifteen months ago.

Andy shouted his baby talk and raised his arms.

"I've got ye." Molly untied the little boy and carried him to his father.

Jamie jumped down and examined the beam. "It's too big for the two of us," he said, taking the toddler. "I'll have to ask Clay Ramsey another favor and get him over to help finish up. Ye may be strong, but setting roof beams is a man's job."

Molly surveyed the clearing they had grubbed together in the hill country full of piney woods. Most of the logs, fat ones as well as saplings, had gone into building the two small cabins. A stack of cedar shingles, about half of what they needed, waited for the beams and crosspoles to go onto the roof.

"Surely we can try again," Molly said. "I'll help. I know I can share the burden."

Jamie shook his head. "The Good Lord's been a' watching out for us, but I don't want ye to get hurt. I'll ask Ramsey and Pappy Hanks's boys up to help soon. I should have all the shingles made by then."

The animation sagged out of his eyes, and his skin seemed to go thin as the bleakness he had worn for so long took hold again. "It's not like she'll be here to see it."

"But ye picked a good site," Molly said. "Just what Sarah wanted." The living cabin was on the right, the cookhouse cabin ten feet away on the north side, leaving a space big enough for three dogs to trot between. She hoped one day to have a cabin like it with a man of her own.

"Aye, this style cabin works best in Texas. Soon enough, we can put up the roof to join the cabins, and this homestead will be done."

Molly shook her head. "Maybe your part will be done, but I'll be hauling mud from the stream to chink out those logs all summer."

Jamie set his son onto wobbly legs and tousled his hair. "This young'un can help. He'll like getting his hands in the mud. 'Sides, he needs to start earning his keep."

"You're starting him to work young, like Pappy."

"You don't know how long you got with 'em. We be blessed Ma and Pappy started us working young."

The half-built cabins sat in a clearing that sloped gently down to a trail through the dense underbrush and woods that sheltered the watering hole. Green leaves stirred in a scrap of breeze and alerted Molly's senses. Injuns raided this countryside. Her ma had warned many times—you never saw 'em until too late.

Belle's barking turned to a gruff bay, and Jamie thrust Andy to Molly. "Hie ye to the cookhouse, and bar the door."

"Hush, Andy." Molly scurried with him to the roofless cook cabin. Jamie grabbed his rifle.

She crouched beside Andy and stared through the log gaps toward the trail. Belle bounded from the woods, making enough noise to flush out every bird within miles. The dog paced before the cabins, teeth bared. Jamie waited in the breezeway.

A ragged, dirty Tejano man, dressed in the sort of clothing worn by Texas Mexicans, pushed out of the woods, leading a lame satiny black stallion. "*Vaya, perro*," he shouted at Belle.

The dog paced left and right, growling and barking. The man stopped. "*Qué es eso?*"

Jamie walked toward him cradling the rifle in one arm and holding up the other hand in greeting. "*Buenos días.*"

"Good day," the Tejano's deep voice held only a trace of Spanish accent. "Call off your dog."

Jamie slapped the side of his right leg, and Belle joined him. The dog quieted but did not take her eyes off the stranger.

"I have been away. You are new here." The man removed his faded cloth hat and untied the red scarf from around his neck. He wiped his forehead in the June heat, and Molly noted his handsome features. His blue-black hair shone in the sunlight as he glanced around the clearing.

Jamie shifted. "Ye be from around here?"

"I am Luis Vasco de Carvajal." He gestured north. "My family has lived on this land for three generations."

Jamie extended his hand. "Jamie Faires. Ye be our neighbor, then."

The man's eyes swept to Molly, and he nodded. She picked up the toddler and joined them.

"This be Molly and my boy, Andy."

Luis Vasco de Carvajal swept into the bow of a Spanish gentleman. "The countryside always welcomes beautiful women."

"Thank ye," Molly said. His obvious weariness caught her heart. "Have ye far to go? May I get ye and your horse water?"

Coal-black eyes stared. "We drank at the stream."

"Your English be very good." Molly shifted Andy in her arms. "May he pet your horse?"

"*Sí.*" Carvajal motioned the horse forward. "I had an American tutor who visited over the years. It is important to speak with Anglos in a language they understand."

The horse's tongue stretched to explore Andy's fingers. He giggled. Molly smelled the sweetness of the woods in the horse's mane and sighed. "Don't you miss having a horse, Jamie?"

He nodded.

"What's his name?" Molly asked.

"Maximo." Carvajal frowned. "How do you hold this land?"

Jamie set the rifle on the ground beside his boot. "Bought it. We traveled with a party from Tennessee and settled the land this spring."

"How much land?"

"As head of household they only let me have forty-six hundred acres. I share with Molly."

Molly watched the Tejano calculate their holdings. She wanted to grab Jamie's arm and warn him not to say too much. But she was nineteen to his twenty-four; surely he knew better.

The man's jaw tightened, and his dark eyes flashed. "This is fine property," he said. "I have liked it since my father gave it to me."

Jamie flushed. "We paid hard cash for this land."

"Perhaps you paid money," Carvajal said. "But you are squatters. I will have my land back." He turned on his heel, tugged the horse's bridle, and headed into the dense undergrowth.

Before they could reply, he disappeared.

Chapter 2

Who did this? Luis thought as he stalked toward the family *ranchero* he had left three years before. Who would have sold his property to Anglos?

He didn't have to think long: Manuel.

Luis had received only one letter from Mamacita during his time in the south, and that letter had announced his father's death and his teenage sister's marriage to Manuel Gomez, a man ten years her senior. Luis knew in his absence Manuel would try to control the family property. But would Mamacita have allowed him to sell Luis's land? Didn't she follow the instructions he sent from Mexico City?

Anglos. Luis had had his fill of the greedy, proud Americans who had flooded his Texas the last fifteen years. To have them live nearby could be troublesome, even if the war was finally over and Texas a republic in its own right. Luis set his lips. The land belonged to him, no one else.

He paused when Maximo nickered. The stallion had carried him all the way to Santa Ana's government in Mexico City and back. What a shame he'd turned up lame only half a day from home. "We will put you in the pasture and let you grow fat again on Carvajal Ranchero grass," Luis said as he stroked the horse's powerful neck. "I will find you beautiful mares, and we'll live on our ranchero in peace."

But where? Luis had planned to clear the land and build his own house on the exact spot the boyish Anglo had chosen.

I will need a wife, too.

But who? Would Carlita have waited for him? Did Carmen still flutter her fan with wanton skill? And what about a blond woman with bluebonnet eyes?

Luis stopped. What had made him think of the Anglo's wife? He shook his head. He had been away from his people too long.

May I get your horse water? He thought about her soft voice, a slight burr to her English words. It jiggled the memory of a story he had heard once, about a man who married a woman because she volunteered to water his animals.

Crazy Anglos. A horse requires much water. The Anglo girl would grow tired very quickly if she tried to water Maximo.

And why did her husband allow her to speak to him? A Mexican *señora* would have worn a *mantilla* veil across her face and wouldn't dare address another man. Luis would deal with that boyish husband. They were children and he a man of horse and cattle, a *vaquero*. Luis would get his land back.

As he strode through the mottled sunlight of the forest floor, Luis tried to slough off the horror of the last years. He knew and loved this land, so very different from the dry, cactus-studded ground beyond the Rio Grande. Since the day he'd left, his soul had yearned for green woods threaded with streams and filled with game.

When the trees thinned, he came to a broad clearing dominated by a wooden ranch house with a deep porch and steep roof to keep off the east Texas rains. Smoke rose from the cookhouse chimney, and colorful lantanas grew below the porch in welcome. He sighed: El Ranchero de Carvajal, home at last.

Mamacita dashed from the house as quickly as her tiny feet could move. Tears streamed down her plump cheeks, and dazzling earrings caught the light. She clasped her hands before her heart and babbled his name: "Luis, Luis, *mi caro*, Luis."

"Mamacita." He kissed her on both cheeks and then knelt at her feet.

She dropped her hands onto his head and murmured, "*Gracias a Dios*"— thanks be to God—"who brought my son back to me."

A squeal from behind announced his sister Maria. "You have returned, Luis! Where have you been? Why were you gone so long? We thought you were dead."

"Dead? Did you not receive my letters?" Luis frowned.

"No, mi *hijo*," Mamacita said. "Many thought you dead, but I prayed for your safe return. My heart, mi *corazón*, it overflows with gladness to my Creator."

Maria grabbed her mother's hands. "No, Mamacita, Manuel doesn't like it when you talk about God like Anglos."

Luis stood; he towered over the women. "You have spent time with Anglos? Who sold my property?"

"We thought you were dead," Maria cried.

Mamacita clapped her hands. Two servants with narrow black braids scurried from the *casa*. Mamacita gave directions accented with cries of thanks to God. The women stared at Luis. Mamacita clapped her hand again, and they ran off.

"Mi corazón, I will have them kill the fatted calf."

He scrutinized his mother. He had never heard her use such terms. The words reminded him of verses from the Bible his tutor Tomás had made him read all those years before.

"*Dónde está* Manuel?" Luis scanned the area for his brother-in-law. Hens scratched near the fence. Several head of cattle foraged in the pasture near the cookhouse. The property appeared neglected; no men were in sight.

"He went yesterday to Nacogdoches to sell livestock. He will return soon, if God wills," Maria said. "Where have you been, Luis?"

"I have been to Mexico City, Bexar, Coahuila, and other places against my will. I was forced to fight, drafted into a war I did not want. That is behind me now."

"What happened in your battles?" Maria twisted the beads around her neck.

He shook his head. "I do not wish to talk of war. It is not safe with so many Americans around. I want to know why those Anglos are on my property. A boy has built a cabin."

The women looked at each other. Mamacita wrung her hands. "We received no word, no letters in all these years. Manuel said you must be dead. He sold the property because he said we needed the money."

Luis rocked back on his heels. All the politics, all the time he had been forced to fight when he wanted nothing more than to come home. And for what? To lose his land at the hands of a greedy brother-in-law and a young American?

"But I am not dead. Americans may have defeated Santa Ana at the Battle of San Jacinto, but they have no right to my land."

"Manuel says many things are changing," Maria said. "How will you fight the American for your land?"

Luis shook his head. "I am tired of fighting. I want peace."

Mamacita touched his shoulder. "I am sorry, mi hijo. But if you do not wish to speak of war, perhaps we can talk of the greatest thing: love. Have you seen a woman to catch your eyes and steal your heart in all your travels? Perhaps a fair-haired *señorita?*"

Luis stepped back in surprise. What had happened to his mother in the last three years? And could she now read his mind?

Chapter 3

July

A scream from the woods yanked Molly awake. Her racing heartbeat choked her as she stared between the unchinked logs. Dawn's faint glow cast a blue-gray light over the clearing. Jamie sat up from the floor and grabbed his long rifle.

Another high-pitched cry shivered through the air. "Who is she?"

"No woman," Jamie said. "That be a panther."

Across the breezeway, the cow mooed in the north cabin where they had penned her for the time being. The half-dozen chickens clucked their worry. Belle howled.

Jamie pushed past the sleeping Andy and peered out. The screeching faded into the north woods, and Belle quieted. Andy muttered and rolled to his side, thumb in mouth.

"Dear, Jesus, please protect us," Molly prayed.

"Always does, always will. I'll be glad when we get the roof on, though," Jamie said.

"You don't think?"

"Panthers climb trees. Good thing the Ramseys are coming today." He nudged her foot. "Are you sorry now you asked us not to finish the whole cabin when the Hanks boys helped me raise the walls?"

Molly pulled the quilt to her chin. "I figured we could live without a roof longer than most. With Lily's pregnancy, the Ramseys needed a home before us. I'm glad you agreed. It was the right thing to do."

Jamie grunted and poked at the white oiled canvas stretched across the top of the cabin as a makeshift roof. "We'll need to get this down before everyone arrives."

An hour after sunrise, Clay and Lily Ramsey rode up in a wagon with their three children. "Jamie, ready to raise a roof?" the red-faced Clay called in a cheery voice.

"We all are." Molly took the toddler from Lily's arms. "When is your next babe coming?"

"Fall." Lily retied her bonnet. "We be blessed Jamie helped finish our place first."

"Believers do good for each other," Jamie said. "Willie and two Hanks boys will be here right soon. I figure to have the whole roof on today."

Clay eyed the rough cabins. "What made ye build both rooms so soon? Couldn't ye get along in one?"

"We built on the midpoint," Jamie said. "Molly has her cabin, and I have mine."

"And what happens when your sister marries and doesn't want to share half a dogtrot with ye and Andy?" Lily asked.

Molly's lips twitched.

"She hates to burden anyone. Molly can follow her new man home." He winked at her.

Molly led Lily to a stump by the cook fire while she stirred up the corn pone in the three-legged iron frying pan. She slid a piece of fat around the inside and then mixed in water and cornmeal. Molly put on the lid and shoveled coals around the sides and top. The pone would bake into a brown cake by the time the menfolk got hungry.

"That Sarah's spider ye cooking with?" Lily asked.

Molly couldn't trust her voice. She nodded.

"Sure is something to see her babe running with mine." Lily blinked rapidly. "'Twas a bad night when we lost Sarah."

Molly studied her. "Ye scared of the same thing?"

Lily's eyes followed the children. "Ma Hanks will come; Pappy Hanks should be back from circuit ridin', and he'll pray. God numbers the hairs on our heads, and he knows Clay and the children need me. I'll trust Him."

"I be praying for ye, too." Molly picked up the empty water bucket. "We need more water."

Lily waved her away. "I'll watch the young'uns and the cook fire."

"Thank ye." Molly collected two buckets and followed the thin path through the clearing's coarse grass. She brushed at nettles and remembered her Scottish ma's affection for tea made from steeping the flowers. Molly stopped and closed her eyes, willing a memory of her parents and four brothers sipping tin mugs of tea in the Tennessee cabin. The image shimmered like the wings of a dragonfly waiting to light, but then snapped shut, empty.

Molly sighed. "Thank ye, Lord, I've still got Jamie and Andy. Help me serve 'em well." She continued on her way.

Heat had risen with the sun, and Molly felt the cooling drop in temperature when she entered the dense wood. A hare startled and disappeared into the brush. The chattering stream called greetings when Molly dipped the buckets.

She checked over her shoulder as she knelt by the water. She loved the leaf-patterned light and the splashes of wildflower color, but the thicket, for all it provided, could hide as well. A hoot, a whistle, the warble of sapsuckers, made her uneasy. Birdsong or man-made?

When both buckets were full, Molly stepped carefully in the direction of the clearing. She paused at the muddy path. A heel mark in the mud caught her eye; boots she didn't recognize had passed this way.

❄

Luis did not mean to spy on the woman with the corn-colored hair, but he needed to know what the Anglos were doing. Their shouts and thudding hammers rang through the forest, sending a tremor through the wildlife of his woods; indeed, even through his heart. The foolish girl had knelt before checking. He knew the hoot hadn't been real and stepped behind a tree to watch.

Her body stiffened as she grasped the bucket handles. She moved back to the trail with steady steps, before stopping and searching the clearing one last time. Her pretty face crumpled with uncertainty, and then she left.

Luis waited, counting to two hundred as his father had taught him. Soon a red man slipped out of the thicket, watched after the girl, and then blended back into the forest. Luis pointed his long gun north and followed the Indian; he knew how to hunt men.

Wild grapevines twined across the deer path Luis followed. He cursed when a pawpaw branch smacked him in the face and he lost sight of the red man. He shouldered the long gun and turned toward home.

The ranchero buzzed with activity. He stopped one of the servant girls. "What has happened?"

"The master has come; we must hurry."

"*Señor* Gomez?"

"Sí," she said with wide eyes. "The master."

Luis marched toward the house. Where had his brother-in-law been the three weeks since Luis's return?

A bulky man with a bushy black mustache, Manuel leaned back in a chair on the porch, his feet on the railing and a pungent cigar between his teeth. Maria fluttered about him while Mamacita sat upright nearby. She beckoned to Luis.

"You are back," Manuel growled. Two chair legs thudded onto the floor.

"Where have you been?" Luis kept his voice even but firm.

Manuel took the cigar from his mouth and picked at his teeth. "I ask you the same."

"I have been to war. How did you come to sell my property to Anglos?"

The man shrugged. "You were not here. They wanted land. We needed money. Cash. Your father would have done the same."

"My father never would have sold his land. Where is the money?"

Manuel gestured with his cigar. "Gone. The livestock has thinned. Things are not what they were."

Luis narrowed his eyes. "Show me an accounting. Now."

"Accounting is for Anglos." Manuel dropped ashes onto the porch. "You were dead. I am the man of the ranchero, and I make the decisions."

Luis glanced at Mamacita. With her eyes closed and her lips moving, was she praying? About what? He climbed the three steps to the porch and stood over Manuel. "I am Carvajal. These are my ancestral lands. I want an accounting, or you will leave."

"But this is our home." Maria clutched her husband's broad shoulders so hard her knuckles turned white.

Luis raised his eyebrows. "Manuel owns land northeast of Nacogdoches. That became your home when you married."

"Mamacita," whined Maria.

Mamacita opened her eyes. "If you cannot answer Luis's questions, you must leave, Manuel. A good steward provides an accounting to the owner. Luis is correct. You have a casa. With Luis returned, I do not need you to manage the ranchero."

Maria fumbled for a handkerchief. Manuel's face distorted into rage. "I cared for you, Mamacita. You cannot throw us out."

"I asked God to send someone to help you see the error of your ways. A workman is worthy of his wage, Manuel. You have not been a good steward of our family property. Now you must return to your own."

"You cannot send me away," Manuel thundered.

Maria's hands went to her belly. "What about my baby?"

Mamacita sighed and folded her hands. "If Manuel cannot explain how he has handled the ranchero's finances, you will go in the morning." She rose. "Dinner is served."

Chapter 4

With the new roof overhead, the cabin was dimmer—light only shone through the gaps between the logs. Molly didn't mind because now she had a place of her own. With winter still months away, she could take her time chinking the cracks.

On that July afternoon, however, she couldn't imagine the cold and excitement of Christmas. Molly lifted the thick braid off her neck. Right now she'd be thankful for anything to stir the languid mugginess.

She moved about the small, square cabin setting things aright. Jamie had built a shelf on the long wall above her straw tick mattress. There she placed her mother's thick leather-bound Bible, her oldest brother John's drawing of the family, and her grandmother's sewing kit, which had crossed the ocean from Scotland. Molly touched each precious treasure in turn, remembering.

When the pain of their loss finally eased to acceptance, she grabbed the twig broom and set to work.

Across the breezeway in the south cabin, Andy muttered. Molly stopped sweeping the hard dirt floor to check on him: still asleep on his father's straw tick. Down the rise, she saw Jamie carrying a bucket of water in one hand, toting his rifle in the other. She went to meet him.

"A roof makes a difference, don't ye think?" Jamie handed her the bucket.

"It makes the cabin more secure and finished."

"I'll cut windows soon." Jamie removed his straw hat and fanned himself. "Raisin' a cabin and startin' a farm takes a lot of work."

"Ye don't remember building the claim in Tennessee?"

"I was a young'un, maybe three, afore ye were born. John and Samuel, they did most of the helping, even though they were young'uns, too. Billy was a babe," he sighed. "All passed on to glory now."

Jamie set his jaw, and Molly knew the bleak expression would thin across his eyes. She touched his sleeve. "They'd all be proud of your hard work. Ye be a good man, Jamie Faires."

He squinted toward the sun. "Thank ye for coming with me, Molly. I talked to Steele Hanks back in Tennessee about leaving ye behind in Tennessee. But Sarah said family needs to stick together. She said it was the right thing to do.

I'm glad I listened to her."

"Aye. Sarah was a wise, godly woman."

"But she's dead gone like all the rest. It be time to move on."

Molly shook her head. "I don't understand."

"Ye be a fine sister, but a man gets lonely." Jamie tucked the rifle under his arm and reached for his ax. "Ye remember to carry Samuel's long rifle with ye into the forest, 'specially when you start chinking. I'm going to clear more trees. Belle?" He paused and looked around. "Where be that hound?"

She watched him return to the woods. He'd deal with his sorrow by work. "Help him to fear no evil, Lord, for thou art with him."

Molly hauled the water back to the cabin and poked her head into the south side of the dogtrot. The toddler slept, but between the unchinked logs, a sinewy hand stretched through to pat Andy's back. As Molly reached for Samuel's rifle, the figure on the other side of the log wall shrieked. The savage laughter ricocheted through her skull, driving out everything but the high-pitched horror.

Andy rolled over.

Her heart racing and feet tripping in panic, Molly snatched the rifle. By the time she got to the corner of the cabin, however, only the fluttering branches of the undergrowth indicated where the Injun had fled.

Late in July, Luis crept along the stream on the side opposite the trail and heard singing from the water hole. He did not understand the words, twisted as they were with her "ye" and "thee." The Anglo, Molly, had hitched her skirts high and waded into the middle of the stream, where she doused a faded rust-colored dress in the water. Luis frowned at the immodesty of her bare legs and told himself not to stare.

A hoot pulled his eyes away, and he scanned the brush. She heard the call and stopped, and then she stepped toward the bank. Luis saw the action before she did.

The red man snatched up the *niño* and dangled him by the heel. The child screamed, and Molly flung the dress at the shore. "Put him down!"

The red man advanced toward her, chattering in a guttural tongue. The child wailed, and the red man swung him like a pendulum.

"What do ye want?" Molly staggered to the embankment and reached for the child, but the red man wrenched him away.

He pushed his lips into a pout and pointed at Molly.

"Give the baby to me," she shouted.

With a hissing laugh the red man swung the boy's head close to a nearby tree trunk.

Luis raised his rifle and stepped from the shadows. "*Alto.*"

"Thank ye, Jesus," Molly said.

In the seconds they glared at one another, Luis registered the sturdy length of the Anglo's white legs, the red man's scrawny strength, the niño's terror. He felt the weariness of his own soul; he didn't want to shoot anyone ever again.

"What does he want?" Molly's voice quavered.

The red man righted the child and clutched him to his chest. As Luis stepped closer, he smelled the red man's rank skunk scent.

The child whimpered. Molly frowned. "He's thin. Do ye think he's hungry?"

Luis steadied his rifle. Were Anglos so foolhardy they didn't recognize danger?

As she gazed at the red man, Molly's lips moved, but Luis couldn't hear anything. He stepped into the stream.

"Do ye speak his language?" Molly asked. "I got hot corn pone at the cabin. I'll feed him if he'll give Andy back."

"*Comida?*" Luis tried. "*Maíz,* casa." He pointed in the direction of the cabin.

"What did you say?" Molly released her skirts.

Luis watched the red man. "Food, corn, house."

The red man secured his hold on the toddler and whispered to him. When Molly reached for the child, he shook his head and gestured toward the clearing. She patted the boy's back.

"Ye be safe, Andy. The Injun will carry ye home." She picked up her woven laundry basket and walked up the trail. The red man followed.

Luis did as well, rifle at the ready. When they reached the clearing, he saw the boy-man cutting a window in the cabin wall. Jamie flung away the bow saw, grabbed his firearm, and started in their direction.

"We be fine, Jamie. I'm going to serve tea," Molly called.

"What?"

"I met our neighbors in the woods and brought them home. Nettle tea and corn pone. I know ye be hungry, too."

Luis heard the tremor in her voice, but Molly appeared calm when she lifted the lid from the iron skillet. The red man dropped the child and snatched the corn pone. Before anyone could react, he sprinted away.

Molly soothed the little boy with kisses. She matched her cheek to his and closed her eyes on a moan. Luis saw tears slip.

"Did he hurt ye, Molly?" The boy-man hovered, his hands apparently not sure what to do.

She shook her head, swaying with the child. She cleared her throat. "I guess the Injun be hungry."

Luis nearly dropped his long gun.

"Will ye join us, Mr. Carvajal," she said, "for a cup of nettle tea?"

Louis's mouth dropped open in surprise. "Yes."

Chapter 5

August

Molly squished her fingers through the sand and wet clay in the bucket. She mixed in small sticks and moss, picked up the chinking sludge by the handful, and pushed it between the gaps in the log. It didn't take much skill if you could stand the smell.

Molly didn't mind the job; the cool chinking felt good on her hands in the summer's heat, and the work gave her time to think.

Andy tottered about the north cabin beside her. Belle lay across the dogtrot breezeway, her eyes on Jamie hauling wet mud up from the creek to fill Molly's chinking bucket.

In between mud buckets, Jamie constructed shutters for the cabin windows using rawhide hinges and leftover shingles. "I want to shut us in real good the next time Injuns come."

"Luis said they haven't had a lot of Injun trouble in the past." Molly smoothed the chinking with the palm of her hand.

"Call him Mr. Carvajal, not Luis," Jamie retorted. "He may have saved your life, but I don't trust him. He wants this property back."

"He's a lonely and sad man with much on his mind. I wonder if he knows that Mexican woman, Ana, who comes to the camp meetings?"

"I be telling ye, Molly, don't let your tender heart get ye into trouble. That Injun could have killed all of us, and ye would be inviting him to tea." Jamie hit the peg so hard it split. He threw it on the ground and reached for another. "I'll need to whittle more pegs."

"Just like Pappy Hanks says, God be watching out for us. He sent Luis in time."

"Maybe, but Carvajal watches ye too close. What was he doing at our watering hole, anyway?"

Molly ducked her head. Over that first tea, Luis had watched her with an intensity that had made her feel both hot and shy. He'd stopped by several times since then for no apparent reason. Or at least no reason to satisfy Jamie. Molly smiled as she pushed a twig into the space between two logs and smoothed mud

312

around it. "Luis has a sister—that's why he be concerned for womenfolk."

"Right."

"What would make ye trust him?"

Jamie snickered. "If I see him at a camp meeting, I might trust him. But the only Tejanos I see at camp meetings are older women like Ana."

"If we invite him, maybe he'll come."

"Bat your eyelashes and invite him yourself." Jamie split another peg.

When Andy stuck his pudgy hands into the chinking, Molly showed him how to spread it along the logs. She hummed as she worked, thinking of how unsettled she felt in Luis's presence. Her faith told her to soothe his troubled soul. Wasn't that why she wanted to reach out to him?

Of course Luis was their nearest neighbor, and a handsome one. Molly squirmed. She enjoyed watching him, too.

Molly began to sing, "Come Thou Fount of Every Blessing." Jamie joined in. After they sang the final verse, Molly sighed. "When be the next camp meeting?"

"Soon, at Ma and Pappy Hanks's clearing out toward Ramsey's. It'll be good to see folks again."

"Aye. I wonder if there be any new folks in the area." Molly scraped the contents of her bucket into an empty spot. "Time for more mud."

❄

"You are brooding, mi corazón." Mamacita took Luis's arm as they watched Manuel train a colt.

"I should have sent him away despite Maria and the baby," Luis growled.

"Your heart is too easily swayed."

"Perhaps yours is too hard," his mother whispered. "Manuel acted in good faith. He thought you were dead. He apologized; he showed you what information he had. Your father would not have liked his choices, but you were not here. We are called to forgive one another, remember?"

"I will not forget what Manuel has done. I don't trust him."

"For good reason, but if he is here, we can harness his strengths."

Luis didn't like it, but he agreed. Manuel could be useful if Luis kept him in line. The man handled horses well. "He owes us much. I am sending him to round up mustangs soon. We will work together breaking horses."

"What will you do with new ones?"

Luis remembered how Molly had fussed over his stallion. "Anglos love horses. I can trade with them." But what did she have to trade? His heart skipped as he wondered if the boy-husband would trade his wife. Luis snorted. Ridiculous.

"Manuel has skill with horses," Mamacita agreed.

"Why did you let him marry Maria? With so few women around, surely other men offered marriage."

Mamacita sighed. "Maria is a silly girl, but she loves him. A priest was in Nacogdoches to celebrate the *posada* two years ago and available to marry them. You and your father were both gone; I thought it would be good to have a man run the ranchero. I know Manuel can be difficult, but why should we condemn her to his hovel when we have room here?"

"A married woman belongs in her own home with her husband, not her mother."

"When you bring home a bride, we will send them to their own place. Perhaps you will find one at the camp meeting next week."

"I have no time for women. I must put the ranch in order and reclaim my land." Luis frowned. "I did not think they would close the land records office in Nacogdoches because of the revolution. Someone must be in charge. But who?"

"You said you wanted to live in peace without fighting. Can you not let it go?"

"And do what instead?" he asked.

Mamacita rubbed his arm. "You need to come with me to the camp meeting. She may be there."

"Who?"

"The woman who will fill your heart."

He stared at his mother. "Camp meetings are for Anglos. You would curse me with an Anglo bride?"

"I would bless you with a woman after God's heart who will cherish yours. It is not good for a man to be alone."

"Bah."

"I heard your voice when you told of the red man threatening the beautiful Anglo with the gentle heart. Perhaps the love of a good woman could soften yours."

Luis picked up a rope left by his slovenly brother-in-law and coiled it. His mother didn't know about the ugliness in his heart. "I thought Maria was going with you."

Mamacita's lips flattened to disappointment. "Manuel said she could not attend; he fears for her health. With the red men in the woods, I cannot go alone."

Luis looped the coiled rope over a fence post. "I will take you to the meeting, but do not expect anything else."

"I put everything into God's hands," she said. "He knows where your life belongs. Someone will welcome you at the meeting."

"I doubt even God will want me there," Luis muttered as he joined his brother-in-law in the paddock.

Chapter 6

M olly gal, it be good to see ye." Ma Hanks's face wrinkled in pleasure as she reached for her grandson. "How be my Andy?"

"He be a good strong boy. Sarah would be glad."

The older woman dipped her chin. "It be good of ye to care for the young'un. How be Jamie? Where be his heart?"

"He will always love Sarah, but he be ready to wed again."

Ma Hanks nodded. "That be the way of a man." She brushed the blond curls away from Andy's face. "Eighteen months be a long time for a man. He was a good husband to my girl."

Molly thought of Sarah, buried along the trail from Tennessee. "There be few womenfolk for him to wed."

Ma Hanks slipped Andy a handful of blackberries. "That be changing. A new family took a claim on Hat Creek, and they've got two marriageable daughters with red hair. Their neighbor be that recent widow, Hunter, whose husband left a nice spread. They all be coming to the brush arbor meeting today. You can meet 'em and see for yourself."

Ma Hanks buried her face in Andy's curls and whispered. "Jamie, too."

Molly left the toddler with his grandmother and joined a group of women standing beside a row of trimmed logs. Children stirred up dust in a game of tag.

"Did ye hear Pappy Hanks be a few days late?" Lily asked.

"Aye," Molly said. Everyone knew the gregarious Pappy Hanks was always getting caught up in events that delayed his return home: weddings, baptisms, even a pretty piece of east Texas acreage for sale.

"Jamie told us about the Injun who grabbed Andy." Lily hugged her. "How did ye get him away?"

"Luis saved us. He was hunting in the woods. I don't know what would have happened otherwise."

Lily rubbed Molly's hands. "Luis who?"

"Luis Carvajal, our neighbor. The Injun was hungry. He snatched corn pone out of the spider, and I never saw him again."

"Luis sounds like a Tejano name," Lily said. "Be he friendly?"

"Aye."

"And he saved ye from an Injun. God be praised." Lily turned toward the dense woods not far away. "You never know if they be out there, lurking and watching."

Molly shivered. "Not on a noisy day like today." Molly scanned the wide clearing. Joy brimmed in her heart when she saw Luis help Ana dismount from a beautiful mare. Molly hurried to greet them.

"*Bendiciones a usted*," Ana said. "Blessings to you."

"And ye, too," Molly replied. "Luis, how do ye know Ana?"

"She is my Mamacita."

Molly clasped hands with the dimpling woman. "Mamacita suits ye."

Luis pulled rope picket lines from the saddlebags. "Where have you met my mother?"

"At the spring camp meeting. She be very wise, particularly when the Holy Spirit falls upon her."

"The Holy Spirit?" Luis's glance flicked between the two women.

"Are ye a believer?"

"I have read the Bible many times," Luis finally answered. "There is truth in that book."

Molly felt breathless at the sight of Luis and his elegant, spotless clothes. His short black jacket highlighted his broad shoulders and trim waist. The startling white shirt emphasized his dark complexion. Ana wore a blue silk dress. Dangling earrings flashed from under her broad-brimmed hat as she inspected the gathering.

Beside them in her best calico homespun, Molly reminded herself that God cared about her heart, not her appearance. All the same, she wished Christmas was sooner so she would have her annual new dress.

Luis examined the clearing like a bird of prey. "What happens now we are here?"

"Pappy Hanks be not yet back from riding the circuit, so one of his sons will lead the singing as soon as they finish building the brush arbor. He'll bring a message from the Good Book. When he tires of speaking, or the Holy Spirit pauses, we'll eat."

He nodded toward the basket strapped to his beautiful stallion. "Mamacita brought *tamales* enough for all. These are special; we usually eat them to celebrate the posada, your Christmas."

"Tamales?" Molly's tongue twisted on the word. "Is that the spicy food you brought last time?"

Mamacita nodded.

"Much better than corn pone," Molly said. "I remember so much flavor bursting when I bit into one, my eyes filled with tears."

Luis laughed. "Do you mean the *chiles*?"

"I don't know what they were, but my mouth burned." Molly caught herself. "I be not complaining. I'll enjoy the tamales."

Mamacita murmured, "I'll enjoy seeing God at work."

❈

Luis had been to the area before with his father, retrieving lost cattle. On that day a few wagons huddled together while oxen and a half-dozen tethered horses cropped grass. Not far away he saw the preacher's dogtrot, new since he'd gone away three years ago.

As he walked around the clearing, he listened to the conversations. Three men discussed the formation of the new Texas Republic as they tied up their horses. He paused when he overheard two couples talking about the closed land records office.

"We came to Texas because of the cheap land," one of the women said. "I just hope no one snatches away our chances."

"Land rights always get mixed up in revolutions. It takes years to sort it out," the man beside her said. He looked speculatively at Luis, who stepped away.

Luis stopped in the shade on the edge of the clearing to watch a group of Anglo men erect a spindly structure of wooden poles with branches laid across the top. Brush arbor, Molly called it. Arbor sounded like the Spanish word *árbol*, for tree.

Several men, Jamie Faires among them, rolled large logs under the arbor for seating. His neighbor nodded when he spied Luis, and Luis returned the greeting.

Mamacita brought him a tin cup of water, which Luis gulped in gratitude. "You must meet people," she murmured in Spanish.

"You have attended these meetings before?"

"Sí. Your father met the preacher long ago." Mamacita dimpled. "He returned after you went south, and your father brought him home for a meal. We had many conversations. The preacher was the only one who made sense to me when your father died. He told me I would see him again if I believed. So I believed."

"Believed what?" Luis asked.

"The words written in the Bible. It helps me to know God is the husband to the husbandless."

A soothing harmony came from the women standing under the arbor. Luis recognized the song as one Molly sang. Luis narrowed his eyes against the sunshine to find her. Mamacita waved her old Spanish lace fan.

Jamie Faires stopped to speak with a blushing young woman with bright red hair. Luis frowned. Where was Jamie's wife?

The boy-husband moved to the front row log, where a weary woman in a dusty black dress rocked a small babe. Faires sat beside the woman and bowed his head, nodding at her words with an intensity that irritated Luis all over again. Flirting with two women?

He heard Molly speaking to her little boy not far away while an older woman watched. "Can ye say my name, Andy? Say Molly."

"Ma. Ma." Andy danced at her feet.

Molly crouched at his eye level. "Molly. Ma Hanks wants to hear you talk."

"Ma-LEE!" Andy shouted. The women laughed.

Luis scowled. Anglos. Didn't they understand a boy should respect his mother at all times? What was he doing among them?

Molly came toward him, her laughing face rosy from the heat. "Andy can say my name."

Mamacita applauded.

"Why do you want your son to call you Molly, not Ma?" Even Luis could hear the harshness of his question.

Molly flinched.

He felt a pang of guilt, but she began to laugh, her fingers touching her lips. Molly stepped closer, and he could smell honeysuckle. "Andy be my brother Jamie's son, not mine. Andy be my nephew."

Luis nodded, clicked his heels together, and stomped into the woods, his emotions awhirl.

Embarrassed, he shoved aside the branches and bushes that snagged his coat. So she wasn't married to the boy-man. How had he missed that?

Luis trampled through wild grapes and blackberries on his way toward the creek, but by the time he reached the water, the bubbling inside his gut had spread to his lips. He smiled, and then he laughed long and hard. Never had he been so happy to be found a fool.

Chapter 7

During the week-long camp meeting, Molly would stay at the roomy Hanks dogtrot cabin the Tennessee party had built when they arrived in east Texas a year and a half ago. She and Jamie had wintered there with the infant Andy, sharing grief over Sarah's death with her parents, that first year. The Hanks clan was her second family. Along with Jamie and Andy, they were her only family now.

Molly loved camp meetings. The sweet hymns sung by the women reminded her of her own mother's songs. The Bible stories captured her imagination and made her feel closer to God. Camp meetings were opportunities to fellowship and swap stories; "sparking" often went on between young couples.

They were fortunate to live near Pappy Hanks, both in Tennessee and now in Texas, so they got to attend more often than most folks on the frontier. When Pappy Hanks was home from riding the circuit, he welcomed all believers to study the Bible with him. Almost everything Molly knew about the Good Book came from Pappy Hanks's teaching.

❄

Pappy Hanks rode up two days late to the meeting. His arms spread wide for a hug when he saw Molly. "Ye get prettier every day, Molly gal. I don't think ye will be long without a husband."

"Are ye prophesying, Tom?" Ma Hanks joined them for an embrace of her own.

"Nay, just saying the obvious. Christmas be not long a'coming." Gaunt with the leathery skin of a man who spent many hours in the saddle, Pappy Hanks swept into the cabin and sniffed. "Got ye any food?"

Ma Hanks slathered butter on a wedge of cold corn pone and set it on the table. When Andy scrambled up beside him on the bench, Pappy Hanks took the boy onto his lap to share.

Pappy Hanks filled them in on his travels. "People are on the move, trigger-happy and scared. It be good to be home."

"Ye be safe here," Ma Hanks said.

He smiled. "I be safe wherever the Spirit leads me." He finished his food, set the boy on the floor, and held out his hand. "Come, Andy, let's go tend Grandpa's horse."

Molly cleared the table and picked up the broom, happiness humming in her soul. Luis would get to hear Pappy Hanks preach. She'd pray the Spirit would move in Luis's heart and smooth away the sadness he wore like a blanket. Or maybe a *serape* since he was Mexican. She smiled to think of their different cultures.

"Ye sure like to sweep the floor, Molly." Ma Hanks stirred the cauldron suspended over the cooking hearth.

"It be a pleasure to sweep a wood floor. The dirt floors be fine at our place, but I feel like a better housekeeper if I can push the dirt out the door, rather than stomp it back into the ground."

Ma Hanks laughed. "Your work be done, gal. Go visit. I'll finish up here."

Molly set the broom in the corner and grabbed her bonnet.

"Mind ye, Ana's son," Ma Hanks said. "He holds sorrow to his soul. His heart be gentle in the past, but it could be calloused now. Be he washed in the blood of the Lamb?"

"Why ask me?"

"He been coming the last two days."

"He escorts Ana," Molly said.

"His eyes follow ye, gal. Does his heart rest well with ye?"

Molly sighed. "We be very different. I be not sure what he believes."

"I be praying for ye," Ma Hanks said. "God often uses unlikely vessels to get our attention. Or to test our character."

Molly tied on her bonnet and went outside. She paused when she reached the stretch of ground where the horses cropped at the late summer grass. On the dusty road from Nacogdoches, she spied a rider cantering on a roan gelding. He tugged the black hat from his head when he stopped before her.

"Eli Parker," Molly said.

"Molly, sweetheart, just the woman I longed to see. Are you wed?"

"Ye still be full of nonsense. I be not wed."

His green eyes twinkled in his charming sunburned face. "Have you changed your mind since last winter? I'm headed west, Molly. Bring your pioneer spirit with me, and see fresh land. That young'un must be old enough to leave by now."

She shook her head. "Ye be too much an adventurer for me. We don't want the same things."

"How can you be sure? I'll buy you a horse."

Molly patted his horse's neck. "Ye be tempting me with a horse, but no."

She heard the leather of his saddle creak as he leaned down. "What do you want, Molly? You're always giving to others. I remember when you traded your mare for a milk cow on the trail."

"Andy needed milk more than I needed a mare."

"You can't give everything away. You're too fine a woman to sacrifice her life for others. What's the matter with the bucks around here? Or are you too particular?"

Molly shook her head. "Are ye staying for the meeting?"

"If I can watch you and eat vittles, sure." He swung out of the saddle and reached for her.

Molly easily spun away and joined Ana at the back of the arbor fluttering an elaborate lace fan. Luis stood nearby, arms crossed over his chest. "Who was that?" he asked.

Molly scrunched her nose. "Eli Parker from Tennessee. He rode with us in the wagon train."

"Does he live around here?"

"Nay. Eli be going west. He doesn't want to settle down." She took a deep breath. "Ma Hanks asked if ye be washed in the blood of the Lamb."

"What does that mean?"

"Ye confess Jesus as your Savior and the forgiver of your sins."

Luis looked away. "You don't know the sins I carry."

"I can see ye be burdened," Molly said. "Do ye seek God's will, Luis?"

Mamacita's fan slowed.

He answered after a thoughtful pause. "There's a place in the Bible about beating swords into plows. That's what I'd like to do. I won't worship a soft God, but I'll follow the will of a just God."

"He be a just God. The Bible tells of a just God who be firm with those who fight against him and his people."

He narrowed his eyes. "Would not a just God expect his people to return what has been taken away from a man?"

"Aye," she whispered. "But if a man bought and paid for something with his sweat and blood, believing the authorities who said it be his, God would see that different."

"I wonder."

Molly wished Pappy Hanks were near to help. What words did she have for such a question? "I would give ye back the land be it in my power and if it would make a difference to your soul. It would please me to see the stranglehold of disappointment ye carry given to Jesus so ye could be free and forgiven."

His face softened before he whispered, "Would you like me better if I believed the same way you do?"

"I already like ye mighty fine."

Pappy Hanks stood beneath the arbor and shouted out a verse from his open

Bible. "Come now, let us reason together!"

"Ah, Pappy," a man shouted from the back. "Let's eat first."

❄

Three Anglo men, including Eli Parker, surrounded Molly during dinner. Luis settled Mamacita with two Tejano women and then drifted off to discuss livestock with the men. Several Anglos wanted horses. Luis could turn this week into a profitable business venture if he and Manuel broke a few horses.

His father had told him many times, "You must understand the Anglos and what they value before you can do business with them." Two days of camp meetings had given him insight into the Anglos' business interests, even as it expanded his unease with his own past.

His Anglo tutor had insisted Luis read the Bible for his English skills, but also for his spiritual life. Their many discussions had convinced him God existed, but Luis knew he no longer measured up. He also realized Molly saw too clearly what he didn't want to acknowledge—the personal disappointment and sadness he had brought home from war.

The men who'd fought and died beside him in the south had spoken of God in harsh voices of anger or with whimpers of fear. Luis felt exhausted whenever he thought of them. He tried not to remember lest he feel their pain all over again; or at least that's what he told himself. Unfortunately the camp meeting stirred the ghosts from the graves where he thought he'd buried them.

After dinner, folks gathered under the pine-scented arbor for hymns. It was a pity Molly made such an appealing saint, Luis thought as he watched her sing. Her face glowed with the ardor of her enthusiasm and made her even prettier.

He wasn't the only one who noticed her, either. Eli Parker didn't bother pretending to sing; he stared with such interest that Molly blushed.

The music washed over Luis, swirled around his sore soul, and trickled into his brain. He picked out a refrain:

> The sorrows of the mind,
> Be banish'd from the face,
> Religion never was design'd,
> To make our pleasures less.
> Hallelujah,
> We are on our journey home.

What does it mean? he wondered. He examined the other bachelors; were they here for the religion or the pleasure?

Luis could guess.

Mamacita tugged on his arm as the chorus ebbed away, and pointed to the front. The man they called Pappy Hanks took the wide-brimmed hat from his shaggy silver head and opened his Bible. "Now, we will reason together as God ordained in the Good Book. Let us pray."

Luis bowed his head as the preacher prayed about his thankfulness for returning safely and God's blessings for the meeting. But the man's voice jostled a memory, and Luis leaned forward to hear this Pappy Hanks better.

"Lord, the trials of this new Republic have wounded and killed both the souls and the bodies of too many people, but we thank Ye there is no sin too big for Ye to forgive. We pray for those who died along with those who did the killing. None of us can ever hit the mark of perfection Ye demonstrated. We all are lost without the shed blood of Jesus. We cast ourselves upon your grace and mercy, resting in Jesus and know we be saved. Amen. Thanks be to God."

Luis bolted upright and stared.

Pappy Hanks opened his eyes and gazed directly at Luis. His mouth broke into a wide grin.

"Mamacita," Luis said. "It's Tomás!"

Chapter 8

October

Molly raked the embers into the back corner of the rock fireplace, setting the iron pot close enough to warm. Jamie had eaten his fill of rabbit stew before heading to Hat Creek. He'd stay several days with other men and finish the harvest for the widow Hunter. At least that's why he said he went. The days would stretch lonely unless Luis stopped on his way past, but she hadn't seen him in weeks.

Andy sat on the hard dirt floor beside the old family trunk and played with blocks his father had whittled for him. Molly touched his sweet blond head as she reached above to open the shutter and peer out the window. The sky stretched clear above.

Andy pointed. "Outside?"

"When I'm done." She returned to the wooden table Jamie had fashioned from thick planks, and tied up wild lavender with willow string. She hung the flowers to dry on pegs on the roof beams. With bunched herbs and flowers drying overhead, Molly often felt like she lived in an upside-down garden.

She sighed in contentment. Cooking implements hung on the wall. The colorful quilt she'd pieced as a child covered the straw tick. Molly straightened it with a tug on a green calico corner—a friendly scrap from her mother's best dress.

With the nights turning colder and the fireplace burning constantly, Molly examined the chinking daily to ensure it hadn't gaped to let in cold air. She wanted to make sure the cabin was tight before clay became too difficult to dig. Everything appeared solid, so she pulled a warm shirt over Andy's head and opened the door.

The boy ran before her, headed to the log shed Jamie'd built to house the livestock when they roofed the dogtrot cabins. Andy loved to chase the chickens that evaded his chubby hands with squawks and fluttering stubby wings. His simple words made Molly laugh.

"Chick," he said as she let them out. The cow lowed when Molly set the bucket down to milk.

The routine chores were nearly done when Belle barked, and she saw Ma and Pappy Hanks approaching on two brown horses. "Neigh-neigh." Andy pointed in their direction.

His grandparents swooped him up for kisses before hugging Molly. "We thought we'd visit ye since Jamie's off to help with the end harvest."

"Are ye staying long?" Molly felt relief at the thought of a long visit.

"Until he gets back." Pappy Hanks studied the property. "Ye have prospered the place."

"Jamie be a hard worker." Molly picked up the milk bucket. "It be a good farm."

"Aye." Pappy Hanks scratched Belle's ears. "Jamie be enthused to go to Hat Creek. Which one do ye think he means to wed, the sassy redhead or the Hunter widow?"

Molly turned away. "I don't know."

"Surely ye prefer one o'er the other?" Ma Hanks asked.

"I don't really know either one."

"They both be fine Christian women," Pappy Hanks said. "I expect to be marrying several couples come Christmas. How about ye? Ye get much help with the harvest here?"

Molly stopped in surprise. "How did ye know?"

"How many of them were bachelors?" he teased.

"Enough to get the work done. I didn't see ye here."

"I don't need to be here," he laughed, "as long as Jamie has an unwed sister."

Molly put up the milk while Pappy Hanks inspected the dogtrot. "I hear Clay Ramsey helped with the roof. I can see his careful fitting at the peak."

"Aye."

"Lily's baby be coming soon," Ma Hanks said.

"Aye, she looked done in at the camp meeting." Molly's questions burst from her. "Ye spent a lot of time with Luis Carvajal at the camp meeting, Pappy. What did ye say to him? Where did he go?"

"He be hunting wild mustangs. He's probably breaking 'em now."

"Don't tease the girl, Tom," Ma Hanks said. "Tell her about Luis."

He took off his hat and rubbed at a worn spot. "I suppose I can tell Molly. Can ye keep a secret, gal?"

She nodded.

Ma Hanks drew a circle in the ground and showed Andy how to toss pebbles into it while Molly and Pappy sat on stumps nearby.

"I been riding the circuit into Texas since 1821. Until this year, preaching the Protestant Gospel was against Mexican law. Up here near Nacogdoches, the officer said we weren't doing nobody any harm, so he let us have our meetings."

Molly nodded. Pappy Hanks's comings and goings were familiar events in her childhood.

"Still, I was breaking the law, and it made things easier if I had an excuse for being here when the officials stopped me. I met Antonio Carvajal early on. His wife, Ana, loved God but had no priest in the neighborhood. He invited me to stay at his home. He wanted me to pray with her and talk about God and the Bible. He also wanted me to teach the whole family how to speak English. Antonio was particularly concerned about his son, Luis, who was maybe thirteen years old."

"Ye were his tutor?" Molly said.

"Aye. He reminded me of my own boys. I spent many months, broken up by circuit riding, with the Carvajal family. It be one of the reasons we settled here. Antonio invited us."

Molly gasped. "You bought the land legal?"

"I bought mine from Antonio long before we came. But I don't know about yours. Jamie told me about his worries over the land's title."

❄

Weeks on the trail with his brother-in-law would try the patience of a saint, and God knew Luis was no saint. Manuel's ego knew no bounds, and his drinking grew out of control until Luis seized the wineskins. Fortunately, they found a half-dozen wild mustangs immediately afterward, and Manuel's hands were soon filled with more important activities.

"Three mares, two yearlings, and a filly; we split them, no?" Manuel asked.

Luis knew better. "We'll discuss it when we return."

Luis had plenty of time to think while they drove the horses home, and his mind often returned to Tomás and Molly.

Anglos! First they invaded his homeland, and now they tormented his mind.

Except what they said made too much sense to be denied. Brain warring with heart warring with culture warring with experience. "I'm a vaquero," he said aloud. "I can make my own decisions."

"*Qué es eso?*" Manuel asked. What is it?

"*Niente.*" Nothing.

Nothing for Manuel, but for Luis a revelation. Tomás, the man who had taught him to speak English and read the Bible, had listened to his nightmares about the last three years. To no one else could Luis have spoken with honesty and admitted so much. Even his father would not have understood.

Tomás had been in the south. He had seen the chaos and the horror. He knew men who had died as well as men who killed. Tomás did not blink when

Luis told him what he had done. Over and over, Luis reviewed the conversation with relief.

"We read the scriptures all those years ago, Luis. What did you learn about God's thoughts on forgiveness?" Like Molly, Tomás went to the heart.

"If we confess our sins, he is faithful and just to forgive us our sins, and to cleanse us from all unrighteousness," Luis remembered

"Ye got it right with your words. Ye have confessed your sin to me. As an ordained servant of God, I, Thomas Hanks, pronounce ye forgiven. Believe the truth, and it be yours."

Riding Maximo through the falling orange and golden leaves, Luis savored his release from killing guilt. Consequences remained; he would never forget the faces of those he'd consigned to death. But he claimed the cross for his forgiveness and no longer feared God's judgment. Who would have thought an Anglo could help him find peace?

But then, how could he have known the one Anglo he trusted would return to his life?

Only one?

What was he going to do about the woman with the rosy laughing face and bluebonnet eyes? The one who liked him mighty fine?

"What are you smiling about?" Manuel asked. "The ponies?"

Luis inspected their new stock and nodded. The palomino filly would do very well.

Chapter 9

November

The harvest moon rose full in the east and shone a dazzling light across the clearing bright enough they could work long after supper. The frosty air nipped beneath her shawl when Molly stacked the cow's winter straw. As they worked in the livestock shed, Molly wondered if she would need to bring the chickens into her half of the dogtrot for the winter.

She pondered the fowl huddled together on their roost. "Remember how cold it got last winter at Pappy Hanks's place? Will the chickens survive?"

"They should be fine." Jamie raked up more straw. "Look there."

A fat raccoon ambled across the stubble field, pausing to turn his bandit face in their direction before skittering into the woods. "Belle be inside with Andy, or she'd be after him," Jamie said.

"That old dog be slowing down. I'd best check on 'em." Molly picked up a wicker basket of dried corn and headed to the cabin Jamie shared with the little boy.

Andy lay with his arms spread wide on the straw tick, quilts pushed off. Embers burned in the fireplace, just enough to take the chill off the air and let Molly see. She tucked in the boy and prayed about the changes ahead. She tried not to think of the redheaded Eliza from Hat Creek living here and mothering the young'un Molly had cared for since birth, but she knew it would have to be. Jamie had decided. Andy would have a new ma by the spring planting, and Molly would. . .

She swallowed back a lump in her throat. Molly didn't know what she would do.

Belle sprawled before the hearth, and Molly rubbed her ears. The dog moaned and squirmed onto her back. Molly obliged with tummy scratching. "What do ye think happened to Luis?" she murmured. "Have ye seen him in the woods? Do you think Pappy Hanks scared him away?"

Belle wagged her tail, Andy shifted, and embers settled. Molly patted the dog a final time and rose. She had chores to do yet.

She closed the door and paused near the neatly stacked firewood in the sheltered area between the cabins. An owl hooted, and bats flew over the shed where Jamie soothed the cow. The night poised on a moment of change. Molly sighed.

"Bring the rifle." Jamie's hushed words seemed more like a feather brushing her ears than an actual request. Sounds carried on the silent night, and in the icy moment Molly heard rustling and a dampened shuffle from the woods. She eased into the cabin and plucked the loaded rifle from its pegs.

She stayed in the shadows. Was that movement along the edges of the clearing?

"I'm going to run to the cabin," Jamie whispered. "Cover me."

Belle began to bay.

"Now!"

He dashed across the moonlit area between the shed and the cabins. A scratchy shriek echoed from the woods, and Molly glimpsed a line of skulking figures. Injuns.

Jamie grabbed the rifle, and they hustled inside. Andy sat up, and Belle growled. Jamie shoved open the shutters and crouched on the bed, rifle ready. Molly bolted the door and retrieved brother Samuel's gun. She propped it within Jamie's easy reach and pulled Andy onto her lap, rocking to calm him. "Quiet," she ordered Belle.

They watched the moon rise high over the clearing, an owl's silhouette in its light. The rustling eased. They neither saw nor heard the Injuns again.

Jamie finally breathed a sigh of relief and relaxed his shoulders. "Carvajal said Injuns be headed west about now. That must be 'em going."

"Thanks be to God." Molly's heart raced. "Where did you see Luis?"

"Over to Pappy Hanks's place when I got the news about Lily and her baby."

Her heart ached. She'd think about Lily later.

"He said they often travel at night when passing settlers' cabins. Easier to steal chickens," Jamie said.

"Where has Luis been?"

Jamie drew in his rifle. "Rounding up horses with his sister's husband. He's breaking 'em now and hopes to sell 'em. Pappy Hanks says the Carvajals have always been good businessmen."

Molly nestled the now-dozing Andy into a more comfortable position.

"Them Injuns be headed west," Jamie said with confidence. "They be giving up."

"Going to new lands," Molly agreed. "Like Eli Parker."

Jamie pulled the shutter closed and latched it. "You could do worse than Eli. He's a good man."

Molly smiled as she caressed Andy's rounded cheek. She could do better, too.

❄

Luis rode through the woods toward dusk the last week in November. While faster and possibly safer to take the main road home from Nacogdoches, he liked the tranquil and less dusty path through the foliage. He also welcomed a chance to see Molly. He tried to discipline himself to going by once a week, telling Jamie it was wise to keep track of neighbors and their needs in that sparsely populated area.

He traveled with mixed emotions. He'd finally found the land surveyor who had given him the news he'd hoped for. Without Luis's signature, Manuel could not sell the land; thus Jamie Faires farmed land that legally belonged to Luis. He could contest the false sale and refund the money. "But good luck getting it to stick," the old Tejano had muttered. "Mexico's days are over. The Americanos have won. You have plenty of land north of that parcel. Take my advice, and let that property go unless you want to use a gun."

Luis carried his long rifle in case of emergencies but never shot anything except game. The southern battles had snuffed ambition's fire from his heart.

Maximo nickered as they neared the Faires farm. Jamie had cleared the land all the way down to the creek now; they no longer had to venture into the woods to their former watering hole. He had lined the bank with stepping stones to make it less muddy when they drew water. Luis admired initiative, particularly in contrast to his brother-in-law Manuel's sloth around the Carvajal ranchero.

He gritted his teeth. Forgiveness toward Manuel didn't always sit well.

Luis saw Jamie sitting on a stump not far from the water with his rifle across his lap, his eyes scanning the forest as dusk grew. Andy played beside him, and the dog, Belle, rustled in the undergrowth at the clearing's edge. The two men raised their hands at each other.

Molly sat beside the creek watching the water flowing past. She shrugged when Maximo stopped several feet away. Luis tipped his hat.

Her eyes were swollen, her cheeks striped with tears. He dismounted. "What has happened?"

Her hands twisted in her lap. "Ye heard my friend Lily Ramsey died?"

"Mamacita told me. I am sorry to hear of your loss."

Her head jerked up. "My loss?"

"Was she not a good friend? It is difficult for a woman to make friends on the frontier; a terrible grief when a friend dies."

She shut her eyes, and her shoulders slumped. "Do ye understand?"

The faces of lost friends flashed through his mind—vivid, laughing men who went to death in a rain of Americano lead bullets. "Too many senseless deaths? I understand very well."

"How long do ye mourn them? Jamie grieved Sarah more than a year. One day he decided he had mourned long enough and moved forward. He hopes to wed before spring."

"What will you do?"

"That be the question." Molly stood and buried her face in Maximo's mane.

Luis took a step closer to her. "Would you live here with your brother and his new wife?"

Molly cleared her throat. "Clay Ramsey came today with his young'uns. His three children be under five. They need a ma."

A sickening feeling drained through his gut. "His wife and babe are not long dead."

"No. Three weeks gone." Her hand moved across Maximo's coat as if she gained comfort from the roughness under her palm.

He forced the words through cold lips. "What will he do?"

Molly sniffed. "He said his young'uns need a mother. He knows I fostered Andy. He said Pappy Hanks could wed us at Christmas. Clay comes in two weeks for my answer."

"Do you want to marry him?"

Molly hesitated then stamped her foot. "What do ye want from life, Luis?"

The frustration in her voice surprised him. He answered carefully. "I am like most men. I want a family, a wife, a place to live in peace." As he spoke the words Luis recognized their truth. He clenched his fists.

The haunting call of a night dove echoed around them. Water rippled over rocks, and the horse's head came up, eyes wide, as he shuffled nervously.

"Ye have a home and Mamacita. Ye own land that has been in your family for many years." She took a deep breath and lifted her chin. "If your life be not at peace, maybe it be the fault of those who choose not to forgive others." Belle trotted over to lean against Molly's leg and whimper. She rubbed the dog's ears.

Luis faced north in the direction of his ranch. Manuel's presence made peace impossible. But if Manuel and Maria didn't leave before the baby came, they might never make a home of their own. It was past time. Manuel could take his share of the new horses.

But even as Luis beheld Molly's beautiful face, he knew a house empty of his brother-in-law would not fill the hole in his heart. The words came unbidden: "*Te adoro.*"

"What does that mean?" She hooked a lock of her pale hair behind her ear.

"What do you see in Ramsey, Molly?" Luis whispered. He tugged the reins to steady both the restless stallion and his own flash of rage. Luis stepped closer.

"He offers a home, but it's a home Lily made. I want young'uns, and he offers me Lily's children." She put her face into her hands and wept. "All I see is Lily. Her home. Her life. Not mine. But they need me. How can I say no to children without a mother?"

Belle growled from deep in her throat.

"Molly." He struck his open palm against the leather saddle, the pain to his hand as sharp as Molly's words to his heart. Maximo whinnied and jerked. Trying to find the words to make her understand, Luis squinted up at the towering trees. The first star shone through empty branches, and a black shadow with shimmering yellow eyes alerted his instincts. Luis grabbed for his rifle.

The dog yelped. The snarling scream of the panther made Luis fumble with his gun. "Get the horse between you and the cat," he shouted, raising his rifle as the panther sprang.

The panther landed, claws extended, on Maximo's flanks. The horse screamed and took off toward the woods, knocking Molly to the ground. Belle chased after, barking. Luis sighted the animal riding the horse's back, steadied, and shot. Another scream, a shot from Jamie's rifle, and the panther fell.

"Got 'em!" Jamie shouted. He ran after the horse and grabbed the bridle. "The panther's dead."

"Ma-lee," cried Andy.

Luis knelt to clasp Molly to his chest. "Are you hurt?" He smoothed back her hair and stared into her beloved face.

She shook in his arms, and he drew her to his chest, holding her tight.

"My body be fine," she whispered. "It be my heart that stumbles."

Chapter 10

December

M olly's shoulders ached from the churn's up-and-down motion. She didn't have much milk to churn, but with Christmas coming she wanted butter for the feast at the Hanks's cabin.

Andy played with pinecones on the bed, giggling at her churning rhyme:

"Come butter, come,
Come butter, come,
Andy standing at the gate
Waiting for a buttered cake,
Come butter, come."

Molly wondered if she should find a word to rhyme with corn pone since Andy had never tasted cake. "Andy riding on a roan, waiting for some warmed-up 'pone?" She shook her head; Andy wasn't likely to ride a horse soon either.

A hot fire crackled in the fireplace, warming them against the December chill. Bean soup simmered in a small iron kettle. The scents mingled with the pine boughs Molly had hung over the door and gave the small cabin a festive feel. Fabric for her new Christmas dress peeked from behind the feather pillow on the bed. She'd already finished sewing new shirts for Jamie and an entire outfit for the fast-growing Andy.

Molly quietly sang the opening verses of "Oh, Come, All Ye Faithful." When Andy looked up, she reached for him and crooned, "Oh, come, let us adore Him."

"Door," he repeated and fell back against the straw-stuffed mattress.

How did Luis and Ana celebrate Christmas, Molly wondered. And those words Luis had whispered last week, te adoro, what did they mean? Adoro, adore—could it be? Her heart lifted, and her lips twitched with delight.

Belle started up and barked just before a knock on the wooden door. The dog's tail wagged. "Who be there?" Molly called.

"Luis Vasco de Carvajal."

Andy pointed at the door. "Luis!"

Molly's shyness at seeing Luis disappeared at the excitement of Andy's word. She opened the door with a delighted smile. "He said your name. Come in."

Luis swept his hat from his head and entered. Molly noted his elegant clothing as she shut the door behind him. If only she had a nice dress.

"Good morning. I have come with an invitation. My mother requests your family join us tomorrow for noon dinner. I met Jamie outdoors, and he agreed."

Molly's heart danced. "Thank ye. We would be pleased to come. But Luis, did you hear? Andy said your name. He knows ye."

Luis nodded at the little boy. "Very good." He inspected the room. Molly flushed when she saw her sleeping chemise and old rust-colored dress hanging from pegs beside the bed.

"You sleep here?"

"Aye. Andy and Jamie have a bed across the breezeway."

Luis took two steps farther into the room, nearly reaching the fireplace. "What are all these plants hanging from the roof?"

"Herbs." Molly touched a braided strand of wild garlic. "These flavor stew. The chickweed and sassafras make good tea."

"Which are the nettles for tea?"

"Already put away. These still be drying. I collect seeds, too."

Andy stood on the straw tick. "Luis."

Luis steadied him. "What is this drawing on the shelf?"

"My brother John drew it: Ma and Pa, Samuel, Billy, and Jamie. I'm the little girl."

"Where are they now?"

She swallowed. "All passed on to glory."

"I see."

"Do you, Luis?" Molly trembled as she clutched his arm. "The only brother I have left has built this homestead. It's all we have. He and Andy are all I have. I know the cabin be simple, but we've worked hard to make it secure. He's poured his life into this property."

"But now your brother weds again?"

"Yes. He'll wed Eliza when she returns from visiting family in San Antonio." Molly dropped beside Andy.

"And Ramsey? Have you decided?"

Molly shook her head. "I have eight more days."

Belle's tail waved, and Jamie opened the door. "I've done as you asked, Carvajal. The horses be cobbled."

"What horses?" Molly opened the shutter. Luis's Maximo, Mamacita's gorgeous mare, and a brown stallion she didn't recognize cropped at the few tufts of grass remaining in the clearing.

"Can you ride sidesaddle?" Luis asked.

"Yes."

"Then you have a horse to ride to my ranchero. I will see you all tomorrow. *Adios*, Andy. Good day." Luis clicked his heels and left.

Jamie flung himself onto the bed beside Andy. "What do ye think this invitation is about?"

Molly knelt to unlock the padlock on the family trunk. "Did ye see his clothes? What am I going to wear? If only my Christmas dress be finished. Jamie," she bit her lip and looked at him. "May I wear Sarah's dress?"

Jamie frowned and sat upright. "What do ye think he's up to?"

❄

Ever since Luis had come home with the news of Clay Ramsey's proposal to Molly, Mamacita had bustled with energy. Orders flew to the servants; she banished Manuel's cigars outdoors and laid out Luis's finest clothes for airing.

Cleaning went on with a vengeance: rugs beaten, candlesticks polished, floors scrubbed. Luis had had to remove his mother from a precarious balance on a chair as she tried to knock down cobwebs from the ceiling in the *sala*—the main living space in the house.

"Why must we work so hard because Anglos are coming to dinner?" Maria whined.

Manuel stomped outside.

Mamacita drew herself tall as she watched her son-in-law depart. "Now maybe he will prefer his own casa." She clapped her hands. "Set the table."

Luis grew uneasy. He had not realized how humbly the Faires family lived before he entered the cabin yesterday. He wondered what Molly would think of the relative grandeur of the ranchero. His mother spread an embroidered cloth across the table and placed her most cherished possessions, two candlesticks, in the middle. He'd often heard the tale of his grandmother's journey from Spain with the heavy silver candlesticks tucked into her luggage.

"Mamacita, perhaps a simple meal in a less grand setting would be better?"

The woman shook her head. "Molly needs to see she would eat meat and be surrounded with beauty here."

"She is a hard worker," Luis said.

"That is why I like her. She could help you rebuild a strong home to honor our family as well as hers. You can give the beautiful girl children of her own in a real house."

Mamacita was wise. Luis hoped she was right.

At noon on the appointed day, a servant scurried into the house. "They arrive, señor."

Luis strode to the porch and watched the two horses he had left with Jamie Faires stop at the fence. Jamie swung off from the brown horse and tied the reins. He touched the brim of his hat at Luis before securing Mamacita's mare.

Luis had eyes only for the beauty wrapped in a dark cape and perched on the mare's saddle. Molly clung to the pommel with one hand and controlled a giggling Andy with the other. He hurried down the steps to reach her just as Jamie took Andy from her arms. "May I?" Luis asked.

Jamie thrust the boy at him and helped his sister dismount.

"Chick." Andy squirmed to get down. Maria followed Mamacita into the yard and held her arms out to the little boy when Luis set him down. Andy ignored her and headed toward the scruffy chickens pecking through the flower bed.

"Hello, Luis." Molly smiled at him and then grasped Mamacita's hand. "Thank ye for the kind invitation." She reached into a pocket of the cloak and pulled out a small package wrapped in softened bark and tied with willow string. "I brought ye sassafras tea."

"Gracias. Please come inside." Mamacita introduced Maria and Manuel. Molly tendered a shy smile and ducked her head.

"Thank ye for the use of your horses," Jamie said. "I hope to have one of my own soon."

"Let me know if I can help." Luis followed the women into the house, anxious to see Molly's reaction. Jamie went after his son.

Molly handed her cape to a servant and gazed about the sala. Maria joined her immediately. "Your dress is beautiful." The woman fingered the smooth blue fabric. "Is this what they are wearing where you come from?"

Molly lowered her voice. "This be the wedding dress of my brother's late wife."

"Beautiful." Mamacita took her arm and led her to a painting. "This is a portrait of my Antonio. Luis resembles him."

Luis watched Molly's eyes grow wide as Mamacita introduced her to their home. Maria sidled up to him and whispered in Spanish, "Why is Mamacita showing her everything? What does this mean?"

He replied in the same tongue. "Only God knows."

She slapped his wrist. "Now you sound like Mamacita when she comes back from camp meetings. What happened at the camp meeting?"

"Tomás reminded me of the Bible truth." He crossed his arms. "That includes turning the other cheek when men insult you and forgiving people who do not deserve to be forgiven."

She flushed. "You don't understand Manuel."

"No. But I want the best for you." He searched his little sister's round face for understanding. "That is why you must go to Manuel's ranchero. You need to have your own life."

Maria pouted and blinked her eyes rapidly. "Mamacita needs to come with me."

"She will come in time for your confinement."

Mamacita looked in their direction. "You all must be hungry. Luis, call the men, and we will eat." She clapped her hands and led her guests to the dining table.

Molly sat quietly beside Luis, gazing about the room and at the brightly lit candles in the gleaming candlesticks. "We will pray," Luis said, and bowed his head. He saw Maria gesture to Manuel, and the sullen man bent his head. Luis blessed the food in both English and Spanish. Manuel did not speak English.

Jamie sat stiff and upright beside Mamacita. Molly kept her head down as they dined. Andy gave up trying to eat with utensils and picked up the tortillas and roasted pork with his fingers.

"The food be delicious, Ana. I have not eaten like this in a long time. Thank ye for inviting us to dinner," Molly said.

Mamacita beamed. Manuel nudged Maria, who translated.

"Aye, thank ye," Jamie said. "Ye have a very nice spread here."

"This was part of my grandfather's land grant from the Spanish king," Luis said.

"Do ye live here as well?" Molly asked Maria.

"We leave next week to move to town. Manuel's family owns a casa in Nacogdoches, and we will travel there soon for the holiday celebrations and our baby's birth. In the spring we will go to my husband's ranchero," Maria said. "Do you celebrate the posada?"

Molly shook her head. "Tell us about it."

Maria glowed with importance. "We remember Joseph and Mary traveling from house to house in Bethlehem, trying to find a place for Mary to give birth to the baby Jesus: the *natividad*."

"And they found no room at the inn," Jamie murmured.

"We have *fiestas*, and visit our friends as if we are seeking a home like Mary and Joseph. We eat the delicious food, sing the songs, and remember the birth of the Christ child." Maria rubbed her hand along Manuel's sleeve as he ate, oblivious to the conversation. "It is my favorite time of year. We were married the final day of the posada two years ago—Christmas Eve."

Mamacita handed Molly a bowl of pecans. "How will you celebrate the natividad?"

"We will roast a wild turkey, read the story of Jesus, and share small gifts, mostly whittling Jamie did for Andy," Molly said. "On Christmas Day we will visit the Hanks family. Pappy Hanks always performs weddings on Christmas. He likes to begin new families on the day of Christ's birth."

"A lovely idea." Mamacita raised her eyebrows at Luis.

At the end of the meal, Luis stood. "I have an announcement to make." He nodded at Jamie. "I met the land surveyor in Nacogdoches. I have thought and prayed about his answer. I will not fight you for the land; it is yours."

"Praise Jesus," Molly said.

Jamie stood and shook Luis's hand. "Thank ye."

"I have one request."

"Ask it," Jamie said.

"I would like to court your sister with an aim toward marriage, sooner rather than later."

Molly's fork clattered to the table. She looked down to hide her blushing face. Jamie, however, knocked over his chair as he picked up his son.

"Get your things, Molly. We be leaving." He glared at Luis. "My sister is not for sale."

Chapter 11

Christmas Week

As Clay Ramsey trotted up to the farm on Pappy Hanks's horse, Molly approached her brother.

"Ye know what ye need to do." Jamie shaved smooth the wooden donkey's back. He'd sat on the stump whittling and watching when Luis came to call every day for the past week. Jamie wouldn't allow him to visit Molly in the cabin, so the couple strolled about the clearing in the chilly afternoons.

"It pains me not to be at peace with ye, Jamie," Molly said.

Her brother shook off the fragrant cedar shavings and looked directly at her. She saw a glint in his eyes. "Ye be worth more than a piece of land. Clay be a good man; he could give ye a good life."

She gazed steadily back, tears blurring to match her brother's. "What did ye feel when ye looked at Sarah? When ye look at Eliza now? I don't feel that way about Clay. But when I see Luis, when I talk with him, my heart be fluttering."

"Marriage be not built on fluttering."

"No? On need then? Luis needs me as much as Clay."

Jamie frowned. "How so? He's got a fancy house and horses. If it be horses ye want, Clay can provide. Look, he be coming on a horse."

"It not be about horses."

"Do the right thing," he said.

Scrubbed and beaming, Clay dismounted and tied the reins to the fence. "I borrowed the reverend's pony so I could get here faster. I've come for your answer."

Jamie scowled. "Don't ye want to take her for a walk and whisper sweet words?"

"Nay. This be a business arrangement, though with a gal as pretty as ye, Molly, I know it will grow to love right quick." He peered at the ground, bashful almost. "Lily always thought mighty fine of ye."

"Thank ye. Lily's love for ye speaks well of your character, Clay. I know ye be a hard worker and good father."

Now Jamie scowled at her. "This not be about Lily."

340

"No, it be about my heart. I be sorry, Clay, but when I see ye and your little'uns I think of Lily. It be not fair to ye or to them for me to join your family with my heart divided."

"Molly, don't be a fool," Jamie said.

Clay straightened his shoulders and met her eye. "Our hearts be sad, but what can we do? My little'uns need a ma. Can ye think on them? I may not be a handsome man, but I would work hard for ye and any children of your own."

She yearned to erase Clay's disappointment and to appease her brother's anger, but Molly knew marrying Clay wasn't the answer.

"Carvajal be twisting her mind, filling her head with ideas about a fancy house and horses," Jamie said.

Clay's eyes narrowed. "I knew about Eli Parker sparking for Molly, but what be this about the Mexican?"

"He's been here courting the last week," Jamie said.

"Ye would wed a Tejano?" The horror in Clay's voice pricked her conscience. "Be he a believer?"

Molly nodded. "Aye. He's known Pappy Hanks since he was a little'un. I been thinking about what God wants me to do."

Clay's shoulders slumped, and he rubbed his eyes. "What will I do? If ye don't wed Carvajal, will ye consider me? I got time; there be not many women I would wed if not ye."

"Thank ye kindly, Clay. I be sorry, but no." Molly took Andy by the hand and walked down to the stream without looking back.

Luis rode up to the dogtrot later that day while the woods rang with the fury of Jamie's two-sided axe. She ran to meet him.

"Did you see Ramsey?"

"Aye."

"Well?"

Molly felt guilty as she thought of Lily's motherless children. She sighed. "He be patient."

Luis dismounted. "What does that mean? What did you tell him?"

"It be not good to enter a marriage if I think of the first wife whenever I see the husband."

"True. What do you think of when you see me?"

Heat swept through her body. Standing close to Luis made her legs shaky.

He grinned. "Or should I be encouraged you won't look at me?"

She didn't dare look at him.

He lowered his voice to a caress. "I know your tender heart. What did you tell him?"

"I told him no."

He stepped closer. "Good. Then will you marry me?"

Molly tried to swallow her smile. "I still be thinking. We come from very different ways of living."

"It's only now you realize I'm Tejano and you're Anglo?"

"Nay. But I didn't realize ye were rich when I—" She paused, flustered.

He leaned toward her. "When you fell in love with me?"

Molly gasped. Luis laughed and drew her hands to his lips, where he settled a gentle kiss. "It didn't stop me from falling in love with you."

The sky may have been overcast, but the day Manuel and Maria took their possessions and left for Nacogdoches was a bright one for Luis. They'd stay in town for the winter and move to Manuel's ranchero in the spring. Luis would finish training the mustangs and then hand over a mare and a colt to pay off his lazy brother-in-law.

He didn't approve of giving the horses to Manuel, but reading the Bible influenced his decision. He could let Manuel go, forgiven.

"You have become an Anglo," Manuel growled when Luis and Mamacita announced their plans to stay at the Carvajal ranchero during the posada.

"Someone has to mind the property. Enjoy the fiestas." Luis helped his sister onto her mare. One of the ranch hands drove a cart with their luggage.

"Why will you not come with us, Mamacita?" Maria asked.

She touched her heart. "Having my son for the natividad blesses me more than anything. I will stay with Luis now and come to you at the New Year. I will be there for your baby's arrival."

Manuel crossed his arms over his chest. "It also means Mamacita can be a *dueña* for Luis and that Anglo girl."

"Her name is Molly. It does not hurt to have a chaperone."

Manuel snickered as he climbed onto his horse. "*Feliz navidad. Vaya*, Maria. Let's go."

Mamacita fluttered her handkerchief after them while Luis retrieved Maximo.

He rode through the thinning winter brush until he came to the Faires clearing. A line of smoke rose from the chimney, but he heard the chunk of an ax farther south. Luis nudged the stallion in Jamie's direction.

The young man's buckskin jacket lay on the ground beside a growing pile of kindling and small logs. He grunted at Luis and continued chopping at a dead loblolly pine. Luis dismounted and tied Maximo to a nearby sapling. A damp fog slid along the ground, and he hoped this would not take long.

Jamie pointedly ignored him. When it became clear he would not take a break, Luis tossed his cloak onto Maximo's saddle and began piling wood. They worked together through three stacks of logs before Jamie stopped to catch his breath.

"I would speak with you, Jamie."

"There be nothing ye can say to me, Carvajal. I'd give ye back the land if I had another option."

Luis wiped his arm along his sweating forehead. "I have been reading the Bible. Tomás suggested I study a passage in the book of Romans."

Jamie's eyebrows came together and he looked uncertain. "When did ye see Pappy Hanks?"

"Several weeks ago"—Luis paused—"about a personal matter. He told me about a passage that says 'if it be possible, as much as lieth in you, live peaceably with all men.'"

"That be right." Jamie kicked at a pile of sawdust, stirring up the pine scent.

"I made peace with my brother-in-law. He now has left my ranchero, and I believe my sister will be happier."

Jamie looked up. "Why do ye tell me this?"

"Because I do not like the man my sister married, but she loves him. I could continue to make her miserable, or I could do whatever was in my power to live at peace with him. He did not deserve my forgiveness, but I gave it anyway."

Jamie reached for his ax and examined the blade. In the silence they heard the tapping of a woodpecker.

Luis cleared his throat. "I love Molly and want to make her my wife. But she loves you and Andy. Without your blessing, she will not marry me. What do I need to do?"

The young man's shoulders sagged. "Tell me. What made ye change your mind? Why did ye really decide not to fight me for the land?"

Luis paused, trying to think of how to explain. He was a vaquero, strong and confident, but the answer was simple. He shrugged. "It is the right thing to do."

Jamie jerked back as if bitten. He blinked rapidly and swung the ax into the stump so hard it shuddered. Luis did not move. Jamie stared at the stump a long time, long enough for the frigid December air to prickle Luis's fingers.

Luis tugged his cloak around his shoulders and untied his horse. "I ask you, please, to tell me what I can do. This has nothing to do with who owns the land. I love Molly and would do anything for her."

Jamie stared into the forest. Luis climbed into the saddle. "Good day."

"Wait, Luis. I understand now." Jamie blinked rapidly. "I loved a good woman who always steered me right about Molly. I can give ye my blessing."

"Qué? What?" Luis pulled the reins taut.

Jamie reached up to shake Luis's hand. "Come to dinner on Christmas Eve."

"The final night of the posada?"

"Aye. Bring Ana with ye."

Luis gripped his hand. "Gracias, mi *amigo*."

As Luis turned Maximo toward his ranchero, Jamie called after him, "And bring a change of clothing. Pappy Hanks likes to perform weddings on Christmas Day."

Luis looked back over his shoulder and grinned.

❄

The rich smell of roasting turkey filled the small cabin as Molly turned the spit. She wore her old apron over her new blue Christmas dress and hummed "Joy to the World." Andy held open the door while his father carried out her straw mattress. They needed more room in the cabin to fit everyone around the table.

Everyone, Molly sighed in satisfaction. Jamie had kissed her forehead when he'd told her Luis and Mamacita would join them for dinner. "Sarah always wanted ye to be happy," he explained. "If Carvajal be who ye want, then letting ye go to him is the right thing to do."

"Do ye mean that, Jamie?"

"Aye," he'd replied. "It be the right thing to do."

The dried flowers had been stowed away and replaced by fresh pine boughs dotted with red berries. She had covered the small table with woven reed placemats and set precious china bowls in the center—four bowls her grandmother had carried all the way from Scotland. They had five forks and spoons—one for each diner. The candles, which Molly had made herself, stood upright on a flat stone, melted into place. She put finishing touches on the room with pride. The rough rock fireplace, peeled log walls, and sitting stumps could not compare with the Carvajal's sala, but she and Jamie had made the home themselves, and they were thankful.

They heard singing as dusk settled. Molly, Jamie, and Andy opened the door when Luis knocked. Luis had written out their lines, and at his request for a posada room, Jamie played the traditional part of the innkeeper and turned them away.

Andy sobbed. "Luis!"

The adults laughed, and Jamie reopened the door. "Come in, pilgrims."

He took Mamacita and Andy with him across the breezeway to set their cloaks and baggage in the other cabin. Luis loomed tall in the cook cabin, and Molly's heart leaped. His dark eyes gleamed, and she gazed back with pleasure.

He handed her a basket. "Tamales."

"Do we eat them with the turkey?"

"Why not?"

They nestled around the table, knees to knees, said grace, and ate their meal, a mixture of Anglo and Tejano tradition. Andy's face squinted at the hot chiles. Mamacita tasted the dried apple relish carefully and pronounced it *muy bien*. Jamie and Luis ate with gusto while Molly picked nervously at her tamale.

After dinner, Jamie handed Luis the Bible to read the posada story of Mary and Joseph looking for a place to stay. Luis read clearly and with emotion, transfixing them all. When he finished, he placed the Bible back on the shelf. Jamie reached into a basket at his feet and pulled out the pieces of a whittled nativity scene: Mary, Joseph, sheep, wise men, and several donkeys. Andy's mouth fell open, and his eyes grew wide. He reached for the figures, and they all laughed when Mamacita presented him with the tiny niño whittled from a pecan shell.

Luis touched Molly's hand. "Come outside with me. Perhaps we can see the Christmas star tonight?"

She raised her eyebrows at her brother.

"Go." Jamie waved an indulgent hand. "Ye have my blessing."

"Aye?"

"Aye," he laughed.

She kissed him on the cheek. "Thank ye." Molly put on her woolen shawl and followed Luis out to the wide breezeway between the cabins. They faced the pasture, where the horses huddled together against the December wind. Stars twinkled white in the ebony sky.

"I have long wanted to ask you about something," Luis said. "Why did you offer to water my horse that day I met you?"

"My parents always said to watch for opportunities to do the right thing." She shrugged. "Ye looked so tired and discouraged, I wanted to do something for ye."

"Thank you." Luis touched Molly's arm. "Have you decided about my offer?"

Molly ran her hand along the cabin's rough logs. "I been thinking about how different we be, but as I listened to ye read about Mary and her faith, it reminded me of how much faith it takes to live in Texas."

Luis nodded. "Making a life from scratch took a great deal of faith for you and your brother. Like Mary and Joseph, you traveled a far way to make a home."

"As did your family, and that took faith. I think we be like this dogtrot cabin. We each have our own way of living, our own cabin." She pointed to both sides of the breezeway.

"Sí."

"Like a dogtrot cabin, a marriage combines two different people to shelter one family. Do ye understand?"

Luis took both her hands. "Yes. Do you believe God's love can cover our traditions and cultures to unite us?"

Her lips parted, and joy filled her voice. "I know what ye say be possible."

"You have my heart, mi corazón. I love you, Molly."

She looked him in the eye. "Te adoro, Luis. I love ye."

His laughter rumbled low. "Then will you marry me?"

"Yes."

He touched her cheek, tipped up her chin, and kissed her. Molly's knees gave way, and he hugged her close. "When?" he whispered.

"Tomorrow."

Luis laughed.

When Molly began to hum "Joy to the World," he tucked her hand into his elbow and led her out from under the dogtrot roof toward the paddock. "Let me show the golden filly you'll ride tomorrow, mi corazón."

"A horse for me?"

"A present for my beloved to ride to her Christmas wedding."

A direct descendent of the Reverend Thomas Hanks depicted in *The Dogtrot Christmas*, Michelle Ule is a writer, genealogist, and Bible study leader. She graduated from UCLA with a degree in English Literature and married a navy submarine officer whom she followed all over the world with their four children. Michelle lives in northern California with her family.

A Grand County
Christmas

by Debra Ullrick

Dedication

This book is dedicated to my eighty-seven-year old mom, who fluently speaks low-German and whose parents were Germans from Russia. Thank you, Mom, for answering my many questions about our heritage and for helping me with the German. God bless you, Mom. I love you.

Chapter 1

Awnya O'Crean hoisted her rifle, took aim, and eased the hammer back. Just as she narrowed her gaze through the sight and fingered the trigger, a large gloved hand covered her thumb and raised the barrel of her gun. "What are you doing?" she hissed through a whisper, not even looking at the person who had the nerve to deny her a much-needed meal. "You trying to get your fingers blown off?"

"*Nein.* But that animal you vill not shoot."

Snapped into the reality that some stranger had his hands on her rifle, Awnya's gaze swung toward the man with the thick German accent. Her gaze trailed upward a foot or more before landing on the face of the barrel-chested giant standing beside her.

Her heart raced fast and hard, but she would not let him catch sight of her fear. That's one thing her pa had taught her. Well, kind of. Pa had referred to wild animals not sensing her fear, but this man was big enough to be an animal, a two-legged version, so the lesson held true. She glanced at the deer that had raised its head and stared straight at her only twenty yards away. "Let go of my rifle."

"Nein. I vill not. That deer is my pet."

Pet? She lowered her gun. She couldn't believe she'd almost killed someone's pet. She wasn't that hungry. Okay, she was, but she would never kill someone's pet to fill her stomach. She slid her face upward and fought not to notice the bluest eyes or longest lashes she'd ever seen. "Your pet? Are you serious?"

"*Ja.*" He stared back at her from under a snow-covered cowboy hat.

Defeat settled into her weary bones. Now what would she do for food? Hunger cramps stabbed her stomach.

Snowflakes floated down like an erupted feather pillow. She needed to hurry and find some other game and get back to her cabin before she got stranded. But how? She'd burned up all her energy hunting for her next meal and had wandered around in circles for hours until she no longer knew which way was home.

Oh Pa. If you were still alive, there'd be plenty of food, and I wouldn't be out in this blizzard hunting. Before her pa's death seven weeks back, he had filled their meat cave, but somehow wild animals had gotten the latch open and stolen every bit of it. Awnya had her suspicions about wild animals stealing it, and so had her pa, but proving it was another thing. No sense dwelling on that now. She needed to get food, and soon, or she might very well end up buried beside him.

With no money to buy supplies, her only other option was to hunt. If only she could trap animals like her father. Then at least the pelts would give her enough money to put food on the table. But that took more skill than she possessed.

Her gaze wandered toward the deer still standing there but no longer looking at her. She stared longingly at the animal. Despite the fact the doe was this man's pet, she still pictured turning it into a large pot of venison stew. Her mouth watered, and her gut rumbled, sending sharper more painful cramps than before.

With no warning the man's hand came to rest on her shoulder, now piled with at least a half-inch of snow.

She glanced at his hand then up at him. Snowflakes melted against her bare face.

"Since I am responsible for you not getting meat, come to my cabin, *und* I vill give you some."

Tempting. Mighty tempting indeed. But she didn't know this man. She looked around for a cabin and saw none. How far was his place? Did she dare trust him? For all she knew he could be a crazy person or a murderer. Well, she'd take her chances dying in the wilderness or starving before she would go anywhere with him.

Awnya stepped back, putting distance between them. "No thank you. I'll keep hunting until I find something."

He glanced upward at the snow falling heavier now then back down at her. "You must come to my place und stay the night."

"What?" She put even more distance between them. "Are you gone in the head? I am a God-fearing woman, mister, and I won't have my reputation tainted. I'll take my chances getting home, thank you kindly." It would be a chance, too. A huge one. If only she'd paid attention to where she'd traveled, but she hadn't. She'd been too intent in her search for food. And now every rock, every draw, and every tree looked alike—stark white. Awnya's heart dropped.

Things sure were simpler when they'd lived in the Colorado flatlands. Down there, she used the Rocky Mountains as her guide. She could find her way anywhere because the mountains were always west of where she'd lived. Here in the high country, she was surrounded by them. Aside from all that, she still loved living in Grand County. Or she had until her pa died.

Oh, Lord, why didn't I pay closer attention to where I was going? Please help me out of this situation.

Her stomach rumbled again, and her body was getting weaker and colder by the moment. The only thing left at home to eat was flour and lard, and there was barely enough to make even a small batch of biscuits—biscuits without milk.

"*Fräulein,* I assure you. You are perfectly safe with me." His deep, gentle voice pulled her attention off her dire situation and onto him. "I am a God-fearing man myself, und we vill not be alone. My children und *meine mutter* live with me."

How many children could this man have? He didn't look a day over twenty-five.

Her insides screamed at her not to go with him. Oh dear. What to do. Should she go? He said he wasn't alone. And the snowfall had increased significantly.

In the short time she'd lived here, one thing she'd discovered was a person never knew what the weather would do. She could venture out in a cloudless sky and within an hour find herself in a blizzard. Like now. This morning she'd started out under a clear blue sky. Now the clouds hung low, and it would only be a matter of minutes before things turned into a complete whiteout.

She swallowed the lump of indecision stuck in her throat. No other sane choice remained but to take this man up on his offer. Trying to find her way home in this storm would be certain death. And not a pretty one either. "Is your place nearby?" she asked with a tilt of her head.

"Ja. Over the hill. We need to hurry, fräulein, before we can see no longer."

"I've only been in this neck of the woods a few months, and I'm already finding that out."

He chuckled. And what a nice chuckle it was.

A gust of wind slapped icy patches of snow onto her nearly frostbitten skin. Awnya wrapped her scarf around her nose and mouth and tucked the edges deeper into her coat. With a new resolve to do what she had to do to survive, she pulled her shoulders back and looked up at him. "Lead the way, mister."

Rifle in one hand and her lodgepole pine in the other, she followed him. She used her pole like an oar and lifted the toe of each snowshoe upward, forward, and then down.

Thank the good Lord, when she and her pa had first moved here, Pa had purchased two pairs of Norwegian snowshoes and two lodgepole pines. The long snowshoes made maneuvering through the trees and deep snow much easier.

At the top of the hill the man extended his hand toward her. "Here. Take my hand."

Because it was slippery, Awnya reluctantly complied. Her small hand disappeared in his.

Down the hill she and the stranger traipsed.

Stranger.

Awnya realized she didn't even know his name. Apprehension crawled up and down her spine like a million spider legs. She yanked her hand from his.

He glanced at her. Then as if he understood her hesitation, he continued walking sideways down the hill, peering back often.

Awnya continued to follow him. She prayed for God's protection from the weather and the elements but mostly from the brawny man who had piqued her curiosity.

He stopped at a corral gate, opened it, and then motioned for her to precede him. She stepped through the gate and paused. Since when does one go through a corral to get to a house? What was this man doing anyway? Was he even taking her to a house?

The urge to whirl and flee as far away from him as possible hung in her brain like a large icicle until the hazy shape of a cabin came into focus.

Several yards in front of her stood a log cabin with another log cabin on top.

Very strange. Very strange indeed.

The top cabin had a door with a window on each side, but the bottom cabin had no door, only an opening. What kind of person would build a doorway without a door? Just then a cow stuck its head through the opening.

"Oh!" She stepped back. "You share your home with animals?" Awnya couldn't keep the incredulousness from her voice.

"Nein. We lived there until I built that cabin." He pointed upward to the cabin sitting on top of where the cows were housed. "We live there now."

"Above the animals?" This man was nuttier than a sack full of walnuts.

"Ja. Their body warmth rises und helps heat my home." He smiled, revealing white even teeth.

"How many animals are in there?"

"Eight dairy cows."

How big was that place? She really wanted to peek inside to see, but with the increasing snowfall, now was not the time to go exploring.

"Come, fräulein. We must hurry." He clasped her free hand and led her through the corral.

On her left, nestled against the trees, stood a large barn. A single fence separated the corral they were in from the one with the plank wood barn. They stopped at another gate and went through it. Once he had it securely latched, they headed around the side of the lower cabin to a set of stairs that went to the upper place.

Before going up, she removed her snowshoes, tucked them and her pole securely under her arm, and then draped her rifle sling over her shoulder.

Up the slippery stairs she climbed, struggling the whole way to keep her footing. Partway up, a strong gust of wind pushed her body sideways. Her foot slid out from under her.

"Careful." His strong hand clasped hers, pulling her upright.

Her foot slipped yet again.

"Forgive me, fräulein, for taking liberties but. . ." With that, he scooped her up into his arms, and Awnya's breath fled. "This way we can quicker get there."

He was right, and the quicker the better, so she let him carry her. Through her bearskin fur coat, the strength of his muscular forearms on the back of her legs and shoulders both frightened her and made her feel safe at the same time.

Horse, soap, a heated body, and crisp air drifted from him. Without trying to be too obvious, she studied the man.

Underneath the brim of his black cowboy hat, a lone strand of brown hair lay against his forehead. His masculine nose had a slight hump in the middle, and a day's worth of stubble dotted his square jawline and upper lip. Having never been kissed before, she wondered what it would be like to feel his lips on hers.

His mouth curled into a smile, accompanied by two dimples, and his chest vibrated against her as a deep chuckle escaped. Oh dear. Had he caught her studying his mouth? Her gaze darted upward, clashing into his.

The mirth in his eyes said, yes, he had caught her. Her cheeks, no longer cold, burned with mortification.

Awnya yanked her attention away from him. She wanted to release her arm from around his neck, but she had no choice but to cling to him as he continued up the steps. If she were honest with herself, she really didn't mind. Being held in his arms felt nice.

A little too nice. Cozy. Snuggly even. She could get used to this.

Amadeus Josef wanted to slow his pace. A long time had passed since he had held a woman. Lye soap, forest floor, mixed with damp animal hair teased his nostrils.

Since his wife's death four years before, loneliness followed him like a yapping puppy. For two years now he had prayed for a mother for his children and a loving wife. Could this woman in his arms be God's answer?

He was not sure. Deep inside something had stirred when he'd noticed her staring at his mouth. He knew the moment she realized he had caught her. Her green eyes widened, and her cheeks turned redder than they already had been from the cold. The temptation to laugh again came strong, but he didn't. Women were inquisitive creatures. To have to admit his instant attraction toward her and how he wanted to feel her rosebud lips on his would not do.

He forced his attention from her and finished climbing the stairs. At the landing, he noticed a loose porch rail and a missing piece of chinking above his mother's bedroom window. Tomorrow morning after chores, he would fix the rail. But the other, he had no choice but to wait until the ground thawed to mix mud and clay together to fill in the hole. For now, he would stuff a rag in the gap.

"Uh, you can set me down now."

He looked at her amused eyes. He did not wish to put her down. He enjoyed holding her.

"I don't even know your name."

"Amadeus Josef. Und yours is…?"

"Awnya O'Crean."

"Pretty name. You are Irish, ja?" He set her on her feet.

"Yes."

"That explains the red hair." He reached over and brushed at a lone strand the wind had blown across her face.

Their eyes connected and lingered longer than a moment.

"My mother's hair was the same color." Awnya turned her face from his, but not before he saw her glistening eyes.

The past tense usage of her mother indicated the woman had passed on. What about her father? Was he dead also? Seeing how upset Awnya was, Amadeus chose not to ask. He would not risk upsetting her further.

"Where are you from?" Those green eyes were back on him, skipping his heart several beats.

"I was born in Austria. My papa was Austrian, und my mama is German. Fifteen years ago, to America we moved."

"That explains your accent."

"Ja. I try hard to speak the American well. My papa insisted we learn to talk like the Americans, but I do not always succeed."

"You speak English very well. It's just sometimes your *w*'s sound like *v*'s, and your *t*'s sound like *d*'s, and you toss in a German word here and there." Her body suddenly shook with the advancing cold. "Brrr."

The poor woman is freezing to death, und you stand out here like an idiot in a whiteout carrying on a conversation? What is wrong with you, Amadeus?

"Forgive me for keeping you in the cold." Using the porch rail as a guideline, he led her to the front door of the cabin. "Let us go inside where we can get warm und get something to eat." *And where I can much better get to know you.*

Chapter 2

Awnya stood to the side so she wouldn't be in Amadeus's way while he opened the cabin door. Snow swirled inside, onto a braided rug and the knotty-pine flooring. He stood back and motioned for Awnya to precede him.

She stepped inside under a low ceiling that sloped upward. Warm, inviting heat greeted her along with a mixture of faint animal odors, baked bread, food, and two identical small boys that resembled their father.

Amadeus hurried inside and shut the door. "Ethan. Jakob. Give the lady some room."

Immediately, the brown-haired, blue-eyed boys took three large steps backward.

"Here. I take that."

The weight of her rifle lifted from her shoulder. She wanted to snatch it back, but Amadeus hung it above the door right below another one. Not having it nearby made her nervous, but surely he wouldn't do anything to her with children in the room.

That thought helped her relax a bit.

He hung her snowshoes on a nail, placed her pole below, and faced the room. "Where is your *grossmutter?*"

Next to a kitchen table stood a seven- or eight-year-old girl with fawn-colored hair and sea-blue-green eyes—eyes that frowned at Awnya then swung toward Amadeus. "*Oma's* taking a nap. She wanted me to wake her up when you got in." Her attention swiveled back to Awnya.

"Isabella, this is Fräulein Awnya O'Crean."

"Nice to meet you, Isabella."

The girl said nothing, only turned questioning eyes up at her father.

"Tonight she vill stay with us."

The girl frowned, eyeing Awnya warily. The two younger boys moved alongside their sister.

"These are my sons." He pointed to the one on Awnya's right. "That is Ethan."

"Ethan." She smiled at the child.

His little shoulders hiked, and his gaze dropped to the floor. "Ma'am," he whispered before shuffling back to his sister's side.

The boy on her left pressed his shoulders back, raised his head high, and stepped forward.

"That is Jakob."

Yaycob. She loved Amadeus's accent and how his *j*'s sounded like *y*'s. Like when he'd told her his last name was Yosef.

"Pleasure to meet you, ma'am." Jakob smiled, and so did Awnya when she noticed his two upper front teeth missing. Jakob returned to his sister's side. "Welcome to our home, Fräulein O'Crean."

Isabella jabbed him in the side with her elbow.

Jakob's gaze flew to his sister. "What did you do that for?" He elbowed her back.

Awnya would have liked to hear the answer to that question, too.

"*Das ist genug.*" Amadeus's stern voice took Awnya back a bit.

The children stopped and whirled their gazes up at him.

"Isabella, go und wake your grossmutter. Boys, clean your mess, und wash your hands for supper."

"Yes, Papa," they both said before heading over to the river-rock fireplace, where they gathered wooden train cars, railroad tracks, checker pieces, and a fold-up checkerboard, placing them in buckets.

Not knowing what to do, Awnya removed her other glove, her wool hat, and her scarf. She folded them neatly and placed them on the honed-out tree bench under the window.

Amadeus moved behind her. He held the bearskin coat she and her pa had made while she removed her arms from the sleeves. He hung it on a peg near the door.

"Your feet must be cold." He reached under the bench, grabbed two pairs of hand-stitched, fur-lined slippers, and handed her the smaller leather pair.

"Sit, und put on these, ja?"

"Thank you." She sat down and found the smoothed-out surface surprisingly comfortable. Before she had a chance to finish unlacing her boots, Amadeus had his off and his slippers on. She finished removing her wet boots and slid her feet into the warm, furry footwear.

"I need to add logs to the stove und fireplace. You make yourself at home, ja?"

"Thank you." She stood.

Amadeus gave a quick nod, loaded his arms with logs from a nearby wood-box, and strode over to the fireplace at the far end of the large room. His shadow loomed large against the log walls.

Orange and yellow hues from a kerosene lantern sitting on a corner cabinet, along with coals from the fire, shed some light into the dusky room. While he tossed logs onto the grate, she stepped farther into the room and took in her surroundings.

A buckshot rifle, identical to the one her pa had, hung high above the fireplace mantel. A wave of sadness washed over her. She never found her pa's gun. It had been nowhere near his body. She wondered where it had gone. Something about her pa's death had never set right with her, but she wouldn't dwell on that right now. It hurt too much.

She switched her focus to the open fireplace and the three slatted, straight-back rocking chairs in front of it. How she'd love to sit in one and rest a bit. Her muscles ached from traveling so far in the thick snow. Even sitting on the round top of the steamer trunk against the wall sounded good at this point.

She lifted her gaze. The room appeared distant and moved like clouds pulled by the wind. Having very little to eat for several days was taking its toll on her. Before the light-headedness sent her to the floor, she needed to find a place to sit. She didn't want to get in Amadeus's or the boys' way. Surely it would be all right to sit at the kitchen table in one of the knotty-pine chairs or on one of the benches. They looked mighty tempting. Mighty tempting indeed. Amadeus had told her to make herself at home. The decision was made.

Blinking back the fog, she made her way to the closest kitchen chair and lowered herself onto its hard surface. Flames from the two lanterns on the table danced and twirled in her vision, making her dizzier. She pulled her attention from them, and within minutes her vision cleared.

Heat from the nearby Glenwood cookstove worked its way into her bones, warming her and making her eyelids heavy, but she would not allow herself to be rude and fall asleep. She blinked twice, forcing her eyes to stay open, mentally making notes to keep herself awake. To the right of the stove stood a breadboard counter with drawers, cabinets, a pull-out flour bin, and gray-and-brown crocks that must hold baking powder, sugar, molasses, honey, spices, coffee, and tea.

Her attention swayed as sleep dropped over her once again. She shook herself and forced her mind to continue the litany of kitchen items. Next to the breadboard counter stood a shelf with two blue, speckled dishpans. Hanging on the wall above it were towels, a knit dishcloth, and a bucket. Next to that stood an open-face cabinet filled with dishes.

The boys headed toward her. One of the twins dropped his head and scurried past. From his earlier shy behavior that had to be Ethan. The other flashed her a wide smile with two front teeth missing. That boy had to be Jakob.

She shifted in her chair. Balancing their toy buckets, they climbed the built-in ladder between the two bedrooms up to a loft. The only things she could see there were a single mattress, a trunk, and a few clothes on the wall.

Butted up against the farthest bedroom wall were shelves loaded with bottles of tonics, jugs, lanterns, jars of canned fruits, vegetables, fish, and chicken.

She'd never seen so much food and supplies in one place before. Her stomach growled just thinking about all that fare.

"You warm now, fräulein?" Amadeus asked beside her.

She looked up at him and nodded. "Yes. I am. Thank you. The heat feels nice."

"Das ist *gut*." He smiled.

"Excuse me?"

"Sorry. I forget sometimes. I say, that is good."

"Oh. Okay." She smiled her understanding.

With a half nod, he moved to the cookstove and raised the iron lid. After stirring the ashes, he added logs.

When he finished, he turned and peered over her head. "Did you sleep well, Mama?"

"Ja."

Awnya spun in her chair.

A short woman with gray hair pulled back in a bun, wearing a navy wool dress with an apron, ducked under the line of laundry and headed toward them. Isabella followed, her face scrunched as if she'd just eaten a sour apple.

Awnya stood on weak legs.

"Mama, this is, Fräulein Awnya O'Crean. Awnya, this is Louissa, my mama."

"Nice to meet you, Awnya. Such a beautiful name. Und such beautiful red hair."

"I think it's ugly. It looks like marmalade jam," Isabella's whisper reached Awnya's ears, but she pretended she hadn't heard it. Her father didn't though.

"Isabella. What is wrong with you?" He glanced at Awnya. "Again, I apologize for my daughter's rudeness." He looked back to Isabella. "Apologize to our guest."

Isabella's gaze lowered. "Sorry."

Even though she knew the girl didn't mean it, it didn't matter. Awnya would forgive her anyway. "It's okay. I've always thought my hair looked like marmalade, too. I wish I had pretty hair like yours."

Isabella jolted her gaze to Awnya's. She twirled a strand of her own hair around her finger.

Awnya followed the movement around and around and around. Suddenly, she didn't feel so good. The room appeared dimmer than it had a few minutes before, and even the glow from the kerosene lanterns had dimmed. She reached behind her and felt for the chair she'd been occupying but couldn't find it. White dots pranced in the dark shadows around her. "I think I'm going to. . ."

"Isabella, get water." Amadeus carried Awnya's limp body into his mama's bedroom and laid her on the feather mattress.

"Did I cause her to faint, Papa?" His daughter's eyes, filled with fear, shifted between Awnya and himself.

"Nein, nein, *liebchen*. Lack of food has made her weak. Go und get water now, please."

"Yes, Papa." She fled the room and within seconds returned with a glass of water.

"Will she be all right?"

"Ja." He took the water from Isabella, raised Awnya's head, and laid the glass against her lips. "Come, Awnya, you must drink." He let the water run into her mouth.

She stirred as the liquid trailed down her chin. Her eyes opened. "What—what happened?"

"You fainted."

"Oh dear," she whispered.

Seeing Awnya faint had resurrected a heartbreaking memory, one Amadeus wanted to forget. The image of his wife slumping to the floor and never regaining consciousness crashed in on him. He forced the image from his mind, knowing there was nothing that could be done for Georgina, but for Awnya there was.

Though he had just met her, she stirred something inside him he had not felt since Georgina's death. His arms ached to hold Awnya, to explore his feelings toward her. But now was not that time. "Isabella, ask your grossmutter to bring Awnya food please."

"Yes, Papa."

Awnya sat up, but not without bouts of swaying, which she tried to hide. "Please don't. I'm fine."

He hiked one brow then turned to his daughter. "Tell Oma we are ready to eat. Und help her set the table."

Isabella nodded and left the room.

He faced Awnya. "I vill help you to the kitchen."

"No, no, that's okay. I'm fine. Really."

Not believing it for a moment, he stood, draped his arm securely around her shoulders, and led her to the kitchen table.

She felt good tucked under his arm. A perfect fit.

He missed having someone to talk with. To wake up to. To share his life with. Yes, he had his children and mother, but it was not the same. He wanted a companion. A wife. With Christmas only twelve days away, he silently prayed, *Lord, for Christmas, the only gift I want is Awnya.*

❄

Awnya bowed her head while Amadeus said grace. When his prayer ended, Louissa filled their bowls and passed them around. Braided bread came next. Each person tore off a chunk. When everyone had their food, they began to eat.

When she took her first bite, chicken, carrots, celery, onions, and little clumps of dough similar to heavy dumplings melted in her mouth. "This is delicious, Mrs. Josef. What kind of soup is this?"

"Please, call me Louissa. It's chicken rivel soup."

"Rivel? Is that what the little dough balls are?"

"Ja. It was my Oma's recipe. Meine mutter teach me to make it, und I teach Isabella."

Awnya looked at Isabella. "You made the soup?"

"No. But I helped."

"Well, you did a very good job of helping. My mother used to make great soup, too, but this is one of the best I've ever eaten."

The little girl beamed. Then a shield of nonchalance fell over her.

"You said 'used to'." Amadeus's voice pulled her attention to him.

"Yes. My mother died several years ago."

"Und your papa?"

She put her spoon down and placed her hands in her lap. "He passed away, too."

"I am sorry for you, Awnya."

"Thank you."

"Any brothers or sisters?"

"No. No one."

"No one at all?" Ethan blurted.

When she looked at him, he dipped his head.

"If I do, they're in Ireland, but my parents never mentioned anyone else." She picked up her spoon and shoved soup into her mouth, hoping they would take the hint and move the conversation in a different direction.

"Papa, Awnya could become part of our family. You could marry her, and she could become our mother."

Awnya gasped at Jakob's boisterous suggestion. A vegetable chunk stuck in her throat. She coughed and hacked, trying to dislodge it.

Amadeus rushed to her side and patted her back until her airway cleared. Then he leaned close and for her ears only said, "Sounds good to me."

Her gaze flew to his. She searched his eyes to see if he was serious; after all, they'd just met.

Sincere blue eyes smiled at her, making her wonder if it might very well be possible.

Chapter 3

In the shadowed bedroom, Awnya stretched her arms under a tied, patchwork quilt. One of the taut ropes underneath the mattress pushed a chicken feather through the sheet, pricking her skin. She shoved it back through and tossed the blanket aside. "Brrr." Cold air penetrated the flannel nightgown Louissa had lent her, the one an upset Isabella informed her was her mother's.

Awnya slid her legs over the wooden frame and stood. She leaned over and tossed the covers into place and then shoved her bed under the frame of the one above it, the one Louissa and Isabella had shared the night before.

She rubbed her arms, hurried to the window, and pulled aside the quilt curtain. Very little light filtered into the room due to the heavy cloud cover.

Snow swirled around the window, adding inches to the drift against the porch rail. Unless things changed, Awnya wouldn't be going home today. She let the curtain fall back into place.

She felt her navy and brown wool dress to make sure it was dry before getting dressed. At the bedroom door she paused, savoring the aroma of coffee and bacon that wafted from the room beyond.

Isabella stopped talking to her father and scowled at Awnya.

Amadeus turned toward her and stood. "Morning, Awnya."

"Morning." Awnya focused on the pine knots in the floor.

"Come. Join us."

She picked up her gaze.

"Ja. I have a plate ready for you." Louissa smiled, adding more wrinkles around her eyes and mouth.

"Move over, boys, to let Awnya sit," Amadeus said.

Ethan offered her a small smile before lowering his gaze to his plate.

Jakob's bright face split into a wide grin. "Sit next to me." He scooted over so fast and hard he almost knocked Ethan off the bench.

Awnya's heart warmed at his acceptance of her. She sat down. Syrup and plates of bacon, eggs, and some crumbly looking stuff in a bowl was placed before her.

Awnya took two pieces of bacon, a scoop of scrambled eggs, and a small portion of the other stuff. What was the syrup for? She sneaked a peek at Jakob's bowl. Syrup coated the crumbles. Ah, so that's what it was for. She drizzled the warm liquid into her bowl and took a bite of the crisp yet chewy morsels. "This is wonderful. What is it?" she questioned Louissa.

"*Verhackertes.*"

"Far-hawk-tuss? What's it made of?"

"Flour, milk, egg, und a little salt."

"How did you get it into such tiny pieces?"

Isabella huffed and took over for her grandmother. "You fry it in lard or oil and keep chopping away at it until the pieces are little. Don't you know anything?"

"Isabella. Your behavior is unacceptable. Apologize to Awnya. *Jetzt!*" Amadeus ordered sternly.

Isabella turned narrowed eyes at Awnya. "Sorry."

Again, it was obvious the girl didn't mean it. Awnya didn't care. She only wished she knew why Isabella disliked her so.

She nodded. "Thank you for telling me how it's made."

"Welcome."

She knew Isabella didn't mean that either.

"Now finish your breakfast," Amadeus said to his daughter.

"Yes, Papa."

When everyone finished eating, Amadeus dressed for outside while Louissa and Isabella worked at clearing the table.

Awnya rose to help, but Louissa stopped her. "Nein. We get this. You are guest."

"An uninvited guest," Isabella murmured near her.

Awnya sneaked a glance at Amadeus to see if he'd heard his daughter's comment. He continued to dress for outdoors, so he must not have, which was fine with Awnya, as she could well forgo the insincere apologies.

Unsure what she would do now, Awnya tugged at her lower lip, pondering her choices. One thing she didn't want to do was stand around and watch Isabella glower at her. She'd rather face a raging blizzard than put up with the girl's insolence.

In that instant, the decision was made. In record time, she readied herself for outdoors, grabbed her pole, and reached for the door handle.

❅

Amadeus turned, shocked at what he saw. "What you doing?"

"Going outside to help with chores." Her eyes held hope. He did not blame her. Isabella's disrespect had not gotten past him. But he had no idea how to handle his daughter. A talk would be good to find out why she was being rude to their guest.

He nodded and opened the door. Cold and snow blasted his face. "You certain, Awnya?"

She stepped past him onto the snow-covered porch.

"Ja. I guess so." He chuckled.

Around the house and down the stairs, he shoveled a path for them to walk. While still not good, the visibility was much better than yesterday. He would not need to put up a rope to guide them.

At the bottom of the stairs he asked, "You got animals to feed, Awnya?"

"No. None."

He sighed with relief. He could not bear the thought of any animal going without food. But that also meant the woman was more destitute than he'd thought. She needed someone to take care of her. And he wanted to be that someone.

His attention darted behind her. "Ah, there you are. I wondered where you were."

Awnya turned. She gasped and leaped backward.

Amadeus chuckled and ran his hand over the deer's neck. "Sorry she startled you. She is come for grain."

He left to get the doe's feed, and when he came back, he shook his head and grinned.

"Aren't you the sweetest little thing ever?" Awnya cooed, scratching his pet behind the ears. "And to think I almost shot you. I'm so glad I didn't."

"I bet she is, too, ja?"

Awnya looked up and chortled. He joined her.

They trekked through the snow to the shelter underneath his cabin. He motioned for her to go first. Then he ducked inside, keeping his head low so his hat would not scrape the ceiling.

"I'm surprised the cows come in here. The ceiling's so low. How tall is it?"

"Six und a half feet."

"Why'd you make it so low when you're so tall?"

"Heat rises to the top, und a low ceiling makes less space to heat."

"When you built the cabin above, why didn't you make it low like this one then?"

"Several reasons." He counted them off. "With the roof sloped it helps to keep snow from accumulating und the roof from caving in. I did not wish to duck all the time. Plus the boys needed a room, und the loft provides that. I knew the heat from the animals would rise und help heat the cabin."

"I see." Awnya stepped farther inside and looked down. "Is there a wood floor under all this dirt?"

"Nein. No time. Winter come too soon."

One of the cows butted him, knocking him into Awnya. She stumbled, but he shot his arm out and caught her. Touching her made his heart race. The yearning to hold her came strong, but the restless cows needed to be fed and milked.

Amadeus forced thoughts of holding Awnya from him. He secured the cows while she pulled the rope on the grain chute, filled the buckets, and fed each cow grain while he milked.

"What do you do with all this milk?" She grabbed a stool and a bucket and started to milk the cow next to him. He hated seeing her work, but she had insisted on helping.

"Most of it I sell. I transport it to the relay stage stop, und they haul it to the train depot. But today, the snow is too deep. The horses vill not make it. So Mama vill skim the cream und make butter. The rest, I vill store."

They finished the milking, and against his wishes, Awnya helped carry the buckets to the house.

"Hi, Papa." His children greeted him from around the kitchen table, where they were playing jackstraws.

"Who is winning?"

Isabella successfully removed one of the long thin sticks he had whittled. "I am." She raised her chin.

He had to ask.

He and Awnya removed their outer garments then stood in front of the blazing fireplace. Awnya extended her hands toward the flames. Shadows of yellow and red danced across her beautiful face—a face he would not mind seeing every day.

Awnya tilted her head, and her lips slowly curved. This time, she had caught *him* staring at her. But instead of looking away, he allowed his gaze to roam over her face, over the most beautiful eyes he had ever seen, and down to her rosebud lips.

"I make hot cocoa. Here." His mother's voice behind him pulled his attention from Awnya. She handed them each a cup.

"Thank you," they responded at the same time.

"Welcome." Louissa chuckled. "Sit, und get warm."

He moved the rockers closer to the fire. "Mama, vill you not join us?"

"Nein. I make butter."

"Oh. Let me help you with that." Awnya shifted to rise, but his mother laid her hand on Awnya's shoulder.

"Nein. You sit. It will give me something to do, und I use that time to *beten*."

"To what?"

"Pray," Amadeus answered for her.

"Oh, I see."

Mama headed to the kitchen.

Awnya faced the fire and took a sip of her drink. "Ummm. Your mother makes great hot chocolate."

"Ja. She does."

In comfortable silence, they drank their cocoa.

Awnya raised her legs and pointed her toes toward the flames. Her woolen stockings looked like a moth had eaten them.

"Awnya, why did you not say something?"

She whirled her face toward him. "Say something about what?"

"Your stockings."

"My stockings?" She looked at her feet. Her eyes widened, and she quickly planted them back on the floor and tucked them under her skirt hem. Red flooded her cheeks. He felt bad, embarrassing her by mentioning something so delicate, but the situation needed attention.

"Had I known your socks were like that, inside I would have insisted you stay. I am sorry."

"Sorry for what? There's no way you could have known I ran out of thread. Besides, I'm used to it." She stopped suddenly. Her gaze shot to his then back to the flames. "Can we not talk about this, please?"

He would not discuss it further, but he would definitely do something about it. In his wife's trunk were many pairs of stockings. Later, he would have his mother give them to her.

"Papa, we're bored. Can we make ornaments?" Isabella asked from beside him.

"Ja. Good idea, liebchen." He faced Awnya. "You wish to join us?"

"Papa! I don't want her to join us." Isabella planted her hands on her hips and pursed her lips.

Once again he made his daughter apologize. He needed to talk to her about her attitude, and soon, but not now. They had ornaments to make.

"Oma, you want to help make ornaments?" Isabella skipped over to his mama's side.

"Nein, meine *schatz*." She patted Isabella's cheek with her wrinkled, age-spotted hand. "I am tired und need a nap. But you go ahead, ja?"

Isabella's smile dropped, as did her hands to her side. "Okay." She looked at the floor.

His heart ached for his daughter. Mama tried to do what Georgina used to, but lately she seemed to tire faster. Isabella needed a young mother. He glanced at Awnya and once again told God the only present he wanted was her.

Awnya hadn't made a single ornament since her mother's death. No need to. There had been no Christmas tree to put it on. Pa wouldn't hear of it, nor would he let her decorate their home. He apologized often, saying it hurt too much because her ma loved Christmas and had always made a big to-do about it. Awnya missed celebrating Christmas. So right or wrong, she would not allow one disgruntled little girl to stop her.

"Awnya. You have ideas for ornament making?" Amadeus asked.

"Oh yes. Lots of them."

"Good, good."

Awnya turned to Isabella and the boys. "I could make both gingerbread and salt dough that you could shape into something Christmassy. Then I'll bake them."

"I don't want to do that," Isabella snipped.

"I do," both boys said. Shy Ethan jumping in made Awnya's heart happy.

"All right. If you will help me get the ingredients, then I'll make the dough." She looked over at Amadeus for his approval. He gave a quick nod. She smiled, feeling like a kid again.

After the ingredients were gathered and hands were washed, Awnya made the dough and rolled it out. Isabella sat at the table with her arms crossed, eyes narrowed, and her lips pinched.

"You sure you don't want to join us, Isabella? We could use your help."

Her eyes brightened, and then she rolled them. "I suppose." She sighed heavily, uncrossed her arms, and leaned forward.

They all sat at the knotty-pine table, and Awnya placed a slab of rolled-out dough before them.

"What shapes do you recommend?" she asked Isabella.

Isabella closed her eyes and sighed, but Awnya could tell she was pleased.

"How about snowmen?" Jakob blurted.

Isabella's eyes darted open. "Jakob! She was asking me."

"So? I'd like to make some snowmen."

"That's boring." Isabella snorted.

"Not to me."

"Das is genug!" Whatever Amadeus said, the children stopped immediately. "Jakob, you und Ethan can make whatever you like, but Awnya asked your sister a question."

The boys groaned, and Isabella smirked at them.

"Is—a—bell—a." Amadeus's voice held a warning.

She briefly dropped her gaze then faced her father. "I think we should make a nativity scene. With animals, baby Jesus, the three wise men, and gifts."

Awnya hid her shock. "That's a lovely idea."

Isabella never took her eyes off her father, but her face brightened.

"I get to make the animals," Jakob blurted.

"I want to make them," Ethan whined.

"How about we each make one?" Isabella once again stunned Awnya, only this time with her ability to handle the situation.

"Then who'll make the rest of nativity stuff?" Jakob hiked his hands.

"We all will, okay?" Isabella took charge, and Awnya sat back and let her. They nodded. Amadeus stoked the stove and sat back down.

Once the misshaped nativity, stars, snowmen, hearts, and the other ornaments made from both gingerbread and salt dough were finished, Awnya baked them. When they had cooled, the little mismatched family ran string through the holes.

"Now what are we going to do with them? We don't have a tree," Isabella said.

"We vill. But until then, we can. . ." Amadeus rubbed his chin.

Awnya scanned the room. "I have an idea."

Isabella hiked a brow and dipped her chin, her eyes straining upward at Awnya.

Awnya pretended not to notice. "Why don't we set the nativity up in that box?" She pointed to an empty cubby hanging on the wall. "We can string the rest together and hang them above the fireplace mantel. Then maybe another day we can make ornaments from clothespins and empty thread spools and string them in the windows."

"You won't be here in a few days."

This time she couldn't ignore the girl. Isabella was right. In a few days she wouldn't be here. And that saddened her.

Amadeus spoke from behind her. "With any luck, meine *weihnachtsgeschenk*, you vill be." His breath warmed her ear, and chills skittered down her back.

What did—how did he say it? 'vie knoxs goo shink?'—mean anyway?

Supper consisted of homemade buttered noodles mixed with fried potatoes and some oblong ground meat thing mixed with rice and onion. Earlier that day, Awnya had helped Louissa roll the ground meat mixture in softened cabbage leaves and was shocked when the woman had poured homemade canned sauerkraut on top. They were really quite delicious, and she barely tasted the sauerkraut. Buttermilk grebble sprinkled with sugar topped off the meal.

Afterward Amadeus placed several large pine and aspen logs into the cavern of the river-rock fireplace, making the room toasty and inviting. The children sat on the floor Indian style, and the three adults sat in the rocking chairs.

Amadeus opened a Bible and read a scripture in German. "*Also hat Gott. . .*" He continued reading in German, but the words were lost on her. He looked up from his Bible and asked, "Does anyone know what scripture I just read?"

Awnya had no clue. She didn't speak a lick of German.

His mother nodded, and the children raised their hands.

"All together, *kinder*. Name the reference."

"John 3:16," they all three said in unison.

"Very good. Now together, quote it."

"'For God so loved the world, that he gave his only begotten Son, that whosoever believeth in him should not perish, but have everlasting life.'" They spoke slowly and clearly, and Awnya was amazed they knew it so well in English.

"Now, each of you tell me what it means to you."

"It means Jesus gave His life for me so that I could live in heaven with Mama," Isabella said softly.

Though one side of her face was shadowed in the dim room, the side Awnya could see showed a little girl who missed and needed her mother. Awnya's heart reached out to her. She knew what it was like to lose a mother at a young age.

"Very good, Isabella. Und you, Jakob?"

"God gave away His only boy so I could go to heaven to be with *Opa* and Mama and God." Jakob's gaze rose to Amadeus. "You wouldn't give me up like that, would you, Papa?"

Amadeus ruffled Jakob's head. "Nein, mein liebchen. I would not."

The little boy's chest heaved, and he looked upward. "Thank you, Jesus."

They all laughed.

"Your turn, Ethan."

"I wouldn't have wanted to be Jesus. They hurt Him really, really bad." Ethan kept his voice and his head down.

"They sure did. But He allowed them to because He loves us. Just think, we would not celebrate Christmas if He had not."

"What?" Jakob's eyes darted open. "No Christmas? No Christmas tree? No gingerbread ornaments? No gifts?" He slung his small hand onto the side of his face and shook his head. "*Ach du lieber*. That would be terrible!"

Ethan, Isabella, Louissa, and Awnya giggled, but Amadeus only smiled briefly, and then his lips slid into a grim line.

"Jakob." Amadeus leaned forward and looked at his son and then at his other two children. "*Weihnachten. . .*" He glanced at Awnya. "Um, I mean Christmas"—he looked back at his children—"is not about ornaments or trees or presents. It is a time to celebrate our Savior's birth. Ja, we do those things in celebration, but the only gift that matters is Jesus. He is the best *Geschenk* ever."

Awnya's breath hitched. There were those words again. Only now she knew what they meant—Christmas gift. Amadeus had called her his Christmas gift. She'd never been anyone's gift before. Her heart warmed with the thought and what it implied. *Thy will be done, Lord.*

Chapter 4

At twilight Awnya stood at the wood-framed window near the kitchen, watching snowflakes accumulate on the porch rail and listening to the fierce winds rattle the glass. Shivers rippled through her body. She wrapped her arms around her, trying to block out the cold and the feeling of being trapped at the Josefs' another day.

Who was she kidding? She didn't feel trapped at all. In fact, she rather enjoyed the idea of having to stay another day and dreaded the idea of going home to an empty house. The last three days here with Amadeus and his family had helped lessen the pain of missing her pa. The only disadvantage to this whole thing was Isabella, who obviously didn't want her there. She pulled herself away from the window.

While Louissa and Isabella made supper, Awnya churned the last of the cream into butter. Earlier she had helped Louissa make cheese. She found the whole process interesting. They had first scalded the milk and strained it, added soda and butter to the curds, and then let it sit for two hours before cooking it again in a pan over water. Next they had added salt and soured cream and cooked it a third time until the curds dissolved. After making sure they got most of the whey out, they molded the resulting blocks.

Awnya had learned when Amadeus couldn't deliver the milk for days that Louissa made cheese and stored it in large crocks in the cooling shed. Before she could serve it, she had to remove the mold that had formed around the outside of the cheese balls.

"Supper is near done," Louissa announced.

Awnya cleaned her churning mess and helped ready the table.

After they all sat down, Amadeus prayed.

Awnya enjoyed the homemade German sausage known as *wurst*. Even the *glace*, which resembled tiny heavy dumplings with onions fried in lots of butter and a generous amount of cream, was surprisingly delicious. The only thing she did not enjoy was the sauerkraut on top of the meat. Eating it wasn't something she could do without losing her supper. She didn't mind when it was on top of the things Isabella had called pigs in a blanket. But alone? Eww. Ma's words about eating what was set before her skittered through her mind. Oh dear. What to do? What to do? She removed her elk-tooth necklace tucked inside her dress and fidgeted with it, trying to discern an answer.

"What's that?" Jakob asked.

"It's an ivory elk tooth."

"An elk tooth?" Ethan joined in but quickly dropped his gaze when Awnya looked at him. Would the boy ever lose his shyness around her?

"Eww." Isabella scrunched her face and tsked. "That's *widerlich* und a sin und a *schande*."

"Vee der what?"

"Isabella!" Amadeus barked. His anger toward his daughter made Awnya wonder what she'd said. As if he read her mind, he translated for her. "*Widerlich* means disgusting. Und *schande* means shame. A sin und a schande is something meine grossmutter said all the time of things she did not like."

"A sin and a shame? Disgusting? You think my necklace is disgusting?" That hurt. "This was my mother's, Isabella. Other than her Bible, it's the only thing I have left of her. It is *not* disgusting, and it is *not* a sin and a shame either." Awnya had never spoken so harshly to Isabella before, but how dare the little girl defame her mother's necklace.

"You're wearing an animal's tooth around your neck. That is disgusting." The girl slammed her hands on her hips.

"Isabella. Apologize this instant. Then go to your room, und do not come out until I say so."

"But what about dessert?" She pouted. "Oma made cherry *kuga*. My favorite."

Amadeus said nothing. But the look he gave his daughter was enough. She rose and moped her way to her room.

Awnya felt bad that Isabella seemed to be always getting in trouble on account of her, and she had no idea how to fix it.

"Do not trouble yourself over Isabella. It is not your fault."

She nodded even though she didn't feel any less troubled.

"Can we have some kuga now?" Jakob asked.

"Ja."

Louissa scooted her seat back.

"I'll get it, Louissa." Awnya jumped up and brought the sweet bread dessert with the cherry filling and the tiny specks of crumbled rivel baked on top. "Would anyone like anything more to drink?"

She filled the adults' coffee cups and the children's milk glasses. Awnya savored every morsel of the delicious German dessert.

Hours later, after the dishes were finished and the mess all picked up, Isabella was allowed some kuga before going to bed for the evening. Everyone retired early except for Awnya and Amadeus. Sitting alone with him in front of the fireplace made her wish she never had to leave. But leave she must. It was clear her presence upset Isabella, and she had decided she would not come between a daughter and her father.

❄

Amadeus repaired his tack. Having Awnya near warmed his heart. Only feet from him, she sat rocking her chair, sipping her coffee and staring at the buckshot rifle hanging above the fireplace. "You look miles away, Awnya. What is your mind on?"

"Pa."

He laid his tack on the floor and faced her. "What about your pa?"

She looked at him. Flames danced in her green eyes, along with. . .suspicion?

"I was thinking about how much I miss him and about how he died. I can't help but think his death wasn't an accident. Too many strange things had happened up until the time of his death."

"Like what?"

"Well, all our meat disappeared for one. Pa said wild animals got it, but I never saw any animal tracks near the meat shed, and there was no truth in Pa's looks. I knew he was hiding something. Something he didn't want me worrying about."

"You said many strange things. What else?"

"Besides the feeling of being watched all the time, things kept disappearing. Grain. Tack. The spring box we built into the creek to keep our milk and food cool. A mess of animal pelts. Things like that. Plus, when I found Pa's body, I never found his horse or his rifle." Her gaze traveled to the rifle he'd recently purchased, the one hanging above the fireplace. "He had one just like the one you have hanging." This time there was no mistaking the suspicion in her eyes.

Realization dawned on him. She must think the rifle he had purchased from the traveling peddler was her pa's. Did she also think he had something to do with his death? That thought slammed mountainous pain deep into his heart. He wanted to reassure her he had nothing to do with it, but the only way to do that would be to find out the truth. And he would, starting with the peddler. With Christmas mere days away, the peddler would be back. And Amadeus would be ready for him.

❄

After dinner the next day, Awnya peered out the window and discovered the snow had stopped. "Finally."

"Finally what?" Louissa asked from her rocking chair, resting her mending onto her lap, and Amadeus looked at her from stoking the cookstove.

"It stopped snowing." She faced the window.

Within seconds, Amadeus was behind her, talking over her shoulder. "Too bad the drifts und snow are too deep to go to town. We—"

"Jakob. Stop it!" Isabella cut her father's word short.

"Give it back!"

They both whirled around at the same time.

Jakob tried to snatch a wooden object from Isabella, but she hit him over the head with it.

Jakob grabbed her hair.

"Ow. Stop it! You'll be sorry," Isabella spouted.

"Kinder, that is enough." The sternness in Amadeus's voice stopped them.

Cooped up inside for days, the children's bickering had increased. Awnya thought they needed a distraction. "Amadeus."

"Ja?"

"Could we do a Christmas treasure hunt for the children?"

All three sets of eyes brightened. "Yeah."

"I tell you what. If you nap, Awnya und I vill get it ready."

"Ahhh, do we have to?" Jakob and Isabella whined in unison.

"Ja. Und you have to stop fighting, or no hunt." He and Awnya eyed each silent child.

"Okay. Forget it then." Amadeus turned to walk away.

"No. No. We'll do it." Isabella glared at her brothers, who quickly nodded their assent.

"Okay. Off to bed then."

"I join you, ja?" Louissa set her mending in the basket and stood. All four headed into their grandma's room.

Amadeus gathered paper and an inkwell. He and Awnya sat at the table and got busy making the clues.

"How did your father come to live in Grand County?" Awnya asked.

He stopped working on the clues and turned his attention onto her. If she wasn't mistaken, sadness had shifted through his eyes for a brief moment before returning to normal. "Papa's brothers come to America from Austria. They spoke often about the beautiful mountains in Colorado, und how friendly the people in Grand County were, und how ranching und raising cattle had prospered them. They encouraged Papa to join them, und he did."

"Where are your uncles now?"

"Over the ridge north of my place." He laid the wooden cross she'd watched him construct on the table and looked at her. "You never say where you live."

"Our. . .I mean my cabin." She lowered her eyes and took a deep breath, fighting back the tears.

"Ah meine weihnachtsgeschenk." He stood and pulled her into his arms, cradling her against his chest. His heartbeat pulsed through her ears. "Is hard losing a loved one."

The grief was so heavy, and she had carried it alone for so very long. She lost her fight not to weep.

Amadeus held her close while she soaked his shirt with her tears. After she had her cry, she gazed up at him. "I miss him so much. I don't know what I'm going to do without him. Or how I'll survive out here alone."

He cupped her chin. "Ah, *liebling*, you're not alone. The Lord is with you, und am I."

She didn't know what he meant by "und am I," nor did she have a chance to ask because warm lips joined hers, covering her with the sweetest feeling she'd ever known. She slipped her arms around his waist, liking how they felt there.

Salty tears trickled between their lips, but Amadeus didn't seem to mind because he continued to kiss her.

The need for comfort drove her further into his embrace until she couldn't tell where his heartbeat ended and hers began. She imitated the movement of his lips, caressing them like he did hers. She drew comfort and strength from his nearness and his kiss. Coming to her senses, she pulled back.

Amadeus blinked. His insides trembled. Except for his wife, no other woman had affected him like this. He loved and missed his wife, but it was time to move on. Time to love again. And Awnya could very well be that love.

She stepped out of his embrace. "We'd better get these clues finished before the children wake up." Her voice sounded deeper than normal.

"Ja. You are right."

They sat down and got to work on the treasure hunt.

"I'm not sure where my home is," she said as if it wasn't even her talking.

Amadeus frowned. What did she mean she knew not where her home was?

"You asked me earlier where my cabin is. Truth is, I'm not sure. I was so hungry I didn't pay attention to where or how far I'd traveled."

"Ah." He rubbed his chin. "I know these parts good. Describe your place, und I vill see if I can figure out where it is."

"There's a small waterfall on the place with a rustic bridge where you can stand and watch the water running over the rocks, and trees growing down through the middle of it. The house is small but long. The whole front of it has a covered porch with white poles supporting it. The windows are painted white, and so is the front door. Unlike your cabin, the house was built using hog trough joints."

"How did you know that?" Amadeus interrupted her.

"Pa told me what they were." She smiled sheepishly.

"Ah. I see. Und what else?" he asked even though he knew exactly what house it was now—the very one he had purchased for his cousins, who were to arrive in America come springtime. But just in case there was the slightest chance he was wrong, he would keep that information to himself and not upset Awnya needlessly. Once he got all the facts straight, only then would he tell her.

"Much better." His mother shuffled her way to her rocking chair near the fireplace.

"Papa. Can we come out now?" Isabella's voice floated to him.

"Nein. Not yet, liebchen. We have to hide the clues. I tell you when we are ready."

"Okay."

They hurried to place the clues around the cabin.

"Okay. You can come now."

All three barreled into the kitchen, bringing a smile to Amadeus's face. Seeing their joy brought him joy. Excitement filled the atmosphere as their eyes traveled around the room.

"Look at me. I vill tell you where to start. You must work together." He handed Isabella the first clue because she was the only one who could read well.

"Green is my color; I represent life. You'll find me close to where Oma keeps her bread knife." All three heads turned toward the knife hanging near the breadboard counter. "Look for something green." Isabella took charge. They ran over and searched the area.

"There it is!" Ethan hollered. Halfway down on the left side of the breadboard counter was the stiff Christmas tree Awnya had made by dipping the green yarn in flour paste. Attached to it was the next clue. Their faces beamed, bringing another smile to his face.

Isabella removed the clue and read, "Silent night, holy night, all is calm, all is bright. You need me to give off light."

"The windows." Jakob rushed to the windows closest to the front door and checked them while the other two scurried to check the others.

"I don't see anything here," Jakob said, walking over to Ethan. "Did you?"

"No."

"You, Izzy?"

"No." She sighed. "Wait. I got it. Lanterns are bright, and we need them."

They inspected the two sitting on the table and the one near the fireplace. Finding no clue, they frowned.

"Let's see." Isabella tipped her head. "What else gives off light?" Her brows darted upward. "Candles."

Ethan ran to Amadeus's bedroom. "I found it." He rushed out to Isabella and Jakob.

"I'm up in the sky only at night, but can sometimes be seen in the daylight."

"Huh?" Isabella looked at Amadeus.

"Just think, liebchen." He scanned the ceiling, letting his eyes linger on the star above him.

The children followed his movement. "There it is!" Isabella pointed to the star hanging in the center of the loft. The boys climbed the ladder and removed it then scurried down and gave it to their sister.

"My insides appear silver, and I was first made in Germany in the shape of a fruit or a nut. Only you cannot eat me, or your mouth will I cut."

They wrinkled their noses then put their heads together, discussing what it could be. They came out of their huddle. "Papa, we don't have any idea what this is."

"Okay. Go to the steamer trunk und look inside. Find a small wooden box hidden at the bottom, but do not shake or drop it."

They rushed to the trunk and knelt down. When they found the wooden box, they opened it and removed three pieces of cloth.

"Oh, Papa. These are beautiful." Isabella glanced at him then back at the ornaments.

"What are they?" Awnya asked.

"Bring them here, liebchen."

"Oh, those are beautiful. I've never seen anything like them before." Awnya ran her fingers over the blown-glass ornaments shaped like nuts and fruits.

"They come from Germany. My grossmutter sent them to my children for Christmas." He held one up for each of them to inspect. "See how the inside looks silver."

Each one took a turn admiring them before putting them back into the trunk. The children continued their treasure hunt until only one clue remained.

"You can't have one without the other to be the greatest gift of all. We are the true meaning of Christmas." Isabella frowned. "This one doesn't rhyme, Papa."

"I know, daughter." He gathered all three children to himself. "Meine kinder, when you remember what the greatest gift of all is und the true meaning of Christmas, you vill find your last clue und the real treasure."

Without hesitating, they went to the manger scene. Lying in the cradle with baby Jesus was a heart and the wooden cross Amadeus had made. No note accompanied it.

His children reverently removed baby Jesus, then the cross, and then the heart and brought them to him.

Awnya sniffed beside him.

He blinked to keep his own tears. Pride and love swelled his chest. His children understood the true meaning of Christmas—that Christ's birth, death, and resurrection was the greatest love gift ever given.

Moments of reverential silence passed before Amadeus retrieved his children's treasure gifts. "This is why we give gifts at Christmas, to remember the greatest gift of all. Jesus." He handed the boys each a small bag of the alabaster marbles he had played with as a boy and Isabella his wife's American Bible.

Isabella whirled and fled the room.

Amadeus followed her into her bedroom. "Liebchen, *was* ist *los?*"

His daughter, still so small but growing into her own wisdom, stood huddled over the gift. "It's mama's, right?"

"Ja, und I want you to have it."

She hugged the Bible to her chest. Tears spilled from her eyes. "Thank you, Papa. I'll treasure it always."

"I know you vill, liebchen." He gathered his daughter into his arms, and tears slid down his cheeks as she wept.

❄

The next evening, still touched by the children's understanding of Christmas, Awnya wanted to do something special for them. The joy on their faces when they'd found the clues had brought both joy and sadness to her—joy at being a part of their lives during those brief moments, and sadness from knowing when the weather cleared, she would have to go home to an empty house. If only. . .

No. She would not allow her mind to drift that direction. She wasn't their mother and never would be.

"You ready?"

"Yes."

Before Amadeus had a chance, Awnya opened the door and stepped outside. Cold stung her cheeks and bit into her spine. She shook a chill.

"Sure you want to do this, leibling?" Amadeus asked from behind her.

"Yes. I'm sure." She glanced at the different shades of yellow and pink surrounding the sun, which was minutes away from disappearing behind the mountain.

"Beautiful," she whispered.

"She sure is."

She? Awnya looked up at him. He wasn't looking at the sunset, but at her.

Nothing more was said. They made their way to Amadeus's workshop.

Amadeus unlocked the door and stepped inside. He lit two lanterns and hung them on their hooks, then moved aside for her to enter.

Inside the cramped room, waist-high benches lined two walls. Each had a pinewood stool in front of it. Tools of various kinds hung on pegs above each bench. In one corner of the bench, a cloth covered something. On the floor between the two benches sat a large wooden box.

Amadeus raised the lid, pulled out a bag, and dumped the contents onto the bench.

"Oh, how lovely." She picked up one of the wooden carved farm animals and turned it over, admiring the detail on the horse. "You made these?"

"Ja."

She counted. "Two horses, four cows, six sheep, two dogs, and two cats."

"I have the barn und the fences yet to make for the boys."

"And Isabella?" She let the question hang between them.

He reached over and raised the cloth.

Awnya gasped, and he smiled. "What a beautiful cradle." She tilted her head and frowned. "I don't remember seeing any dolls. Does she have one?"

"Ja." His smile dropped. "My wife made it, but Isabella carried it all the time, und now it barely holds together. She put it in her trunk und vill not play with it, afraid it vill fall apart completely."

"Can it be mended?"

"Perhaps. But mama's hands do not work like they once did. She struggles to get done the mending."

"She should have said something. I could do the mending for her."

"Nein. It keeps her mind busy. She enjoys it."

Awnya played with her lip as a plan formulated in her mind. "Do you think Isabella would mind if I repaired her doll?"

His face brightened. "You think you could?"

"I would love to look at it and see."

"Tomorrow, I sneak it here, ja?"

"Ja," Awnya said without thinking.

They laughed.

Amadeus stepped closer and clutched her shoulders gently. His eyes seized hers. "That is very kind of you, leibling. *Vielen dank.*"

"Feeling donk?" She tilted her head.

"Ja. It means, thank you very much."

"Oh." The softness in his eyes drew her into their depths, holding her captive. "You're welcome," she whispered.

His head lowered, and Awnya's stomach fluttered with the wings of a thousand hummingbirds.

Cool lips captured hers, warming her insides, making it difficult to stand. His arms, strong and comforting, pressed about her, supporting her as his lips tenderly caressed her mouth. She sighed contentedly. She could get used to this.

Chapter 5

Three days before Christmas and still unable to travel down the mountain to deliver his dairy products, Amadeus noticed his mother's puckered forehead. Her hands played with the rocking chair arm, worry scrawled on her face. The children's constant bickering over who got what marble was obviously getting on her nerves. She would never complain or say anything because she loved them dearly, so he needed to do something to ease her discomfort.

"Meine kinder, how would you like to get our Christmas tree today instead of waiting until Christmas Eve?"

The lines on Mama's forehead softened. The children jumped up.

"Wait! Your toys pick up first, und then we vill go."

Toys disappeared off the floor in record time. Hats, coats, gloves were ripped from lower hooks near the front door. He turned his attention away from them and onto Awnya. Her face held the same anticipation as his children. "Would you like to come, Awnya?"

"No," Isabella said, stopping with only one arm in her coat. "I don't want her to come, Papa."

He opened his mouth to rebuke his daughter, but Awnya's voice stopped him. "I would love to, but I don't want to interfere, so I'll stay here and keep Louissa company."

"Nonsense. We want you to come. Right, kinder?" Amadeus sent his daughter a warning glance.

Isabella put on a pout but said no more.

"Yeah. We want you to come with us." Jakob and Ethan beamed their replies.

Jakob ran over to Awnya. "Please. Come with us." He tugged her hand until she stood.

"If you're sure. . ." Though her face showed obvious reluctance, she allowed Jakob to pull her along. She slipped into her outside garments.

Amadeus silently thanked God that Awnya could not see the look of disdain his daughter shot her way. He considered saying something about it but felt it best not to. He still did not know why Isabella disliked the woman so. Every time he had asked, pain filled his daughter's eyes, and she told him she did not know why. Because his feelings for Awnya were growing stronger every day, he could only hope that in time Isabella would come to love her.

❄

Awnya followed the children outside. Large fluffy snowflakes floated gently from the heavens. She opened her mouth to catch them on her tongue. They still tasted like candy to her.

"What you doing?" Ethan asked.

"Catching snowflakes."

"Why?"

Awnya glanced down at him. "Haven't you ever caught snowflakes on your tongue before?"

"Um, uh-uh." He shook his head.

"Try it."

Ethan tipped his head back and opened his mouth. He yanked his head one way, then another, then leaped into the air. Within seconds, Jakob, Isabella, and even Amadeus joined him.

Awnya laughed at the scene before her. Not at the children, but at the gentle giant with his tongue stuck out, lapping up snowflakes.

The children ran ahead of them, giggling and chasing snowflakes with their mouths wide open, disappearing out of their sight. Laughter poured from somewhere deep in Awnya. She hadn't done much laughing since her pa's death. It felt good, so she let it roll out of her even more.

"You think that is funny, ja?"

"Ja," she said through a titter.

Amadeus chuckled, and quick as a bolt of lightning he knotted a snowball and tossed it at her. It splattered on her bearskin coat just above her knee.

Under his hat she could see his eyebrows dancing up and down in challenge to her.

"Why you. . ." Awnya grabbed a snowball and hit him in the arm. Again and again they hit each other with snowballs.

Awnya bent down to make another just as Amadeus's large hand encircled her waist and swung her body toward a deep snowbank. "Oh-h-h no you don't." She yanked his arm, pulling him into the drift with her. She grabbed a handful of snow and smeared his face with it, giggling.

He scooped a handful of white powder and aimed it toward her face. "No, no." She wiggled and giggled until her cheeks hurt from smiling, and her heart pumped from the exertion.

"What vill you give me if I don't?" His smile dimpled, one of his eyebrows rose, and his gaze slid to her lips then jumped to her eyes. "A kiss, ja?"

She peered around, making sure the children were still out of sight.

"Ja? A kiss?" she mimicked him. She raised her lips to his, and right before their lips touched, she swerved and kissed his cheek, leaped up, and ran into the woods, where his children were having their own snowball fight.

He caught up with her. His warm breath sent shivers skittering up and down her spine. "I vill collect later, meine weihnachtsgeschenk."

She sure hoped so.

❊

Amadeus fought the urge to steal a real kiss from Awnya. With his children nearby, that would not be good. But later perhaps. No. Definitely later. He grinned inwardly.

Together they traipsed through the snow, looking over several trees until the children found the one they wanted.

"Can you hurry, Papa? We're cold." Isabella cupped her hands and blew into them.

"I am almost done, liebchen." Within minutes he had the tree felled. Amadeus dragged the tree behind him as they weaved their way back through aspens and pines.

Inside the cabin, Amadeus set the tree while Awnya helped his mother fix hot toddies. He smiled when his mother explained that for medicinal purposes only—like a fever—she would add a hint of whiskey to the hot water, lemon juice, and honey tea mixture.

They sat in front of the fireplace and warmed their bodies, sipping their drinks. When they finished, Amadeus leaned forward in his rocker. "You ready to decorate the tree?" He eyed everyone, leaving no one out.

The boys jumped up and nodded until he thought their necks would break, but Isabella remained seated, staring into the fire.

"You coming?" he asked Isabella.

"No." She crossed her arms and shot daggers Awnya's way. She slung herself around, placing her back to them.

"As you wish, daughter."

Awnya's questioning eyes darted between him and Isabella. He laid his hands on her shoulders, turned her toward the kitchen, and gave her a light push.

She joined his mama at the table, but his boys clung to each side of him.

He opened the small box of ornaments he had retrieved earlier. "Who wishes to go first?"

❊

Awnya was so glad he'd encouraged her to join them. She couldn't wait to be a part of the tree decorating. She didn't know what he meant by who wishes to go first, but she'd wait her turn.

Jakob and Ethan pulled out an ornament.

"Ethan, you go first," Jakob offered.

"Thanks." Ethan held up one of the clothespin ornaments she'd helped them make. It had a white dress and long hair made from yarn. "This reminds me of Awnya. I'm grateful God sent her here." He spoke softly.

Awnya's heart hitched. He looked shyly at her, and she smiled her approval. She took a peek Amadeus's way. His eyes twinkled like the night stars, and his lips curled upward, warming her heart and overflowing it with love for this family.

"Und you, Jakob?"

"What I have to be grateful for this Christmas is. . ." He held up a heart ornament. "That you always taught us, Papa, that God is love, and I love Awnya and want her to be my mama."

Heat rose into her cheeks. She slid her gaze toward Amadeus. He winked, and her heart responded with a wink of its own.

Amadeus pulled out two ornaments, a handmade angel and a small wrapped box. "This Christmas I, too, am thankful that God sent us an angel. She is meine weihnachtsgeschenk."

"Your Christmas gift!" Jakob said. "Can she be ours, too?"

"Can she, huh, Papa?" Ethan jumped in. The hopeful look in the boys' eyes shoved a longing through her heart.

"We vill see. Who is next? Awnya?"

She picked a snowman ornament, and while she hung it on a high branch, she said, "I'm grateful for the snowstorm that led me to all of you and for snowball fights."

"Snowball fights?"

"Yes." She and Amadeus shared a secret twinkling look.

"Your turn, Mama."

Louissa said what she was grateful for and hung her ornament.

Jakob picked up a daddy ornament. "I'm glad I have a daddy who loves me." After he hung the ornament, he threw his arms around Amadeus.

The scene made Awnya lonesome for her ma and pa. Seeing the ornaments finished, she excused herself and headed to the fireplace. Sometimes the sorrow was so very heavy in her heart.

Isabella stood, glared at her, and then darted to the table.

Awnya's gaze traveled over the mantel lined with evergreen branches and red bows up to the cutout North Star hanging below the rifle—the one that looked exactly like her pa's. She glanced behind her to make sure no one was watching.

A Grand County Christmas

Awnya stepped as close to the fire as possible and studied the gun. Her heart sank when her gaze landed on the initials *SPO*—Seamus Patrick O'Crean. *Dear God, no.*

"You look pale. What is wrong, Awnya?"

Awnya jumped at Amadeus's nearness. She looked into his concerned blue eyes. What to do? What to do? Her heart yanked her backward and forward—forward toward the man she'd come to love and backward as far away as possible from the man who could possibly have taken her pa's life.

Chapter 6

Under the clear blue sky Amadeus harnessed the horses to the sled wagon. He loaded the back with dairy products and a two-month supply of food for Awnya. He stopped and rested his hand on the wagon. Ever since last night, Awnya had seemed different. Distant. He'd asked what was wrong, but everything was fine, she'd insisted repeatedly as they had worked on the toys. But if that were true, then why was she so eager for him to take her home?

"I'm ready." The object of his thoughts appeared behind him.

The idea of her being alone tonight ate at his gut. "Are you sure you want to go home, Awnya? You can stay here with us." He opened his mouth to say she could marry him, but her words cut him off.

"I want to go home, Amadeus. I need time alone. To think. To pray."

"Nothing I could say would change your mind?"

"No."

"Even if I asked you to marry me?"

"Marry you?" Her eyes widened, but a shadow fell over her face. "No. I'm sorry, Amadeus. I can't marry you. Please understand I must do this."

He understood, but like it he did not. However, he would give her the time she needed. He nodded his agreement, even though his heart wanted to convince her to stay. How could he refuse her request? With a heavy sigh, he helped her into the wagon.

The silence on the way to the stage stop screamed a warning in his ears that something more than needing time to think and pray was at work here. But he had no idea what.

He dropped off his dairy supplies. Knowing what he had to do next broke his heart. He listened as she gave him directions to her place. All the way there, Amadeus struggled with leaving her alone. Defenseless. Unprotected. *God show me what to do. I cannot bear to leave her there. To let her go.*

He drove the team into the yard. Having been so upset about taking her home, it had slipped his mind that he was taking her to the same place he had purchased for his relatives. The second he saw it that thought returned, and his suspicions were confirmed.

If he told her now, it would solve his problem. She would have no choice but to marry him. But he did not wish her to marry him because she had no choice. No, he would not speak of it until he checked with the deeds office to find out just who did own this property, him or Awnya.

Until then, against his better judgment and wishes, he needed to hurry and get Awnya settled. Three hours of daylight would barely give him enough time to get unloaded and back home before dark.

He leaped out of the wagon and helped Awnya down. Drifted snow blocked her doorway. He grabbed a shovel, cleared a path to her front door, and reached for the handle.

"Please let me. Just give me a minute alone, okay?"

"Ja. I vill make a path to the firewood und bring you some."

"Thank you." Her green eyes locked onto his. Disturbing questions lingered in them. Questions he hoped she would voice. But she did not. Instead she put her back to him, slipped inside the cabin, and closed the door.

Awnya stepped inside and gasped. Her gaze darted wildly about the place. The only thing left in the one-room cabin was the tattered sheet that separated her bedroom from the rest of the cabin and a small field of dead mice lying about. Pa's traps, his handmade furniture, all her mother's dishes, everything, including the potbelly stove, was gone.

She shoved away and ran to her bedroom, ripping back the curtain. Empty. Just like the rest of the cabin. "No-o-o!" she screamed. "Not Mama's Bible." Her most cherished possession was gone. She slid to the floor, wrapped her arms around her knees, and wailed. The only tangible link to her ma now was the elk tooth necklace.

Awnya tugged on the chain around her neck and hugged the polished keepsake to her cheek, wetting it with her tears. Never before had she felt so alone or abandoned. Forsaken even. "God, why?" she screamed.

The door was flung open. "Awnya!" Amadeus's gaze flew around the empty room before he ran to her. Dropping on the ground, he pulled her onto his lap and wrapped his arms around her. She buried her head into his chest and sobbed as her heart broke inside her.

After her tears abated, Amadeus helped her up and wrapped his arm snugly around her. "Come. I vill take you home."

Overcome with grief and knowing there was no way she could even heat her barren home, she numbly allowed him to lead her to his wagon.

As they headed out, she turned in the wagon seat and took one last look at the place she had called home. Just as her cabin was now disappearing from her sight, her faith in a loving God slipped into the empty void. How could He allow this on top of everything else she had suffered? Wasn't losing her parents enough? Why had He abandoned her to the wolves of nothingness and want?

Pain unlike any she had ever known crowded into her heart. She faced forward and laid her hands in her lap. "I don't understand. I prayed and believed God to heal my mother, to protect my pa and my home, and He didn't. Why did He let me down? How can I ever trust Him again?"

Amadeus glanced at her, his face placid. "By faith alone, leibling."

"I don't understand."

The wagon slid forward as Amadeus sighed, his countenance growing heavy. "When my wife died, I struggled with my faith also."

That got her full attention. "You did?"

"Ja. Like you, I prayed to God und believed He would heal her. To this day I do not know why He did not. But what I do know is, during that time I learned that real faith is not about getting every prayer answered the way I think it should be. Real faith says I trust God even though I do not understand why He does what He does und even though things did not turn out the way I thought they should.

"I discovered that faith does not always see my desired results, but it continues to hope anyway. It continues to trust God even in the midst of the times when I don't see Him. Like it says in Hebrews chapter eleven verse one. Now, faith is the substance of things hoped for, the evidence of things not seen. Faith is the thing what gives you hope und keeps you going when things look impossible." He reached for her hand. "Without faith, what else do you have, leibling?"

The memory of the stark empty cabin drove through her, and she put her head down. "Nothing. But right now, I'm having a hard time seeing it. I've just been robbed of everything I ever held dear to me. I have nothing left of my family. Right now, I don't have even the smallest amount of hope."

"You vill, leibling. You vill. Trust me?"

Her heart snagged on that. Could she trust the man who had her pa's rifle hanging in his cabin?

❄

Christmas Eve Day. Where had the time gone? Since bringing Awnya back to live with them, even though she did not talk much and had lost some of her joy, having her around all the time warmed Amadeus's heart and filled the lonely hours he had endured since his wife's death. Today, he would ask her to marry him, not to fix things for her or for himself, but because he loved her with all of his heart. This time, he hoped she would accept.

In tandem, they loaded the wagon and headed down the mountain. The closer they got to town, the less snow they had to traverse. It amazed Amadeus what a difference a few miles made. Up at his place there was several feet of snow, and down here there was maybe three to four inches.

He pulled his wagon into town. Before he dropped off his dairy supplies, he decided to make a quick stop to check on the deed to his cousin's place. He pulled in front of small building that resembled a house more than a business. "Wait here. This vill only take a minute."

Awnya nodded.

Within seconds he had his answer. Amadeus climbed back onto the wagon next to Awnya. He needed to figure out a way to break the devastating news to her gently. Until then, he had supplies that needed delivering.

While he dropped off his dairy products, his gaze chanced across the snow-packed street, and he did a double take. The peddler from whom he had bought the buckshot rifle was standing only yards away, selling his goods to the locals.

"Amadeus, do you mind if we stop a minute? I want to say hello to Mr. Cane, that nice man Pa bought the cabin from." She pointed toward the same man who had sold him the rifle.

His gut jerked. "You sure that is him?"

"Yes. I'm positive. Please can we stop? I won't be but a minute. I promise."

With a quick pull on the reins, Amadeus turned the horses around the corner and reined them to a stop. There was no way to break the news gently and no more time to put off telling her. "Awnya, we need to talk."

"What's wrong? You sound angry."

"Forgive me, but I must be blunt. The rifle above my fireplace. Those initials on it are your pa's, ja?"

Fear and uncertainty flashed through her eyes. "Ja. I mean, yes."

He pulled her hands into his, needing the connection to her when he told her what he must. "I bought that rifle from the traveling peddler."

"Mr. Cane?"

"Ja."

"I don't understand. How did he get Pa's rifle?"

"That is what I am about to find out. But first, there is something else you need to know. You say your pa bought your cabin from him. When?"

"Four months ago. I watched him pay for it. Why?" She frowned.

"Because from the owners, I buy that same place. Mr. Cane never owned it. The Martins did."

"No. That can't be. Pa had the deed. I saw it. He kept it in Ma's Bible." Her shoulders slumped. "It's gone now, too."

"I am sorry, leibling, but the deed he gave him was a fake."

"How do you know this?"

"That's what I was doing when I asked you to wait."

"You knew?"

"I had my suspicions."

"Why didn't you tell me?" A shield of hurt fell across her eyes.

"Because I'd hoped I was wrong. Plus, I wanted to make sure that the deed I have wasn't a counterfeit, too. But the place, the Martins did own, und the deed I have is genuine." Amadeus found no pleasure in knowing he wasn't the one who had been tricked. For Awnya's sake, he wished it had been him. Then using his own money, he would have purchased another place for his cousins. There was only one thing to do now. "Come, liebling, we need to talk to the sheriff."

❅

Awnya couldn't believe her ears. Her body went numb. What else could go wrong? At least before, she thought she could sell the cabin and make enough money to live on until she decided what to do next and where to go. Desperation squeezed her heart, restricting its blood flow, making her feel dizzy.

What had Amadeus said about faith when things looked impossible or we don't understand why? Well, impossible was staring her down right now, and she couldn't think of how things could get any worse than they already were.

Amadeus helped her down from the wagon. Careful to stay out of the peddler's sight, they made their way to the jail.

Too upset and nervous to sit while Amadeus told the sheriff everything, Awnya paced the room, looking it over but never seeing anything until her eyes fell on a wanted poster.

"I've never seen any peddler around here befor—"

"That's him!" Awnya blurted, cutting off the sheriff's words. She pointed to the poster.

Amadeus and the sheriff both yanked their attention that direction.

WANTED DEAD OR ALIVE
Notorious Outlaw Willy Pratt
Wanted for Forgery of Legal Documents, Robbery, and Murder
Reward $500

"You know where this man is?"

"Ja. Here." Amadeus answered for her.

"Where?"

Amadeus led the sheriff to the window. He scanned the street and pointed him out.

"You stay here," the sheriff ordered Amadeus and Awnya. He loaded his rifle and headed out the door.

Minutes ticked away like hours. She fidgeted with her hands.

"It vill be okay, liebling. Have faith."

She nodded, but it wasn't easy.

The door opened, and in stepped the sheriff with a handcuffed Mr. Cane. Rather, Willy Pratt. In amazement, Awnya listened as the sheriff pulled information out of the old sidewinder—how he had sold land to her pa, land he didn't own.

"Yeah, I killed the old man." The devilish gleam in Cane's eyes sent shudders of revulsion through Awnya.

She put her hand over her mouth as her stomach threatened to empty its contents. Amadeus tucked her under his shoulder and away from the evil staring her down.

"Got a pretty penny for them pelts he had on him, too. And his rifle and his horse. Yep. . ." He continued to boast about how he had emptied their meat shed and cabin and how he had sold most of its contents in another town.

"What about my mother's Bible? Did you sell it, too?" She hated asking, but she had to know if there was the slightest chance that he still might have it.

"Nope. Used it for kindling. That's all it's good for anyway."

Burned? The thought of her mother's Bible being used for kindling splintered her heart into millions of tiny pieces. Unable to look at the man any longer, she turned her face into Amadeus's chest.

"She has heard enough. I vill take her home now."

"Wait." The sheriff made sure the outlaw didn't have any weapons on him before he opened the cell door and shoved his prisoner inside. Then the sheriff knelt in front of a safe. He stood and handed a stack of bills to Amadeus and one to Awnya.

"What's this?" She tilted her head.

"The reward for Willy's capture."

"I—" No more words came. All of this was too much to take at once. She needed air.

Seeing her pale face, Amadeus tucked the money in his pocket and led her to the door. Outside in the crisp winter air, away from the jail, he motioned for her to sit on a bench.

His heart wrenched with uncertainty and fear that the woman he loved might very well slip away from him forever now that she had the money to do so. He couldn't let that happen. He faced her. "Awnya, I must speak what is in my heart."

She nodded.

"Now that you have the reward money, I fear you vill leave Grand County und me. That thought I cannot bear." He pulled her hands into his. "I love you, Awnya, und have for some time. Please, do not go. Stay und marry me, ja?"

Awnya stammered, "You. . .you love me?"

"Ja. I love you more than words can express."

She threw her arms around him. "Oh, Amadeus. I love you, too." She pulled back. "But what about Isabella? She hates me."

"Nein. She does not hate you. She just misses her mutter. It vill take time, but I truly believe she vill come around."

"Do you really think so?"

"Ja. Or I wouldn't have said so." He held his breath for what seemed like forever, waiting for her answer.

Slowly she nodded. "Okay. I'll marry you."

"You vill?"

"Ja." She giggled.

"Now, meine liebling?" he whispered in her ears.

"Yes, now." She pulled back. "But first, what does liebling mean?"

"It means *darling*."

"Oh-h-h ja, I like it."

Their chuckle ended when he found her lips. He wanted to take his time enjoying her, but he wanted to get married before she changed her mind. He pulled back and helped her to her feet.

They found the parson at his house and asked if he had time to marry them. "I sure do." He pumped Amadeus's hand. "I'm so happy for you, Amadeus. And you, too, Awnya. It's about time you two found someone special. I'm glad it was each other." He rubbed his hands together. "Now, let me go get the missus as a witness."

Within seconds, he came back into the room with his wife. Amadeus and Awnya repeated their vows after him. "I now pronounce you husband and wife. You may kiss your bride."

"With pleasure." Amadeus cupped her face, and his lips found hers. He deepened his kiss, willing his lips to show Awnya just how much his heart overflowed with love for her. Awnya returned his kiss with equal passion and love.

"Uh, umm."

Amadeus reluctantly raised his head at the sound of someone clearing their throat.

"Congratulations," both the parson and his wife said.

"Vielen dank."

"Thank you."

He and Awnya responded at the same time then laughed.

Everyone hugged and said their good-byes, and then Amadeus and Awnya headed for home.

"I cannot wait to tell my family we are married. After dinner we go for a sleigh ride und tell them then, ja?"

She hooked her arms through his and leaned into him. "That sounds so romantic."

"Ja." He leaned down and kissed his wife. *Wife.* That word sent his heart dancing.

❄

The wide eyes on everyone's faces when Awnya stepped into the house tickled her. The boys ran up to her and hugged her.

"We're so glad you came back," Jakob said with tears in his eyes.

"Ja," Louissa added and smiled.

"I didn't want you to go," Ethan whispered.

"Thank you. I'm glad to be back."

Isabella glared at her.

Awnya quickly looked away, hoping that everything would work out as Amadeus thought it would.

After dinner Awnya watched her husband—*husband*. . .she loved that one word—hitch the horses to the sled.

The children climbed in the back and sat on a bed of straw. Amadeus draped blankets over their legs.

His hands spread across her waist as he hoisted her up into the wagon and tucked a blanket around her legs. Louissa didn't come—she didn't want to get out in the night air—so they had taken her aside and told her. Awnya smiled thinking how happy Louissa was for them. When Louissa asked Awnya to call her mama, Awnya held back her tears—tears of joy that she had a new mother, and tears of sadness that her ma wasn't here to see her happily married.

Under the full moon, they headed out for a sleigh ride. Bells jingled along with the jostling tack. Snow crunched under the sled runners, and snow powder dusted Awnya's face as she sang Christmas carols with Amadeus's family. Her family now. She sighed and closed her eyes.

"Silent Night" drifted through the darkness in German from the children and Amadeus. "*Stille nacht, heilige nacht. . .*"

Awnya listened to Amadeus's deep voice and strong German accent. Goosebumps rose on her flesh. Not from the cold, but from the reverence in which he sang and from the mere presence of the man next to her.

The song ended when they crested the hill.

"Whoa, boys." Amadeus pulled on the reins. He smiled at her then shifted in the wagon seat, facing his children, still smiling.

"What you smiling about, Papa?" Isabella asked.

"I am happy, liebchen, und I have wonderful news." He reached for Awnya's hand. "Today, Awnya und I got married."

The boys tossed their blankets aside. Jakob threw his arms around Awnya's neck. "Can I call you mama, now?"

Ethan shoved Jakob aside and hugged her, too. "Can we, please?"

"No!" Isabella shouted.

All four swung their attention toward her.

The girl's head swayed back and forth, and tears splattered onto her cheeks.

Seeing Isabella cry crushed Awnya's heart. She had no clue what to say or do. Prayer would be good, but her faith in the face of impossible was still so weak. Then she remembered Amadeus's words, so she silently prayed. *Lord, I do believe, but help my unbelief. I love this little girl. Please work this awkward situation out.*

The ride back to the cabin was quiet. Amadeus squeezed Awnya's hand often.

"Do not fret, liebling. God vill work it out."

Back at the cabin, for the rest of the evening Isabella sulked. The family tried to draw her in, but she refused. When they took communion together, which Awnya learned was a custom they did every Christmas Eve to celebrate not only Christ's birth but also his resurrection, even then Isabella refrained from partaking, saying her heart wasn't right. Awnya was glad when Amadeus announced it was time for everyone to head to bed. She and Amadeus were the last ones up.

Her husband pulled her into his arms and whispered against her lips, "I love you, liebling."

"I love you, too."

His lips captured hers. He kissed her until her knees gave way, but Amadeus caught her. With his lips still on hers, he swept her into his strong arms and carried her to his. . .their. . .bedroom.

❄

The next morning Awnya awoke to her husband, leaning on his elbow, staring down at her.

"Good morning, meine liebling."

"Good morning, *geliebte*."

"Sweetheart," he whispered, pleasure sparkling through his eyes that she had learned a new German word.

"Ja." She winked.

He pulled her to him and kissed her softly.

Noise from the kitchen snagged Awnya's attention. "We'd better get up."

He sighed. "Ja."

Breakfast consisted of bacon, fried potatoes, and *blinna*. When she bit into the blinna, it reminded her of the crepes her mother used to make. Joy mixed with a generous dose of grief washed over her, making her heart wish for those long ago days spent with her mother.

The feeling stayed with her through the morning even when they all went and sat near the fireplace, facing the Christmas tree.

Amadeus handed the boys their presents first.

Jakob and Ethan untied the string around their flour sacks and yanked out the hand-carved farm animals. Their eyes widened. "Papa, these are *wunderbar!*" They took turns hugging their father. "Thank you."

Awnya smiled. She loved being a part of this.

Amadeus scooted a package toward Isabella. She raised the cloth half-heartedly and stared at the empty doll cradle Amadeus had made. Her eyes held confusion and sadness.

"Isabella? Open your other gift, liebchen." An understanding tone filled his voice.

She nodded and sullenly tugged the string off her package and then removed the cloth. She blinked. Reverently, she picked up the doll her mother had made—the very one Awnya had spent evenings repairing with Amadeus in his workshop. With each stitch Awnya had fought back tears, knowing exactly how devastated and heartbroken Isabella felt losing her mother. With awe in her eyes, Isabella faced her grandmother. "Oh, Oma. You fixed Lilly. And you made her clothes, too. I love her. Thank you. Vielen dank." She tucked the doll to her chest and rocked it. Tears slipped over her eyelids.

Awnya turned her head away and discretely brushed the tears from her eyes. All her hard work had been worth it just to see the joy on Isabella's face.

"Liebchen." Amadeus pulled Isabella onto his lap. "Oma did not fix Lilly. Awnya did."

Isabella tilted her head, frowning, blinking, and staring at Awnya. Her chest heaved, and without saying a word, she rose from her father's lap and slipped out of the room. Awnya's heart fell.

Amadeus stood, and Awnya placed her arm on his. "Let her go. She needs time alone." He nodded and sat back down in the rocker.

Minutes later, as the boys bustled with their toys, and Louissa admired the potholders Isabella had crocheted for her, Isabella stepped out of the bedroom carrying a small book in one hand and her doll in the other. With her eyes lowered, she came and stood in front of Awnya. "I'm sorry I didn't make you anything. Here. I want you to have this." Her hand came up, and in it was a small black Bible.

"Oh sweetie, I can't take that." Awyna's eyes filled at the mere thought of the precious gift. "That's your mother's Bible. It's yours."

"I know. But Papa said a bad man stole your mama's Bible, so you can have my mama's. I want my new mama to have it."

Like a broken dam, tears flooded Awnya's cheeks.

"Don't cry." Isabella's voice trembled, and fear filled her little face. "I'm sorry I was so mean to you. It's just that when I saw the way Papa looked at you, I was afraid he was forgetting my mama, and I didn't want him to. But—" She dropped her gaze. "You're my mama now, so I want you to have her Bible."

"Oh, Isabella." Awnya put her arms around the child, singing praise to God for His goodness in her heart. She accepted the gift with reverence and amazement. "Thank you so much." She pulled the Bible to her chest and clutched it there. "You will never know what this means to me. I won't let your papa ever forget your mama. I promise."

Isabella nodded and swiped the tears off her small cheeks. Awnya pulled her daughter into a hug. A love unlike any she had ever known pulsed through her.

"My turn." Amadeus pulled his daughter into his arms.

Isabella pulled back, grabbed one of his hands, and joined it with Awnya's. She smiled up at them and then went and joined her brothers.

With the children occupied with their gifts, Awnya slipped her arms around her husband and pulled him close.

"I love you, meine vee-not-goo-shank."

His chest rumbled against her ear. "Vie. Nacht. Ga. Shinkt."

"That's what I said. Vee-not-goo-shank."

He shook his head and laughed. She shut him up by joining her lips to his.

Love flowed through his kisses as he returned hers. *Lord, thank You for my vie-not-goo-shanks. Vie-nacht-goo-shints. Oh piddle. For my Christmas gifts. My husband, my new mama, and my new children. But most of all, thank You for the gift of faith. Amen.*

Debra Ullrick is an award winning author who is happily married to her husband of thirty-seven years. For over twenty-five years, she and her husband and their only daughter lived and worked on cattle ranches in the Colorado Mountains. The last ranch Debra lived on, a famous movie star and her screenwriter husband purchased property there. She now lives in the flatlands where she's dealing with cultural whiplash. Debra loves animals, classic cars, mud-bog racing, and monster trucks. When she's not writing, she's reading, drawing western art, feeding wild birds, watching Jane Austen movies, *COPS*, or *Castle*.

Debra's other titles include, *The Bride Wore Coveralls, Déjà vu Bride, Dixie Hearts, A Log Cabin Christmas, The Unexpected Bride*, and come January 2012, *The Unlikely Wife*.

Debra loves hearing from her readers. You can contact her through her website at www.DebraUllrick.com.

Christmas Service

by Erica Vetsch

Dedication

To the Sorensen family, Kevin, Ann, Rebecca, Jonathan, and Elizabeth, who know a thing or two about serving in church and chaotic Christmas programs.

Whether therefore ye eat, or drink,
or whatsoever ye do, do all to the glory of God.

1 CORINTHIANS 10:31

Chapter 1

You'll just have to tell him no. I'm not interested." Beth Sorensen wet her finger and tested the bottom of the sad iron. No pop and sizzle. Still not ready. She mentally ran down her list of Saturday chores.

"I don't understand you, Beth." Her grandpa laid aside his glasses and pinched the bridge of his nose. "Todd Rambek is a fine man. Why won't you let him call on you? Or for that matter, the three others who have tried to court you. You're going to wind up a spinster if you're not careful."

She laughed and crossed the puncheon floor, bending to kiss his bald head. "I'm barely twenty-one, Grandpa. Hardly on the shelf yet. You've always taught me to listen for God's leading. None of the men who have asked permission to court have been the man God wants for me. Especially not Todd Rambek. He's a blacksmith, of all things."

"What's wrong with being a blacksmith? It's an honorable profession. He makes a good living, and more importantly, he's of good character—a deacon in our church. I had such high hopes that you might look favorably on him." He tapped together his sermon notes and tucked them into his Bible. "I do wish your parents were here to give you counsel. I'm hopeless with this sort of thing."

Returning to the stove, she threw another log into the firebox and tested the iron once more. Perfect. The smell of hot cotton pricked her nose as she went to work on the wrinkles in Grandpa's best shirt. She wished Mama were there, too. She'd understand. After all, it was Mama who had most often said what a wonderful preacher's wife Beth would make someday.

She shook her head. A blacksmith? No, she couldn't abandon the calling she had been born to, not even for a man as handsome as Todd Rambek— deacon or not. Grandpa was a preacher, her father had been a preacher, and if she had been born a boy, she would've gone into the pastorate as well—the next generation of Sorensens to serve in a little log church somewhere in the American wilderness. It was a family tradition, a calling. She didn't know when God would bring a single preacher into her life, but He moved in mysterious ways, and she was confident He could accomplish the task.

"Did you shovel a path over to the church?" Last night's storm had decorated the Minnesota woods with a fresh half foot of snow. "I should get over there to freshen things up before church tomorrow."

Grandpa opened a newspaper and adjusted his glasses. "I didn't have to shovel. Todd took care of it first thing this morning. He's thoughtful that way." He eyed her over the top of the *Grand Rapids Gazette*.

"Nice of him." She kept her voice neutral. "Did you decide on the opening hymn?"

He flipped open the cover of his worn Bible and consulted his notes. " 'O, Sacred Head Now Wounded.' If you could, play 'When I Survey the Wondrous Cross' for the offertory, and we'll finish with 'O Come, All Ye Faithful.' That should get folks into the holiday spirit."

"So should practice for the Christmas Eve service. I'm excited about how we've switched things around. I think the adults will enjoy putting on a pageant for the children for once. We certainly had a lot of volunteers when you announced the idea last week."

"I think you've taken on too much. You'd best consider delegating some of the responsibilities. You can hardly direct the choir, the play, and the gift giving, and see to all the food by yourself."

Beth shook out the shirt and held it up to the morning light streaming through the small window set in the heavy log wall, examining the sleeves and collar for any stray wrinkles. "Perfect. I've already brushed and sponged your suit. Will you need me to polish your shoes?"

Grandpa shifted and crossed his legs. "I'm capable of polishing my shoes all by myself. You fuss too much. I don't think the church roof will fall in if I have a scuff or two on my boots or a wrinkled cuff or collar every once in a while."

She wagged her finger at him. "Nonsense. You must look the part. You're very handsome when I get you all spiffed up, and you must command the respect due your office of pastor. We can't have you looking less than your ministerial best when it's time to preach God's Word." With quick, efficient motions, she folded the ironing blanket and placed it in the cupboard under the washtub.

Cutlery and plates clinked as she set the table for lunch. "I've got stew simmering, and as soon as I get back from the church, I'll make some biscuits. How does that sound?"

"Like you work too hard. I can make the biscuits, or we can do without. I wish you'd slow down. You don't have to tackle everything in a day. Between your household responsibilities and all the things you take care of at the church, you've no time to relax and enjoy life. You've no time for gentlemen like Todd Rambek."

She lifted her coat and bonnet from their peg by the door. Clamping the edge of her red bonnet between her teeth, she shrugged into the sleeves of her dark-green coat. Once she had the wooden buttons done up, she settled her bonnet on her head. Checking her reflection in the looking glass, she smoothed dark-brown hair off her temples and tied the bow under her chin. Neat and tidy. She gave her reflection a cheeky wink. "That's right. I don't have time for men like Todd Rambek. Now, I'm off to the church. I'll be back before lunch. Don't worry about me. I'm quite content to 'Do with my might what my hands find to do' and wait for the *right* man to come along. He's out there, and I'll know him when I see him."

Just before she closed the door, Grandpa muttered, "Be careful you don't miss what's under your nose because you're too busy staring at the horizon."

❅

Todd Rambek pumped the bellows and shoved the tongs into the white-hot coals of the forge. A bead of sweat trickled down his nose, and he swiped at it with his shirtsleeve. A little more hammering and shaping, and this peavey would be done. He had been blessed to pick up extra work from the nearest logging camp, repairing and making peaveys and cant hooks.

The camp blacksmith had gotten kicked by a horse and broken his leg, but he should be back on the job just after Christmas. Until then, Todd had all he could handle keeping their horses shod and tools in good repair as well as meeting the needs of the settlement. The money wasn't bad either, especially since he was hoping to have need of a bigger cabin in the near future.

His hired man, Billy Mather, brought in another bucket of water. "Do you want me to haul these tools out to the camp tonight, or will they come and get them?" He tugged off his cap, leaving his hair a spiky mess.

"The Push said they'd send someone, but first thing on Monday, he wants me out there to work on the water wagon and to fit a pair of ice shoes to their best team. Can you hold down the fort here if I have to stay overnight?"

"Easy. Who is the Push this year? It isn't McGowan, is it?"

"No, a new man. Caffrey, I think? To hear the loggers complain, he must be the slave-driving-est foreman they've ever worked under, but I hear they're looking to fell more than a million board feet before the spring log drive. Their blacksmith going down hampered them some. They offered me good money to move out there until he was healed up, but. . ." He shrugged and pumped the bellows again.

A grin spread across Billy's open, likeable face. "But. . .lemme guess. You didn't want to leave our little settlement without a blacksmith?"

"I have a lot of work to do here, and not just in the shop. I have other responsibilities, too. They just made me a deacon at the church. Wouldn't look right to abandon my post so quickly, would it?"

"Could it be you didn't want to leave a special someone?"

Wielding the long-handled tongs, Todd yanked the peavey spike from the flames. He hefted his favorite hammer, so familiar it was almost an extension of his arm. Laying the spike on the horn of the anvil, he pounded the glowing metal and sent a shower of sparks toward the floor. Billy didn't miss much that happened in this hamlet. A few more whacks, and Todd stuck the hook back into the coals.

"So, am I right?" Billy swept his hat across a stump and examined it before taking a seat—a wise move, for any surface in the shop might have a hot coal or piece of cooling metal on it. Todd kept a sign over the forge that read SPIT BEFORE YOU SIT to warn customers.

"Right about what?" Todd wiped his hand down his leather apron.

"Don't play games. I'm talking about Beth Sorensen. You like her. I think you more than like her."

He did, and he had for a long time, but he wasn't ready to spill his longings to anyone, much less Billy Mather, good friend though he might be. Todd had finally reached a financial position to consider marriage. He'd gone to the preacher to ask if he might call on his granddaughter, and waiting for the reply had driven him to distraction for most of the day. Even as cold as it was, he'd kept the door propped open so he could see the path to the preacher's log cabin. He pumped the bellows again. "Don't you have some chores to do?"

"Sure, but what happened when you called on Pastor Sorensen? You asked him if you could court Beth, right?"

Todd whipped around. "You know about that?" His tongs clattered off the front edge of the forge, and he sprang backward to avoid getting burned.

"I do now. You just confirmed my suspicions." Billy grinned. "I saw you talking to him up by the church this morning when you were shoveling snow, and I figured you might be asking permission to call. So, what's the verdict? Is she willing?"

A groan started somewhere around Todd's toes and worked its way up. He throttled it before it squeezed through his teeth. "He said he'd ask her and get back to me, but he didn't say when that would be."

"Did he sound like he thought it was a good idea?"

Todd shrugged. "He said he'd ask but not to get my hopes up." Which was ridiculous, since if his hopes weren't up, he wouldn't have asked in the first place.

"That doesn't sound positive. What if she says no? Will you try to get her to change her mind?"

"You're worse than an old woman wanting to gab when there's work to do. Suppose you take those buckets of ashes out and spread them on the pathways to and from the church? Melt some of that snow and ice and make it safe for the old ladies." Todd didn't worry that Billy would be offended. Nothing seemed to offend him.

Billy craned his neck to peer through the open doorway. "Wouldn't you rather do it yourself? Beth's coming over to the church from the parsonage right now." He shoved his hands into his pockets and leaned back against the log wall by the workbench. "It'd give you a chance to say hello and maybe test those courting waters." The grin spread across his face irked Todd for a moment.

Sweat slicked his palms, sweat that had nothing to do with the forge or hard work. His heart popped in his ears like gunpowder under a hammer. "Maybe I will. Anything to get me out of here and your old-woman nagging." He flung off his leather apron, snatched up the buckets of ashes from beside the door, and strode out into the cold, not bothering to put on his coat.

❄

Beth spied the giant of a man approaching and wanted to sink into a snowdrift until he passed by. He dangled two buckets from his hands, and in spite of the cold, he wore no coat, only a plaid shirt with the sleeves rolled up.

Todd Rambek. Why did she have to run into him before Grandpa had a chance to talk to him? She cast about for some place to. . .not exactly hide, but rather to avoid him. Knee-high piles of snow blocked her escape. Like it or not, she was going to have to speak to him.

He drew nearer, his stride eating up the ground. At almost six and a half feet tall, he dwarfed Beth by more than a foot. Hours bending over a forge, molding metal to his will, and wrestling recalcitrant horses into submission for shoeing had given him a physique not too far off the tales of Paul Bunyan.

She shook her head at that fantasy, clasped her hands at her waist, and composed her countenance. "Good day, Mr. Rambek." Better to speak to him first.

"Miss Sorensen." His rich, deep voice sent a tickly sensation through her middle. She looked up—way up—into his equally rich dark-brown eyes. "On your way to the church?"

Knowing this man wanted to court her caused her to see things, to see him, differently. Hoping her appraisal didn't show, she collected his features—the broad shoulders, well-muscled neck, square jaw, lashes thick and straight, and a smile that made her heart bump. She'd known he was handsome, but standing this closely, knowing he would like to call upon her, that he had sized her up and found her to his liking, that heady combination took her breath away.

"Yes," she managed to get out, gathering her scattered wits and reminding herself not to be silly. He might want to call upon her, but she had turned the offer down. Not that he knew of that yet, but he would. And her reasoning was sound. Her life had been mapped out long ago. Marry a minister, and serve God in the church. No blacksmith, not even a deacon blacksmith, had any part of her future.

"Would you like me to go with you? I could light the fire in the stove if you're going to be there awhile. The church will be too cold for you to play the piano."

"Thank you, but I don't want to take you from your errand." She motioned toward the buckets.

"No trouble. I was heading to the church anyway. Thought I might spread these ashes on the path to melt some of the snow. I'd hate to see anyone slip on the stairs." He turned on the narrow path and headed back the way he'd come, his buckets clanking.

Beth followed in his wake. It was thoughtful of him to think of the safety of others. Very thoughtful. Too bad he wasn't a preacher.

Chapter 2

At the end of the Sunday service, Beth closed her hymnal and lowered the keyboard cover on the piano. She turned down the kerosene lamp next to the music stand before rising from the bench. Congregants stood in little knots in the aisles and amongst the pews, chatting, greeting one another, everything harmonious.

Grandpa gathered his Bible and papers and strolled toward her.

She offered her cheek for his kiss. "Wonderful sermon, Grandpa."

"Thank you, dear. You played beautifully." He took her arm and steered her to the back of the log church. They took up their accustomed places, side by side, shaking hands and giving each parishioner a personal greeting.

Beth loved this part of her duties, a substitute for her grandmother, who had passed away in the same epidemic that had taken her parents, leaving her an orphan and her grandpa a widower.

Mrs. Sophie Amboy tottered up, leaning hard on her cane. "Pastor, thank you for opening the Word for us today. We surely appreciate having a fine pastor like you to lead us." She offered her gnarled hand in its fingerless lace glove. The scent of lavender drifted off her rusty-black dress. "And Beth, the music lifted my spirits. So festive. Well, I won't keep you, but I will see you this afternoon. Looking forward to taking part in this program you're planning. I haven't been in a Christmas program since I was a girl."

"I'm glad you're looking forward to it. I'll see you back here at 2 p.m. sharp." She held out little hope that Sophie would be on time. She, like many of the members of the congregation, had a rather fluid take on timetables and was apt to show up late more often than not.

"Miss Sorensen."

She jerked. Mr. Rambek stood before her. A rock lodged in her throat, and heat rushed into her cheeks. A quick glance at Grandpa told her he had yet to speak to Mr. Rambek about her refusal of his suit. Grandpa became engrossed in the story the grocer's wife told.

"Mr. Rambek." Beth held out her hand, and his came up, clasping it and dwarfing it between his palms. His work-roughened skin rasped against hers, warm and tingly. Beth smiled politely and withdrew her fingers.

"I'll see you for lunch." His brown eyes so mesmerized her she failed to take in his words. "Thank you for the invitation."

Finally what he was saying penetrated her fascination. "What?" Her voice shot high, and her mouth fell open.

Brows bunching, he tilted his head. "Your grandfather invited me to share the noon meal with you."

"Oh, he did?" She tore her gaze away and sought out Grandpa's face.

Shrugging, a sheepish grin on his lined face, Grandpa stepped closer. "Didn't I tell you? I meant to, but I guess I forgot. Must've had my mind focused on my sermon. No matter. Beth always makes plenty. A great little cook, she is." Grandpa put his arm around Beth's shoulders and hugged her.

She painted a pleasant expression on her face. Grandpa would hear about this, but not in front of the blacksmith. "Of course, Mr. Rambek. You're most welcome. If you don't mind, I believe I'll head home now to make preparations. You can come with Grandpa as soon as he's done here."

"No, child," Grandpa cut in. "Todd here can escort you to the cabin, and I'll be along shortly. He can help you lift that roast from the oven. I won't be long."

Neatly hemmed in unless she wanted to cause a scene, Beth acquiesced. Perhaps it was better this way. Grandpa clearly hadn't spoken with Mr. Rambek about his desire to call upon her, so it was up to her to disabuse the blacksmith's mind that there could ever be any feelings between them.

He helped her with her coat and held her Bible for her while she tied her bonnet strings. When she went to take back her Bible, he shook his head. "I'll carry it for you." He held the door and took her elbow to help her down the stairs. Her boots crunched on the cinders he'd spread yesterday, and with the thin winter sun filtering through the pines, they made their way along the path to the parsonage.

With every step, she knew she should tell him. But how did one get started? Just blurt it out? *Mr. Rambek, you're welcome to lunch with us, but after that, I don't want you to call ever again.*

Wouldn't that sound lovely? A fist of tension pressed under her ribs, and she wished she had her Bible to hang on to, something to do with her hands. It might not sound lovely, but the man had a right to know. *Stop dillydallying, and just say it.*

"Mr. Rambek—"

"Miss Sorensen—"

They spoke at the same time, and she stopped on the trail.

"Please, go ahead, and I'd be obliged if you'd call me Todd." He ducked under a low-hanging branch—a branch that she'd walked under with no trouble—and waited.

Her mouth went dry, and she tugged her lower lip, letting the scratch of her woolen glove distract her for a moment. Finally, she mustered her courage. "Mr. Rambek—Todd—my grandfather informed me that you asked his permission to call upon me...socially." Warmth surged through her cheeks, further intensified by the light that leaped into his eyes. "While I am flattered, I must decline the offer." There, it was out.

"You don't care for me?" He tilted his head, the gleam dying from his eyes, leaving puzzlement and hurt behind.

"I don't really know you."

He shifted his weight from one great boot to the other and switched the Bibles to his other arm. "Then why turn down the request? You could get to know me better before deciding. That's what courting is for, to spend enough time together to see if we would suit one another." Thankfully, he kept his voice low so none of the people walking home around them would hear.

And while what he said sounded reasonable—and would be if she weren't so sure of God's calling on her life—she knew she had to stand firm. "I'm sorry, Mr.—Todd, I have my reasons."

"Does someone else have your affection?" He crossed his arms over her Bible and his against his chest.

She blinked. "No. Not yet."

"Then I see no valid reason why you shouldn't allow me to call upon you. We're both believers, of good health, near enough the same age."

His logic made her feel rebelliously illogical. "Really, this is silly. You've asked to call, and I've declined. I would prefer not to go into why. I was trying to be polite, to break it to you as gently as possible, but I can see I must be blunt. I do not wish you to call upon me socially. I could never have tender feelings for you. You're obviously well qualified to make someone a wonderful husband, but you will not be mine." She turned and marched up to the parsonage door, flung it open, and closed it in his face before she remembered he was supposed to dine with them.

Pastor Sorensen was right in one respect. Beth Sorensen was a fine cook. Roasted beef and vegetables with thick, brown gravy, hearty wheat bread, and dried-apple pie with a crust so flaky it shattered when he cut it. Todd forked a portion into his mouth.

Beth held herself so stiffly he thought she might shatter like the pie crust. She picked at her food and avoided looking at him.

Pastor Sorensen alternated between amused tolerance and exasperation, smiling and frowning by turns. He kept the conversation going but had to ask

Beth questions point-blank to get any response.

Todd pressed the tines of his fork into the bits of syrupy apple filling and crusty crumbs on his plate and savored the last bite. Pushing his plate back, he rubbed his stomach. "An excellent meal. Thank you for your hospitality. As a bachelor, I don't often enjoy such fine cooking."

Beth rose and began clearing the plates. She lifted an apron from a peg beside the washtub and tied the strings into a perky bow at the back of her tiny waist. Moving efficiently, completely at home in her kitchen, she poked the fire, poured water from the kettle over a cake of soap in the washtub, and began washing dishes.

Everything about her spoke of what a great wife and homemaker she would be. Why had she spurned him? Was she being coy? That didn't line up with what he thought he knew of her.

Pastor Sorensen cleared his throat, jarring Todd, making him realize he'd been staring. Winking, the pastor inclined his head.

Todd grinned, a spark of hope lighting his chest for the first time since Beth had slammed the door in his face. Though her response had set him back for a while, he knew himself well enough to know he wasn't finished yet. He loved a challenge. If Beth could just get to know him a little better, she'd see what he'd known for a long time. That they were meant for each other. If she thought she could just brush him off and he'd fade away, she had another think coming. "I'll dry." He scooted his chair back and plucked a towel off the counter.

Pastor Sorensen chuckled and opened his newspaper.

When Todd reached for the first wet plate, his fingers brushed hers, sending forge-hot sparks up his hand.

Beth flicked a glance up at him from under her long lashes, giving him a glimpse of the blue-green depths of her eyes. "Thank you."

"My pleasure. Not long now until practice." The clock on the mantel nudged past one thirty. "Seems like everyone I spoke with this morning was looking forward to the service. Are you?"

She whisked dishes through the hot water so fast he was hard-pressed to keep up. "Of course. It will provide something different for the children. I'm sure, come Christmas Eve, you'll be surprised at what we've come up with." This time her eyes looked right into his.

So, she didn't intend for him to be part of the cast? A grin tugged at his lips. "Oh, but I won't have to wait until Christmas Eve. I plan to be there for every practice."

Before she could protest, Pastor Sorensen broke in. "That's terrific, Todd. I'm sure you can help Beth in so many ways, like building the set and hanging the decorations. She's told me some of what she's planned, and I have to say, it's an ambitious undertaking. I've told her she might be flying too high for the time and people she's got to work with, but with you helping her out, it's sure to be a success." He beamed on them over his half glasses.

Todd didn't miss the twinkle in Pastor's eyes, nor the exasperated sigh from Beth.

"Really, there's no need." Beth added more hot water to the dishpan. "I can handle the decorations, and I thought perhaps Billy Mather would build the stable for me. I'm sure you're much too busy with the shop to volunteer for the Christmas service."

"I'm never too busy to serve in the church. I've been looking forward to it. Billy can give me a hand if I need it, but it won't be any trouble at all for me to volunteer wherever there's a need."

She plunged her hands into the dishwater, and a fluff of soap floated up and clung to her eyebrow. Blinking, she tried to rub it with the back of her wrist, but Todd grasped her arm.

"Hold still. You'll get soap in your eye. Let me." He stepped close, inhaling the scents of cinnamon and apple that clung to her. The top of her head came to about his collarbone, and the bones of her forearm were light and small. He swallowed. "You'll have to look at me, so I can wipe that soap off."

She turned her face upward so slowly he thought his heart would stop completely. No woman had ever affected him like Beth did. Her blue-green eyes held a challenge, but the way her breath hitched told him she wasn't immune to his nearness. Carefully, he dabbed her brow with a dry corner of his dishcloth.

Pastor Sorensen cleared his throat, and they sprang apart. Beth handed Todd a fistful of cutlery and edged around him to put away the dry dishes. Pastor yawned and stretched. "Todd, you'll walk Beth over to the church, won't you? I think I'm going to take a nap."

"Yes, sir. And I'll see her safely home, too." He wanted to laugh at the look on Beth's face, as if she'd somehow been betrayed.

Her mouth was set in a straight line, and her movements were more jerky than smooth as she snagged his coat from the hook and shoved his hat into his hands. "We might as well go then. It wouldn't do for me to be late." She took her own coat from the peg and stepped away from him before he could offer to hold it for her.

Here's your hat. What's your hurry? Yep, courting Beth Sorensen was going to be a challenge.

Chapter 3

I want to thank you all for coming." Beth turned up one of the lamps hung between the windows on the log wall. Though it was midafternoon, the log church sat in a grove of pines that—while protecting the structure from howling blizzard winds—blocked out a great deal of sunlight. "If you'll find a place in the front pews, we can get started." She took her place behind the lectern and consulted her notes, flipping through the pages while men and women jostled and settled, some still chatting while others stared expectantly.

A bubble of anxiety lodged in her stomach. Was she up to the challenge of shepherding a dozen adults through a program? Most of whom were nearly twice her age? Todd took a seat at the end of a row, crossed his arms over his broad chest, and watched her. She turned her shoulders a bit to put him on the edge of her vision and mustered her best "in-charge" voice. "I thought it might be easiest to break the service down into the different areas. We have the choir, the living nativity, the Christmas tree, and the food. First, the choir."

A hand shot up. "Who's going to direct the choir?" Mr. Hampton inclined his head.

"I had thought to direct." Beth toyed with her pencil and leaned on the lectern her grandfather used when he taught Sunday school.

"How can you direct when you'll be playing the piano? I don't mind directing." He tucked his thumbs under his braces and leaned back.

Mr. Hampton direct the choir? She consulted her list, buying time, searching for a way to say no that wouldn't wound him. "Mr. Hampton, that's very generous of you, but if you're directing, the choir wouldn't have your fine tenor voice. I had planned to have the choir stand behind the piano, so I can play and direct at the same time."

Mary Kate Bormann raised her hand. "What kind of food were you thinking of having? We always have *krumkake* on Christmas Eve."

"I don't want any of that foreign food. Plain old shortbread cookies should be enough for anyone." Clive Jenkins rubbed his round middle and stuck his red whiskers out. "Maybe some cider."

"Cake would be nice. Maybe fruitcake?" Sophie Amboy piped up. "I've got a new fruitcake recipe that I would love to try. I just know it will be the right one this year."

Beth's stomach knotted. Sophie had been trying—and not quite succeeding—at making Christmas fruitcake for the past several years. One year they would be hard as bricks, the next squishy and oozy.

Suggestions and counter-suggestions flew through the group, and a dozen conversations blossomed. "Please, if we could all be quiet and handle this in an orderly manner. . ." She might as well be talking to the white-pine log walls for all the attention her words garnered.

"Excuse me." Todd's deep voice rolled over the conversations. Talking ceased. "Maybe we should move on to something else. The menu for the treats doesn't have to be decided this minute." Heads nodded, and Todd waved for Beth to continue.

She took a deep breath and consulted her lists again. "I'd like to move on to the living nativity. I need a Mary, a Joseph, a couple of shepherds, and some wise men. Of necessity, we'll have to have some of the choir members do double-duty in the play. There will be time to shed the costumes before the last choral piece."

Immediately the chatter started again. Everyone seemed to know who should be doing what, and there were several volunteers for each part in the play.

"I think Mary Kate should be Mary. She's got such pretty yellow hair."

"Everybody knows Jesus' mother didn't have yellow hair. She was Jewish. It's only in the paintings and such where she's got yellow hair. Maybe Mary Kate should be an angel. Everybody knows angels have yellow hair."

"Are we having angels in the play?"

"I thought angels were boys in the Bible."

"Christmas tree angels are girls."

"Please, if we could quiet down, I have a few ideas—" It was like trying to herd butterflies. Beth rapped her pencil on the lectern, but no one paid any heed. Except Todd, who remained silent, never taking his eyes off her face. Chatter continued.

"That doesn't mean Mary Kate wouldn't make a good Mary. She's already got the name."

"I don't know if I could play that part. I mean, all those people looking at me. Mary is the center of the whole play."

"I thought Jesus was supposed to be the center of the whole play." This dry remark from Mr. Hampton caused both frowns and a ripple of laughter.

"Perhaps we should focus on—" Beth tried again, but the discussion didn't stop. How could she prove what a good pastor's wife she would make, how excellent her organizational skills were, if people refused to stop talking and listen?

Mary Kate's face flushed, and she smacked Mr. Hampton on the arm. "You know I didn't mean that Jesus wasn't important, but are we going to have a real baby to play Jesus? Last year they tried that when the kids put on the Christmas service, and little Arnold Harrison screamed the rafters down the entire time. I thought he was going to break all the new glass windows and we'd have to go back to those drafty wooden shutters again. Maybe we should just use a doll or wrap a towel in a baby blanket."

"Please, everyone, if we could just quiet down." Beth raised her voice and slapped the podium. The sound ricocheted off the log walls, and heads swiveled. Heat swirled in her cheeks and ears, but at least everyone had stopped talking.

She cleared her throat, trying to ignore the smile teasing Todd's lips. How dare he laugh at her? She narrowed her eyes in his direction and pulled back her shoulders. "I'm going to ask you to all remain quiet. I've given each aspect of the service considerable thought, and I believe, if you'll just listen, you'll agree it is a plan we can all work with."

Without waiting for any comments, she barged ahead. "For the choir, we'll be singing three songs. 'Silent Night,' 'Hark, the Herald Angels Sing,' and my favorite, 'Joy to the World.'"

"I like 'O Little Town of Bethlehem.' That would be the best one to sing, since we're doing the nativity play." Clive scratched the hair over his right ear.

Todd cleared his throat and rose. His head almost brushed a crossbeam. "Folks, we all seem to be laboring under the idea that this service is still in the planning stages. Miss Sorensen says she's got it all mapped out. Why don't we listen to the director all the way through before we throw around any more opinions?"

Beth's lips trembled, but she grasped the edges of the podium and gathered herself while Todd resumed his seat. "Thank you. Now, I'd like to explain how the gift tree will work, then the food we'll serve, and finally, I'll assign parts for the play."

She plowed ahead, and for the most part, folks stayed quiet. Until she started casting the play. Nobody was happy. If she put people in, they declared themselves unfit. If people weren't cast, they took umbrage. Her head spun, and through the entire process, she could feel Todd judging her, weighing up her lack of skill in corralling this renegade congregation.

She glanced out the window at the fading sunlight and realized they'd been thrashing things out for over two hours. And they hadn't even managed to practice one song yet. Nothing had gone the way she'd planned.

Shuffling her papers, she blew out a breath. "Folks, it's getting late. The last thing on my list is the schedule of practices. We've got two weeks until Christmas Eve. In that time, we'll have four evening practices and one afternoon dress rehearsal the day of the service. We'll also meet on the twenty-third to decorate the church and build the stable for the play."

Once more everyone jumped into the conversation, objecting to or agreeing with the schedule. The room swayed. Beth closed her eyes as a wave of tiredness washed over her. She hardly dared look at Todd to see what he thought of this turn of events. The noise tapered off.

She opened her eyes and found herself staring right at Todd, who had stood once more. His eyebrows rose, and a smile quirked his lips. "I think the schedule sounds just fine. I'm sure we'll all do our best to fit in with what you've got planned."

Billy Mather's hand went up. "You're gonna need help getting all the pine and holly and the Christmas tree and such. And the lumber to build the stable. Maybe you need an assistant director. I'm thinking Todd is your man."

At his phraseology, heat charged up Beth's neck and pooled in her cheeks.

"Todd's a fair hand with a hammer," Billy went on, "and he'll be driving through the woods nearly every day between the logging camp and here. Lots of time to scout out a Christmas tree and the decorations you might need."

The only thing the entire group agreed on that night was that Todd would make an excellent assistant for Beth.

❄

"Are you all right?" Billy got up from the table and flopped into the chair before the fireplace in Todd's cabin. "You haven't said a word since the practice ended. Are you mad because I volunteered you to help Beth? I figured with you two starting to court, you'd be happy to have an excuse to spend more time with her."

Todd scooped leftover ham and beans into a crock and covered them for his lunch tomorrow. He was no great shakes as a cook. Their supper had tasted nothing like the flavorful roast he'd eaten this noon at the Sorensen table. What would it be like to eat that well every day? And how much better would the food taste if he could look across the table and see Beth there? "I'm not mad."

"You're sure not happy. What's wrong?"

Stowing the crock in the cupboard, he returned to straddle his chair backward. The wood creaked, but he'd built it strong, and it fit his long frame so he could cross his arms across the back and rest his chin to stare into the fire. "She said no. She doesn't want me to come calling."

"What?" Billy struggled upright. "Why not?"

He shrugged, feeling the tug of his suspenders. "She didn't say. Just a 'no thank you.'"

"I'm sure sorry. I thought, from the way you were watching each other and how she blushed every time her eyes lit on you, that she'd said yes."

She had blushed every time she'd caught his eye, but it wasn't from pleasure and anticipation or the beginnings of tender feelings. It was embarrassment, pure and simple.

His chin dug into his forearm. The optimism and challenge he'd felt before had faded with each of her attempts to pretend he wasn't at the rehearsal. What had started as a drizzle of doubt that he could win her heart had developed to a downpour in his chest the more he thought about things. "She had her hands full today."

Billy laughed and plonked his elbows on his knees. "She sure did. Seemed like we'd just get headed down one road and somebody would make a break for it down another. If all the practices are this chaotic, I don't imagine we'll be ready for the service in just two weeks."

Two weeks until Christmas. "We might need more than just a few practices between now and then."

"You'll get to spend a lot of time with her, especially if you're helping with the decorating and set building. Maybe you can get her to change her mind. . . see what a terrific fellow you are. A real catch."

"A man can't do his courting with all those people around." Todd grimaced. "With Clive and Sophie sniping at each other, and Mary Kate arguing with every word that comes out of Hampton's mouth? Not exactly the most romantic of settings."

"Pshaw! You're not trying. I bet if you put your mind to it, you can find ways to show her you care, and there won't always be so many people around. Don't give up so easy."

Was he giving up too easily? How did a man go about courting a woman who wouldn't be courted?

"What you need is a little outside help." Billy studied his fingernails. "I bet if you asked them, every last person in the Christmas service would be happy to nudge things along."

A spark of hope lit in Todd's chest, but he shook his head. "Would that be fair?"

" 'All's fair in love and war.' Beth wouldn't stand a chance if the whole group was working to get you two together. You do love her, don't you?"

He did. And he had for a long time. Since the first time he'd laid eyes on the preacher's granddaughter. He'd scoffed, telling himself he didn't really know her and that being pretty wasn't enough of a recommendation to be a wife. But the more he watched her, the more he learned of her character, the more his love grew. As did his certainty that she was the one God wanted him to marry. Was all fair in love and war? "Let me think about it. I thought she was perfect for me, but maybe God has another plan."

His friend rose, stretched, and yawned. "I'd best head home. The boss will be after me tomorrow if I'm late and droopy from staying up." He grinned and got into his coat. "Thanks for supper. Don't give up on Beth. She might not know what she wants until you show her. Think of some ways to romance her, show her how much you care. No woman can resist a man who is truly in love with her."

The door closed, leaving Todd alone in his single-room log cabin. He stirred up the coals and added more wood. Firelight pushed the shadows to the corners of the room.

How did one go about romancing a woman? The dead of winter was a rotten time for flowers.

He could give her a Christmas gift. But what? He could purchase something from the store, but if he made something, that would be more personal, right? What could he make? She was hardly in need of a new cant hook or wagon wheel rim. Ice skate blades? A bridle bit? A string of harness bells?

He thought up ideas and cast them aside until a flash of inspiration sparked. Bounding up, he went to the bed, knelt, and fished underneath. He dragged out a flat-topped wooden trunk. His father's toolbox. He carried it to the table, lit his kerosene lamp, and opened the lid. Ranks of picks, screwdrivers, tiny calipers, delicate chains, and ingots of silver and gold. His father had worked with metal, too. But where Todd used hammer, anvil, and forge to bend steel and iron into implements and horseshoes, his father had been a silversmith, a jeweler.

Lifting the tools from their places one at a time, he examined them. He couldn't make her jewelry. That wouldn't be proper. No girl would accept jewelry from a man she wasn't engaged to marry. But he could make her a gift. A Christmas ornament for her tree.

As he laid out the tools and sketched ideas on a scrap of paper, he prayed. "Lord, You know my heart. You know how much I love Beth. I'm asking You, if she's the one for me, that You'll make it plain to her and to me. And if she's not. . ." He sucked in a breath and made a few more pencil strokes, gathering his courage to say what needed to be said. "Lord, if she's not the one for me, I'm praying that You'll make that plain to me, too. If she's not Your best plan for me, then I'm asking You to take these desires from my heart."

Even as he said the words, he knew how hard it would be if God chose for him not to have Beth. And yet, he had to trust that following God's will, even if it meant a future without Beth, would be better than going his own way.

In the meantime, he would concentrate on making something beautiful that showed what was in his heart. Surely if she knew how much he cared, she'd consider his suit. Patience usually wasn't too hard for him, but where Beth Sorensen was concerned, he couldn't seem to lay hold of any.

Chapter 4

Todd strode toward the log church. Light streamed from every window, and through the panes, figures moved. He shouldered open the heavy church door, his arms wrapped around a bundle of pine boughs, stomping in the entryway to rid his boots of snow before entering the big room.

Feminine laughter and the pounding of hammers greeted him. Church folks clustered at the far end, busy transforming the stage into Bethlehem and a piney bower rolled into one.

Tomorrow was Christmas Eve, and he'd made little headway with Beth. Perhaps tonight would be different.

"Hey, you finally made it." Billy reached for the branches. "I thought you'd never get here. What happened?"

"Sorry. I got held up out at the camp. Half the logging chains decided to break today." He shrugged out of his heavy coat and hat and ran his fingers through his hair to straighten it. "Did I miss much?"

His eyes sought out Beth, bright as a cardinal in a red dress. Lamplight shone on the smooth wings of her hair pulled into a fancy knot high on the back of her head. Color danced in her cheeks as she laughed at something one of the ladies said.

"Hello? Are you listening?" Billy tipped his head to the side and nudged Todd's elbow.

He jerked his attention away and focused on his friend. "Huh?"

Billy rolled his eyes. "I said we were waiting to do the rafters until you got here, but it doesn't look like you've shown up, even though you're standing right there." He grappled with the branches and wound up dumping half of them on the floor.

Beth and several others looked over at the noise.

"I'll get 'em." Todd bent and scooped up the fragrant limbs.

"Follow me." Billy made a beeline for the women. "Think they'll work for the rafters?"

The ladies pounced on the decorations Billy carried and began weaving them into wreaths and tying them into long strings.

Todd stood there with his arms full, feeling like a bull moose in a herd of graceful deer. His heart thudded against his shirtfront and stopped altogether when Beth turned away from draping the piano with a crimson cloth and looked right into his eyes.

God, if this is You taking away the desire to be with Beth, I don't think I've quite got the hang of it yet.

Skirting a group of men hammering together a set of risers for the choir, she came to stand before him. "Here, let me take those. We thought maybe you weren't coming." She sounded like a teacher scolding a tardy student.

So she'd noticed he was late. That was good news, wasn't it? She gathered the boughs he held, and when her hand brushed his, his heart leaped into a gallop.

"Sorry I'm late. Where would you like me to help?" A board clattered to the floor, drawing his attention to the stage.

Beth sighed, her mouth twisting. "Help Mr. Hampton. He insisted he knew how to construct the stable, but he's been at it all evening, and he won't take any direction from me. 'A little lady like you couldn't possibly know one end of a hammer from the other.'" Her voice, though low enough that only he could hear, wavered in a perfect imitation of Hampton's nasally twang.

"Sure thing. Glad to help. And I'm sorry I was late." But she'd already turned away to direct the hanging of the wreaths in the windows.

Hampton heaved and shoved, his face turning purple as he struggled to lift a plank over his shoulders and brace it on a crosspiece.

"Let me help you." Todd grasped the rough wood and hoisted it onto his shoulder. "Go ahead and nail it to the supports. I've got this."

Hampton growled and hefted a hammer. Instead of whacking in the nails, he tapped and tinkered and took his time. Though Todd could hold the heavy plank easily all evening, he had no desire to, and after a few minutes of Hampton messing around, Todd lifted the hammer from his inept hands. With two mighty blows, made awkward by still holding the plank on his shoulder, Todd sent the nails home, anchoring the roof of the stable to the wall of rough-barked pine logs that he'd helped raise into place when they'd first constructed the church three years ago. The pine still gave off a resin scent and leaked pitch when the weather got hot. "There. That should do it."

The shopkeeper's mouth puckered like he'd just kissed a sourball. "Thank you." He snatched the hammer out of Todd's hand and marched away.

Todd shrugged and stood back to survey the construction. The plank he'd nailed formed the roof of the "stable" and was supported by another upright board that formed the side wall of the temporary structure. Todd stood a foot taller than the peak of the stable roof. Since he was supposed to play Joseph in the nativity scene, he'd have to kneel or sit. Standing would make him look like a lone pine in a pasture.

Beth seemed to be everywhere, overseeing everything, and though she kept her distance from him, he supposed he was the only one who noticed. She remained tactful and calm, juggling opinions and quirks. And she'd planned a very nice program. The only problem he could see was that she tried to control everything and wasn't much for delegating, not even to her assistant director.

After the stable was completed, Beth kept Todd and everyone else hopping with projects. Hanging more lanterns, moving the piano, and finally winding yards and yards of pine and fir garland around the exposed rafters crossing the sanctuary.

Since the peeled-pine logs that formed the rafters were only a few inches above his head, Todd had no need of a ladder. Billy fed him ropes of boughs. When they'd finished the next-to-last beam, Todd lowered his arms and flexed his shoulders. The quietness of the room caused him to turn around.

Nearly empty. Only Beth and Billy remained. A mischievous glint lit Billy's eye. He stretched and let go a fake-sounding yawn. "I sure am tuckered. I think I'd best get home. You can finish up here, can't you?" Before Todd could comment, Billy sprinted for the door, snatching up his hat and coat and slamming the door in his wake.

Todd grimaced at the obvious ploy. He turned to where Beth swept up loose pine needles and bits of ribbon, his collar growing tight. Would she think he had conspired with Billy to be left alone with her?

But her expression was clear of accusation when she looked up. She stacked her hands atop the broom handle and rested her chin on them. Candlelight reflected in her blue-green eyes. "It's starting to look like I imagined it would. It's beautiful."

He swallowed hard and took a steadying breath. Better get busy before he did something stupid. Like giving in to the urge to kiss her. "I'll just finish this last rafter."

Without his having to ask, she took Billy's place, handing up the garland and lengths of string. They worked in such harmony Todd had a hard time believing she had refused his suit. Again he petitioned God to make it work or make these feelings stop.

When the last bit of greenery was in place, he stepped back to survey their work. A wreath hung in every window. Red ribbons decorated the greenery. Fat, white candles stood on a tray atop the piano. "What about this corner?" He pointed to the only empty space in the room.

"That's for the Christmas tree." She laced her fingers under her chin and breathed deeply. "You'll bring that tomorrow to the dress rehearsal?"

Mention of the tree reminded him of her gift. Her present was complete, a delicate silver ornament, a tiny nativity scene inside a heart frame. He'd labored over it for hours, calling upon every skill he possessed and drawing upon every lesson his father had taught him. It was the finest, most detailed metalwork he'd ever done.

Would she like it? Would she think him too forward? Would she even receive it? Maybe he shouldn't give it to her at all. Maybe it had been a dumb idea from the first.

She stirred. "I had no idea the decorating would take such a long time. I'm sorry to have kept you so late. You don't need to stay. I can finish up here. You've probably got a lot of work to do tomorrow." Picking up the broom once more, she dabbed at the floor.

"I wouldn't dream of letting you walk home alone. Let's just blow out the lamps and go. The sweeping can wait until morning." He lifted the glass on a wall lamp and snuffed the flame.

Walking with Beth under the stars. Like a courting couple. He grinned to himself. Not much she could do to stop him.

Beth reminded herself as she accepted his help with her coat that they were not courting and that the thundering of her heart was ridiculous. He was seeing her home, a gentlemanly gesture, nothing else. Even Mr. Hampton would do the same. Todd had been helpful and steady at every practice and had done nothing to indicate he hadn't taken her refusal in his stride, which she had to admit both relieved and perturbed her.

He doused the final light and took her elbow. "It's bright tonight. We shouldn't need a lantern." He guided her out the door and jiggled the handle to make sure it was closed.

She puffed out her breath in a white plume, testing the air. Ice crystals formed instantly and hung like a cloud before drifting away. The starlight made bluish shadows on the snow under the trees. Everything lay under an expectant hush. Anticipation lodged in her chest, and she couldn't dispel it. But, she assured herself, the feeling had everything to do with Christmas approaching and nothing to do with the fact that she was alone with Todd Rambek.

"Thank you for walking me to the parsonage. It isn't far, though. If you want to head home, I can make it by myself." The instant the words were out of her mouth, her shoes hit an icy patch and shot out from under her. If it wasn't for his quick action and his firm grasp on her arm, she would've gone down hard.

He grasped her like she weighed nothing, saving her from a tumble but hugging her against his chest. "Whoops. Be careful." His arms remained about her, solid as tree trunks. "Are you all right?"

Except for the fact that he was squeezing the breath out of her lungs. Then she realized her breathlessness wasn't because he was holding her too tight. His arms were gentle. It was her lungs that refused to work properly.

Moonlight shone on his face, outlining his features. He bent, and for a moment she thought he was going to kiss her, but he smiled and released her. "I guess I'll have to spread more ashes on the path tomorrow."

When his arms dropped away and he clasped her elbow again, disappointment coursed through her. And if that wasn't plain ridiculous, she didn't know what was. She sought to get things onto a more normal footing. "You'll be on time for the dress rehearsal tomorrow?" Great, now she sounded as if she were scolding him about being late tonight.

"I'll be there. And I have a little surprise for you. Something I think will really lend authenticity to the play." His boots crunched on the snow.

"Really? What?"

"No, it's a surprise. You'll find out tomorrow. And if you don't think it is too late, there's something else I wanted to show you."

She stopped on the path, trying to formulate a refusal. It *was* late, and she didn't want to give him the wrong impression. If she agreed, he might think she really did want him to court her and was just being coy saying no the first time.

As if conscious of her hesitation, he said, "It's related to the Christmas service, I promise. And it won't take long."

Relief poured over her. If it had to do with the service, she had a legitimate reason to prolong their time together. That thought brought her up short. She did *not* want to linger in the snow with Todd Rambek, did she? "If it's church business and it won't take too long, then that's fine."

"This way then." He plunged off the path and headed toward the river. "Step in my footprints. I'll break the trail."

The snow was shin deep to him but clear to her knees. "Wait." She floundered a few steps. "Your strides are longer than mine." She giggled and clapped her hand over her mouth at the sound of such girlish silliness coming from her.

He turned back, a grin tugging at his lips. "Sorry about that. I forget." He took her hand and shortened his steps. "You're so tiny—I must seem like a clumsy giant."

Giant yes, clumsy no. The way he'd made short work of assembling the stable tonight and the deft way he'd handled the garland proved he wasn't clumsy. But how did she answer without revealing that she'd been watching him? "Where are we going?"

"To see something I came across when I was heading back from the logging camp this evening. I thought it would be just right for the service."

"Is it far?"

"Not too far." He led her around a stand of white-trunked birch trees. There, in the center of a little clearing, the moonlight reflected off the prettiest little pine tree she'd ever seen. Pillows of snow clung to its branches.

She stopped walking and drank in the sight. "Perfect."

"I thought so, too, the minute I saw it." His voice rumbled in his chest, and when she looked up, he was staring at her instead of the tree.

Her heart beat fast, and an empty, quivering feeling started in her middle. Her lips parted to say something, but she couldn't think what.

Todd stepped closer and lifted her hands in his. Even through their gloves she imagined she could feel the engulfing warmth of his fingers. "Beth, I . . ."

She should stop him. She should hold firm to her resolution. She had a calling she couldn't ignore.

Then he gathered her close, and despite everything her head was telling her, she went into his arms willingly. His lips came down on hers, so soft and warm, drawing a response from her that sapped her strength and infused her with feelings so strong she thought she might cry. Her arms entwined about his neck, and she allowed him to crush her to his chest.

So, this was love. . . .

Reality hit her like the whiplash of a snowy branch to the face.

She struggled, and he immediately loosened his hold. His chest heaved as if he'd run a long distance.

"Todd, I'm so sorry." She put her gloved fingertips to her lips where she could still feel of his kiss. "I should never have let that happen. Please, forgive me."

"Beth, you've nothing to apologize for. You felt it, didn't you? You have to know I love you, and you feel something for me. I know you do. You can quit all this nonsense about us not courting." He grinned. "I knew we were meant for each other the moment I laid eyes on you."

Aghast at what she'd done, what she'd allowed to happen, she stepped back, floundering in the snow. "No, Todd. Please. We're not meant for each other. I can't let myself be in love with you. I'm sorry!" She flung the last words over her shoulder as she turned to get away from him, to outrun her conscience and her mother's words.

"You'll make a perfect pastor's wife, someday, Beth. You were born to it."

Tears blinded her vision, but she didn't stop until she reached her cabin.

Chapter 5

How could she have been so foolish as to let her guard down and fall in love with someone she *knew* wasn't right for her? Beth asked herself that question a hundred times throughout a sleepless night. Scratchy-eyed and with nerves bare and twanging, she managed to fix breakfast for Grandpa.

"How are the preparations? Will you be all set for the service tonight?"

She dished up his eggs and ham and set his plate before him. "We'll be ready. Just the dress rehearsal to manage."

"You were awfully late getting in last night. I'm sorry I dozed off. I should've walked up to the church for you. You didn't walk home alone, did you?"

Not alone. Not really. Not all the way. "I was fine, Grandpa. One of the men walked me most of the way home." She dug in the cupboard for the flour and molasses. "I've got ten dozen cookies to bake before tonight. Gingerbread with icing. I best get cracking." If she could fill her mind with all the details of the program, maybe she could stop thinking about what a fool she'd been.

"Ten dozen? Who else is bringing treats?"

Beth sorted through her spices until she found the ginger. "No one. I've got it under control. Mary Kate is bringing the cider, but it was easier to do the cookies myself. Sophie offered to bring her fruitcake." Her lips twitched. Grandpa had been the recipient of more than one of those chewy bricks when on visitation.

He grunted and finished his ham. "Cookies will be good, but don't you think you should've spread it around a little? You're doing so much. There are lots of good folks in the church who are willing and able to help you out. Though I'm glad we're not having fruitcake tonight."

"Sometimes it's just easier to do it myself."

"Maybe, though I don't see how taking on so much yourself is easier. Easier doesn't always mean better."

She dropped a kiss on his head as she passed behind him to take down her mixing bowls. "You do talk nonsense sometimes. Easier is always better."

After spending the morning baking and the early afternoon spreading icing on dozens of cookies, trying all the while not to think about Todd and what she

426

would say to him when they met again, rehearsal time loomed. Beth mustered every ounce of courage she possessed to force herself to walk into the church.

Happy faces greeted her, along with the aroma of pine needles. "Here she is." Mr. Hampton came forward, took the box she carried, and breathed deeply. "Gingerbread? My favorite."

She scanned the small crowd, but Todd wasn't there. Strangely, her heart didn't calm. Here she'd hoped to get the first awkwardness behind them, and he wasn't even there. Guilt clawed up her chest and smothered her racing heart. Her foolishness had sent him all the wrong signals, and now he couldn't face her. Not only would she not have a chance to apologize, but if he stayed away, who would play Joseph in the pageant, and who would anchor the bass section of the choir? Had she ruined the service by failing to control her feelings?

"Honey, are you all right?" Sophie patted Beth's arm. "You look a little. . . distracted. I'm sure you must've worked too hard making all those cookies."

"I'm fine, really. Everything's under control." She shrugged out of her coat and bonnet and smoothed her hair. "All right, folks. How about we all get into our places, and we'll run straight through the service without any stops. Let's see if we can make it mistake free."

The door behind her opened, sending a gust of cool air swirling through the room. Beth whirled to see who had arrived, hopeful and fearful that it would be Todd.

Those hopes and fears were confirmed. Todd stood in the doorway, the trunk of a pine tree over his shoulder and a rope in his other hand. "Sorry I'm late. Can someone give me a hand?"

Beth froze. She'd thought she was prepared to see him again, prepared to be an adult, to apologize as soon as the situation afforded an opportunity, and move on. But she'd been wrong. She wasn't prepared at all.

Her knees went a bit wobbly, and she grabbed the back of the closest pew while several men hurried by to help with the Christmas tree. They dragged the pine up the aisle and set it up in the corner, chattering and laughing.

Todd remained by the open door, talking to someone outside. Beth did a quick head count. No one was missing. Who could he be talking with? If whoever it was would go away, perhaps she could talk to Todd in private before the rehearsal got started. She'd just peek and find out who it was.

A strange sound stopped her midstride. Todd flicked a glance over his shoulder and pulled on the rope in his hand. The sound occurred again, preceding a black face and a pair of marble-like eyes. Four hooves and a mass of wool.

Her jaw dropped. "Wha—" She gulped. "What is that?"

Todd's eyebrows rose. "It's a sheep. Goldenrod, to be specific. I told you last night I had another surprise for you." He patted the animal's shaggy head. "Don't you think she'll add authenticity to the stable scene? I borrowed her from Anders Granderson's kids. They keep her as a pet, and she's as gentle as"—he shrugged, a grin teasing his lips—"a lamb." He led the ewe a few more steps into the church and shut the door on the cold afternoon air.

Beth tugged at her lower lip and studied the sheep. The ladies in the cast and choir huddled together, whispering and frowning. "I don't know, Todd. A live sheep?" His name slipped out easily. At least the animal had managed to break the ice between them—though Todd didn't seem to be out of sorts at all.

"Don't you think the kids will like it?" His eyes held a challenge as if to ask if she was going to let personal feelings interfere with the reason for the service.

Her chin went up, and she folded her arms at her waist. "Be my guest. Just remember, you're the one who will need to clean up after the animal." If he wanted to pretend nothing had happened, that was fine by her.

Todd led Goldenrod up to the stage. The animal let out a single bleat and folded her legs to subside in a gentle heap on the straw under the stable overhang. She looked bored with the proceedings. Perhaps all would be well after all. Certainly a sheep would entertain the children.

"All right, folks. Let's start from the top. Straight through just as if this was the final performance. Don't stop, even if something goes wrong." Beth sat at the piano and began the soft opening strains of "Silent Night." Perfectly on cue, the choir came in. She smiled and nodded. Sweet harmony filled the church, and she could almost see the happy faces of the children beaming in the candlelight. The choir continued into "Hark, the Herald Angels Sing" without a pause.

Billy Mather stepped to the pulpit and opened his Bible while the nativity players donned their rudimentary costumes and took their places. A quick peek at Goldenrod—eyes closed, slowly grinding her cud. Any minute now, the ewe might begin to snore. At Beth's nod, Billy began reading from Luke chapter two. Todd knelt beside Mary Kate and the manger, and Sophia and two of her friends in white robes held their arms up when Billy got to the part about the angels appearing to the shepherds. Mr. Hampton and Clive, dressed as shepherds complete with crooked staffs, moved from near the piano to crowd into the stable area to see the Baby Jesus. Everything was subdued with Billy's voice the only sound in the room.

Beth, from her position on the piano bench, couldn't have been more pleased. Not one single stoppage of the program, no arguments, no suggestions, no helpful advice. The dress rehearsal was unfolding nothing like the previous practices, where she couldn't seem to get any continuity for the interruptions.

Everything was all coming together. Billy read slowly, as if savoring the story, just the way she'd asked him to, giving the players time to move without seeming rushed, which would allow the audience time to soak in the sights and sounds.

Billy closed his Bible after the last verse, and solemnly, the cast stepped onto the risers beside the piano. Time for the finale. She poised her hands over the keys, meeting the eyes of her singers, asking them to give this closing song their very best. Determination glinted in each expression. She raised her wrists and crashed down on the opening chord as the choir launched into "Joy to the World." The sound was loud and joyful, nearly deafening her with their enthusiasm.

A very *un*-joyful noise erupted from the stable area, drowning out the choir, who stumbled to a halt. Beth's hands faltered on the keys, adding several sour notes to the cacophony. The plank ceiling of the stable rocked, creaked, and disappeared downward with a crash. Necks twisted and craned, and a look of horror shot over the faces of the back row of the choir. Beth was halfway up off the bench when a wool-covered tornado plowed into the singers, sending shepherds' crooks, angels' halos, and sopranos' songbooks skyward.

Mary Kate screamed and threw herself into Mr. Hampton's arms. Together they toppled into the bare Christmas tree. Sophia fainted. Fortunately Clive was able to grab her and ease her to the floor. Billy lunged for the rope dangling behind Goldenrod, swinging wildly but coming up empty. Todd leaped after the wooly beast, but she bounded away from him straight toward Beth.

Beth scrambled backward to avoid the onrushing sheep and stumbled. Her foot caught on the edge of the piano drape and dragged it half off the instrument and right onto Goldenrod's head. Beth tumbled to the ground, smacking her backside on the puncheon floor and toppling backward against the log wall.

The candles and holly wreath went flying, and Goldenrod—seemingly enraged by the red cloth now enveloping her—went entirely berserk. Bleating and crying, she dashed here and there, plowing into people, pews, and party decorations. In seconds the church was in shambles, and Beth could only sit and watch as her carefully erected plans exploded.

Mary Kate continued to emit scream after scream. Choir members huddled and scattered according to their personalities, and through it all Todd and Billy ran and dodged, shouted and pointed, trying to corner the demented sheep long enough to at least drag the piano drape off her head.

The final coup de grâce occurred when Goldenrod managed to shake loose from the cloth and, looking for a target for her rage, barreled into the refreshment table. Jugs of cider, a punch bowl, ranks of punch cups, and ten dozen iced gingerbread cookies defied gravity and hovered in midair before plummeting to the floor in a cinnamon-spicy, glass-shard-inducing crash.

The sheep skidded to a halt, wheeled, and lowered her head to charge in another direction. Before she could move, Todd pounced on her and brought her to the floor near the door, where Billy caught up to them and added his weight to the kicking ewe. He wrapped his arms around her legs while Todd leaned on her neck.

Thus subdued, Goldenrod gave one last bleat and stopped squirming. This turn of events did nothing to stop Mary Kate's screams, though the rest of the choir seemed to relax a fraction and stop contemplating climbing to the rafters for safety.

Beth blinked, ran her hand over her eyes, and stared at the disaster. "What happened?" she shouted to Todd over Mary Kate's screams.

"I think we scared her." His reply seemed a bit strangled.

"Of course she's scared. A sheep just launched herself into the middle of the choir." Beth rounded the piano and patted Mary Kate on the arm. What she'd really like to do is clap her hand over that mouth and muffle the shrieks. The danger had subsided. It was time for Mary Kate to quit peeling bark off the walls with her ear-piercing wails. Beth pushed herself up and headed toward the pile of men and wool on the floor near the door.

Billy choked and snorted and then gave up the fight, collapsing into laughter. Todd grimaced and appeared to be trying to hold it in, but he, too, lost the battle. His loud guffaws echoed off the log walls and nearly lifted the rafters. "I meant"—he managed between bouts of laughter—"that we scared the sheep."

A river of sticky-sweet cider raced toward them, carrying soggy gingerbread cookies like life rafts on a current. Snatching up the piano drape, Beth stemmed the flow. The fabric darkened as it soaked up the beverage.

From her position by the door, Beth assessed the damage while trying to hold on to her temper. Christmas carnage greeted her eyes everywhere she looked. Praying for patience, she tried to hold back the wave of despair building in her chest.

"Enough!" Beth spat the word at Mary Kate, who had just sucked in another enormous breath, ready to let loose another screech. Mary Kate swallowed her scream with a hiccup. "The animal is subdued. There is no reason to go on with your hysterics. Pull yourself together." She rounded on Todd and Billy, who still laughed uncontrollably, pinning Goldenrod to the floor. "You, too. Stop laughing. It's not funny. Todd Rambek, this is all your fault. You brought that beast in here deliberately to ruin my Christmas service. After all my hard work."

The sob she had tried to quell forced its way up her throat and past her clenched teeth. Horrified at losing control, she stumbled outside, slamming the door on the debacle.

Chapter 6

Todd levered himself off the floor and made sure he had a firm hold of Goldenrod's rope. Billy rolled off her legs and sat up, still chuckling, though he had a guilty tilt to his shoulders. He grasped Todd's offered hand and allowed himself to be pulled upright.

Goldenrod lumbered to her feet, bent her head to sniff the puddle of cider, and lapped a few tonguefulls. She lifted her head, shook herself, and looked around the room with a quizzical expression as if to say, "What happened in here?"

Todd shrugged and rubbed his palm up the back of his head. "What a mess." At that moment, one of the carefully constructed wreaths hanging in a window gave up the fight and dropped to the floor, taking a string of garland with it.

"What are you going to do?" Billy shoved his hands in his pockets and grimaced.

Guilt, his constant companion since he had lost his head and kissed Beth last night, stomped through his chest and set up a racket near his conscience. Why did it seem that everything he did with the intention of pleasing her ended with her running away from him? He gritted his teeth and called himself all kinds of a fool.

"We're going to get this cleaned up." He handed the rope to Billy. "Stay here, and don't let go of that sheep." Marching to the front of the church, he began issuing orders. "All right. This little disaster is my fault, and we don't have much time to get it cleaned up before the program is supposed to start. Beth is really upset, and I know she must be thinking there's no way we can have a program now, but that's not true. We can, but not without her. First, we all need to pitch in and get everything put to rights. Clive, you and Hampton rebuild that stable. Mary Kate, are you all right?"

She sniffed and swallowed. "I think I've hurt my wrist." Still trembling, she held up her arm, bracing it with the other hand.

"I'm so sorry, Mary Kate." He motioned to one of the ladies. "See if you can help Mary Kate out. The rest of you, get cracking on the cleanup. Salvage what you can; throw out the rest. Be careful with that broken glass." Todd turned to Sophie. "I don't suppose you have any of that fruitcake available, do you?"

Sophie gave him a gamine grin and patted his arm. She motioned for him to bend down so she could whisper in his ear. He had to bend a very long way to hear her. "I made up a big batch this morning, just in case. I was planning to give them out as Christmas gifts, but this need is more pressing."

He engulfed her little hand in his. "That's great. Why don't you head home and get the cakes? Take someone along to help if you need to. And round up some cider if you can. If not, we'll serve water."

As soon as everyone set to work, Todd returned to Billy. "See what you can do about hanging up that garland and stuff. Set that tree up. You can start putting the presents on it when everything else is done. That was the last thing we needed to do after the practice anyway."

"What are you going to do? And what should I do with her?" Billy lifted Goldenrod's rope.

Todd took the rope. "I'm going to tie her up outside, and then I'm going after Beth."

Billy pulled a face. "She was pretty upset. Don't you think you should give her a little time to cool off?"

"We can't afford to. There will hardly be time for us to finish here, get home for a quick supper, and get back before the service is supposed to start. We can't let Beth down. She's worked so hard." He lifted his coat from one of the back pews and shouldered his way into it. Giving the rope a tug, he scowled at the sheep. "C'mon, you. Let's get out of here before you start another riot."

Stepping out into the frosty air, he noted that the sun had gone down. Faint stars winked through the treetops, and as the darkness intensified, the stars glowed brighter. He made Goldenrod's rope fast to a hitching post out front and studied the snow around the church. Hundreds of footprints pocked the path, but one fresh set caught his eye, a set that veered toward the track he and Beth had taken last night to see the Christmas tree.

His heart beat thick. She hadn't headed home. And she had no coat. He hurried inside and tossed through the stack of coats on a back table until he found the green plaid he'd know anywhere.

Tramping through the woods, he tried to formulate what he would say to her, but everything after "I'm sorry" got stuck. He walked faster as the cold settled in and flowed over his face like icy water.

He found her standing in the snow, arms wrapped around her waist, chin on her chest, beside the empty place where the Christmas tree had stood until he'd removed it to bring into the church. Her look of utter defeat ran him through like a peavey spike. His lungs sent plumes of frosty breath into the air.

When he stood only a few feet from her, he called her name, not wanting to frighten her. There'd been enough frightening going on today. "Beth?"

She flinched but didn't look up.

"I brought your coat." He stepped closer and held up the garment. When she didn't move her arms to slip it on, he draped it around her shoulders. "Beth, I'm so sorry. I had no idea Goldenrod would go mad like that." At the mental image of the maniacal sheep wearing the piano drape, a chuckle bubbled into his chest, but he stifled it. "If you think about it, it *is* a little bit funny." He tilted his head and invited her to laugh with him.

Nothing. Not a trace of humor. In fact, her lower lip trembled in a way that made his insides turn to water. Surely she wasn't going to cry? And what on earth would he do if she did?

"Beth, please. I truly am sorry. Don't cry. Everyone's pitching in to clean things up. We can still have the service tonight. Nothing's really ruined." He scratched his head. "Well, the cider and cookies are, but we're taking care of that."

She gave a strange hiccupping sound and clutched the edges of her coat. "You don't understand."

He spread his hands. "Then tell me. I want to understand. I want to make everything all right—with the church service and with us." Moving to stand before her, he put his finger under her chin and raised her face to look into her eyes. Starlight softened her features, and tears hung like diamonds on her dark lashes. "Beth, I stood right here last night and held you in my arms, and I *know* you felt something for me. You have to know that I love you. If we could just talk this out, you'll see that everything is going to be fine."

She rocked back, jarring his finger from her chin. "You don't get it, do you? I can accept your apology for the sheep disaster, but I can't accept your love." She took a couple steps back, putting distance between them. Her coat slid from one shoulder and trailed in the snow. "I can't allow myself to love you, because I've been called to serve God."

He blinked. Somewhere his chain of thought had broken a link. Or hers had. He squinted and shook his head. "How would loving me mean that you couldn't serve God?" Though thoroughly puzzled, a spark of hope fanned to life in his chest. She hadn't said, "I can't love you," but rather, "I can't let myself love you."

"I'm not supposed to fall in love with a blacksmith." She grappled with the coat and hunched it back over her shoulder. "I have to marry a preacher and serve God in the church."

His jaw went slack as he struggled to make sense of her words. "Who told you that? Your grandpa?" That didn't mesh with what he thought he knew of Pastor Sorensen.

"It's been my destiny since I was a little girl. My mother always told me so, and I come from a long line of preachers. If I had been born a boy, I would've joined the pastorate. That's just how it is. It's a calling, a responsibility. The Sorensens serve God in the church."

Disappointment trickled through him as he began to understand. He folded his arms and braced his legs. "So do the Rambeks." He spoke slowly, so she wouldn't miss a word. "We always have, though there's not a preacher among us." Shaking his head, he took a deep breath. "So a humble blacksmith isn't good enough for you because he isn't a preacher? You think preaching is the only kind of service that counts in the church?" He swung his arm wide in the direction of the log church. "What do you think the people who have volunteered for this Christmas Eve program have been doing if not serving in the church? What do you think they're doing right now?" A scornful growl rose in his chest. "For someone who comes from a long line of preachers, you sure don't know your scripture too well."

She gasped as if he'd slapped her, and though it hurt to be so blunt with her, she needed to hear the truth.

"Doesn't the Apostle Paul tell us that the church is like a body, made up of all kinds of members that have all kinds of jobs? If one of those members doesn't do his job of serving in the church, the whole body is less effective. We're warned against elevating one role in the church body over another. You've done that to such an extent that nobody else in the church matters." He pursed his lips. "Just how do you think you'd even put on a Christmas Eve service without those volunteers? Without Clive and Billy and Hampton and Sophie and Mary Kate and all the rest? Without this blacksmith?" He thumped his chest with his thumb. "You've been so busy organizing and dictating and being in control, you've lost sight of not only who was doing all the work, but also who the work was being done for."

Knowing he'd said more than enough, and with his heart like a wound in his chest, he turned away from her to go back to the church. He might not have been able to mend his relationship with Beth—most likely, his words, though truthful, had slammed the door forever on her loving him—but he could help mend the damage caused by the renegade Goldenrod.

❄

Beth clutched the edges of her coat around her as Todd disappeared into the woods. The tears on her lashes lost their hold and tumbled down her cheeks in warm streaks that turned icy almost at once.

His words hit like darts, piercing her. The disgust on his face when she told him her reason for refusing to let him court her—she squirmed at the memory.

How she wished she could curl up in the snow, sink down, and make herself as small as she felt. Because he had been right. And the truth, spoken through the scripture, straight from his own lips, shamed her.

Beth sought to maintain her hold on her firm belief that her destiny lay in being a preacher's wife, but the threads of that argument had already frayed and broken under the weight of Todd's words. She bowed her head and her heart to whisper a prayer in the frosty night.

"God, I'm so sorry. Everything he said was right. I—" She choked on a sob and sniffed. Whispering didn't seem appropriate, as if she still sought to hide her confession. Bracing her shoulders, she slipped her arms into her coat sleeves and dug in the pocket for her gloves. "God"—she tilted her head back to address the heavens—"I've been so wrong. I've been prideful. What I should've been using for Your glory, I've used for my own. This Christmas service, it wasn't about sharing the joy of the Christmas season with the people in our church." It hurt to admit, but she had to say the words. "I was using it to prove to myself and to others what a good preacher's wife I would make someday. I discounted the service of others and elevated myself." The tears flowed freely now as she opened her heart. Her feet moved, carrying her in the direction of the church, but slowly, for she wanted to thrash everything out with God before she faced anyone.

"God, I wounded Todd, too. I made myself out—at least in my own mind— as being too good for him. And the opposite is true. He's too good for me." At this admission, her heart burst wide open, and her legs gave out. She dropped to the snow, hugged her knees to her chest, and begged for God's forgiveness. Peace flooded her insides, a weight lifted from her, and after a while, she became aware of the cold seeping through her coat. Wiping her cheeks, she stood and brushed at the snow clinging to her clothes.

She frowned, her stomach muscles tightening. How long had she been out here? Surely it had to be nearly time for the service to start. Did she have time to run home and change? What about the mess at the church? Had they gotten everything squared away?

Brushing through the trees, getting dumped on with gouts of snow each time she encountered a low-hanging branch, she hurried toward the church. Along the way, she reminded herself of Todd's words. The good people she'd yelled at were cleaning things up. They were serving, and they were just as capable, and in a lot of cases more capable, of taking care of things as she was.

When she reached the church, everything was dark. She ducked inside and lit a candle, checking the clock on the wall first. Forty minutes until the service. She hurried up the aisle. The stable, a new piano cover, the Christmas tree.

Everything that could be put to rights had been. One would never know that disaster had struck only a short while ago.

She turned to the refreshment table. Six new jugs of cider sat at one end, flanked by a row of shiny tin cups. The floor beneath the table shone dark and damp from a recent mopping. She lifted the corner of a tea towel gaily embroidered with poinsettias and holly. Eight dark loaves of spicy fruitcake stood all in a row. Beth poked one of the loaves. It gave way like a sponge and sprang back. Not dry and crumbly, but moist and redolent. It appeared Sophie had finally hit on the right recipe for Christmas fruitcake after all.

The clock showed the half hour. In the candlelight she glanced down at her wet coat and the soaked hem of her dress just brushing the floor. If she hurried, she'd have time to change and be back for the service.

Her breath hitched. If she thought it took a lot of courage to face Todd after he kissed her, how much more would she have to muster after their latest confrontation?

Chapter 7

Her fingers shook with a trembling that had nothing to do with the plummeting temperature or the falling snow. Light shone from every church window, and dark figures made their way from the cabins of the settlement toward the pine structure. Lines of chinking stood out white between the solid logs, and overhead, pointing to the sky, a cross stood atop a small cupola. The church bell sent out round, reverberating rings, calling everyone to worship.

Grandpa put his hand under her elbow to help her along the path. "I sure am looking forward to tonight. It isn't often I get to sit with the congregation. I'm going to enjoy being ministered to by the members of the church."

Her heart pinched. How had she missed understanding the truth of the whole body ministering and working together? Grandpa clearly believed it and had probably mentioned it many times, both in their home and from the pulpit. And yet, she'd been blinded by her own pride. But no more.

She entered the church, her nerves playing a fugue in her stomach, and laid aside her coat and bonnet. Brushing her hands down the polonaise of her new, burgundy dress, she took a few steadying breaths.

A low hum of excited conversation buzzed in the room, enhanced by the many lanterns and lamps brightening every corner and the heady scent of pine boughs and cinnamon. Billy and Clive ushered the children to the front rows, and several of the choir members and cast stood off to the side awaiting direction.

Though aware of his presence from the moment she stepped into the building, Beth had avoided until the last possible minute looking directly at Todd. When she did, her heart did an unpleasant flip and jumped up into her throat. He stood talking with a group of men, a full head taller than they and heart-stoppingly handsome in a black suit.

"You'd best get up there." Grandpa nudged her arm. "It's time to start."

As she walked up the center aisle, conversations ceased and the choir assembled. Taking her place at the piano, she didn't know if she was glad or sad that she hadn't any time to speak to Todd before the service. Her mouth was as dry as pillow ticking, and her fingers froze on the keys. Every choir member looked at her expectantly. She sent up a quick prayer.

Of their own accord, her fingers played the introduction to the first song. The singers harmonized beautifully, coming in when they should, even remembering to repeat the last line and hold the last note. How many times had they stumbled over that in practice?

Billy's rich voice reading the Christmas story while the cast members acted out the nativity play sent gooseflesh marching across her skin. The faces of the children in the front rows all attentive and illuminated with candlelight made her heart glow. These were the ones they had come to serve. Mary Kate with a maternal expression, Clive with his Adam's apple lurching with each swallow, Mr. Hampton, face shiny with pleasure, Sophie, hunch-shouldered with age but singing with gusto. And Todd. Broad-chested, tall, strong in body and in spirit, big in stature, and big of heart. Every last one of them had come to serve the body of Christ.

Todd, as Joseph, stared right at her. She blinked, caught off-guard, and looked away. A cold fist wrapped its fingers around her chest and squeezed. What if he was so thoroughly disgusted with her that she'd lost any hope of his love? She swallowed as Billy finished the scripture passage and closed his Bible. What would she do if Todd didn't want her anymore?

She concentrated on the hymnal in front of her. The notes swam and danced and made no sense. They were supposed to sing about joy, but at that moment, she could muster none at all.

The actors shed their costumes and took their places for the final song, shuffling along the risers and opening their songbooks. In spite of her efforts to the contrary, her eyes found Todd's once more. Chocolate brown, warm, and caring. The corner of his mouth lifted in a hint of a smile, and he nodded ever so slightly. A promise that they would talk later.

The fist around her heart eased, and her fingers found the right notes. When the choir crashed in on the first words of "Joy to the World," she wanted to laugh at the memory of poor Goldenrod frightened to the point of panic and rampaging through the church. She didn't dare meet the eyes of any of the choir members. How she wanted to call down blessings on that poor demented animal. If it wasn't for that crazed ewe, she might never have told Todd her foolish thoughts, and he might never have had the chance to show her the error of her ways.

When the last strains of music faded away, a rustle went through the crowd, centered mostly in the front rows. It was time for the giving of Christmas gifts from the tree. Beth rose, covered the piano keys, and moved to the side of the room to watch. Her grandpa and several helpers surrounded the tree, reading off names and passing out bags of candy and small gifts that had been delivered to the church all week. Eager hands received toys, books, games, puzzles. Cheesecloth bags of hard candy—donated by Mr. Hampton—spread happiness amongst the small-fry.

Todd didn't come near her, instead helping with the distribution of gifts. He lifted a small child onto his arm so the little girl could see the tree better. A hard lump formed in Beth's throat, and she willed the time to pass quickly until she could speak to him.

Billy Mather sidled up to Beth, a grin revealing a great many of his teeth. "This one has your name on it."

She blinked and took the small packet of tissue paper. Turning it over, she read her name in bold, black letters. Who could this be from? She and Grandpa had agreed to exchange their gifts tomorrow. Beth untied the ribbon and edged back the paper.

Lamplight gleamed on a beautiful silvery ornament. Delicate whorls and flares of metal formed a heart, and in the center, a silhouette of Mary, Joseph, and a manger. The ornament hung from a red velvet ribbon. The workmanship was so fine it took her breath away.

She looked up to ask Billy who had given her such a fine gift, only to find Todd before her. Everything she wanted to say to him flew right out of her head. Her tongue became a wooden thing, and the sound of her heart and breath collided in her ears.

"Do you like it?"

She nodded.

"I made it for you after the first practice."

Before he knew what an idiot she was. Was he sorry now that he'd given it to her in light of the words they'd exchanged earlier?

Heat prickled her skin. She opened her mouth to offer the gift back to him and to apologize, but before she could, he took her hands in his, engulfing her fingers and the ornament.

"I'm sorry, Beth. I feel terrible chastising you like that. I should've found a more gentle way to say what I was thinking and feeling."

His apology loosened her tongue. "Todd, you have nothing to apologize for. I'm the one who is sorry. Everything you said was true." She moved her hands inside his. "I'll understand if you want the gift back, since you made it before you knew. . ." Her gaze dropped along with her voice, too embarrassed to go on, but she gave herself a mental shake. *No shirking.* Lifting her chin, she swallowed and forced the words out. "Todd, I apologize for the way I treated you. You are a good and kind man, and you are right. You do serve God in this church, much better than I have. I'm only sorry I realized it too late." Tears stung her eyes, but she forced them back.

A ridge formed between his eyebrows, and his hands tightened on hers. "Too late? Too late for what?"

He was going to make her say it. Well, it was no more than she deserved. "Too late to do anything about the fact that I've fallen in love with you."

His lips spread in a grin, and his hands crushed hers. "I don't think it's too late for anything."

She put all her love for him into her eyes. He leaned down to whisper in her ear, and the low rumble of his voice and the warmth of his breath on her temple made her shiver. "If we weren't standing in church surrounded by all these people, I'd be kissing you right now."

"Maybe, if you're free, you could walk me home after the service, and we'll see who kisses whom." She gave him a saucy grin.

"I'm going to hold you to that." He tucked her hand into his elbow and escorted her to the refreshment table, where Sophie served up slabs of fruitcake and Mr. Hampton poured cider. Beth tasted the rich, dark cake, and her eyes widened as the flavor burst on her tongue.

"It's my new recipe. I never could quite get it right until this year." Sophie winked at Beth. "I was hoping to have a chance to share it, and thanks to that ridiculous sheep. . ." She shrugged and winked again.

An hour later, Beth and Todd walked arm-in-arm through the woods. Grandpa had given his hearty blessing on Todd seeing her home, slapping Todd on the back and kissing Beth's cheek. "I'm glad for you, Beth." He flipped his hat onto his head and left them to close up the church.

When she and Todd reached her cabin door, Todd took her face between his palms and kissed first her eyelids then her nose. His arms came around her, and his lips descended on hers. She sighed as he deepened the kiss.

When he finally released her, he smiled down into her eyes. "Merry Christmas, Beth. May it be the first of many for us."

Erica Vetsch was Kansas born and raised, but this award-winning author now makes her home in Minnesota. This wife and mother of two teens is thankful God gave her a wonderful imagination that helps to weather the storms of life and contributes to great stories set mostly in the nineteenth century.